STUMBLING OUT THE STABLE

SEAN PRAVICA

Stumbling Out the Stable by Sean Pravica

ISBN-10: 1938349334

ISBN: 978-1-938349-33-1

eISBN: 978-1-938349-34-8

Library of Congress Control Number: 2015948826

Layout and book design by Mark Givens

Author photo by Danelze Strydom

First Pelekinesis Printing 2015

For information:

Pelekinesis, 112 Harvard Ave #65, Claremont, CA 91711 USA

www.pelekinesis.com

Stumbling Out the Stable

Sean Pravica

PART I

IT

1

Seamus knew that college did not matter. He knew that his degree would be a meaningless piece of paper that only served to justify his place among the rest of the graduates in the school of Establishment Values. He, like all the rest who bought into the empty promises of higher education, was being coded with the social binary of contemporary American culture. Class by class, all were tested and debugged until the big day came when they walked across a well-lit stage to the applause of friends and strangers alike, having proven that they could take it on the chin for four years. They had survived the first 13 years of indoctrination after all. And before they all knew what hit them, they would wake up in the middle of the night, sweating, unsure what had woken them on an insignificant Tuesday, the drapes open and the moon looking bizarrely foreign, and their partner beside them, sleeping soundly, looking suddenly like a person they had never met. This dark night of the soul, Seamus knew, would be the moment of clarity, passing and dying away with the restless submission to a troubled sleep, that one encounters when enrolled in the lifetime course. And once encountered, nothing outwardly would change. They would know something, but never be able to say what it was.

Seamus did not know what that meant for him when his time in school was through, but he knew he sure as hell did not want to move back in with his parents full time and work some damned job that would most likely be even more soul-sucking than the one his degree might help him land.

So to pass the time of his academic sentence, Seamus did what a significant number of college kids do and embarked on a consistent diet of drugs and poorly executed sexual activity while alternately pointing the finger at the all-pervasive system and its millions of brain-dead constituents. College life can be expensive for hedonists, however, so he begrudgingly took a summer job at Singing Pines Country Club where his high school classmate, Jamie Caballo, worked.

The two boys were never close but got high together when paths crossed at parties. Because their parents lived within a half mile of each other and Seamus did not drive, Jamie would pick him up for work often. Seamus had not logged a minute at his new job when Jamie's influence upon his work habits already began to percolate.

"Whoa, there went a glitch," Jamie said under his breath.

Seamus looked in the distance, though not sure where. "What's up, man?" he said.

"My man. What is happening?" Jamie looked nervous.

"You said something about a glitch?"

"Oh, yeah, never mind man," Jamie said and rubbed his mouth.

"Okay."

He looked at Jamie who looked only at the road ahead and was silent for the duration of their short commute. As they neared the main road to Singing Pines, Jamie swerved unexpectedly to the curb and parked.

"Get out of the car," he said.

"What?" Seamus laughed.

Jamie did not laugh with him. "Get out of the car." He repeated.

Seamus was uneasy but he obeyed Jamie and followed him off the main road into land not as heavily manicured by the local home owner's association.

"Sit down on that rock. Let's have a talk," Jamie said.

The houses in Singing Pines' neighborhood were surrounded by A-list flora and fauna. Jamie took his seat on a log and looked out over a pond. A pair of ducks floated serenely across its green-blue surface. Birds chirped wildly before he spoke, to which his eyes turned askance into the density of leaves overhead.

The whistling ruckus ceased. Then, "Now that that's over with, I have a question for you."

"Shoot."

"Watch your mouth." he hissed. Leaning in closer he whispered, "Did you see something strange happen when I picked you up today?"

"No. But I wasn't really looking."

Jamie pointed his index finger at Seamus and released a righteous growl.

"You weren't really looking. They don't want you to really look, otherwise you'd know," he said.

Whatever Jamie meant by that, Seamus knew that there was a wide-ranging network of intelligentsia that did not want anyone to be in on what was really going on behind the screen. Not only did the Emperor wear no clothes, there was no Emperor.

Most importantly, Seamus also knew that he had found a friend for life.

"Listen Jamie, I know damn well they don't want me to look, but that doesn't stop me and it sounds like it doesn't stop you. They want to coddle you into some kind of neutered state that resembles sleepwalking much more than it does living. They want you to work their jobs and make just enough money, which you never have enough of because you always owe it right back and then some. I don't know what you saw back there but I'd guess that if it's anything like what you're hinting at, I've probably seen it too, one way or another."

Seamus stared pensively at a rock. His phone rang and broke his concentration, but did so only once and before he could answer it.

He looked at its screen. "Missed call from number unavailable. Strange."

Jamie nodded slowly. "Glitches often are strange."

Seamus considered. "A glitch? What, like from *The Matrix*?"

"No one can say for sure what the Matrix is."

Seamus understood. "Is that what you were looking at when you picked me up? A so-called glitch?"

"If by so-called you mean watching the exact same car drive past me for the second time within thirty seconds, then yes, it's an apparently shoddy day in the so-called mainframe."

"What if the person was just lost?"

Jamie shrugged. "I can only lead you to water."

Seamus smiled. "Okay dude, whatever you say. It's your trip."

"Yeah, it's a trip all right! And you haven't even met Barry yet." Jamie stood up, waved his thumb back in the air, and said, "C'mon Seamus. Let's get to work."

2

Other than Jamie, Angela was the first person at Singing Pines Seamus met. She was a young woman who giggled and fidgeted often. There were dark circles under her eyes, which were curiously expressive. They betrayed an inner world of unanswered questions and compromised ambition. He looked into them during his interview, answering questions more about his personal life than anything else. Angela asked about his ability to get along with other people, emphasizing "conflict resolution" and "the ability to see from multiple perspectives." He entertained the notion of telling her that he had held multiple perspectives many times before while tripping off his face, but knew such a remark, though tongue-in-cheek, would likely not warrant him a realistically hirable candidate. And though the last thing Seamus wanted was a job, if he was going to be able to afford to trip off his face over the summer he was going to need an income.

"We learn how to think critically in college. I don't know what's it like to be a bat, as Thomas Nagel famously said, but I can use deductive reasoning to understand that your experience may not be very different from my own. In the workplace, we're all operating under the same basic goal. In this case, I'd be happy to help you make the customer happy."

And so it was Angela that gave him a quick tour of the country club his first day. He met, fleeting and briefly, the secretary, the wedding planner, and the wedding planner's assistant. The GM, Howard, could not be reached nor disturbed. His door was closed but Seamus could hear a faint human murmur from the other side of it.

Next, when taking a quick look at the member's grill, a part of the country club Seamus was told he would never work in as he was part of the banquet staff but should see anyway, Seamus met Steve, the club's finest bartender.

"Sorry, Angie, but I couldn't track you down anywhere. It takes a pack of bloodhounds to sniff you out sometimes, I tell you."

"Steve, you know not to take the liquor from up here. Once I'm done showing Seamus around I can go to the storage room for you."

"Well I know that, Angie, but then I'd have to wait for you."

Angela removed her keychain from her pocket, its long rubber cord neon green and shiny, and ran her fingers around it nervously.

"Don't do it again, Steve, okay?"

"No promises but I'll take what you say into consideration when my bar's understocked and I'm preparing it for a big ass night. Now, what in the hell kind of name is Seamus? Your parents from outer space or something?"

"It's Irish," Seamus said.

"Boy, you're Irish?"

Seamus shrugged. "Genetically. I was born here."

"Then why the hell your parents name you that? Should have given you an American name. Like Steve."

Seamus considered. "I think they just really liked the name Seamus."

Steve nodded his head. "Yep! There's no budging some people. C'mon Angie, Seamus."

As though he was now in charge, Steve led the way down the stairs. Angela, probably regarding this exchange as a conflict, spoke up, "Now Seamus, remember that Steve is the number one bartender at our banquets. He's very important to us, but no more important than anyone else. He just acts that way."

"Oh boy, Seamus, go back into Angie's office and fish out some of those stupid cards with the spilled ink on 'em and tell me what you see. I tell you, this one is all about the touchy-feelies. Didn't go to college to study the human mind because it's baloney. Nope, one hundred percent hard science."

"You're a psych major, right?" Seamus asked.

"Yes, Seamus. Good memory."

"So watch what you say, Seamus. She'll look you up one side and down the other and then she'll ask you if everything is okay. Isn't that right, Angie?"

"Steve! Listen, Seamus. Steve is a bit of a colorful man."

"Hey don't worry, Angie. We all love having you around. Beats the ice queen, Wanda. You meet her Seamus?"

"Yeah, for a second."

"For a second is all you get. She's up in that office and never associates with the help. Too much time planning weddings and ordering her assistant around. Hell, the only person from the upper world you'll see is Angie. The Banquet staff brings in more goddamn money than anything else here but that's not how they see it. They see it as Wanda. That's what Howard will tell you, except he'll never tell you because he never talks to anyone in real time. The man is a hermit in his office. Spooky place, if you ask me."

Downstairs, Steve immediately shot into his bar, a small hole of a place with a large, cut-out window guests would visit throughout the night. Throughout the rest of the room the banquet crew was working on setting the final touches on the tables. Seamus met the clubhouse's second-most colorful man, as Angela put it, when she introduced him to Barry.

"Now Seamus, if Steve wasn't enough, you're just going to get a kick out of Barry. He's your captain. He really runs things down here. And he is instrumental to making every banquet run smoothly."

"Did you get his fingerprints, blood samples, urine samples?" Barry asked Angela without color in his voice nor expression on his face. He was busy straightening silverware laid askew, and never lifted his head to make eye contact with either of them.

"Yes, and I got his hair samples, too," she said, laughing, though all mirth that exited her mouth sounded as forced as her smile looked. Her eyes were sad and weary, rung darkly. Though they were not as sad as Barry's.

"Hey now. You know that's a sensitive subject with me."

"Oh Barry. You're such a clown! Okay Seamus, just do what Barry tells you to, okay? I know you'll do great."

"Sure will," he told her, though despite his best intentions he assuredly would not. He was new to working with food. Save for a pair of work-study jobs he pulled his freshman year that involved little more than sitting in a chair and saying the occasional "hello," he was essentially new to work in general.

And so his first night at Singing Pines, busing and serving a room full of 380 people in a raucous wedding party, was hell. And when the work was not troublesome enough, Barry was always there to make his night worse.

"For a young stud with a head full of hair you show all the urgency of an old man with low T," he said early in the evening.

"Since when does this place hire the first person who applies, anyway?" he asked later.

"You better make it a real quick smoke because your tables look like shit," he said after dinners had been served. Other than Barry, only Steve the bartender worked with any degree of focus. Seamus' tables were a mess of picked over plates and dirty glassware.

Seamus did not smoke but he gladly accepted a cigarette from Christine. It was dark outside when the entire crew, Barry included, took a break on the deck. The moon was thin and the fountain on the ninth hole was alight in shifting colors. Seamus, being of a particularly dreamy ilk, looked over at it and reflected on his evening so far. Seamus thought about thinking often, which usually meant thinking about himself.

Christine said to him, "It's always a tough night at first, Seamus." Then, "He'll do fine, won't he Barry?"

"Fuck no," Barry said. He was sitting on the railing, his head down and his feet raised up on the lower bar, a scrawny gargoyle. He smoked quickly and nervously. As the captain, he did not have to serve tables or bus, but only delegate responsibilities and talk often, sometimes quite often, with the mother of the bride.

"Okay, break's over, let's get back inside," he said and leapt off the railing in much the same way a monkey does off a tree branch at the zoo.

Seamus watched in awe as everyone ignored Barry and remained at ease. Whether they smoked or not, the crew always met outside and talked. Seamus listened to them and beheld an orgy of work-related anecdotes, movie lines, song lyrics, accounts of recent sexual conquests or lamentations on dry streaks. He heard laughter, he heard yelling, and he heard the united voice of a crew that felt no urgency to return to work despite Barry's stern directions to follow him inside. Seamus would soon learn that this was the nightly standard.

Back inside, Seamus did his best to keep up with his busing duties while he woefully watched his coworkers behave as though the reception was held in honor of them. Felipe was moonwalking on a wet rubber mat in the service area while Jamie beat boxed the bass line to *Billie Jean*. Isabelita watched on and clapped.

Later, Jamie helped Seamus clear his tables of their unnecessary wares. Seamus marveled as Jamie bounded through the room with a spring in his step and a smile on his face. While Barry had looked only miserable all night, Jamie had looked only happy.

"Don't worry, my man. Barry's tough on everybody. Especially at first," Jamie told him.

"He loosens up after a while?"

"No. But you will."

Jamie bounced away to the service area. Seamus gave a few more minutes of miserably slow busing before the two caught up again.

"You want some advice, Seamus? The key to working with food when you're only getting paid hourly is to keep your captain happy, not your guests. And when you keep your captain happy, you'll be happy. Call me crazy, but this place grows on you."

Barry was decidedly unhappy with Seamus at the night's end and gave him a G, meaning "good," on the captain's report. While Es were nearly obligatory, Gs meant that something went wrong. Rarely did one earn a P, though it did happen on occasion.

The following night Seamus received another G. He watched Barry write it. Despite his earlier protests, Seamus had submitted to Jamie's insistence that they stick around after work and have a smoke with the captain on the deck. Jamie promised it would be worthwhile.

"I don't care if it's only your second night, Seamus. Your tables looked like hell all over again."

"Now Barry. His tables looked like hell but I wasn't there to bail him out. They looked like hell on his own, and that's progress."

"Shut up Jamie. You've been flapping your gums at me all night about this guys' virtues and all I see is a floppy-haired asshole looking as out of place as Felipe does with a girl on his arm."

"Felipe just lacks confidence. Much like Seamus here, but I'm telling you Angela found a diamond in the rough with this one. He's going to make you proud."

Barry put out his cigarette and completed his captain's report. He stood up quickly from the deck table, as though the wedding was still wilding away inside and the mother of the bride was experiencing a moment of unhappiness. Seamus started after Barry, but noticed Jamie was already disappearing into the shadows the other direction, down the outer reaches of the deck around the building and towards the parking lot. When Barry noticed Jamie was missing, Seamus was no help.

"I don't know Barry. He just disappears."

"No shit he disappears, faster than my wife when I have a

boner."

Seamus, sensing an opportunity to smooth things out with his adversary, asked, "Married, huh? What does your wife do?"

"Jack shit. She used to cut hair but her salon shut down."

"Bummer. Is she looking for work elsewhere?"

"Of course. She doesn't want to work at Supercuts but I'm telling her there aren't many options in this economy. We can't all be artists. But what do I know? I'm just a 32 year-old loser."

Seamus considered. "Well, at least she gets to practice on you. She cuts your hair, right?"

"I'm going bald, Seamus."

"She could still cut the hair you do have."

Barry did not respond to Seamus for a long time. The two walked upstairs to clock out. Suddenly, Barry said, "You know what, Seamus? For a young man who goes to a private school like yours, you're kind of a dumb kid."

When they got to the time clock room, Jamie was standing there holding three flower centerpieces he had lifted from the tables near the reception's end. He gave one to Barry and Seamus both.

"Got the pick of the litter, boys."

Barry held Jamie's floral gift limply in his hands and frowned. He asked, "So you stick around with me after all the other guys went home already just to give me one of the free centerpieces I could have picked up myself?"

"I didn't want them to get jealous. This was the best one."

Barry looked at Seamus' and Jamie's. They could have been

cloned.

"Just quit milking the clock out and punch out, moron."

"Oh I already clocked out sir. I'm not getting paid to pick out flowers for my favorite captain."

Barry sighed. "One of these days, Jamie, one of these days."

Driving home, Jamie rolled through several stop signs as usual. He took off his shoes and socks which caused some minor swerving. He rolled down his window, stuck his left foot out and said, "Sorry my man but my dogs need some air after long nights like that one."

"Looks like a good idea."

"Oh it is!" Jamie leaned over Seamus and rolled down the passenger window for him. "Go on," he ordered.

Seamus stuck his right foot out and leaned back in his seat.

"No man - get both feet out there! You're not driving."

He had to admit it. The open air on his sweaty toes was relaxing. And though his field of vision was low from the compromised posture, he could still see his parents' house pass by them as Jamie kept driving. Another detour. This time, to Jamie's.

"You don't have anywhere to be right now I'm guessing?" Jamie asked.

Seamus looked at the clock on the car's dash. It was ten after two in the morning.

"Nothing I couldn't do later."

Jamie chuckled and answered, "Yeah I'll bet. C'mon in man. I've got something for the both of us."

Jamie stole two bottles of champagne from the reception,

which he justified taking since they were already paid for, but remained corked.

"You can't have them selling these things twice, or even three times. I won't have it," he explained. "But that's the moralist in me."

At Jamie's house, there were horses everywhere. Paintings. Ceramics. Tin baking sheets. Needlepoint pillows.

Seamus smiled. "I guess with a last name like Caballo a lot of your decorating sense is made for you."

"The truth is, Seamus, my mom has a thing for horses. Even before she met my dad she had all this shit in her place."

"Wow! What are the odds of that?"

"They say love is strange. Anyway, Seamus, check the freezer. I'll be back."

Jamie disappeared and Seamus obeyed. A pair of mugs frosted over sat side by side next to a box of waffles. Clearly, Seamus saw, this evening's meeting was premeditated. He filled the glasses with the lifted champagne and waited to drink until Jamie reemerged from whatever wormhole he shot down this time. With little to do but admire the walls of equestrian kitsch, Seamus realized just how much work Jamie had done to prepare his parents' home for a massive party one weekend their senior year in high school. Jamie had cleaned out the living room and covered the couches with layers of trash bags. Outside, a ten-person tent sat in the middle of the lawn, constantly leaking smoke. Seamus wondered if he had even seen Jamie that night. Everyone in their class must have been there.

Jamie returned with pot.

"You still get high, Seamus?"

"Every day."

"That a boy. Cheers."

They clinked glasses and drank, followed by wincing.

"How is it?" Jamie asked.

"Oh it's top shelf. '09 really shines when it comes to this varietal."

"Jesus, you sound like my dad. He and my mom are big wine drinkers."

"Mine too!"

"Yeah? They go on wine tasting vacations up north?"

Seamus considered. "They don't really go on vacation too often...who knows though. I don't talk to them much during the school year so maybe they get into trouble then."

Jamie shrugged. "Well maybe they should go with my parents sometime, paint the town red."

"They'd probably have a great time."

"They would. Let's get high."

Jamie's backyard was large and grassy. A single tree bearing pink blossoms rested off center, and even at this late hour the boys could hear a bird call from its branches. Seamus began appreciating bird chirps ever since he started meditating during winter break his freshman year. The following semester, his mediation practice interfered with his classes but he never felt guilty. Seamus learned a great deal that had nothing to do with any subject offered in college, vindicating his absences further. He was onto something. He knew it.

He never skipped his photography classes, however. He learned things in the darkroom and studio alike from his professor and classmates that he could not learn on his own.

"I'll have to show you some of my photography sometime, Jamie. I've got some cool bird shots."

"Yeah? Are they fucking or something?"

Seamus had never thought about it that way. "I guess they're not that cool. They're just birds."

"That's still cool. I'd love to see your work. You're a photography buff then, huh?"

"Well man, I enjoy it more than anything else. I like philosophy too. Maybe get a double major in art and philosophy, photographic emphasis."

"Yeah? Then what?"

Seamus leaned back and put his arms behind his head to think. Then what indeed. About all he knew was what he did not want.

Seamus shrugged. "Hell I don't know. School is just a little rat race to gain position in a bigger rat race. Between you and me, man... I don't know how I'll pull this off quite yet, but I think I'd like to hitchhike."

Jamie packed a small bowl and smoked, saying nothing and staring at a reddening Seamus. Finally, he said, "so you'd be like a philosophizing, hitchhiking photographer? That's what you want to do with your degree?"

Seamus took a large, awful drink of champagne and blinked hard. "Boy, this stuff is rough. Thanks for picking it up, but—"

"You're changing the subject!" Jamie snapped.

Seamus shrugged. "Ah, I don't know. It's a thought. I've just come across a couple hitchhikers. Chill as all hell, pretty enlightened too."

Jamie smoked more and stared longer. Then, with a voice

slowly rising in volume and enthusiasm said, "That has to be the coolest thing I have ever heard of!"

Seamus brightened. "Yeah?"

"Dude! I've never had a philosophizing, hitchhiking photographer in my backyard before."

"Thanks dude, but I've got a long way to go 'til I get there. Truth is, I don't want to race with the rats all my life, you know?"

"Hell no you don't! Boy, congratulations! I know it's early in the game, but so help me God, I'll do whatever I can to get you on the road."

"You're serious?"

"Goddamn it, Seamus. I wouldn't pull your leg! You've been unplugged already. I can't just leave you to learn Kung Fu by yourself. Hey, I believe in you."

"Jeez. Maybe it's not so far-fetched after all. You're a hell of a dude, Jamie. I know we never kicked it much before, but man I feel like I've been missing out on a good friend."

"You're telling me. But don't worry about all that. We're friends now and that's what counts. You keep doing as I say at Singing Pines. If you really want to hitchhike, you're going to need to get your eyes a little wider, if you know what I mean."

Seamus took a sip and nodded. "I have to keep my eyes open for glitches."

"Yes man, yes! Now you do as I say and you'll see them for yourself. So-called and all."

Seamus shook his head. "I didn't mean it like that. But if you think a misdial from some restricted number is an assault on consensus reality, I'd say there are probably bigger holes gaping through our illusions."

"Assault on reality or an agent accidentally showing his face from behind the curtain?" Jamie said and drank. "Anyway, no one's going to lose sleep over missed calls, Seamus. I just want you to notice breaks in the patterns."

Seamus nodded. "Like when people do things that are out of character for them."

Jamie snapped his fingers are pointed at him. "Now you're talking."

"I took a class called 'Sociology of Deviance.' We talked about this stuff all the time."

"I bet you did. School is good for talking. It's not much good for anything else."

Seamus mimed the motions of tipping a hat. "Now you're the one talking."

"That's right. I don't know what you're doing at school, hell, maybe some of it will even help you to be a hitchhiker. It's gotten you this far. But a whole new education is waiting for you at Singing Pines. You stick with me and I'll show you."

So Seamus would, no matter what that would come to mean.

3

It took another week but Seamus started earning his Es on the Captain's report. He developed a working pace more akin to his coworkers. He was also getting to know them better and joked with them often. He joined the fractured conversations during smoke breaks and the later night observations made about the women dancing and occasionally freaking and the drunken guys who thought they could keep up with them. The single people, guys especially, were easy to pick out at weddings and provided voyeuristic entertainment for the crew. For Seamus, Singing Pines had become a second home of sorts. The job was a grind, but as long as he stayed on pace, there was always time for a joke, a story, a laugh. Angela, noticing the uptick in the Captain's report, smiled when she saw him and told him to "keep it up."

Jamie noticed the uptick too. But his grading was based on something entirely different than Barry's.

"I saw you out there, Seamus. You're not giving these people an inch. That's what I like to see."

"Yeah, that lady was asking me for coffee already."

Jamie dropped dirty dishes hard into a bus tub and leaned face first against the wall. His left knee was bent parallel to his elbow. His head was down, shaking. Seamus knew this look. It was taken from every debt forgiveness service commercial he had ever seen.

Jamie turned and said, "The sun is still out, Seamus."

"I know! I said coffee would come out later with the cake.

She looked at me like I had pulled her granddaughter's shirt down and sucked on her tit in front of the whole table."

"These people think they run the place, Seamus. But they don't. Never forget that."

"I know man."

"Don't placate me. If a bus ran me over tomorrow I would want to know that you were still holding things down. You hear me?"

"Yeah dude. Don't worry. I asked her if there was anything else she wanted and she just looked at me."

Jamie shook Seamus hard on the shoulders. "Thatta boy. You give her the business, not the other way around. Now how are your tables?"

"One more round of clearing on table 17 and I'm off to the races. A few slow fillies are still licking their feedbags, but the finish line is a nose away."

"That's right. It only takes a few slowpokes to bring the night down to its knees. It's early in the game but remember those people come dinnertime. Some nights you have to take their plates when they aren't looking. They'll try and ring your bell later but that's not important. Barry's going to look out there and see nothing but clean tables, and you're going to get an E. Angela's going to scan the report in like two seconds. So long as you got an E, you're invisible to her."

Jamie opened the lid to the ice machine and pulled out a Modelo. He chugged it and tossed the can into the trash. He picked up a broom and pushed the evidence down and out of sight.

"And invisible here, my friend, is everything," he said.

Barry returned from talking to the mother of the bride. He

pulled out his pack of cigarettes and was about to speak when the woman of the hour poked her head into the service area.

"Barry, one more thing," she said and invited herself into the room. She clopped through it on thick high heels and spoke in a raspy kind of whisper that seemed better suited for a library than the raucous tenor of her already drunk daughter's wedding party. Barry fumbled with his cigarettes and shoved them hastily behind him on the employee rack.

"Melissa and Stephen are toasting with Dom, not the house champagne."

"Yes they are. We have a bottle on ice for them."

"That's fine but we need to make sure that your workers know who they are."

Barry looked sadder than he usually did and paused before he answered her. It was probably a good idea.

"I'll make sure they know who Melissa and Stephen are."

"Okay because we ordered that bottle just for them."

"I'll pour it myself."

"You would?" The mother of the bride brought her hands together and smiled satisfactorily signaling that she was getting what she was after.

"Yes, just leave it to me."

"Oh thank you, Barry! Oh, and make sure they get poured last, I don't want them to be sitting there waiting for everyone else to get their glasses filled. Everyone is waiting for *them*, after all."

"Sure. We can do that."

"Thanks Barry, you're the best."

After she left Barry stuck a cigarette into his mouth as though just tasting the filter would calm his nerves.

"Hear that boys? Leave the bride's glass alone. She's in a white fucking dress if you get confused. I'll be on the deck." He then disappeared as quickly as he had appeared.

Jamie poured grounds into the coffee machine and jabbed the brew button with his thumb. "If the mother of the bride asks you for coffee, make an exception. Don't worry about that other old bag, though."

He then took a cigarette from Barry's pack and ran upstairs. The kitchen crew hurled their usual shit talk at him in Spanish and English alike. He understood little of the Spanish, but he gave them back what he could. He picked up a mop, held it like a machine gun, and sprayed them with imaginary ammo.

"Muere, pinche putos."

A couple prep cooks flung themselves over the open counter space. Jamie tossed the mop aside and said, "Vaya con dios," and kicked the back door open violently. Dying sunlight bled over the floor behind him.

Finally alone, he visited his favorite place at Singing Pines. The garbage area was large and despite the rank odors it always smelled sweet to him. Fresh air could do that for a stir-crazy boy like Jamie, who only tolerated the indoors as society demanded that he did.

A ladder hung down from the wall at the back of the area. He jogged into a stutter-stepped gallop and leapt for the bottom rung. He made it, as he always did, and climbed to the roof.

The view was not high enough to give cohesive meaning to the winding streets that snaked through the canyon. Tree tops cut in and across the road, creating partial visibility of the cars that traveled into sight and out again. Some drivers hugged the corners while obvious visitors rode their brakes. Nearer, Singing Pines members whizzed by in golf carts around the perimeter of the clubhouse and trickled through the course.

"All's well in the neighborhood, I see," he said aloud and lit his cigarette.

In the distance a flat, gray smog saucer stretched wide across the sky. It hovered as Jamie imagined an alien ship would before destroying an entire city with a single column of otherworldly laser death.

In the part of the country where Singing Pines was located, golfers rarely had to cancel their tee times over bouts of inclement weather. Though what they gained in sunny days they paid for with their health. Their course was surrounded by mountains, which corralled traffic exhaust and rarely received the rain to wash it away.

Jamie watched the cars and carts drive beneath his feet, and then shut his eyes to listen. The swooshing hum of family-filled SUVs and sedans coupled with the insectoid murmur of golf carts sang a chorus together. He took special satisfaction in knowing that none of the people contained in his visual and aural panorama would ever know he existed. To him, that was Godlike.

4

Late in the summer Seamus joined Jamie and another old classmate, Cameron, on a trip to Venice beach. No sooner did they enter the boardwalk when they encountered a Hare Krishna parade.

Shirtless, copper skinned men danced exuberantly among slow marching elephants saddled with red and yellow canopied seats. They looked like they could do so forever. Their whirling bodies spun on a different dial than the rest of humanity. To Seamus, they looked as happy to be alive as sunflowers reaching to the sky. He knew that he knew how they felt. He had felt the joy of being a sunflower when burying himself face first in a field of them a few months prior while high on mushrooms. He smiled at the memory of writhing like a newborn and lifting his head finally to feel the dirt falling in crumbs from his face in a spring breeze.

"We come in peace!" Jamie yelled to the paraders.

An aged and sun-bronzed man looked down from his elephant, his face wrinkled and cracked. His nipples sagged and the hair on his chest sat tussled in ashy clumps. And yet, against the ailments of his years, his posture was proud. His spine straight and his eyes steady, he raised a thin arm, waved down, and smiled. His gray teeth had sunk into the fermented apple of death long ago. He understood the inevitability of impermanence better than most people ever would. Seamus knew it.

"That's a Godman," he said.

Not everyone agreed. A handful of fat, white men wearing cow costumes followed the parade and held signs with Bible verses written on them. Their rubber utters flopped jovially as they walked along behind the parade, yelling to each other about where to get the best steak dinner later that evening.

The cows argued with the Hare Krishnas when the parade was over. Cameron yelled at the cows to give peace a chance. Seamus listened to the Hare Krishnas and considered their reasoning for not eating meat. Jamie was smoking a joint with a homeless kid somewhere, the boys had lost track of him.

When Jamie returned, his shirt was off and wrapped around his head like a turban. He told the Hare Krishna whom Seamus was speaking with, "Take me to your leader."

The Hare Krishna smiled like he could never be hurt. "He's in here," he said and patted Jamie's chest.

Cameron covered his mouth, muffling his giddy approval. Jamie was wide eyed in swollen wonder. He patted his own chest and looked to his friends. Seamus' eyes were tearing.

The Hare Krishna nodded peacefully and walked slowly, yet spryly, back into a circle of the other sages who were sopping up lentils with sprouted bread. His eyes were small like a bird's, precious pearls containing the visions of a fulfilled inner life. Seamus looked into them and saw a man free from the modern rules, a stomach free from animal products, and an ego free from the need to be more than it was.

"A Godman," Seamus said.

Jamie unwrapped the shirt from his head and pulled it back over his body. "A Godman," he said. "I guess we all are."

Cameron shouted, "He set you straight, boy! Take me to your leader, well shit! Why don't you look in the mirror! Man that's deep." His smile was not totally unlike that of the wise

Hare Krishna. At least in that moment, he had found his leader.

Seamus knew that if he was ever going to get anywhere in life, it was not going to be from taking college classes or landing a big paycheck when his hair was starting to thin and his metabolism was adopting a leisurely work ethic. He remembered the story of Siddhartha encountering age, sickness, and death, and knew that time was ticking always. What could he do?

He was not going to become a Hare Krishna. That would just mean more rules, a different version of hierarchical authority, another approach to man's endless search to tame the inherent abstraction of consciousness. But until he graduated college and got on with his hitchhiking, which would be his real vocation, he wanted to do something that mattered.

School would be back in session soon. Just another week and he would return to the dorms. There was something special about this summer, things he would hold close - like bonding with Jamie, the money he had saved up at Singing Pines, and his exposure to people much different than those in the intellectual circle jerk he knew in college.

Barry and his condescensions. Felipe always staring at the dance floor saying he just wanted "to have a girl like that one." Isabelita and her eyes always dull until Jamie came near, though he never made a move and would never want to. Jamie had a girlfriend already though no one knew it. He saw her like he did everything else in his life: on his own terms.

Indeed, Seamus knew that no matter what happened he and Jamie would be friends. But what better way to see Jamie, to learn from him, than to keep working at Singing Pines? And so Seamus knew, lighting the bowl for Jamie while Cameron held the bong steady, both aiding the boy as he drove them all home, that Singing Pines would be more than just a summer job. Seamus had much to learn still, and taking a cue from the display he saw earlier, understood Jamie to be part of his Karma.

Jamie's feelings about Seamus were just as strong. After Seamus had moved back to his dorm Jamie told him that he would continue giving him rides to and from work anyway. It was much further from Singing Pines than their parents houses but Jamie was undeterred. He only made Seamus promise to continue doing just as he said.

"We're drinking at your place after work tonight, and I couldn't be more excited," Jamie said.

"Me too, man!"

"That's why tonight, we celebrate."

Jamie revealed some lifted champagne he had put aside early in the night. He poured two Styrofoam cups full and hid the bottle back into the ice machine. Seamus had his reservations, but a promise was a promise. He did as Jamie said and drank.

Jamie shut his eyes as he chugged his champagne. Seamus squinted nervously towards the doorway, his heart anxious. But no one came.

Jamie took Seamus' cup into his and placed them innocently on the employee's rack next to someone's purse. They were in clear sight and still foaming inside with telltale bubbles.

"Not bad. In fact, I can think of worse places to be right now." Jamie had a wide, satisfied smile. Seamus was calming. Jamie patted him on the back. The eyes were still wide and fixed, sizzling with the look, but it was a controlled burn. They were eyes that looked at the world as though nothing bad could happen to him ever. No pain, no loss, and even more striking, like there was nothing to lose.

"C'mon Seamus, let's get to work."

"Let's get to work, Jesus Christ what a couple of winners you are. How about, let's get to the crew meeting?"

They were no longer alone. Barry entered the service area quickly, frowning.

"My man," Jamie began.

"Shut up. I told you two idiots the meeting was in the kitchen today. Sancho had to show us what the plate lids are marked with indicating chicken or beef."

"What, are they written in Hebrew or something?" Jamie laughed.

Barry shook his head. "C is for chicken. Just get to work. C'mon, let's get to work," his voice was mocking.

Seamus and Jamie indeed got to work busing appetizer plates along with everyone else. Though their assigned table sections were far apart, they crossed paths in the lobby often.

"Do these broads wear Victoria's Secret for a living or what?" Seamus asked.

"It's an ass and tit show tonight, that's for sure. Felipe and Alfredo are going to have a hell of a time with this one."

It was work, but as Jamie said earlier, Seamus could also imagine worse places to be. He had mixed feelings about returning to school, for instance. Though he was largely excited to live on campus again, even that could be occasionally painful. Limited privacy, campus security harassing peace-loving drug users, and shitty music from down the hall. And most of all the cliquish mentality that pervaded a small campus littered with people from all across the country who nonetheless congregated with other students of the same religion or race, or those who held the same political and philosophical beliefs, or just happened to like playing hacky sack after class. It was a melting pot all right, but one in which the flavors still separated.

Singing Pines had its own cliques in the forms of departments, and those were often divided still. But Seamus knew it was different somehow. Somehow his life was simpler and yet more real at Singing Pines. The Singing Pines environment was less forced, carried no pretense nor promises of a better tomorrow. Once he was home from work he was free to do and think whatever he wanted. There was no homework nor looming midterms. He had plenty of what he considered to be deep and meaningful conversations with his classmates, but there was something inherently organic in the conversations he had at work that had their own profound quality. His interactions with coworkers were more real than the obligatory hellos to classmates in the dining hall, the protests that never saw light past the campus that organized them, the awkward jokes and obscure references to material he had never heard of by professors out of touch with his head let alone his heart. Singing Pines with its rogues, heroes, and miscellany alike meant more to him than any professor's lecture.

"Let's get to work," he said to himself and smiled his way back into the service area with dirty plates in hand. He shot a quick glance at the cups. They remained untouched.

"Seamus, what the hell are you smiling about already?" Barry asked.

"This lady at my table farted right in front of her boyfriend and he gave her this look like he would never fuck her again."

Barry laughed. Seamus loved to hear him laugh. He knew where to light the fuse now. The laughs were rare, but they were always elicited in the same cynical spirit that all the captain's criticisms arose from as well.

"Oh God, tell me it was that guy with the spiked hair. Although that chick with him looks like she doesn't even eat so I don't know where a fart came from."

"That was them! I think he's a musician and she's a lingerie model or something."

"Yeah right. They probably make coffee for a living," Barry said and headed towards the dining room, adding, "Okay Seamus, that's enough fun. Get back to work. No more laughter, no more smiles..." His voice faded into the rising chatter from the wedding guests.

Alfredo was still laughing though, and as he often did, began his rant with one emotion and transitioned into another by the time he said his piece. "She farted! Fucking Seamus, why don't you go poke her in the stomach. Man, that chick is fine, too. I saw that culo earlier and was like, 'Damn! Look at that!' Shit man, I don't need some farting bitch in my bed. C'mon Seamus, keep it to yourself man."

He walked away with Felipe, who was telling him, "Disgusting, dude. I never heard a chick fart."

Alfredo told him, "That's because you've never heard a chick talk to you."

Jamie remained by the sink, grinning with his hands folded together.

"Bravo. You really have Barry's number."

He walked to the ice machine like he had all the time in the world, poured another round, and raised his cup to Seamus.

Only Isabelita walked back to see them, who shook her head and said, "You boys." And with the same smile she always gave them, asked, "What are we going to do with you?"

While her lines never changed, Jamie's never remained the same. "Sweetheart, you're not going to do a thing about us. Tonight's about you. Give me those goddamn bottles."

She did. He then pulled out a chair from underneath the cake cutting table and told her, "Have a seat. Your tables are mine and Seamus' now."

And in one quick trip, they poured for her remaining guests. This compromised their time as they barely finished pouring for their own. Racing back and forth between the service area and the dining room, it was the fastest Seamus had ever served the toast. He felt proud of his accomplishment though back in the service area Barry had his hands on his hips. He eyed Seamus coldly. Seamus glanced at the cups. They remained untouched.

"Do you and Jamie want to give Isabelita the night off then?"

Jamie was by the ice machine. He was grabbing the bottle of champagne behind Barry's back and pouring it into the cups again.

"Isabelita needed a break. It's not easy being a single mother of two in modern America," Jamie said.

Barry ignored him. Seamus struggled to look the captain in the eye, his periphery capturing a slowly moving Jamie, and behind him, a returning Alfredo and Felipe who were laughing and pointing.

"You think you can just disregard everything and mix tables around? What if you didn't manage to pour all your tables, Seamus? Seriously, you don't have enough to do already? What should I do, tell Angela you and Jamie count for four people?"

"It was just a gesture," Seamus said.

"It was a gesture that could get us way the fuck behind while you and Jamie are trying to be a couple of Don Juans or whatever the hell it is you think you are. But you're not Don Juans. You're Cheech and Chong."

Alfredo and Felipe laughed and then Barry turned. They were clapping and yelling at Barry's joke, pretending to smoke joints pressed hard between their fingers. Jamie was at the elevator, directing the exiting Christine and Isabelita where to position the salad carts. The salad carts, like everything at Singing Pines, always went the same place.

Barry yelled at Jamie, walking directly past the two newly poured cups of champagne. Jamie and Seamus drank them in spurts between serving tables. Barry was plating trays as he always did, and suddenly Seamus realized how foolish he was to ever fear getting caught at all. Barry could only see so much. Anyone could only see so much.

As far as Jamie was concerned, glitches were the exception and not the rule. Most people acted the same way most of the time. So long as their behavior could be counted on to remain static, then he was free to act as he pleased. Such was Jamie's secret knowledge, a cracked code that was further validated now that he could share it. Seamus was his Karma, indeed.

Later, during a self-designated break, the boys had the deck to themselves since they had finished busing before everyone else. They needed the privacy, too, since Jamie hid an extra bottle of champagne under the exterior stairwell.

As Jamie was passing the champagne back to Seamus the door kicked open. Seamus impulsively hid the bottle but it was just Steve the bartender. Jamie asked him for a cigarette. He gave one to him and to Seamus too.

Steve sensed something. He watched Jamie and Seamus, who were looking in different directions, grinning but not saying anything. He took violent sucks on his cigarette. He had thin arms and thin fingers, like Barry, but his frame was more imposing, more wiry. His step was quick like Barry's too, but in a different way. His was hostile whereas Barry's was anxious. And, like Barry, Steve was in his early thirties. As far as Seamus and Jamie were concerned, that age was impossibly far away, a certifiable product of adult-land, and a sign of supposed stability. It did not matter to the boys that these two men shared their occupational environment with relative adolescents. They had been through many a something the rest had not. So when a rambling man like Steve spoke, the boys listened.

"You two knuckleheads hit some sauce or what?" Steve asked, jamming a cigarette into his mouth and inhaling hard.

"I only like ketchup," Jamie said.

"It's true. I've seen him get quesadillas from Taco Gordo, covers those things in ketchup. It's awful looking."

Something triggered a thought for Steve and he looked away and into the night. Then, "Taco Gordo... yep!"

When Steve said, "Yep," he was either beginning a story or ending one. His head would jerk back as though that single word was an incantation that summoned a storytelling force within him that could not be stopped once it was started. Steve told stories the way a shaman enters a trance.

"You boys know about the Red Door Tavern on Towne?"

"Hell yeah, I go there all the time," Jamie said.

"The hell you do. You're not 21 yet. But when you are it's something. There's nothing to do. No darts, no pool, some shitty juke box where all the CDs are burned. Yeah! And no dance floor to go with it. But that's okay. You see some bar snakes slither between the high tables and the back wall, ready to shed their skin, you know what I mean. I was in there talking to them one night getting smashed, because that's all you can do at the Red Door. This chick, whatever the hell her name was, comes up to me and we start getting goofy, and next thing I know I'm in the car. I don't remember how I got home. But I wake up and I've got wrappers all over me from Taco Gordo. And I'm thinking, 'Shit, what in God's name?' So I take my morning piss and I nearly hit the ceiling. There's this chick, passed out in the bathtub, and a Taco Gordo burrito, completely untouched, lying in her crotch. I nudge her awake with my foot, my head is crazy hammered throbbing, and I yell at her, 'What's his name!' She freaks awake, cries almost, 'What are you talking about?' I say, 'You tell me. That bastard in your lap sure isn't talking!'"

Steve took a deep drag on his cigarette and tossed it over the railing. He was reliving it all again, and said, "Yep! That's what I think about when I hear Taco Gordo."

Jamie and Seamus went in after Steve while everyone else joined Barry outside. Barry's eyes were holding something back while he addressed them in passing.

"Your tables were done first and you're not taking a half hour smoke break? I guess I *should* tell Angela you count for four people."

Jamie and Seamus delighted in the juxtaposition of reality and projected value, until they turned and saw Angela standing directly behind them in the service area holding two bottles of cranberry juice and a handle of vodka. She was smiling tepidly. It was a rehearsed, false smile that sickened Seamus and Jamie both. Her obvious need for power was alarming.

"So you boys are really getting the job done tonight I hear?"

Steve popped out of the bar, the small sliding door rolling rickety on its rusty tracks, and ripped the bottles from Angela's hands.

"Thanks Angie, but for God's sake I could have used this yesterday. These broads think they're on *Sex in the City*!"

He shot back into his bar and when Angela turned back, Jamie and Seamus were gone. She scuttled out to the floor and saw the two leaning against a wall, holding hand trays and watching the drunks dance under the disco ball, the DJ throwing his hands unnecessarily in the air like he was in the tent at Coachella. She reached for her rubber coiled key chain and rolled it around between her fingers. She glared at them but they paid her no heed. This nervous display persisted for a few ugly moments until one of the guests asked her for coffee. She gave the guest her plastic smile and a few placating words and then immediately shot her eyes right back to Jamie and Seamus, intending to motion them over to help. But once again they were gone.

She hurried to the back door and called for someone, anyone to get this lady some coffee. Jeff, who was working his first shift, immediately jumped up to help.

When Angela turned back inside, she saw Jamie and Seamus again, crossing the room and headed towards Steve. They were carrying hand trays full of dirty glasses.

"What a night, Angela," Jamie said.

"Yeah Angela, these people know how to tie it off. Boy."

"I know you two are having a great night but earlier I saw you were doing nothing while this lady over here needed coffee."

"But that lady was not at any of our tables. These glasses were," Jamie said.

Angela's lips twitched and she looked ready to say something but paused. What could she say? The boys were taking responsibility for their tables. That was their job.

"Okay, I understand. But if you ever get a chance when you're not doing anything, it's okay to help out others."

"Get off their tail, Angela. These two served Isabelita's tables champagne earlier. Their hands are plenty full with their own people, trust me."

It was Barry. And in one fast moment, Steve again shot his red face out the bar. "Jamie and Seamus, boy you two are something else. I just ran out of Martini glasses."

"No problem my man. Tonight's about you," Jamie said.

"Every night is," Steve said as he grabbed both trays, one in each hand, and yanked them back with him into the bar, sliding the door shut with his foot. The boys expected to hear breaking glass, he had taken their trays so manically, but all they heard from the other side of the thin door was, "You're telling me bro, but your girlfriend is trying to make me jealous all night dancing with you that way!"

Angela reached for her keychain and rubbed it as she nodded her head nervously. "Okay boys...keep it up."

At the night's end, Jamie once again disappeared while Seamus was left to make small talk with the captain.

"You stood up against Angela, Barry. You really are looking out for us," Seamus said.

"I'm not looking out for you anymore than I am for me, Seamus. Angela doesn't come down here squeezing the shit out of her keychain, slow with the liquor and pretending to know what she's doing just to get on my crew. I get on my crew."

"Damn straight."

"Damn straight," Barry mimicked. "Are you patronizing me, you little bastard?"

Jamie reappeared in his undershirt holding his tuxedo shirt and vest against his chest. Seamus flushed, but quickly assessed that what were clearly champagne bottles to him just looked like a bundle of dirty clothes to Barry.

"Oh look, it's Seamus' ride," Barry said without so much as looking at Jamie as he walked quickly past him and up to the time clock room. "Whose parents' house are you partying at tonight?" he continued as the boys followed him up the stairs.

"Neither, my man. Seamus is back in school now, you know."

"You're still in school? I thought people like you flunked out their first year." Barry said.

"I almost did."

"I can believe it. What'd you do, spend all your time writing about unicorns or something?"

"No. But I did write an essay about seeing a big ass rainbow."

"Are you serious?"

"Yeah. I had a mystical experience afterwards."

Barry paused before he punched out his time card. Then, "Seamus, are you an only child?"

"Yes, how'd you know?"

"I didn't, but I feel bad for your parents. They better have low expectations or else they're going to be really disappointed."

5

Rachel did not consider Seamus' writing about rainbows disappointing. Instead she found it attractive. She liked to paint, camp, and smoke pot. When she met Seamus in Purgatory during a trilevel dorm's Heaven and Hell party, their connection was immediate. Drunk and talking about nature, Seamus impressed Rachel with his bullshit.

"Sometimes, when I look at the stars on a clear night I swear I can see lines connecting them to each other, making constellations."

"I've seen them too!" Rachel said and grabbed his knee.

She leaned closely into him while he sat back, considering his situation. They had met once before for all of five minutes one day when Seamus was leaving the campus darkroom. Though they were strangers, Rachel asked him how his prints turned out. She could be friendly that way, as some college students sometimes are. When he showed her his work, she complimented the angles he took his shots from and started to talk about her painting. Seamus watched her big lips as she spoke and took note of her body which was curvy but positioned in an awkward way. She wore jeans with holes in the knees and a loose-fitting tee shirt that hid her shape but could not suffocate her braless breasts that bounced when she shifted her weight from one leg to the other. Her legs were skinny but her ass was not. He was interested in her physically but did not care about her paintings and did not particularly feel like seeing them, though he told her he would like to sometime.

He saw them, or at least photos of them on her iPhone, as he sat on the couch with her talking at the Heaven and Hell party. They were okay, he thought. A part of him was almost turned off, but when they started making out, any such feelings dissolved. Rachel could really kiss, and Seamus wanted more of whatever he could get from this strange girl who took to him for no discernible reason other than what was probably little more than a hunch. How else, Seamus reflected later, does romance usually begin?

However it began for her, she had decided that she liked him enough to invite him to her apartment. While this was a win, meeting her roommates later was not. The one named Imogene was the driver. Seamus could not tell if she was in a poor mood because she had drawn the short straw and could not drink for the evening or if she was always that cold. Despite having all of their essential needs catered to, some college students never seemed happy. In any case, she was willing to bring him home with the four of them and for that Seamus was grateful.

Rachel's room was small but the bed was big with throw pillows and a comforter and soft looking sheets and looked very different than what Seamus slept in every night. She had posters on her walls that celebrated Jack Kerouac, Miles Davis, Vincent Van Gogh, Salvador Dali, Gustav Klimt, and The Beatles, including a separate print featuring just John Lennon. Seamus was suddenly irritated as just an hour ago she had been complaining about how everyone at school was the same. Still, she came into the room softly and wrapped her arms around him from behind, kissing the back of his neck and working her hands over his chest and stomach.

He turned to kiss her and again the things that he did not care for about her were forgotten and brushed over. She really was a good kisser, and gave him what he really felt was a good boner. Later, it fit quite well down her throat as she lacked a gag reflex. To be sociable, he reached over her ass and played with her from behind, though he did not feel like it. He was having a fine time letting her work on him. He needed it. It had been a phenomenal summer after all, and the initial rush of being back in the dorms gave way to the shock of having homework. But school was back and here he was, making the most of it.

Rachel went into the bathroom after Seamus finished and he took it upon himself to scroll through her iTunes, changing the artist from Feist to Phish. He turned the speakers louder.

Rachel came in hurriedly and shushed him to be quieter. "My roomies are snoozing," she said in an exaggerated whisper and turned down the volume.

"Good. I think they should snooze all the time," he said.

"Ah!" she slapped him playfully. "They said you were cute."

"That seemed to be about it. They were pretty unimpressed with my Hare Krishna costume."

She smiled. Her teeth were perfect. Her lips really were big. "That's because you just wrapped a bed sheet around you. It had squares all over it, totally Bed Bath and Beyond."

"I drew an Om on my hand."

"I like that," she said and kissed it. He kissed her neck and she kissed his chest and then he kissed hers too. They went on this way, exchanging pecks and giggles until Seamus was ready again. He did not bring any condoms and was thankful that she had some. He put one on and got to work.

Afterwards they talked well into the morning about school, people they both knew, the music and movies and books and art they liked, the food they ate, and even a couple of anecdotes related to work. Rachel had never held a job like Seamus had, but for all he knew Singing Pines was the most inspiring place on Earth. She liked that he worked, probably he knew because it made him sound responsible. He looked forward to his shift the next night. After what ended up being a dry summer, he could not wait to tell Alfredo he got laid again, or to see what kind of celebration Jamie would drag him through now. He even anticipated warmly the thought of Barry's ridicules. He imagined his captain questioning what was wrong with all the other guys at the party or asking what indeed was wrong with her. And if anything told him he loved Singing Pines, it was that. Something about the place, he knew, was bringing out the best in him.

6

Seamus was well aware that life lacked inherent meaning but lately he was charmed by the tremendous uplift that a life seemingly full with purpose provides. He and Rachel were dating and not just sleeping together and when she told him that she wanted him to come over to her parents' house for Thanksgiving so "my family can meet my boyfriend," he immediately accepted the invite though it was not yet Halloween. He had other girlfriends before her, but Rachel was his immediate favorite despite that they had been together for little more than a month.

Rachel listened to Seamus as he philosophized and shared in it, too. While she was sympathetic to his desire to hitchhike, she had many stories of her own from actual travel that crystallized her world view. Their physical chemistry was strong in the beguiling way that it is with some people and not with others. Early on, Seamus tried to conceptualize a concrete reason why their mutual attraction was so, as the hints were many but the certainty of just how it all fit remained elusive. But when no sufficient reason emerged from his heart-drunk thoughts, he gave up worrying about it and settled into the gooeyness of the whole damn thing. Strangely, all else seemed to fall into place after that.

Classes so far were all going well and he was on the bizarre verge of earning a GPA higher than a 3.0. As of midterms he was in strong academic shape and should he continue to attend just the right amount of classes and put just the right amount of time into completing his assignments, then his next report card would be his best so far by a long shot.

He was going to get an A in photography and he always felt competent and happy behind a camera. Resistance to Monoculture was also a good bet for a high mark since the teacher graded soft and cared more about students being honest in their papers about why globalization is evil, Monsanto is evil, and how the public school system is probably evil than he did about the references they cited to support their arguments.

He did not believe he would have what it took to get more than a B in Probability of Games and Gambling and more likely would earn a C, but that did not matter because the course fulfilled one of his math credits for eventual graduation. Should he get a C he would make up for it with his other classes including Philosophy of Art, which was the best course he had taken outside of photography. All he had to do was consider what art was and why, and read anecdotal essays about eccentrics like Damien Hirst and Dan Flavin and Andres Serrano and contrast their work against that produced by older, canonized artists before them. Other questions were posed regarding mass produced abstract art that could be found at stores like Target, if advertisements could be considered artistic, and what role media and academia both had in determining how artists gained exposure.

Because Rachel liked to paint, she enjoyed it when Seamus talked about his philosophy course. On a date to a museum in the city, they smoked a joint on the drive over and explored the sculpture garden while at their most stoned. Seamus talked about ideas for wire and wood sculptures he had which he hoped to make someday soon, perhaps over winter break and if not then maybe over the summer. Because Seamus was young it did not matter that he would never bring any of these ideas to fruition. He was at the age where, by all reasonable accounts, he very well could if he chose to so merely talking about them was impressive enough to Rachel and provided Seamus with an afternoon that further increased his sexual stock as an attractive partner.

Of course, life at Singing Pines remained wonderful. It provided Seamus with an escape from school. Even at its best, a class was still a class and the teacher leading it was still getting paid to lay judgment, whether good or bad, to the intellectual output of a young man like Seamus, and for that he remained suspicious of the institution as a whole. Singing Pines was at least a place he could feel good about when he snuck by producing the least amount of work possible while getting as altered as he reasonably could. In fact, though he was not one to admit or even notice it, life was going so well for him that he even stepped up his banquet serving game and did out-of-character things like serve coffee without much delay or argument, refill water pitchers without being asked to do so, and make small talk with Angela that was almost genuine even if it was secretly condescending.

"I like that necklace, Angela."

"Oh, well thank you Seamus."

"It's subtle and doesn't go against what you're wearing."

"Doesn't go against, but doesn't go with?"

"You're saying that, not me. Sorry, I just noticed it. I'm in a philosophy of art class and we talk about aesthetics. You might have a good eye."

And for someone who was largely ignored by her employees and coworkers alike save for Jeff, who talked to her more often than even she would like, Angela appreciated what sounded like a compliment from Seamus and though she still got on his case about how long his hair was or the fact that he needed to shave, she did so with loose authority that signaled to Seamus that he was winning. Jamie could not have been more proud of him.

With this much momentum greasing their collective wheels, the boys decided to engage in an activity that would be universally frowned upon by all varieties of authority figures when they ate psychedelic mushrooms before one of their shifts.

From their perspective, this was no ordinary shift, but the perfect shift. It was a rare Friday without a wedding. Jamie, Seamus, Isabelita and Christine were scheduled to set the main dining room accordingly for the wedding the following night. Barry had the night off and Mack, the man who captained most of the upstairs weddings, pulled the captain assignment this evening.

The boys would never dare to trip off their faces around Barry. But Mack was no Barry. He was a large man, and by most accounts, a lazy man. He was a self-described gambler and an ex-con, his crimes being tax evasion and fraud. He had an angry ex-wife and a young child. He had an overbite, a lazy eye, but was otherwise an average looking white dude in his early thirties. He appeared to the boys to be one of life's many losers, but that did not mean they disliked him. They simply underestimated him, just as they underestimated the effects of psilocybin in their systems while working a routine shift. Seamus had made strides, but not that many. And Jamie, master of the Singing Pines universe, was about to learn that he by no means knew it all. For one thing, the silverware at the country club was not new.

"Oh Jamie, no they're not," Christine said.

"Yes they are."

"Jamie, I've told you already they are not new!"

"Christine, you can lie to me all you want but look how shiny these things are. I'm not stupid."

Isabelita, wary of Jamie's insistence, asked Seamus for the second time in a whisper, "What did you boys *do* before you came in tonight?"

Seamus, wide-eyed, said, "We played some basketball. Why?"

"You played basketball?"

"Yes." Seamus quickly walked to the service area for no definable reason and traced his hands along the cake cutting table. Wood grains moved like river water back and forth in a nauseating but entertaining pattern. Pen markings spiraled in and out of each other, mimicking the flighty motions of fish swimming in a school. A psychedelic ecosystem was flourishing at his fingertips, and for a moment he was having fun again.

But he heard yelling out in the dining room, which was strange because other than short sentences, everyone was being little more than silent. Seamus could not recall when the turning point was, but there was a moment earlier in the night when it appeared certain everyone knew. Of course, to one on a mushroom trip, everyone always knows. Trip paranoia was not new to Seamus, but this situation seemed more real than imagined.

"What's wrong?" Seamus asked as he reentered the room.

"Well hell, Seamus, that's what we'd all like to know," Mack said.

"Oh. I just heard yelling."

"No one's yelling," Mack said.

"Oh. Well..."

Jamie cut in, sensing his friend was in trouble.

"I'm about to yell myself, homeboy, if someone doesn't come clean about this silverware."

"They're not new Jamie, get off it already," Mack said as he walked by them carrying another tray full of silverware and placed it on a chair. "But all these are."

"Let me see these things!" Jamie yelled and threw down the handful of spoons he was holding onto a table. "Ah, but these are just as shiny as the other ones...they are new! They're all new!"

Mack laughed, though it was a terse sound. "I'm just playing with you Jamie. None of this shit is new. This is Singing Pines we're talking about here. Just look at the curtains, they haven't been replaced since 1991."

Seamus looked at the curtains and shuddered. The room descended back into soundlessness as Jamie finally quieted and stared into a spoon for an indeterminable amount of time. Seamus rigidly continued setting tables, but he was troubled. He was thinking about his identity and he was thinking about his father. He was conceived in 1991. His father entering his mother made him recoil, and suddenly, he needed to the leave the room again. He ran to the bathroom and looked into the mirror. He watched his face shift shapes, widening, narrowing, widening again. He stared into his eyes. They had fear.

Seamus considered a passage from *Zen Mind, Beginner's Mind* where Shunryu Suzuki said, "What we call 'I' is just a swinging door which moves when we inhale and when we exhale."

Indeed Seamus breathed in and out, and as he opened the bathroom door he reflected that his identity was merely an illusion anyway and that he was dying each moment to be reborn again. Feeling the best he had all shift, he walked calmly back to the room and figured that everything would be okay.

Then he saw Angela, who turned and said, "Oh Seamus, there you are."

Seamus considered. "Here I am," he said, Zen like.

She laughed her nervous, fake laugh, and said, "Yes you sure are. Listen, I was just telling everyone to put what pumpkin centerpieces we have on the tables for now. We're short but the mother of the bride is going to bring the rest of them tomorrow."

Seamus nodded and then proceeded past his boss to a table to continue setting it. His motions were deliberate and severe, as though any crooked knife would trigger a bomb that would kill them all.

Angela stood in the entryway watching him. Her keychain was in her fingers. Then, "And Seamus, one more thing."

He lifted his head slowly and met her eyes with his. An unplaced fork remained in his unmoving hand. "Yes?" he asked.

She frowned, perhaps out of habit, or perhaps out of something darker and more suspect. She said, "We really need you to cut your hair. I keep telling you and you never do it. It's time."

"It's time?" Jamie asked.

Mack and the girls kept working but stared at Jamie. The air was suffocating.

"Jamie, I think this is between Seamus and me."

"Than why are you putting my man on the spot in front

of all of us?"

Angela squeezed her keychain. "Excuse me, but I've told, your man, to cut his hair enough times already."

"Well that's fine, but I think he looks great!"

Angela, pulling from her managerial skill set, changed tones. "Well thanks for that Jamie, I love your enthusiasm but this isn't a topic of debate."

"It's not debate. It's about rights. And my man has the right to look good!"

Seamus ran a hand through his hair. It was frizzy as it had not been washed in three days and was grown well past his ears. It hung over his eyes and was inching closer to his shoulders.

"Thanks, Jamie," he said. "I get compliments on my hair you know," he told Angela.

"From who?" she humored him.

"My tables."

"Your tables compliment your hair?"

"All the time. Hey, I apologize though if it's not your bag."

"My bag?" Angela let out a few light chuckles that signaled to Seamus that he was right, everything was going to be okay. "Wow Seamus, you really are trying to play a part, aren't you?"

"We're all playing parts, Angela."

Though the bag comment had appeared to loosen her, his cryptic philosophical inference as to the falseness of human interaction again inspired her twitchy fingers to fumble with the keychain. Now she was defensive.

"Look Seamus, I actually like long hair. My boyfriend has long hair, longer than yours."

"Hallelujah!" Jamie yelled.

"But the rules are the rules. You need to cut it before the next wedding. That's it." Angela turned, looked at Mack and the girls, then back to the boys, and said, "Good work everybody. Keep it up." She then walked away as though Seamus was her boss and she had really stuck it to him.

For the rest of the shift, Jamie's mood took on an aggressive tone. He felt that Seamus had been wronged.

"Seamus man, we all play parts. We all play parts!" He yelled. "You do too, Mack. Let me tell you something, you're my captain only in name. In blood we are no different. No different whatsoever."

Mack ignored him.

"The silent treatment, huh? Well, it appears you've heard this before then. I liked you Mack, and I still do. But you let my man have it."

"Nobody let your man have it, Jamie. Seamus just needs to cut his hair already. And you need to not do whatever it is you did before work today."

Jamie scoffed. The girls were nervous. They cared about Jamie and Seamus both. When Angela was seen in the back area, busying herself with a box of sugar packets, Isabelita forced her way in front of the boys to prevent another run-in with the boss.

"Jamie!" she started, "what's your favorite color?"

"My favorite color?" he shouted.

"Yeah, stay here, tell me what your favorite color is."

"Blue," he said. "What's it to you?"

"I was just wondering."

Meanwhile, Christine was talking with Angela, fulfilling her own part, ensuring that the boss never stepped out again, and instead went back up to her office, sugar packets in hand, and ice tea in the other.

And when Angela came down again to talk to Mack, the girls told Jamie and Seamus to get the glassware.

"Who made you the captain?" Jamie asked.

"Just do it Jamie, please!" Isabelita said. Jamie looked into her eyes. "Fine sweet face. But only because you're my doll."

When they returned the other crew members were talking in hushed tones.

"Oh? Don't mind us, we're just the elephant in the room!" Jamie shouted.

Ignored, Jamie muttered to himself in disgust and got to work setting the tables with glassware. Seamus felt sad. No one spoke. The others looked at each other often, which bothered the boys. It was clear that people they had come to know and like could not be trusted.

When Jamie and Seamus came downstairs again after taking out the trash, which took ten minutes since Jamie ranted to Seamus the entire time about society, rules, and how he felt he had failed his friend, Isabelita and Christine huddled by Mack over the setup sheet. Their eyes were troubled and Jamie was about to say something again, but Mack beat him to it.

"Seamus and Jamie!" he yelled. His voice was a train horn, born from the bottom of his gut, belted out with hammering enunciation and tyranny. The boys, walking with their chests out and ahead of their feet in a zombie-like stride akin to cartoon mice being pulled nearly magnetically across the screen by a tantalizing and surrealistically visible scent, came forward before the committee of suspicious coworkers. The girls looked up from the sheet to look sullenly at them. Christine was shaking her head. There was something very wrong here, the boys knew, and the weight of it broke any hostility that raged within them. Sobering, the girls' eyes were no longer judgmental, and elicited sympathies from the boys, even shame. Mack, still looking over the sheet, was a tougher read. A chronic gambler indeed, his poker face was downright intimidating. The boys stood still and awaited the sentence for their unspoken crimes.

Mack finally lifted his eyes, lazy and all, from the sheet. "You are free to go," he said.

The boys looked at each other, turned on their heels, and broke into a sprint up the stairs. They forgot to clock out as they raced to Jamie's car. Maybe it was the fresh air, maybe it was that so many hours had passed, but Jamie and Seamus both felt suddenly clear-headed.

In the car, Jamie was no longer agitated. He only looked confused.

"What...was *that*?" he asked.

"I don't know man!" Seamus answered, his voice shaking. "But we're outta there now dude."

"No shit," Jamie reversed and shifted into drive with a heavy foot. The stop signs meant nothing to him. "All I know is, that silverware looked new."

"Yeah, that and how unfair it was of Angela to ask me to cut my hair."

Jamie shook in his seat. He laughed loud and hard,

swerving several times over the lane as he did so. "Man oh man, I couldn't believe it! Looking back it was not that big of a deal...but you're my man! You're my main man!"

"And you're my main man, man." Seamus laughed. "We just ate mushrooms at work and kept our jobs."

Jamie quieted, stilled. "We just ate mushrooms at work and kept our jobs."

The boys considered what that meant as they drove to Seamus' dorm. On the way they passed a church. It had spotlights sitting on the lawn. Across the way a homecoming game was in its second quarter at the local high school football field. It was not the high school that the boys attended, it was the public school, the crosstown rival. Jamie and Seamus looked at it reverentially.

"My man, you know what those lights mean?"

"It's homecoming, Jamie."

Jamie took a hand off the wheel and covered his mouth. "Homecoming. It is homecoming, Seamus."

The boys, certain that the homecoming lights were a symbol, felt the need for self reflection. When they arrived at the dorm they stood in an outside courtyard and smoked cigarettes they bummed earlier from Christine.

Seamus said, "You know dude, I think that might have been really immature of us."

Jamie sniffed, and Seamus looked away. He could not see his friend cry right now or he would lose it.

"It's not the world that's the problem. It's me."

"Jamie."

"Seamus, where are we going?"

Sean Pravica

Seamus exhaled. Whatever sense of purpose he had derived from his quaint life was now being held under the microscope of truth. He knew that he had nothing left to do but be honest.

"That's the big question. Are we good people? All we do is go to school and go to work. I mean, that's what we've been told to do. And we're doing it. But people are starving, man. All over the world, starving."

"Starving! Forget about it!" Jamie yelled. "Seamus, we have so much food in this country we can eat shit that makes us hallucinate just for the fuck of it. That's gross."

"That's true! My God man, I've been tripping a lot lately, too. Took Rachel out to that sunflower field where you and I smoked a joint. God, I love that place."

"Out of sight! How'd she feel about it?"

"Had a fucking awesome ass time!"

Seamus pulled out a piece of torn parchment paper from his pocket. Rachel had painted him sunflowers in watercolors. The flowers looked distorted and appeared to transcend a singular dimension and overlap into others, or at least that was how he interpreted it.

"These flowers represent the fact that ultimate reality is unknowable but all around us at all times," Seamus said and knew he was right.

"Yep, yep," Jamie nodded vigorously, agreeing with him. "It's what it's all about," he said.

"What's it?"

"What do you mean what's it?"

"You said that's what it's all about. What's it?"

61

Jamie shrugged. "I don't know man. It's just a saying." He laughed. "It. It's just a saying."

"It's not though. It is something."

"What is it, then?"

"I don't know...except I do. I know it when I see it. It...It with a capital I!"

"Seamus, that's It!"

"That is It!"

"My man, do you know what this means?"

"Yes, except I can't tell you."

"I can't tell you either, but I know exactly what you mean. You know It when you see It."

"Period."

"End of story."

The boys finished their cigarettes in unspoken bliss. Their eyes were full of understanding and their hearts beat at an excited gallop. No one knew what they knew, except for those who did. And they knew that those who knew would know that they knew, too.

"So being in that sunflower field is what It is all about."

"That sunflower field is beauty," Seamus said. "That sunflower field is where I go to remind myself that whatever it is I'm doing, there is something inextricably big that means more than anything here ever will. I can't know ultimate reality, but I can visit it always."

"And everywhere..." Jamie added, staring far away.

"Yes man. It is what matters. Nothing else, not ultimately. Not in the big picture."

"Yes my man, yes. It! Holy hell, how did we not see this before?"

"I don't know man. How does someone miss a glitch when it's staring him right in the face?" Seamus smiled.

"My man!" Jamie pulled him in for a hug and then, "Listen. What we did in there was the right thing."

"Jeez, I mean I get that we pulled it off but how was that the right thing?"

"Look what we're talking about now. It. The Big Picture. That was nothing more than a test. And we passed with flying fucking colors."

Seamus considered. "I don't know man. Could have been a C+ at best."

"Dude, if I got a C+ in a class my dad would probably throw a goddamn party. Hey man, you said it already: we ate mushrooms at work and kept our jobs."

"Hopefully. We still don't know what all that sad-sad stuff at the end was. Dude, Mack and the girls looked like someone had died!"

"Never mind what bug was buzzing in their ear. That's their problem, not ours. I couldn't think straight at the time but looking back they had our backs. And all I did was blame them for my own sins. That's what I mean, it's not the world that's the problem. The world is as the world is. I need to keep my own nose clean is all. That was a little sloppy, but we still made it through."

"True, they wouldn't prevent us from seeing Angela if they were looking to get us popped."

"Exactly. They had their chance but they kept cool. We owe them our gratitude. "

"God yeah we do. Dude, just thinking about, I feel like today we were the glitch. Imagine how that must have looked?"

Jamie clapped his hands. "My man! Hey, even the good guys short some wires sometimes. But that's okay. Today was a good, honest lesson. I'm not going to stop doing what I do at work, but having It might just change my approach."

Jamie wandered into the courtyard, looked up, and smiled wide. "Shit, I think I can even see those goddamn lines you've told me about!"

"Yeah! That's right man, yeah!"

"Fucking beautiful. All this stuff, even this stupid school, beautiful. You're beautiful, Seamus."

"You are my man, you are."

"I know that. You know what else is beautiful?"

Jamie unwound his Singing Pines polo shirt, which had sat crumpled in the planter. He revealed a bottle of champagne.

"You dog!" Seamus shouted.

"I don't care if I was tripping face or sober as a church mouse. You know I get what's mine."

"It's so cold, too!"

"Straight from the walk-in. C'mon, let's toast to It. Our work is just beginning."

And so Seamus drank with Jamie, knowing that their work had indeed just begun, and was sure, though he could not define it if someone asked him, that he knew just what that work actually was.

7

Seamus realized that he was in the business of living a happy, fulfilled life. He had not enjoyed his childhood on the whole, and while his first year in college had its moments, it was more disenchanting than anything else. All he heard beyond the ivory tower of his so-called higher education were reports of a crumbled economy, jobless rates, depression, anxiety, and new directions on shaky foundations. The last part inspired him, but scared him too. It seemed the only way to make it work these days was to forge a new path, both in business and in philosophy. The America his parents grew up in was not his America, and that he knew. And so, talking with Jamie during breaks at work and while drinking afterwards, it was obvious to them that the only answer to today's questions was It. Though undefinable, It had implications, and it was their true work to understand what those were.

The next time Jamie and Seamus were scheduled for a setup shift on a Friday they abstained from drugs of any sort and worked as quickly as possible so they could imbibe immediately afterwards. Besides, Barry was captaining and he would not be a fun man to trip around. Christine was working again with them and her patience would wear thin, too, if they pushed it further. What happened the night Seamus and Jamie tripped on mushrooms became an unspoken anecdote, and the boys respected Christine for keeping her mouth quiet. She in turn told them that the reason she and the others were so upset was because Mack realized only later that all of the tables needed to be set with overlays, a step that had been ignored up to that point.

Not wanting to trigger any drama, Mack cut the boys early and kept the girls to gut through the painful task of resetting everything. The boys rarely worked with Mack, but they had a new appreciation for him, too.

"It's not the world, Seamus. It's you and me. But that doesn't mean we can't manipulate it as needed. Just keep your moral compass due north, if you know what I mean."

"Just follow It."

"My man!"

As for the setup shift with Barry, the reception was on the small side, but the crew set the room in record-time: just under three hours. The shift was scheduled earlier than usual at two in the afternoon, and now that the boys were off the clock they were in a hurry to eat the mescaline that Seamus picked up from his favorite dealer, a young man named Byron. Neither he nor Jamie had ever taken mescaline before and figured that like most things experienced for the first time, they were up for a treat.

They were going to eat the buttons, already divided by an anxious Seamus, on the drive home, but were arrested by the sight of Barry staring at them as he walked to his Isuzu Trooper parked next to Jamie's Saturn.

"Shit, it's the authorities. Hide the stash," Jamie said.

"Take no chances," Seamus said.

Giddy with excitement, they giggled and stirred in their seats, already pretending as children do, transforming their lives with their minds into adventure stories, agents everywhere, glitches alerting them to their presence.

"Look at you two punks, laughing in a parked car in your white undershirts...I bet you get all the chicks," Barry said.

"Yes sir," Jamie said.

"Yes sir," Barry mocked. "Always patronizing me. Punks."

Seamus and Jamie looked at each other. The captain was in a different kind of mood himself. It had to be Friday, a different kind without a reception and the work that was to be done finished so quickly. The boys knew that the captain was proud of them, and they felt proud of themselves. They were eager for what would be an exceptional trip with heads this full of positive psychology.

It was not until Christine arrived that the magic of the afternoon took full affect, when Barry looked over at her and said, "Look at Christine, still wearing her Singing Pines shirt and smoking a cigarette. She must get all the guys."

"There's someone for everyone my man," Jamie said. "Look at you and your Trooper, I bet your wife just sits in the living room chewing her fingernails waiting for you to get home."

Barry laughed and looked away, pulled out a cigarette and leaned against his Trooper to smoke. "Nah. Wifey likes hair." He blew out a thick cloud of smoke. "And I don't have much of that."

"My man!" Jamie yelled and got out of the car. Seamus followed. Christine, spotting the commotion, joined them.

"You tell Wifey that she's gotta pull her weight if you're going to give it to her," Jamie said.

"No Jamie, our relationship isn't like that. You wouldn't understand. You have a full head of bushy hair. And Seamus' is so long he can't see through it. You guys get way too much pussy to relate to a 32-year old loser like me."

"Oh Barry, you're being funny again," Christine said.

"I'm not being funny, Christine. The world's a different

place for us bald guys."

"The hell it is," Seamus said.

"We just grow older and balder until we don't leave the house anymore, and then we stare out the window and creep out the neighbors. It's how it is."

"Barry, why do you run yourself down like this? I think you're very handsome," Christine said.

"You are, and it's time you admit that to yourself," Jamie said.

"You don't have to be nice to me. The world stopped being nice a couple years ago, when I started to lose my hair. It's getting darker every year."

"You rock what you got, dude," Seamus said.

Then, looking at him, Barry said with hopeful eyes, "Yeah, rock what I got. Just like you rock not having a car. Thanks Seamus."

Everyone laughed while Barry just smoked and looked away again into the distance. Seamus could see the mischief. It was rising. And it was palpable.

"Hell, when I do get a car I'm getting one of these things. A red Trooper just like Captain Barry."

"It's not really red as much as it's rust," Barry said. He looked everyone over with his eyes alive in a way the boys had never seen them, and offered mysteriously, "You wouldn't even know what to do with this thing. You're a boy, Seamus. You have all the hair in the world, but you're not man enough for a Trooper."

"Damn!" Jamie screamed into the day. "That's my captain, right here! Sorry my man but he's got your number!"

"What are you getting so excited about, Jamie? Boys who drive Saturns don't even begin to have what it takes to handle a machine like this."

"Are you offering me a chance to drive the Trooper? Is this really happening?" Jamie asked.

"Hell no." Barry stamped out his cigarette. "You want a ride though?"

The boys were quiet at first and their heads rattled with the surprise of Barry's invitation, a look into the captain's world, a close-up of the loser's driver seat.

"C'mon, let's go for a ride," Barry said and pushed up the passenger seat revealing a seatless floor behind it save for a faded blue cooler.

The mescaline was in Jamie's console still and he rolled up his windows and locked his doors.

"We're going for a ride," he said to Seamus, hushed and profane.

"Yes man, yes we are," Seamus answered and followed a diving Jamie into the back of the Trooper.

Barry pushed back the passenger seat into its upright position and said, "Coming Christine?"

She smiled with pursed lips and unfolded her crossed arms. "Why not?"

The trooper was musty inside. And hot. The leather upholstery had cracked in many places, faded everywhere else. The windows were tinted but grimy, casting the world in a wintery light that made an overcast day like this one that much grayer. The engine rattled. The body creaked. And though it was only one part of an afternoon, the ride would be an immortal moment in the boys' minds.

Barry put on a CD. *The Blues Brothers* soundtrack.

"Help yourselves to the cooler. There's no ice in there so the beer is warm."

Jamie pulled out two Bud Lights and gave one to Seamus.

"Holy hell! This isn't half-bad," Jamie yelled over the music. "I'm going to buy a six-pack tomorrow and leave it in the sun."

"Shut up. You're not even old enough to drink beer. And you're probably just going to go home all wasted and tell your mom on me."

"Yeah right, Barry. This is our secret!"

"Well I'm sure it is for Seamus. He'd be too ashamed to tell any of his hippy buddies in college that he took a spin in this gas guzzler."

"Seamus is going places!" Jamie yelled.

"I know he is. I see a methadone clinic in his future."

Barry turned up the music and drove through the neighborhoods near Singing Pines. It was a mystery where he was headed but the boys drank their beers and shoved each other from side to side. Christine smiled in the front seat as she watched them in the rear view mirror.

Outside, children sped by on bikes, skateboards, scooters, Power Wheels. They shot each other with squirt guns, threw water balloons. It was Friday, and they were unplugged.

"Jesus, don't these rug rats play Xbox like everyone else their age?" Barry said.

"These kids know what they're doing, and they make me fucking proud!" Jamie howled.

"Yeah," Barry said inaudibly and turned the music a bit

louder.

A woman watering her lawn looked at the Trooper as it passed. She had twisted columns of cypress, globular shrubs yet to receive water. But she stood, her body rigid, the hose resting in her hand like a prop, and sneered. Her young daughter was just wheeling out of the garage on a tricycle.

Jamie rolled down the window and shouted, "Take a picture!" It was impossible to hear over *Gimme Some Lovin'*.

Barry drove past the houses and to a quieter area in the hills where the public golf course was, the shooting range, the horse stables, the juvenile detention center. He eventually reached a narrow gravel driveway sprouting off the side of the road and sped up onto it, sending dirt clouds blooming behind him. They entered a clearing that was wide and empty. Two mounds of dirt sat like desert dunes. Barry drove over the first which was small enough that even the Trooper handled it gently. The next sent everyone rocking from side to side.

Barry turned down the volume knob. "We're going to see if the gate is open," he said.

"What gate?" Christine asked.

"This way," Barry said and turned the music up loud again.

"Any way you lead us I'll take that ride, captain!" Jamie shouted.

Was this It?

Barry drove parallel to the edge of a canyon that the clearing ultimately led to, the town below as easy to absorb as it was from the roof at Singing Pines. Barry took the Trooper to a narrower driveway yet, unpaved and so rocky that the trip in felt like offroading in a shopping cart. Soon a canopy of trees greeted them and a creek with sunlit twinkling water winked them a welcome.

It was.

Barry turned the track to *Rawhide* and hit the volume higher yet again. His bald head bobbed around while the Trooper crawled over the wet stones and fallen tree branches. Jamie roared words that had no language, hung on the back of the driver's seat, poked an unresponsive Barry in his side, laughed manically at Christine.

Seamus rolled down his window with the thought of throwing his empty bottle at a tree but Jamie beat him to it and immediately launched his own at a boulder. The glass exploded with a sharp pop and the remaining beer fizzed against the rock.

"Hey!" Barry yelled.

Seamus followed suit and sent his bottle hurdling into the brush, clipping a tree trunk along its way.

"Hey!" Barry yelled again. "I thought you'd have a carbon footprint of negative two!"

"It's Friday, captain!"

Barry got another minute out of the trail before he reached a fence locked with a padlock, its copper smirk reflecting the sunlight as it held snugly to its thick chain and turned away all trespassers. Beyond the boys looked haplessly on to a promised land they would not know, but it did not matter. They had made it this far, and that for once was enough.

"End of the line," Barry said and turned down the music. "There didn't used to be a fence here."

"This town is going to shit!" Jamie moaned.

Barry put *Rawhide* back on repeat, turned it loud, and made a u-turn that took many, many revolutions before he was able to spin the Trooper back around and take Christine and the boys to the clearing. There he parked along the canyon's edge. Everyone got out except for Jamie, for whom Barry had to open the trunk door. Jamie somersaulted out and landed in a headstand. It was his first of three.

"Oh God, you are a lightweight."

"That's not it, captain. I just got out of an Isuzu Trooper. I will not be the same."

"Yeah, yeah."

Barry opened the cooler and gave everyone a beer. He took a seat at the canyon's lip, popped open his bottle, and drank, wrapping his arms around his knees afterwards to look out and say nothing.

Jamie rolled into another headstand and Barry turned to watch him wearily.

"Jesus, keep an eye on him, Seamus. You don't want your knucklehead bestie ending up in a missing person's report." He drank. "I'm not taking the heat."

"Jamie knows how to stay out of trouble, Barry. Except when he rides his bike," Seamus said.

"Dude, my ankle is still not the same. I don't know if it'll ever be." Jamie kicked off a shoe swiftly and caught it in his hand. He put it sideways on the ground and slipped half a foot in, rolling the shoe from side to side.

"That's how my ankle was. I could straight up and see the sole of my foot!" He beamed as he recalled his injury.

"See Jamie - this is why I worry about you! I remember when that happened, too. You came into work limping so bad. It just broke my heart," Christine said.

"And this happened when you were riding your bike?" Barry asked.

"I was trying to ride it. I missed my jump. But all I know is that I'm here now, with my favorite captain, looking over my hometown with the bird's eye view," Jamie said with his arms outstretched.

Barry sighed heavily. "You've been warned, Seamus."

"Barry, let me tell you something." Jamie put his arm around him. "If I fall off the side of a cliff today, no one will be that surprised."

"At least try and fall off a cliff when I'm not here feeding you beer. And for the record, there are only two beers left anyway. You and your deadhead friend there will have to fight Christine for it."

"They can have 'em," Christine said, lighting a cigarette.

"Always looking after us, you're a Queen, Christine."

"I bet you want a cigarette, too?"

"Yes, and so does Seamus."

"Okay. But only because you bought me a pack last weekend."

Everyone smoked and stared. Barry looked only a touch less concerned than he did taking a break in the heat of a wedding reception, but a smile, however slight, crept onto his face. Seamus saw it but did not want to look for long. The captain might notice. And Seamus did not want to disturb the perfection of the settling sun, the quiet, the authenticity. He looked to his right at the only other car in the area and saw a couple leaning against each other on a blanket. He took a picture of them with his iPhone and thought the picture was okay but the figures were too far away to be done proper justice. Their bodies made an imperfect triangle. The hillsides of the canyon angled down into the valley at an inverse, nearly mirrored shape. Or at least that was how Seamus saw it.

He tried to take the picture from another angle but Jamie broke the shot. He tossed himself into one final headstand, laughing upside down, and pivoted on his hands so that he fell at an awkward angle with his left leg dragging against the canyon's lip, sending a small outburst of dust and rocks sliding into the shrubs below.

Barry let out an agitated chuckle and said, "Jamie, seriously... be careful."

Jamie only laughed and the crew got back in the car with Barry's wordless lead. He rose, dusted himself off, and frowned at Seamus and Jamie as they tossed their bottles into the canyon. Only when leaving did he ask Seamus if he was worried about being expelled for littering.

"Oh they have ways of finding out," he told Seamus.

"Who?"

"They."

Seamus knew that Barry was joking but also knew that subconsciously he was probably aware that "They" were real and were usually responsible for ruining everything.

"Barry's got It, man. He knows more than he lets on, but he hints around," Seamus told Jamie as they drove to Seamus' dorm.

"Wrote the book."

"And we got one sliver of that reality this afternoon. Just one. But it was sweet man. The guy wasn't born yesterday."

"You see those faded ass stickers on his car? I like the one that just said, 'LIFE.'"

"Holy shit that was inspiring! It was just like, life, take it in."

"And that's just what we did, my man."

Seamus and Jamie ate the buttons and smiled though they tasted awful. Jamie had some orange juice he lifted from the club and they washed away the battery acid taste of the mescaline with big gulps of it. Jamie sped through town while they both let their feet hang out the windows. They tripped on Seamus' campus and felt deeply connected to the many plants, specifically all the succulents, that littered the school grounds. Jamie crouched to the ground and pawed the velvety leaves of a felt bush.

"I had a class last year in environmental studies. My teacher just went ga-ga over plants and now I think I can see why. Feel this thing. You could make a shirt out of it! Hell, I'd wear it."

Seamus did and agreed that it was a remarkable sensation. But he was thinking about something else. "You ever think about going back to school?"

Jamie stood and smiled. "This coming from you? Sure, if that's the way the wind blows. Right now I've got a good thing going at Singing Pines."

"Yeah it's good for now."

"And good for now is good for me. The truth is, Seamus, when I go to work I just do what I want."

This inspired Seamus. The message was clear, simple, direct. It embodied what Singing Pines meant to them, reminded them of the freedom they had available to them if they played their cards correctly and made noise only where it could not be heard by others, even the man who had It but reluctantly represented They.

Whatever Barry was doing with his seemingly dead-end life, the boys hoped it was what he wanted somehow. As far as they knew, that was all that mattered.

8

Seamus felt his life was anything but dead-end, even though by all conceivable vantage points it was incredibly ordinary. Even without a clear notion of the future – save for one in which he would have, until the grave, a valid and special hold on It – his life seemed like it was going somewhere positive. His friendship with Jamie played its part, but then so did love.

Thanksgiving with Rachel's family was a special night for the young man. They were welcoming, warm, and positive. It was a night that helped wash over more troubled memories of Thanksgivings past. Seamus did not especially look forward to the holidays, but this year's was, thanks indeed, shaping up to be different.

Seamus had taken a train and then a subway and then walked for a mile to get to her parent's house. She did not know it. For all she knew he had just gotten a ride from Jamie. But after having spent the previous night high on acid, he was still feeling edgy, but in a positive way.

"I've still got the wanders," he told Jamie.

"Dude, enjoy them. The wanders keep you free."

And they did. The antsy feeling brought on by certain hallucinogenic drugs was not one Seamus minded. In fact he welcomed it. He was, after all, a thinker, and this usually entailed being a walker, too.

And when Rachel answered the door, her slacks charcoal gray and tight to her hips, her sweater maroon and snug, her face in makeup, eyes bright, lower lip full and sparkling, her smile as much an affirmation of his place by her side as it was a welcome, he blushed. He kissed her and she moved into him closing the door behind her but with her hand still on the knob, and kissed him deeply. She pulled her face away, smiling, skin pale and aglow, to tell him that a lot of people were over, and that they would have their time alone later. Then she pushed the door open and he followed.

Not everyone talked to him much but those that did were engaging. Really, it was her parents and her little brother that asked him the most questions. And they listened well. Though he never told anyone his plans to hitchhike, only Rachel knew that and even then it was a light issue, he was given the floor with her father to describe why he liked Jack Kerouac so much.

"Ecstasy through simplicity," Seamus said.

Her dad smiled and meant it, and Seamus suspected he might have It. Her mother meanwhile, talked art. Seamus was well versed enough in contemporary scenes given his philosophy class. Lastly, her little brother was intrigued by Seamus' notion of It, which came across loosely but the young man, being in high school and being at least somewhat open to new perspectives, appreciated the enthusiasm Seamus showed as they spoke privately. Sometimes, enthusiasm is enough for a young man like Rachel's brother. Young people, when enthusiastic, understand a lot of things.

If Thanksgiving was any indication Seamus and Rachel were serious, the inevitability of conflict cemented it. Just a week later they fell into their first real fight. She gave him a ride to work as she occasionally did. Once in the parking lot, a golf-cart driving Jamie zipped quickly in front of Rachel's car, forcing her to brake. Seamus thought it was funny. Rachel was spooked, and then angry.

"Who knows what that was about, Rach! He was just making a joke."

Rachel, still shaking, said, "You think it'd be a joke if I hit him? And what if that asshole in the Jag behind me didn't hit his brakes in time and hit us? Would that be a joke?"

Seamus smiled mischievously. "If he dinged up the grill on that piece of work, I might have a laugh over it."

Rachel grunted and said, "Bye."

"What? Just like that?" Seamus leaned in to kiss her.

"Bye!" she snapped.

"Baby, what's this now? Lighten up, huh?"

"Just go, Seamus."

"For what, for laughing? You're mad at me for not being uptight? This isn't like you."

"You don't get it, Seamus."

Seamus, hearing only It, and not it, was now angry.

"Oh I get It. And I could teach you a thing about It, too!"

She glared at him. "I don't know who the fucking hell you think you are to teach anyone about anything! How about you just stick your thumb out for a ride tomorrow, get some practice?"

Seamus, now steaming, left without saying any more. And later, talking to Jamie, said, "Boy man, I've never really seen any true red flags from her. Everything's been going so great."

"Is she on the rag?"

Seamus was going to answer but a voice behind them said, "On the rag, huh? Yep!"

Steve lit his cigarette. He tossed his head back and nearly shut his eyes as he dragged up a messy memory from a sloppy Saturday years ago.

"You boys know what Oktoberfest is, don't you?"

"I know people drink a lot of beer there and saw logs and shit."

"People saw logs at the good ones. I was at one a few years back where the only goddamn thing there was to do was drink beer. I'm with some buddies of mine and I'm leaving the place and I shit you not but some hot ass redhead comes up to me in the parking lot. Man she's hurtin' for a squirtin' 'cause she starts stroking my arms and telling me all kinds of nasty things and I'm like, seeya fellas - I'm going home with her! So I hitch a ride and I'm seeing double. I don't know where the hell this wild thing is taking me but we get to her place and we start making out right up to the door and I slam her down on her couch and just drop my face downtown. Doesn't take long before I lift my head up and I think what in the world? I go to the bathroom and I've got blood all over my goddamn mouth!"

"No!" Jamie howled.

"Fucked up man!"

"You're telling me! I've eaten some wet tuna before but this chick never warned me it was feeding time in the shark tank! I'm so pissed I go to her fridge, grab this stupid wine cooler she's got in there 'cause it's all she's got to drink and then I pass the fuck out. I feel like shit in the morning but she's making me eggs. So I stick around and get my grub on. Then she starts rubbing my shoulders, my back, hell, gives me a scalp massage. And boys, before you know it, she takes off her panties and no sooner do I finish my breakfast do I bend her over right on the kitchen table!"

"Dude, no way!"

"I did! Right in there with the old kit kat clock on the wall and plaid curtains over the windows. I remember the whole thing like it happened this afternoon. I tell you boys, sometimes all's well that ends well."

Steve put out his cigarette and walked away saying, "On the rag, yep! You ain't seen nothin' yet."

"You hear that man? All's well that ends well," Jamie said.

"Dude, I don't really think Steve's Oktoberfest liaison is the same thing I've got on my hands here. She was mad dude, like really mad."

"True. Well man have you considered that maybe you just weren't leveling with her?"

"What do you mean?"

"I mean, not to sound like I'm on her side because I'm not, but what if you might want to just consider that there's more to the story. I mean, no, it's not like she was going to hit me, but hell, she's a girl. Girls get spooked over stuff like that. I don't know why, so don't blame me. I didn't write the rules."

Seamus nodded. "About that man, just what were you doing on that golf cart, anyway?"

Jamie laughed. "My man, if I told you you'd never believe me. It's all about the glitches. A freak wind and I'm the man with the golden touch. I'll tell you something, hop along with me next weekend. I'll be at it again."

Seamus would. But more immediately, he had to have a talk with Rachel. Jamie dropped him off unannounced at her apartment.

Imogene answered the door.

"How'd you get here, you take a golf cart over?"

"Ha ha. Hi Imogene."

"Hi Seamus. I forgot though, you don't drive anyway."

"I know how to drive a golf cart," he said, entering.

"Really?" she asked, shutting the door. "Since when?"

"Yeah, since when?" Rachel asked from the top of the stairs.

"Hi Rach."

"Since when do you know how to drive?" Rachel asked again.

"Jamie taught me. Anyway, long story. Sorry about earlier."

Rachel invited him up with a glance, a head tilt, an exhalation. Seamus said to Imogene, "Thanks for letting me in."

"Yeah," she said.

Seamus followed Rachel to her room, and while she shrugged off his hand on her shoulder, he kept it cool. Jamie was right. Girls get spooked over strange things.

He continued behind a closed door, "I didn't react the way a mature person does."

"You're seriously just realizing that now?"

"Honestly, no. Just, no. I thought Jamie was being hilarious."

"I know you think Jamie is always hilarious. But seriously Seamus, this isn't even just about me. It's just that there's this whole other world out there you're not always aware of."

Seamus looked at her and then quickly away, as doing so made him less angry and he wanted to hold his ground.

Rachel put her hand on his shoulder and he did not shrug

it off. She said, "You never know..." She rubbed his cheek and they looked at each other.

Seamus considered. "You're right."

She nodded, turned her eyes to her sheets, and looked sullen. But then it happened. Secrets emerged. Old stories. A recent past. This was new ground for Seamus since this was the stuff of intimacy, and he had never been intimate with a girl. He had only had sex.

Rachel told him about getting into a car accident the previous semester while studying abroad in Italy.

"I totally totaled a car in Europe," she said. "It was a fucking Fiat, too." She laughed meekly. Seamus put his arm around her and kissed her cheeks and forehead. She did not shrug him off and said, "It didn't look that much different from a golf cart, baby."

"Yeah I bet. Were you hurt?"

"I was in a neck brace for the rest of the semester! I got really depressed because I went there to paint but I hardly did any of that the whole time. It hurt too bad to sit or stand like I always do at my easel. And my dad was so mad at me. He was so mad," she shut her eyes and a tear streaked down her face.

Seamus wiped it quickly and held her closer. She continued to cry and Seamus looked around her room to avoid watching her, though he felt her stomach spasm from sobs as he held her. It was awful but it was necessary and beat the alternative of her giving him the cold shoulder. But then the conversation turned to him, and the mood took an even worse turn. Her past was one thing. His was another.

"Seamus, can I ask you again why you don't drive then? I mean, why you never learned to drive an actual car, not just a golf cart."

"It just didn't happen," he said.

"How does it just not happen? It's like never learning how to swim."

Seamus shut his eyes and slowly opened them. "That's one comparison."

"Well I mean, it's part of growing up."

For every pale freckle on every minor memory Seamus spent countless hours thinking about, none of his contemplative energies were ever consciously directed towards his childhood. That was a radically different time and he was divorced from it now. He was adult or at least felt like the one he wanted to be, meaning not a child. He had his reservations about the rest of adulthood but then he was still in school. The rest of adulthood was a long way off. So was, he hoped, being a kid.

Rachel pressed him. "Seamus, didn't you want to drive?"

"Just different things came up. We were in the middle of a move, I didn't have money to get a car, all my friends drove. Then I went to school locally here and it really didn't matter anymore."

"Don't you parents want you to drive?"

Seamus let go of Rachel and lied back irritated and quiet. She asked him what was wrong and he told her nothing and then she sniffed and hit him on the chest. She insisted that something was wrong or he would not be acting this way but he knew damn well that she did not need to know what she thought she needed to and would be well advised to just leave him alone. He was thinking, and along lines that were not quieting now that they were going and he needed to go with it and let the storm pass, wait for the muddy water to clear again as Siddhartha had once advised one of his disciples.

She got up shortly after and went to the couch to sit and watch TV. When Seamus found her she was asleep and he hated her. He hated her because none of this was her fault and she would never know that crashing a car in Europe was not a big deal, especially since her dad paid her insurance anyway. He may have been pissed off but parents got pissed off sometimes. Anger beat some alternatives, and Seamus wished he never came over at all.

He was going to leave but thought of Jamie as he looked at Rachel. Maybe she just did not have It. Not everyone did. He sat on the couch beside her and woke her up.

"Let's get to bed," he said.

She blinked slowly and sniffled some more. "You're being distant," she said. "I don't like it."

"I'm sorry," he said.

"You said that earlier but I feel like we didn't get any closer than we were." She began to cry again. "Like maybe we're not working."

"Stop with that!" he said and wiped her face. He picked her up suddenly and carried her to her room. He laid her over her bed and kissed her ravenously all over her body. When she nodded, he entered her quickly and let his tensions out as they made love and stopped talking about the things he did not want to talk about. It ended their argument, and in the morning, except for the fact that something remained unsaid, their chatter and affections appeared to be operating normally again.

Seamus was grateful and with every laugh she gave over the stupid kinds of things they talked about when they were in good moods he was able to walk farther away from the night he just had. It was a close one but she seemed content to let it go herself since it was obviously more pleasant not to press.

And so Rachel continued to drive on all of their dates and Seamus sat happily in the passenger seat where he talked about the world and his theories of its functions, contently set in the ways of his knowledge that flowered open always in the future, the clarity of tomorrow always as brilliant so long as it was not today. Seamus was buying time, but for what he did not know.

9

Some couples who held their wedding receptions at Singing Pines got married there, too. Their wedding package was the "Platinum" option, and included a horse drawn carriage ride from the clubhouse to a gazebo on the far outskirts of the course, overlooking a wide canyon, and back again once all vows were said and the holy wine had been drunk.

The gazebo required some simple set up for those in the Platinum circle, including hanging flowers from its posts and pinning a silk runner to the grass leading up to its steps. A groundskeeper used to do this until he tore the runner. No longer trusted, someone else was assigned set-up duties. And that person, though he would never explain with any degree of clarity to Seamus just how this happened, was Jamie. The next time Jamie zipped through the parking lot in a golf cart, Seamus rode with him.

"All I can say, Seamus, is that I'm proud of you. It took balls to sneak away the way you did, but you're doing like I told you and that's why I can trust you with anything," Jamie told him en route to the gazebo. Jamie had orchestrated Seamus' assistance on the drive over to work, telling him when and where to leave the clubhouse to meet him.

"I appreciate that man, but you should trust me enough to tell me how you pulled this off. How, of all people, did Angela peg you?"

"Seamus, Angela isn't who you think she is."

"What the hell does that mean?"

"There's a reason why I ask you to follow me, Seamus. When you need to lead, you'll lead. I'm more proud of your progress than I can tell you, but you're not a Jedi yet."

"Jesus, dude. I don't think the Matrix existed in the Star Wars universe."

"Well, that's what most people would tell you."

Seamus, understanding that this was one of those secret worlds of Jamie's that he did not have access to, stopped prying and sat back to enjoy the ride.

Once the boys properly, and quickly, set-up the gazebo, they sat back in the cart among the trees and watched, all within earshot, the full wedding ceremony.

The man who married the couple was the same man who married every couple, Jamie explained, and always said the same thing.

"And I still can't get enough of him," Jamie said. "This guy is just outstanding."

"I like to think of love as friendship caught fire," the man said, tilting his head and keeping his mouth open well after speaking, as though thinking to himself that what he said was novel, and that he might be wise to go ahead and write it down some time. "In fact, it's no wonder to people who are in love that 90 percent of song lyrics are written about romance."

"I wonder where he gets his numbers," Seamus said.

"You better believe he does his homework. Listen to what's coming," Jamie said.

"Yes, we simply love, love. It's all around us. In movies, on TV. Goodness, every magazine you open or news site you read online has stories about the latest Hollywood romance."

"Did you know that?" Jamie asked Seamus.

"The man is a student of the human mind," Seamus said.

Those gathered to witness the wedding smiled on as did the couple, their skin glowing in the softening daylight, their faces calm and unmarred by wrinkles from worry or anxiety. As the man went on about other banal generalities and a touch more fuzzy math, Seamus could not help but feel happy himself as he watched the couple signify their commitment with rings and a kiss. Seamus knew that not far away from here, everyone else in the clubhouse was working their asses off.

When it was over, Jamie and Seamus cleaned the site up quickly. It would take multiple trips to the gazebo and back to do so. With nearly a full bottle of white, apparently blessed wine left abandoned, Jamie ensured Seamus that they would need to act quickly before the ousted groundskeeper got to it later. He was still trusted to put away the chairs, after all.

Unfortunately, Seamus was greeted by a furious Angela in the parking lot on the boys' first trip back to the clubhouse. Apparently disapproving of his self-appointed position as Jamie's aide, she yelled at him.

Embarrassed for her given this childish reaction, Seamus gingerly stepped out of the golf cart. "Hi Angela," he said.

"We need you downstairs, Seamus!" she snapped.

Seamus looked back to Jamie who was already carrying out the rolled-up runner from the cart. Jamie tapped his temple with his free hand, and Seamus nodded, though he had no idea whatsoever what it meant.

"Now, Seamus!" Angela barked.

"Okay," Seamus said and walked with Angela down the stairs, her stomping pace like nothing he had ever seen from her.

"You're not going out with Jamie again or there are going to be very real consequences," she told him.

"Hey, at least I cut my hair," Seamus said.

Angela scowled at him. "And it could still use another trim. Just get to work, now!"

"Word," he said, beginning to stew.

But then something happened. It started internally, as most of Seamus' greatest moments did. Thinking of Jamie and what he would do in such a situation, Seamus considered the past. Who was it that bounded through the room that first night, busing for him with speed and will unmatched by anyone else? However he did it, Jamie did not pull set-up duties at the gazebo for being a slouch.

"Let's get to work," Seamus muttered to himself.

And work he did. Rather than succumb to the dour mood that tempted him, he adopted a tone and ethic of robust defiance. In the process he emerged as a model of busing efficiency. He snaked furiously between tables retrieving dirty plates by the dozen. He thought of Pac Man and focused on any suspect plate, even if it might not be time to take it just yet. Even Barry, apart from a single snide comment about his absence, left him well enough alone as he tore through the room. All the while Angela watched on, her brow furrowed, her body stiff, her fingers restlessly lost in her keychain.

When she had seen enough she confronted Seamus for a heart-to-heart that made both feel better about each other and about their jobs. Seamus almost regretted harboring the harsh thoughts he had about her earlier but could never pull himself around to harvest such sympathy due to the fact that he remained convinced they were true.

He saw her coming and initiated the conversation. It was

a tactic Jamie taught him and it usually softened impending aggressions of all colors.

"Boy, these people are hungry today," he said.

"Yes, Seamus," she said wearily. "You know, I see you out there and there's no one better. Why do you have to be so stubborn and difficult?"

Seamus drew another card from Jamie's deck and leaned heavy against the wall. Out of his periphery he could see Angela looking at him, her posture softening. When he spoke again, his words were deliberate and sounded sincere. He watched her eyes as he spoke and stifled a smile. He had penetrated Angela's hard heart and all it took was a little bit of truth and some slight exaggerations, the latter being a necessary evil when dealing with a wrinkle of a problem that had been overblown into a cancerous mole.

"Sorry, I just got dizzy there."

"Are you okay?"

"Fine. I just had to gather myself back up to speed. Anyway, thanks for noticing. I give it my all, whether here or at the gazebo."

"Yeah, Seamus. About that..."

"Actually, let's not dwell on the past. I'm busing now, that's my present reality."

"Your present reality?"

"Ha yeah, sorry. I get kind of Zenned out sometimes."

She snorted. "Well it doesn't take a private eye to figure that out. But I just wish you'd be more Zen about doing what I ask you to do."

"Hey now, I was pretty calm out there earlier when you

rang my bell."

"Seamus, please. You know I mean what I ask you to do in the first place. You know as well as I do that the gazebo really doesn't take two people."

"That may be. But simple doesn't always mean easy, and complicated doesn't always mean deep."

"Thank you, Seamus, for that wonderful insight. But this isn't philosophy class."

"You don't like philosophy?"

"Oh no, I do. My boyfriend got a minor in philosophy. I just don't like it at work."

"Oh he did? I'm considering getting a double major in philosophy. What does he do now?"

She smiled weakly, and looked suddenly distant. "He sells insurance."

"Hot dog! Auto, medical, house, what?"

"Auto," she said, nodding her head.

"Well, that's something else. Anyway Angela, sorry about our run-in earlier, but I've got to keep making my rounds."

He almost got away but she said, "Seamus, before you go back out, just think about what I said, okay?"

Seamus considered. She had not really said anything and this gladdened him, but he did not show it and instead looked thoughtfully past her to the wall as though contemplating something deep. He nodded and said, "I will."

"Thanks Seamus," she said and walked up the stairs to her office, not noticing Seamus behind her stepping softly but swiftly up the stairs and hooking a quick left out the double doors to a waiting Jamie.

"My God you have the timing!" Seamus said.

"I had my tabs on you the whole time, believe me."

"How so man?" Seamus laughed, eager to hear this one.

"It's in here, Seamus," Jamie said and patted his friend's chest.

"Hare-Krishna," Seamus chanted.

"Yes man, yes!"

"Alright, for real though, just good timing or what?"

"Don't bend the spoon that isn't there in the first place, Seamus."

Seamus was going to press, but looked around him and remembered to enjoy the ride. "Goddamn it's a beautiful day for a golf cart ride. And you know what? I never lost faith I'd be back in this thing today."

"You'd be a fool to lose faith, and frankly I don't know what that would mean for us going forward, but you're a man of integrity and you don't live with one arm behind your back if you know what I mean."

"No man. That's not the way you sleep at night, either."

"Sure. Now if we drive around and congratulate ourselves all day we'll never get anything done. I've got a place to show you that you're just going to love. We've got limited time so keep your wits about you."

Jamie took Seamus to the eighth hole and drove into a small clearing obscured by overgrown brush just behind the tees. He took a narrow trail that sent tree branches scraping noisily against the roof of the cart, some stinging the boys in their faces. Jamie abstained from using the brakes until they cleared the brush and abruptly came to the edge of the canyon.

The cart shook hard as Jamie braked, but they remained on level ground, safe, secure, and ready to get high.

Jamie pulled his piece out from his sock and passed it to Seamus.

"Stories to tell my grandkids," Jamie said.

"This would be a great place to pitch a tent," Seamus said.

"Would be absolutely killer."

After getting properly stoned, Seamus confided in Jamie. "I tell you man, it got hairy back there. She yelled at me and I hate to admit it but I was concerned."

"There are going to be uncomfortable moments when you're standing up against authority. I didn't exactly get straight-A's but any history book will tell you that."

"Yeah, well thankfully you showed me the ropes, man. I'm serious. I pulled from what you showed me and just got to fucking work. She watched me the whole time as I bused. But dude, I bused the shit out of that room."

"I know you did. That's the fighter in you."

"I hardly left anything for anyone else to do."

"Sure. You didn't just get the monkey to hop off your back, but off theirs, too. Everyone wins when an ace is in the hole."

"It was like I was the only person working. Barry ignored my ass. Everyone else just sort of looked but didn't really say anything, either. Spotlight was on me, dude, and Angela was captivated."

"We all have our own road to hoe. Now listen, the next time we go on gazebo duty we're doing it right. None of this funny business with Manager Buzz Kill. I want you to take out your own cart. It's gonna make you feel hot under the collar but if you supply your own ride than you obviously mean business."

"Jamie, you're stoned man! I can't do that!"

"Please. You remember Charlie Sheen, don't you? Can't is the cancer of happen."

"He was high as fuck during that interview."

"Okay, bus with the squares. See what I care."

"But how the hell is she going to listen to me?"

"Goddamn it, Seamus! When you ask questions and I don't answer you, you need to remember this conversation."

Seamus considered. "You're right. I've got to remember It."

"Now you're talking like the man I know. Listen, you hitching a ride with me again is like standing on a 12 when the dealer's showing an ace. And I can't take that bet. We're at that point where we draw a line in the sand. If you're going to keep going on these missions, and it's a damn good cause, you're going to have to step up and be bold. Otherwise you're just repeating history and as we saw earlier today, this particular tale has taken a turn for the worst. Evolve or get left behind man, that's the nature of the universe."

Seamus knew Jamie was right. There was not another wedding ceremony at the gazebo for two weeks, and when it finally came, Seamus walked directly into Angela's office and picked up the runner. She looked away from her computer screen and crossly at him. When she began to question him, Seamus was matter of fact in his approach even though his stomach churned and gurgled.

"Jamie's already taking care of the water station. I'm bringing over the runner."

"Seamus, we've been over this how many times?"

"Okay, sorry. I need to at least bring him this thing, though."

"This is stupid, Seamus. You come back and talk to me after he drops you off."

"Oh, he's not dropping me off. I took my own."

"What do you mean?"

"I mean Jamie drove over earlier with the water station and I'm bringing over the flowers and the runner. Big ceremony today."

"Who authorized you to take a golf cart out there?"

"No one. But it's sure saving some time. I was thinking too that I could take people back to the clubhouse after since Jamie's only one man and there are some bigger people out there, older people too, who would like a ride."

"We're not a taxi service, Seamus!"

"Okay. You're right. I'll just drop this stuff off there though and I'll be back."

Angela looked at Seamus in the same hateful way she did that day in the parking lot. Seamus' heart pounded but he never broke eye contact. Still, as she stared at him without even fumbling with her keychain, part of him was deeply worried he had done it this time.

"Seamus, just set up the gazebo then since you're out there anyway."

"Oh, well, okay. I can do that."

"Yeah, of course you can," she laughed bitterly.

"Okay. And I know we're not a taxi service but I could still give rides to some of the older people out there."

"Only if the mother of the bride asks you to, you understand?"

"Angela, if there's one thing I've learned here, it's to always do what the mother of the bride asks."

"No kidding," Angela said and widened her eyes. "This one's drama today, let me tell you."

"Aren't they always?"

Angela laughed. "Some more than others. Just get going now, okay? Hurry up so you can get downstairs faster to help everyone else out."

After setting the gazebo up, Jamie drove Seamus back to the third where they got high again and Seamus told his friend everything.

"Just like that man, she totally buckled! It was like, inexplicable!"

"No, not inexplicable. She just ran out of options. She could either fire you and make a scene, or just go with it. Between you and me, my man, she's not the best manager ever to walk the face of the earth."

"No shit. And we are the benefactors."

"Hey, don't take it lightly, though. You still have every right to be proud of yourself."

"Thanks man."

"I mean it! You manipulated her reality to the point that she'd rather just let the wind blow than have to shake up her crew and go hire someone new, amend the schedule, yada yada. Forget it. And hey, I wouldn't want to do any of that, either. She's got enough on her plate already. Busy lady. Even if she isn't the sharpest tool, her workbench is loaded."

"Just can't believe it's that simple."

"Some things just are," Jamie said softly and looked down at his feet.

"You okay, dude?"

"I'm fine." Jamie rubbed his eyes. "You're just..."

"What man?"

"You're just beginning to lead your own dance, that's all," Jamie said and got out of the cart to look out over the canyon. When he returned, he said, "You're going to be sticking your thumb out on the side of the road better than any goddamned person in this whole stupid world!"

"Fuck man, that's what I'm going for here!"

"Shit. Let's pack another."

Shortly into their next session, a wild golf ball flew into the canyon, followed by a nasty series of expletives from a drunken golfer.

"Jesus! Watch your swing, bud," Jamie said.

It became clear that there were members driving up to the hole behind them. Judging by the terrible swing that shot by them, the boys did not want to linger at the scene. Who knew what was wrong with these people? Still, the polite boys that they were, they did not disturb the game. Jamie spared all sundry the high-pitched beeping issued by a cart in reverse and instructed Seamus to help him push it backwards instead. He did so, and when they suddenly appeared on the other side of the clearing, four golfers looked at them like the boys had crash landed an alien spacecraft.

"Sorry gentlemen, this cart got stuck back there," Jamie said.

"And they made you two get it?" one of the golfers asked.

"We're on cart duty right now," Seamus answered.

"You're in tuxes."

"Sir, this is a country club," Jamie said.

The boys leapt into the cart and drove away sparing further interaction.

"They were nice guys," Seamus said.

"Yeah, but it's pretty late to be out on the eighth."

"You're right. They must just be playing the front nine."

"They better be playing quick because the sun is coming down and I don't want to see any strays on my golf course."

"For sure. This isn't just some free for all."

"No it isn't. This is Singing Pines Country Club." He shook his head. "Some people think they can do whatever they want, and frankly Seamus, it makes me sick."

"It's what's wrong with the world today. We can't act blindly, my man. We need to act with purpose," Seamus said.

"If you're going to start, you had better know why you are. Now let's hurry along. There's a bottle of wine waiting for us back at the gazebo."

"Let's get to work," Seamus said, and they did.

10

In time Seamus would be Jamie's aide whenever a wedding took place at the gazebo. Angela appeared to be content to let them be, as it made all conflicts easier when she just removed herself from them entirely. Barry, scoffing at the whole mess, just belittled them as being "such good boys, such good, hard-working boys."

It was no wonder then that Seamus coasted into his winter break with spirits at an all time high. Rachel would be sticking around town for the entirety of the month-long reprieve since she had scored an internship at a school for the handicapped near their campus. She much preferred staying put in her apartment versus commuting five days a week from L.A. Seamus was not sure what the internship involved because he did not pay complete attention when she told him the news. He was just happy that she would be around and he would have a place other than his parents' house to sleep most nights. Ecstatic, really.

Though Seamus had to give his parents credit. It was a good Christmas this year. The more recent years were not so bad, but there were plenty of meager outings when he was younger. Nothing was quite like the first awful one, when he and his parents ate alone at the dinner table, their first in the rental house, its cork and mirrors plastered to the walls and stuffy living room suffocating. He remembered virtually nothing but the sense of hollowness that enveloped everything around them. They said little, ate little, gave and received little. The evening was whiled away like a long, uninterrupted dream.

Seamus, not yet solidified in his new understanding, was yet poking his head through an egg he never wished to be born from but now there was no turning back. In time the new world would bring its own laws and values that he, like his parents, would come to accept. While the subsequent holiday seasons would always enter as a fog, it was one that thinned with time. But when a year came like this one, Seamus understood what a happy holiday meant.

His parents gave him a DSLR camera, and he knew immediately it was the best gift he had ever received. Seamus looked to his mom on the couch, his dad on the floor, both speaking to him separately, as though taking turns. He hugged them both and wiped his eyes, wiped his mother's too. He never read a thing in the user's manual but explored the camera's abilities with amateur blankness. It boasted more features and megapixels than the school-issued camera he always worked with, and was certainly a departure from the film-based camera he had been using since high school. He still treasured the dark room his dad built for him in the garage and used it every day the previous winter break. This year he used it only once. He would keep that skill alive, he vowed to himself. But time would have its opinion on that, as it always did with private promises. And Seamus would be none the sadder for it. For where Seamus went, his camera often did, too.

Jamie had his own special Christmas since his parents gave him an exquisite tent. They had thrown out his old tent long ago without his consent, its putrid odor offensive to them even as it sat rolled up in the garage leaning against a spider-web laden wall. They were oblivious to their son's bacchanalian heroics while they were away, and the spilled beer and bong water and cigarette ash that marred the tent smelled like nothing more to them than old garbage. It was an appropriate end to what had been a twenty dollar garage sale steal by a younger Jamie. Though he always felt his time with it was ended too soon, his new tent more than made up for it. And so, when his parents left for vacation in the final days of December, it was only appropriate that he throw another tent party all over again.

The new tent was a three-room nylon palace that dwarfed the old tent in its luxury. Calm yellows juxtaposed against gray mesh, the lines strong and dramatic, its poles weaving along the sides and over the roof to give it a deltohedronic shape. Once again the tent was the central hub for the heavier smoking sessions, but this time around those inside spilled far less liquid and ash, and treated the tent with a conscious respect. Not long removed from high school, Jamie and Seamus' old classmates were generally more mature, if even in the slightest ways. It was the first time that any of them had been together in this great a group since graduating. Though individual reunions congealed all around Jamie's backyard, many of the topics each discussed with one another gravitated around the same themes. They asked each other who was doing whom, going to school where, working for what, and wondering with widely varying degrees of ferocity about nearly everything that troubled people of their age from the current job market and its forecast to affordable rent to the better medicinal marijuana pharmacies in the immediate area.

Some old friends were bright and merry with an eye towards the future and a head buzzing with three semesters worth of happy memories and positive experiences. Others appeared tired already, working jobs much like the one Jamie and Seamus did only without the on-the-clock partying. Others yet were going to school and still living at home and did not know when they would not. Others flitted in between, seeming as though nothing had changed even though much had, and if there was something they needed to know about where they were headed they were not bothering to worry about it yet, though they had their hunches about a general direction and followed it, assuming that all would be right in the end, with the end being a vague and shapeless term that they had faith in much like a religious devotee does to a silent god. They were going somewhere, just not today.

Meanwhile, Jamie climbed up to his parents' roof, blindfolded, and leapt into a screaming contingent of old friends below as they locked their arms together in a fireman net of woven limbs. Jamie, Seamus knew, was the one person in the whole party worth knowing if he could know no one else. And so smiling, he wiped up his own spilled bong water and smoked a cigarette outside the tent, and encouraged others to respectfully do the same. He had his boy's back, even as it turned towards the reaching hands below, summoning him with writhing fingers. Of course Jamie jumped backwards. What other way would a young man of his caliber choose?

The tent party, or tent reunion as it were, was almost Seamus' favorite evening of his winter break. But what remained the greatest night of his holiday from the mundaneness of school was also one of the greatest nights of his life. One evening in Rachel's room, she posed naked for him so he could take pictures of something "other than a bunch of rocks, for once."

Rachel did not appreciate Seamus' more natural photographic themes but he was having too much fun to care. He took many pictures over the next couple weeks at her apartment. Though she still wore unflattering clothes, she had no trouble allowing herself to be filmed outside of them provided Seamus leave all the copies with her. He agreed without question and they got to work.

Sometimes they took pictures, sometimes they set up a tripod and filmed themselves in five minute clips. They passed back and forth a joint and stripped each other down, one holding the camera blindly above them and pressing the shutter, ogling over the results later on a computer screen. He cropped images, zoomed in, saturated the colors, added contrast, took away a couple of red eyes. He filmed himself entering her from behind with different body parts, and she filmed him rising over her, going.

He took pictures of her in clothes, too, and experimented with angles while she played with poses. For the most part, she was his only human subject. All else were trees, dirt roads, rocks, street lights, concrete washes, abandoned storefronts, streams, animals, litter, roadsigns, graffiti, fences, train tracks, broken windows. He edited most as black and white images, laying heavy on the contrast as he edited the pictures later in the school computer lab using iPhoto, Aperture, and Photoshop. He played with all three programs and had the most difficulty with the latter. But he was teaching himself a good deal about how to use it and enjoyed the process. The computer lab indeed became his new darkroom, and by his frequency alone anyone who did not know better would think he was a tireless student.

In a certain respect, he nearly was. But in his other classes, even those the previous semester he nearly got A's in, he always fell short. If he could get an A by working hard on a final paper or get a C by not doing it at all, he rewarded himself with the stock he had built up after a good run of successful assignments and took the average grade instead, opening his time again for walks and thoughts, sex, day drugs - always focusing on what he knew mattered most. The spring semester, however, would be shaky throughout. He indeed would focus on what was important, but there were days when he did not know what that was. And right after the night when it all went right, when he and Rachel told each other the big words, the first swing of the ax lobbed itself into his life. Changes were coming, were happening, were having their way. And though he knew change was constant, he only appreciated those of a certain variety. So Seamus changed with them unwittingly, and looked ahead until he could see no further, looking for the place that would not change at all. Finding it would be his goal. And for a young man like Seamus, goals were rare.

11

Rachel and Seamus made more love over their winter break than either had over such a short span of time. Seamus slid his unrubbered hard-on into Rachel more gingerly as the weeks progressed, and winced when it had been a couple days since she last shaved. She goaded him about not being able to keep up. He always did, no matter how chafed he felt afterwards. Then he would exaggerate his wide-legged stance as he lifted himself from her and walked to the bathroom for the jolting first piss post-cum.

And so their bodies reflected the sweat-slick fervor that frequent intimacy produces. Young love is a slop fest and an ego builder.

"You're the best," she told him often.

"You are for me," he said.

"I've never felt so comfortable with anyone," she usually added.

"Me neither," he lied.

The truth was Seamus had never felt so uncomfortable with anyone. He really liked Rachel. He liked everything about her. The plain white sheets that she sprayed with lavender water, the prints that what he imagined all aspiring young artists frame obnoxiously on their bedroom walls, the imitation Calder mobile hanging from her ceiling by a purple tack, the painted flowers on her ceiling fan blades, the beanbag chairs, the assortment of canvases leaning against each other and the walls, the holed jeans strewn over her wooden desk chair, which she had painted and repainted so many times it was chipped all over, revealing pockets of contrasting colors peeking out from past layers.

He even liked her damn artwork. He could not remember when he started to like it, because it did not seem like he even started to in the first place. All of a sudden, he just did. It was like a spider that crawled up his back, except he never knew it was there until the stupid thing entered his ear. Then it was impossible to ignore.

About the only piece he ever consciously liked were the sunflowers. They were psychedelic, but they were also warm. The colors were dark pastel, the lines were blurry. Shapes bled into each other. Physically it was a small piece, pocket-sized, perfectly convenient to carry around everywhere. And it was for him.

Her other work was colder. She painted people often. Tall people, short people, purple people, gray people. Sometimes she painted landscape scenes. While nothing was given a realistic color, trees often had orange or blue bark, pond water was red, there was a certainty to the strokes, a clear delineation of separateness that permeated everything she drew.

Seamus privately dismissed the work as unrealistic because even the most base book on Zen philosophy espoused that nothing, in so many words, could possibly stand alone. To him, the colors were the most realistic part about her paintings.

But then, even the most base book on Zen philosophy espoused that nothing is permanent. And so no longer, apparently, was Seamus' aversion to his girlfriend's art. It still bore a common loneliness, each abnormally pigmented tree so far away from the other, no matter how close they were on the canvas, but he liked looking at it. He enjoyed tracing his fingers along the elongated backs of pink women sitting in uneven groups by the water, staring into the eyes of stodgy men with white patches of hair and gray faces looking suspiciously at blue and yellow children running in the street.

So Seamus wondered as he walked freely around his parents' neighborhood, up to a park to be among the trees of the real world brown and sturdy, sprouted from the ground he walked on and giving him breath, if he was simply losing his own sense of separation from Rachel. She came from a different world no doubt, in upbringing and experience. But if he could lose his aversion to her artwork, was he also losing the grip he held on to the difference between her and him? Was her artwork not just her artwork, but her, as well? And he liked her, after all. He really, really liked her.

Then one night she hit him with it.

"What?" he asked her.

"I love you, too," she repeated.

He had never even said it. But she read his body language, and his added playfulness under the sheets.

He looked at her, longingly, and dove into the expressive tide swelling between them - finally.

"I love you!" he shouted.

"Goodnight," she said and flipped over to her side to go to sleep, smiling devilishly, deliciously.

"I love you," he repeated.

But she remained quiet with her back facing him. Nearly beside himself with her coyness, he threw himself down onto his back and stared at the ceiling. Neither said anything more. Seamus had trouble sleeping. She did not. Seamus looked over at her resting face periodically and wanted to wake her.

At this point he just wanted to party. If he could not sleep he might be better off up all night, drinking with lustful gusto and shoving himself deep into her in the hours that passed, fucking away thoughts about the approaching week when school was back in session, and the doors outside Rachel's room would open again.

He lay awake high with the strongest buzz of his life, his chest warm and his head fuzzy. His stomach fluttered and his mouth was dry. His mind churned through the implications, but they were light and broke on touch. Though he thought about thinking often, his mental patterns groped around in a mush. This was different, he knew. Putting It aside, this was love. They connected somehow, but tonight even It was taking a backseat.

Finally he did sleep, and when he awoke Rachel was straddling his morning wood. They smiled, laughed, kissed, pecked, made love, and then told each other again. They held each other, rubbed cheeks with thumbs, squeezed asses, poked, stole articles of clothing, shoved and pulled.

It was early. Typically it was too early for Seamus to be awake, but he got on with it without hesitation. All went wonderfully afterwards as Rachel made it to her internship on time and Jamie picked Seamus up from her apartment after she was gone. The boys went to a park and smoked a joint, kicked around a soccer ball, had frozen yogurt. They knew that all days should be like this one, save for one trifling bother: they had a meeting to attend at Singing Pines.

The boys knew before their arrival that it would be a farce of an afternoon. There had never been a Food and Beverage staff meeting before and the notion that they needed one now was insulting. But the boys rolled with Angela's feeble punches and showed up on-time though smelling of pot. She gave them her patented distrustful looks as they shuffled past her and made their way to the back table in the circle of four-tops gathered in the Singing Pines restaurant. But she played with her keychain and smiled though her eyes peered gravely, and her stiff body did its best to appear strong, solid, and alive.

She stood beside an oversized notepad resting on a cheap looking easel, thin and plastic with its legs adjusted to uneven lengths. She held a black felt marker. She put away her keychain and wrote a single "P" on the unlined paper. She turned to her crew. What words started with "P" and represented the Singing Pines Banquet crew?

It was a while before anyone said anything beyond a whispered gripe. Finally, Jeff said, "Well, for some of us it's 'positive.' For others…there's a word I'm thinking of…pot…pot…" He scratched his head. "That's all I'm getting on that one."

Angela lifted her chin and said, "Let's go with 'positive.'" She wrote it on the board and said, "Excellent," as though what she had done by writing a word was so, and that everyone in the room was right to feel good about being positive people, and that working at Singing Pines meant something and they were the proof.

"How about something for 'I?'"

Jamie and Seamus immediately nudged each other. But before one of them could test Angela's, and probably the rest of the room's patience, Isabelita offered, "Inventive."

Angela clapped her hands and had new life. "Yes! We need to be inventive in order to do our jobs. Sometimes things don't go as planned. Happens to me and it happens to you. We all need to invent our own solutions sometimes. Excellent Isabelita, excellent!"

Angela wrote the word on the board and Isabelita unknowingly mocked the entire exercise on behalf of everyone by saying, "This is fun. I do anagrams with my son getting him ready for kindergarten."

Steve let out a loud laugh and covered his mouth. He shook with muffled laughter and others laughed with him. Angela looked deflated but pressed on. Eventually the word "PINES" spelled out:

POSITIVE

INVENTIVE

NEIGHBORLY

ENTHUSIASTIC

and lastly, offered by Jamie:

SEXY

"All I know is, there's nothing square about a tux!" he demanded.

Angela had little choice but to go with it. The rest of the room, save for Jeff and a silent Barry, was giving her hell about that being an inappropriate choice.

"All I'm saying is, when you look good you play good!" Jamie yelled over them.

"That's why Beatriz looks at me and is like 'Damn!' every time I walk up to that bitch's window," Alfredo was saying to Felipe.

"That's where you go on lunch break!" Felipe said to him as a revelation.

"Shoot, what do you think I'm doing, eating corn chips?"

"Okay, alright, okay!" Angela shouted over the commotion. "We'll go with sexy." She laughed her forced laugh and said, "Between sexy and Seamus' neighborly, I don't know where you two boys grew up!"

The room was quiet again. She nodded her head and smiled as though presenting the prize pig at the county fair while the eyes of her staff stared back at her with little life.

She stuttered, "O-o-okay, so this is a pretty good list. I think we can all look and see at the very least that we're here for our guests. Positive, enthusiastic, neighborly. We're here to serve."

The group listened while Angela went on for a while, spouting off everything they already knew about their jobs and nothing they did not. The silences were palpable as she took breaks from speaking to write on the board, the marker squeaking, her short breaths just as audible. After a long, drawn out while, she opened the discussion to the crew with the final item on the agenda, the ubiquitous, and in Singing Pines' case patronizing, "Questions and Comments."

"Are we done yet?" Alfredo asked. "I have to go wash my car."

"Almost done, Alfredo. But your car can wait," Angela said.

"Not if I'm going to pick up my hyna on time."

"You're hyna will have to wait then."

Everyone laughed hard and Angela blushed. People began to stand, stretch, push in their chairs. There was a buzz in the room. The meeting felt exhausted. But Angela pleaded for everyone to sit down again. Jeff was, after all, raising his hand.

"Yeah okay thanks, Angela. I just want to say something because I'm seeing everyone stand up and talk about washing their car and stuff, but like I work in the restaurant and banquet department so I have some perspective that maybe not everyone else does."

"Shut up," Steve said.

"Steve!" Angela hushed. "Please, we all have our right to speak."

"Sure thing, Angie," he said and leaned back in his chair.

Jamie elbowed Seamus. "It man, another one with It."

"The barman answers to no one," Seamus whispered back.

"You guys done over there?" Jeff asked.

"Internal temperature of 160 degrees," Jamie said.

Laughter. Jeff rolled his eyes.

"Well what I'm trying to say is that I know we're all young and still trying to find ourselves, but when you come to work you're coming *to* work. I just look around sometimes and I think that gets a little forgotten when we're on our phones texting in the service area and yelling and dancing and stuff."

No laughter. Many eye rolls.

"Teacher, you forgot to assign us our homework," Steve said.

"Steve, please! I'm asking you to knock it off. Jeff has a point."

"Thanks Angela." Jeff gushed. "In the restaurant we do things a little different, and like I said, I get it, I totally do. I'm only 19. I'm like you guys. I just think we could tighten it up, like we do in the restaurant."

Jamie was about to join a conversation that could have gotten out of hand but was stopped silent by a surprising voice.

"We're not all 19. And we can't do things like you do in the restaurant because you have two people working a shift and about as many tables at any given time. We have hundreds of people to serve and a few more workers. We make a profit, and a big one. You're lucky if you break even. Your sole purpose is to serve as a way for the country club members to use their food vouchers and feel the exquisite perk of being able to dine in a place where the public isn't allowed. The next time you want to compare apples to oranges, you should bear in mind that half dozen of one thing is only six of the other if they come from the same tree." Barry leaned back and as usual looked no one in the eyes, until he met Angela's glazed stare without compromise.

Jamie shrieked, "My man!" as he rose to his feet and applauded wildly. Seamus joined him.

"Sit down, this isn't *The Dead Poets Society*," Jeff said.

"Well it isn't our come-to-Jesus moment either," Seamus said.

"Everyone calm down!" Angela yelled over the ensuing uproar. Seamus had not seen her look this rattled since the day she caught him in the cart with Jamie. Struck with a pang of empathy for his dim witted boss, he sat down but stared at Jeff and grabbed his testicles.

"Careful Jeff or your girlfriend's going to be jealous, said no one ever," Steve shouted.

"Steve!" Angela yelled again. "You're not helping anything. I've asked you too many times to knock it off. We all have things to say and we all have points to make. As for you, Barry, this isn't about who makes what kind of what in what department."

"Well said," Steve said quietly.

Angela shut her eyes, and then continued. Her fingers were

knotted in her keychain.

"What Jeff is saying is that we all need to be better. Better behaved, better...we need to work better, not take things so lightly. I'm happy you're friends, I want you all to be friends. But when we come to work, we need to work."

Barry raised his hand.

"Barry?"

"It's hard to work when Steve has a line to the dance floor and I need to hunt you down all over the place for the liquor room key. If you gave me a copy of one, I'd be happy to work as hard as apparently you think I need to."

"Barry, that's really not appropriate at this time."

"Isn't this the question and comment part?"

"You know that key is for management. It's very important that we keep it that way."

"Why?"

"Barry, not now."

"Okay. Well here's another question. How come you insist on hanging around sometimes to help me tray up entrées, which is super arbitrary and unnecessary, when you could go up to the kitchen and get another warmer started to come down the elevator?"

"Barry, that's not my job to bring down the food warmer."

"Well okay. It's not Jeff's job to get on my crew, but he sure gets his rocks off doing it and a free pass from you. Whose idea was this thing anyway?"

"Does that really matter?"

"I'm curious to know if Howard, the GM, is happy that

we're getting paid time and a half to come in for a meeting so we can eat donuts while you dodge any real questions and let a pimpled prick taking general ed classes at a two-year college tell the rest of us we need to clean our acts up?"

Angela only said, "Come to my office now, Barry. Everyone else, you're free to go."

"Captain my captain," Jamie yelled.

"Shut up Jamie," Barry said.

"That's the man I love!" he returned.

Angela wasted no time in packing her notepad and easel up and asking Barry to help her carry them. He did so and they walked up the stairs together not saying a word nor looking each other in the eye.

No one knew what was said in her office but Crystal told Jamie later that Howard asked Angela, not Barry, what he was still doing there. Angela had told Howard that the meeting would only be an hour at most and now it was bordering on two with Barry still in tow. That was all Crystal knew, she said.

In fact, it was all anyone knew as Angela remained by herself in the office during lunch. There she ate her sandwich and her chips that she packed in the morning, her banana and a couple of Hershey's Kisses, before sneaking to the snack bar and ordering onion rings and a piece of chocolate cake. She did not cry much, did not allow herself to stoop that low. She was capable of saving her tears for later when she knew she was safe. It was easier to hide food under her desk than allow mascara to run down her face.

Meanwhile she thought, though she did not particularly like to do so lately. She thought about where she had been and where she was now. She thought that she never even had the chance to tell Barry what she thought he needed to hear, that Howard would be telling her dad about this, and that she would have plenty of time later to cry after all, the phone call awaiting her at home.

Angela knew that being Food and Beverage Manager at Singing Pines would be a challenging job. She did not anticipate the details that would make it so, but only approached the position with the bright-eyed confidence that she could handle whatever came her way. She had been to college, and had even been out already for two years. That meant life experience, such as the backpacking trip through Europe her parents paid for as a graduation gift. She had since spent two years working at the family Mexican restaurant, but wanted more for herself. The job market was difficult, however, even for a psychology major. She found this disturbing. She was told that psychology majors could be anything they wanted to be. Psychology majors understood people, after all.

Her father was one of the people who told her the value not only in studying psychology, but going to school in general.

"If you earn a degree, you can write your own ticket anywhere," he told her.

One day the ticket came. Angela's father's friend, Howard, said to him in passing that the country club needed a new Food and Beverage Manager, and if he knew anyone in the restaurant industry who could fill the position he would be happy to meet her.

Angela was the only person Howard ever interviewed.

Now that she was fully immersed in the position of ordering food, supplies, and managing people, she wondered what exactly her degree meant in the first place. She believed that the best way to manage people was to play to their strengths and not bring too much attention to their weaknesses. Though if she had to go there, she only wanted to address people's faults in a way that tied to some overarching lesson. This had been her strategy going in, a plan devised early on, dreamt up before the day she actually started.

She believed this approach would garner a respect that would make her employees pliable and receptive. She wanted to believe in it still. But days like this one, binge eating alone in her office, her eyes burning from holding back the waves of sorrow that pulsated through her chest, she did not know what to believe. No one respected her. No one wanted to talk to her longer than necessary. Even Jeff just wanted to get ahead. Otherwise he never would have said a word to her.

She had eaten only half the cake, and intended on saving it for later. She still would, she told herself and took a bite. No one was around yet, until Wanda got back earlier than expected with Crystal.

"Cake for lunch, huh Angela?"

Angela gave her weakest fake laugh in response, and headed fast for the women's locker room bathroom. She could not guarantee she would be alone there, but so far it was a light day on the course. She took her chances and let go. She wept. In the midst of her reeling pain, she almost wanted someone to see her. But no one did. No one, she knew, ever did.

12

"Angela is such a loser, Jesus Christ," Seamus said to Jamie as they drove home.

"My man. I felt about as comfortable in that room as a Mormon in a strip club. Watching her try and be tough." He whistled. "It's not for the faint of heart."

"I love how Barry thinks he's a loser. Yeah right."

"Bing! Some people just don't know what being a loser really means. I wonder if they'll ever find out," Jamie said.

Jamie and Seamus were not ready to go home yet. The day was still pregnant with possibility. Cameron Cooper was visiting his family for the weekend. The boys would be meeting him that night to bowl and get wasted. An alley was within walking-distance of Cameron's family home. Seamus was more excited than anyone since Rachel would be joining them. It would be the first time she really spent any real time with his friends. And so it was the first time that, despite all her driving, her recent posing, and her generous sex drive, he felt the relationship was evening up, becoming level. He could barely wait.

Until then, Jamie kept them both occupied with a familiar adventure. He drove up into the hills where Barry had taken them. The Saturn was not good for off-roading, so they toured the affluent neighborhoods and looked at the large houses. They pulled in behind cars that were just entering gated communities and got their eyes full of fountains, luxury cars, and cobblestone driveways. Some of the gardens they saw were so perfectly manicured it made the houses look hollow, like elaborate structures in a set design. The boys wondered what kinds of lives were spent keeping the gardens up and which were spent enjoying them, or if the gardens had simply become forgotten, unappreciated as the status quo, invisible beauties never underdressed.

They passed by one house that had a for sale sign in its yard. Its garden was not so good. There were weeds, patches of dead grass, small piles of dirt. The house looked like it harbored dead dreams, and current HOA nightmares.

The boys kept driving north until they could no longer. There were trails that leaked off from the neighborhood streets, secret passageways to vistas rewarded only to those who dared to explore. The boys found a clearing eventually that gave them a far better view than the one found on the Singing Pines roof.

"Another front row seat to the end of the world, brother," Jamie said. "This is the best ticket yet." He pulled out two cigarettes. "Lifted these from Christine. That dumb broad left them sitting on the table. I gave them back to her and I think she knew I taxed it, but she didn't say anything."

"She was too busy keeping quiet," Seamus said. "She's always gotten along fine with Angela. I thought she might defend the banquet servers' honor a bit. It's her own too, after all."

"Tell me about it! She sat quiet as a mute while Jeff said his share, and let Barry do the Lord's work on his own."

"I wonder if something is up," Seamus said.

"Hmmm," Jamie smoked. He looked over the town. Then, "Some people man...if they sat up here and really looked at the world they live in, right around them, they might just learn something."

"It is not rocket science."

"Right. There's nothing simpler in the world. But some people don't know where to look...or even how."

"I'd hope they would just keep to themselves then. Them."

"Them." Jamie exhaled through his nose. "Poor bastards."

When night came Jamie drove to Cameron's house and Rachel met them there shortly after their arrival. She was shy at first, but Cameron hugged her immediately just as he hugged Jamie and Seamus. They all took a shot of whiskey "for the walk" and carried a 24 pack of beer with them, which they hid in some bushes outside the bowling alley. They took turns leaving in pairs to shotgun beers between frames. Everyone laughed often and Rachel put her hands around Seamus more as the night went on, kissing his neck and whispering in his ear that she was having a good time. It was one of the great nights Seamus had with her, and he would think about it often, much, much more than he wanted to, in the coming weeks.

Jamie and Seamus and Rachel slept in Cameron's living room. No one was up when they got back from the alley and no one was up when they left in the morning.

"How do you feel?" Seamus asked Rachel, her skin flushed and eyes bleary, strips of sunlight coming from the plastic slats drawn over the screen door to the backyard. They were crammed together on a leather love seat. It was warm and they were sweaty. She slid away from him and made the face children make when contending with difficult vegetables.

"We should go before I realize how hungover I really am."

Seamus nudged Jamie, asleep on the couch, with his toe. Jamie shot up, awake to the day with instant energy, saying,

"I'm with it. Dude…Rachel, right on!" he shook her by the shoulders like an old friend from many years ago and she pulled away holding her stomach. Realizing his error, he belted laughter into the room and said, "Sorry, homegirl. Man, good having you!"

She nodded and said, "mmm-hmm," and looked to Seamus.

"We're leaving, man," Seamus said.

"Well so am I! No time to lose."

They walked outside together quickly and Jamie slammed the door behind him, laughing as Rachel blushed and looked at him. "Sorry, don't mean to wake the neighbors. Rooster hit the snooze button today. This place is dead."

Seamus wanted the three of them to get some breakfast but Rachel wanted to go home and sleep in her own bed so he went with her. After saying goodbye to Jamie, she asked him, "Is he always like that?"

Seamus smirked. "Never had a bad day in his life."

His headache slowly creeping forward and his stomach losing its center, Seamus had never felt so great for feeling so bad. He felt like he would never have a bad day again for the rest of his life. School would be back in session Monday, but he feared nothing of its stifled world, its phony teachers and phonier people. Even the thought of Rachel's roommates could not rattle him. He knew he was losing it, in fact, because a part of him even looked forward to seeing them again.

He spent Saturday with Rachel until work that evening, and intended to welcome each of her roommates home. It was a new semester, and it felt like a new world. He was ready. But Imogene did not come back that day. Her sister died skiing in Vermont and she would take a couple weeks off before returning to school. Rachel was on the phone with her often, encouraging her to take the spring semester off entirely. But Imogene was a good student and kept in contact with her professors. She said they said the same thing, except for her favorite among them. Professor Ng, who was Seamus' favorite photography instructor as well, told Imogene to take some time with her family, but to get back to school as soon as she could.

"Ng said you don't heal by making life try to stand still," Rachel told Seamus Imogene told her. "God that girl is brave."

So it would seem that Imogene would not stand still at all. She returned to the apartment that Thursday, missing only a week's worth of classes. Seamus was over, and did not expect to see her. No one did. When she entered abruptly and everything that stood still returned to motion, Rachel shot up with her roommates. The four embraced each other, swayed, and began the murmurs of muffled speech that would rise in volume and warp into even more confused sounds. Their crying was violent. Their hands gripped sides and shoulders. Human claws grasping and tugging. Watching them go on this way made Seamus' stomach squirm and spasm. He backed away rigidly and up the stairs. His mouth was still open like he was going to say something but he did not and went to Rachel's room to wait for her. It felt ten times larger inside than he remembered it feeling. It felt like the ceilings were fifteen feet away.

The four girls had resembled one rocking, cohesive, thing. Limp arms wrapped around skinny bodies, hair down, faces red and eyes squeezing open and shut. Seamus had seen people merge this way at Singing Pines. And so reconfiguring one of his favorite memories, he placed the scene downstairs alongside the mess of bodies dancing late in the evenings, when he took a second from busing to smile at the joy of it. He knew that in sorrow or in joy, emotions melded bodies and danced on relentlessly, paying little attention as to what started the dance at all. "Standing still," he told himself, thinking in the sheets about how minutes ago he stood alone against the wall of the living room, watching again, detached again, from the expressive life that did not stop as it went on without him.

Trying to think of other things but having little luck, he doubled-down on the thought process. He focused on the situation, on the death, even on his own alienation. That, actually, most of all. He tried to cry but nothing came. He knew that Imogene did not know what she thought she did, or truly, did not realize what she should know. She was actually lucky, as he understood it, given the circumstances. Imogene's sister just died, and she had nothing to do with it. There was no absence of mind, no chore left forgotten. There were no doors left open to be shut. There was only a singular event that occurred in a different galaxy of responsibility, one Imogene would never inhabit and so in this whole mess of a tragedy, there were lucky stars she was not counting indeed.

For the rest of the semester Rachel was largely preoccupied with Imogene and her roommates. Seamus spent fewer nights at her apartment. The girls had many girls' nights. Seamus felt like he had finally crossed the impossible threshold of affection, the once-vague concept of romantic love an actual reality in his life. He hated that suddenly so many song lyrics opened in meaning to him. God there were a lot of love songs! And many unhappy ones at that. He got it now. He hated that he did.

Seamus spent time walking and thinking, as he usually did. He was smoking a lot of pot and taking more acid than usual. The sidewalks twisted under his feet, their surfaces rising as separate layers, translucent and moving through him. The hidden dimensions, the sunflowers. He had stopped carrying the little watercolor in his pocket for a while but started again after he and Rachel said they loved each other for the first time. It was a terrible thing to look at on acid. It was like looking at an artifact from a time in his life that felt far away. That the period he longed for was temporally still so near it felt like a different dimension indeed. It was a dimension without death, and without closeness. It was a lusty, light platform with flowers and grass. He felt now like he was picking through the hay-colored straws of a dead lawn. It was winter but it was hot already and felt like summer. And there was no sign of that heat relenting, or of the colors returning.

Rachel just did not seem to have time for him, and when she did, her demeanor was one of chafed disappointment. On a rare night when no one else was home, he came over to see her. They sat in the living room where he drank the worst glass of water he had ever had. Rachel was not in the mood to drink alcohol, lately.

"Imogene is going through hell right now and yet she can still go to class, Seamus. I'm sorry you feel like you miss me but I'm still here. You could try and be a little less selfish you know."

"You're here physically. But I reach out to you and there's nothing there. It's like you're gone somewhere else. I try my best Rach, I don't know what to say though. I try and be sympathetic but your roommates just sort of look at me."

"I don't think quoting the Tibetan Book of the Dead is really what anyone wants to hear right now, Seamus."

"I don't mean anything by it."

"If you don't mean anything than why even start!"

"That's not really what I meant."

Their conversations now revolved around their differences. The things they had in common were only ghosts now, haunting the bedroom that they once shared, but now only visited in, like people who felt they knew too much about each other but were coming to realize they knew very little at all.

Even on Rachel's better days she and Seamus were unable to suture the gap between them. One afternoon she waxed on and on about a student she mentored through her internship. The student had Down Syndrome but Rachel believed she saw natural talent in the girl.

"You think you want to teach, then? You look like you're really in your element, working with these kids."

"Oh I can always teach. You can always teach anything you excel at," she said and looked at him with confident authority. "I don't ever want to stop teaching. But it won't be my career."

It was a bizarre sensation, but now he felt like he missed the melancholy of Rachel's empathic mourning. The tenderness of her heart bled on her sleeve, but he had not witnessed the swell of her ego. This was a new side to her. Another new dimension.

"Don't you know what I want to be?" she asked him.

"Well…you love to paint. I assume that people who love to paint teach others how to paint. But I honestly never thought about your career plans. I hardly think about my own."

"I know that," she said, sounding almost irritated. "I want to be a painter."

"Like houses?"

"You're joking."

"I am," he admitted. "I mean, I'm all for it. It's hard to do, though. Be an actual paid artist."

"Seamus! You sound like all the adults you make fun of

now."

"Well, there's a practical side to things. Even I know that."

Rachel deadpanned. "You want to hitchhike."

Seamus considered. Yes, that still sounded like a good plan.

"I'll have my camera with me. Who knows. Might catch a crime going down along the way. Anything can happen."

"Tell me you're still joking."

"Kinda. But really anything can happen. It's why the idea is attractive to me."

Rachel watched a runaway expression leap across Seamus' face. It was wild-eyed. He could have collapsed into her, losing composure, and maybe his brain. He seemed almost desperately high, stoned suddenly, broken from reality. She had not seen this side.

"You know, you could always consider coming with me."

"And you're not joking," she said. Her voice was quiet.

He released from his mania, and settled again.

"It was worth a shot," he smiled anyway, like he had really shown her.

"Seamus, you're an incredible person. I don't meet people who genuinely look at things the way you do," she told him.

Seamus looked at her. It was the first time he had heard her say something like that to him in what felt like far too long a time.

"Go on," he laughed.

"I'm being serious."

"I hope so! That would suck if you were being sarcastic

about me being so great."

"You are great. And I love you. But it's scary when you start talking about the future this way. It's like you don't have any goals."

"We never even talk about it."

"I know," her eyes were elsewhere, revealing a thinking mind that he did not like. Here was the downside of intimacy: the freedom of another to apprehend another, any way she likes.

"I mean, it's so up in the air. Who knows?"

"It's getting to be a little late to not have some *realistic* idea." Or like you say, the 'practical side to things.' This is why we're in college after all." Her voice was back to being confident, full of itself and the words it hosted in the ether of their dialogue.

"We're in college because we were told to go," he snapped.

"Uh, I don't think so."

"What? That family you have? They didn't drive it into your skull your whole goddamn life to get an education? The hell they didn't."

"Well yeah but I'm here because I choose to be."

"Me too," he submitted. "But it doesn't mean I wasn't...I don't know...lied to along the way."

Rachel had been sitting next to him gently holding his hand, even as her voice grew so boastful, and her grip tensed, she had not let go. But now she had.

"And then you start with the lie talk again." She blushed, her eyes looked hurt. It hurt Seamus. It happened so quickly.

"My roommates make fun of you over it."

"Fuck them," he said.

"Excuse me!" Now she snapped.

"C'mon. I know Imogene is hurting right now, God I do. And I wished I could relate to her, to Beth and Megan, to all of them. But I can't. And just because Imogene's going through a family crisis doesn't mean you and they are her keepers now or something. What did Ng say? You can't heal standing still?"

"You can't heal trying to make life stand still."

"I like my version better." Seamus smiled.

Rachel shook her head. "Seamus, you know I meant what I said. You are a great person. But you don't get it. And you think you do."

"There you go with that again. I'm not an idiot."

"No, but you're just not all there."

"Oh. Is that all then?"

"Seamus...it's like, even last semester my roommates would make fun of you and it would hurt me but I stood up for you."

"How would they do that?"

"Well, one day, like Imogene got this new kind of granola and said it was loaded with omega 3's and how studies show they're so good for brain function and Beth just looked at her and said, 'Studies, huh? Studies are full of lies. Aren't they Rachel?' And the three of them laughed. They have this whole running joke about calling things out as conspiracies or something. And they don't mention your name, but they sure mention mine. It's like they rub my nose in your bullshit."

Seamus did not immediately speak to Rachel but he did

take some time to think. Unfortunately now was not the time to think, but to say. Rachel stared at him imploringly. Somewhere in the outskirts of his intuition, he realized that the most appropriate course of action was to give in to the vulnerability that was otherwise shielded by his flippant attitude and disregard of that which mattered to his girlfriend.

Seamus still regarded his interactions with others as a barometer of his ability to relate to people as a whole. Each interaction was in itself a microcosm of his entire social being. Further, if he really thought enough to break it down, which he did sometimes while meditating, it was obvious to him that his barometer was essentially one of extremes. Interactions were monitored by a gauge located somewhere in his consciousness or brain - he was still unsure if there was a difference. But somewhere a device ticked away, noticing everything: all gestures, all tones of voice, and all words that could really mean anything other than what they appear to be at face value.

So, for all the minutia of human relationship, Seamus' barometer strictly picked up one of two things: whether the conversation was affable and therefore reflective of him in a positive light, or negative in myriad forms, and so cast a shadow over his likableness.

There were those that did not register on Seamus' barometer. These were almost always authority figures, but other times were just flash-in-the-pan passersby. Either way, if someone did not appear on Seamus' scale of concern regarding his own being, it was because he had already dismissed any worth in theirs. Although he had not quite looked at it this way before, it was the truth. He only saw these people as Them, which implied innate dysfunction within their personalities. Them, therefore, were a forgettable and useless people regarding the tedious work of structuring his own ego.

Seamus did not like Rachel's roommates, but they were unfortunately not affiliated with Them. They mattered very much to Rachel, who mattered very much to Seamus, and therefore their opinions of him mattered very much, too. And so something inside him nagged. His intuition bent his ear and whispered that he should admit something. Now. Something told him that this moment, so precious with conflict and raw with truer colors, was the perfect time, and no other time would ever be as perfect ever again. The truth was that Seamus did not like Rachel's roommates because they did not like him. If they did, he would probably like them very much. But instead he never even felt he had a fighting chance. Knowledge of their inside jokes was not illuminating, but only confirming. He felt like they had a running gag going every time he saw them. They never seemed to look him in the eye, but only at his eyes. He felt like a portrait, stuck in a still life, a character on display.

"You know, I really like your roommates. I'm sorry they don't like me. I think they're the ones that don't get it."

Rachel sighed and walked to the kitchen. She put her empty glass in the dishwasher and sprayed off dirty plates left lying on the counter. He looked straight ahead and listened to her movements, shut his eyes to focus on them. Then he heard her ask, "Ready to go to bed?" flatly.

He opened his eyes and shook his head. He had not noticed that she turned off the kitchen light.

"Sure," he said and followed her up the stairs.

He undressed quickly and got into bed and listened to her do the same.

"I love you," she said and got under the covers next to him.

He opened his eyes. "I love you, too," he said, feeling happy relief.

She kissed him on the forehead and rolled over on her side as she did every night to sleep.

13

When the other shoe dropped, Seamus was already bare-foot.

He was cycling through a handful of yoga poses on Rachel's bedroom floor. He looked up from a briefly held down dog to see his girlfriend rushing into the room.

"There you are. I'm getting loosened up," He smiled. She glanced at him. He stood up and watched her blue eyes flit over her cluttered desk.

"That was pretty much the douchiest thing I could possibly say, right?"

"It wasn't sexy," she said with a laugh that was difficult to discern. Was she laughing at him or brushing him off?

She opened a drawer in her desk and quickly began thumbing through stacks of all kinds of things, old journal pages, drawings, articles ripped from magazines, pictures of people she admired, love letters...

Seamus watched her do so. She started talking quietly to herself when she found a stack of polaroids in another drawer. She flipped through them with forceful, fast flicks of her thumbs. Her bony forearms tensed. Her back was so straight it seemed she was poised to shoulder the burdens of all the world. Her ass was hard to see in the loose pajama pants she was wearing but Seamus could detect its curves anyway, if only by memory. He savored a twist she made at her hips, turning on one foot and lowering into the drawer again to pull out another stack of old pictures. However loose her clothes were, he could see the sharp angle of her curving side, feminine beneath the cover-up of sleepwear. It made him fiercely lustful and even more lonely.

The pictures dropped from her hands and she pushed him away.

"Jesus! Are you a caveman or something? You made me drop all the polaroids!"

Seamus looked down at the floor. One picture caught his eye. He knelt down and picked it up. Rachel and two of her roommates sat smiling around a table low to the ground. There was a fourth girl he had never seen. It looked like the shot was taken in a living room somewhere where it snowed. It also looked like a tea party. The girls looked subdued, but happy. They looked like they were posing.

Rachel's eyes brightened. She grabbed the picture out of Seamus' hand. "This is it!"

"That's good."

"Yes it is." She kissed him quickly on his cheek. "I'll be back. Could you pick up all these pictures?"

"I was going to ask you if I could."

"Thank you!" She rushed downstairs.

Seamus was lying on his side in bed when Rachel came back, nearly an hour later. He listened to her undress. She pulled off her t-shirt quickly. It slid against and up her body almost silently, save for a tiny swoosh as she tugged it over her shoulders. He listened to the hangar hook with a dull scratch onto the wooden closet rod. Her pajama pants were too loose to elicit much sound as she yanked them off her soft legs. But they were tossed into the hamper with a clean, wooly thump. She was not wearing any underwear and pulled up the sheets to sidle next to him.

"Thanks for picking up my pictures," she said.

"No sweat."

She kissed him on the cheek again and rolled over on her side away from him.

"Goodnight babe. Love you," she said.

Seamus remembered Rachel telling him she loved him for the first time, and then again the next morning. He remembered exactly how it sounded. And he remembered how it did not sound.

He turned on his side and sidled up next to her.

"Seamus..."

He dug his chin into her neck.

"Ouch! Seamus not now."

He pulled away and felt his eyes watering and his throat burning. It felt like he had swallowed glass. His periphery softened and his ears buzzed. A glass pill and a nitrous hit. The bed felt big and the room felt small.

And he was hard.

He wanted to start jerking off and make a show of it but blue balled frustration pirouetted with a slow death heart break.

"Really fucking glad I came over then. Next time you need some dishes washed let me know."

Rachel turned back to face him. Her eyes were steely and fixed. He softened, hardened, softened, hardened. He felt like ignoring her protests and jerking off over her if he had to. He felt like shaking loose his urge and telling her how sorry he was for not being able to be better, or whatever the hell it was he was supposed to be for things to be different. He felt

like getting smashed drunk, taking a fat line of coke, prefer-
ably with her, and telling all her roommates that he didn't care
what had happened to them, he just wanted to start over. He
felt like running. He felt like lying still.

"So sorry you didn't get laid. Some people are only dealing
with life and death here-"

"We're all dealing with life and death here," he said. "Every
last one of us. It's called being human."

"We're mourning. It's called being human."

She quickly flipped back on her side facing away from him
but Seamus grabbed her and twisted her back to him. She
kicked and got him on his upper thigh. He let out a rolling
whelp. It was close.

"You can't just fucking have your way with me!" she
shrieked. They stared at each other. It was too late - she
caught him. She pushed his hand away from his own face and
wiped a tear away herself. In a hush, she continued, "Baby,
what's going on?"

"I come over to see you and you're spending time with
the girls. I wait like you ask me to and all you do is come in
looking for a picture and ask me to pick up the mess."

"I spilled them because you grabbed me just like you're
doing now."

"You like it when I grab you...you did."

"There are times for things Seamus. It's also called being
human."

"Sure. And I so get that. But making love is also part of
being human. One of the best parts."

"Seamus...that's what you're here for? You're just here to
get laid?"

"No! No. But I'm here for a little more than picking up polaroids."

Her eyes were cold. "You don't know what it's like to lose a sister."

Seamus glared back at her. "You sure don't."

"No. But I have brothers, and I know how to relate." She sighed. "You're an only child." Her voice took on her confident air again, "And you're young."

Older women.

"I'm a few months younger than you."

"It's not biological. It's in here," she tapped his head.

Seamus blinked. "I've reason to think it's in here," he said and patted her chest.

"Seamus...my Seamus. There you go with all that hippy stuff again."

"To be fair I sort of stole that from somebody."

"Well I'm sure it made sense in the context that 'somebody' said to you. But I'm trying to be real. I'm trying to really talk to you."

"I am too. It's just not working, I guess."

Her lips trembled. "It doesn't look like anything's working these days."

Seamus' chest burned cold. Air became difficult to find. He hated this...intimacy.

She wiped another of his tears. "Is anything working?" her voice shook.

"It was working pretty great before all this happened."

"Oh, so what? So life happens? I know we were busy making plans but..." she sniffled and rubbed her nose.

"You took that from someone too."

"It seemed appropriate."

"I think us making love seems appropriate."

"Seamus! There you go again! Is that seriously all I mean to you?"

"You don't even understand what I mean - I said 'make love,' you said 'get laid.'"

"I haven't even had a sex drive since all this happened." she looked coldly at him again. "It's like you're immune."

"I'm not immune. I just miss you so goddamn much."

Now Seamus wiped a tear from her face. "I miss you too," she said. Her lips arched downwards.

"Well I'm right here!"

"And so am I, Seamus."

He put his hand on her lower back and drew closer to her.

"Not now, Seamus! You seriously are only here to get laid."

Her body was rigid and still. Seamus was leaning on his elbow, upright and gently rocking. He thought he was thinking but it was more like stewing, and he could not tell the difference when his emotions began boiling. So he came out with it.

"What's wrong with getting laid? Your other roommates haven't had a dick in them for so long they might as well be cleaning their cunts with dusters."

Seamus got slapped, and it was an impressive slap. He breathed in deeply and felt his cheek pulsate. It throbbed with an icy burn. Rachel's eyes were angled at him like laser beams, watching him reel. He tried to wipe a tear from Rachel's face but she swept his hand away. He winced, gun shy.

"So you think we should all just fuck, is that it? Just forget about the dead and fuck away. Just get a bunch of dicks shoved in us."

Seamus shoved off the bed and looked out the window at nothing interesting. It was raining off and on and no one was outside. Parked cars, closed garage doors. Quiet, damp space.

"I feel bad for you, Seamus, if you seriously think sex is some kind of an issue here."

He turned and sat down on the edge of the bed. His mouth was dry. He looked at her and shrugged.

"We have plenty of love, Seamus. We're hurting right now but we have love, believe me. You're the one who gets so goddamn aloof I feel uncomfortable just having you here. You cry about not coming over but when you do everyone else feels tense."

"I always come over in a light mood. I try and be lighthearted, make people feel good. I only quoted the Tibetan Book of the Dead once. And that was because you told me the last time I was being too flippant. I just can't win."

"Then maybe you shouldn't even try in the first place."

"Excuse me?"

"If you can't win you don't have any business playing."

"I didn't think there was anything to win."

"Well you just said it. And I don't think I can *win* with you either."

Seamus felt like running. There was nowhere in particular

he wanted to run to, he just wanted to exorcise himself of the nauseous anxiety that riddled him in this big bed and tiny room with the buzzing white quiet and invisible roommates who were probably up and listening to his and Rachel's voices fluctuate between anger and sadness and sometimes disbelief.

He wanted to leap out the window. He wanted to throw her polaroids out of it, too.

He wanted to tell her roommates to go to sleep.

He wanted Rachel to get horny, to long unstoppably for him inside her, realizing that it would make all the difference. He wanted to believe that was true.

And he wanted to be honest. He wanted to tell her something personal and great that would make all of this stop. But if there was ever a time for that, it did not feel like now was it. It felt like that time was gone completely, and only this was left. This was intimacy as he now knew it.

When they told each other their I-love-yous, Rachel spoke for Seamus. When it was time for the it's-over, Seamus spoke for Rachel.

"Just like that?" he asked.

"How else is it supposed to be?" She looked tired, like the emotional capacity she had for this exchange was used up and she just wanted to get it over with already.

Seamus still felt hot and dizzy, but now the sensations were amplified. He was used to being in altered states, but this was a maiden voyage to a psychic port he had only experienced in theory, like love had been.

Anchoring at bay within himself, he was able to get out of bed and dress. His movements were calm and composed, and a little slothful. Thoughts were scarce for a change. The only thing he could grasp was that something felt taken from him, and as seamlessly as it had been given. He felt like an entire marching band had stormed into his life, without his invitation, and dragged him along with it, the cymbals clashing louder and louder to abstraction, until the whole production disbanded in one roaring stroke, leaving him in the middle of a street, alone, and the parade beyond him inescapably out of reach.

He knew where it was headed, too: onto the next stop in Rachel's tour of life.

"Do you want a ride home?"

"No."

"It's late. And it's cold."

"I have a jacket."

"It's not much though. And you're skinny."

"I like walking."

Seamus wondered if all of his sentences should be so simple. If dialogues with Rachel were always so straightforward, would they ever have had such communicative problems? Where were the building blocks of their shared ruin? If he knew the exact moments as they connected and formed the molecules of his only meaningful breakup, maybe he never would have had to endure it at all.

But it was too late, both in the night and in their love life, to worry about that now. He knelt down to tie his shoelaces cooly as he did everything else, rose to look at her leaning forward and at attention in bed, and waved his hand like he was calling over a cafeteria attendant to refill the chai tea machine.

"This was real," she said. "And I still think you're an incredible person. We're just not right, or the timing's not right, or something isn't right." She nodded her head. "This is the right thing to do."

"That's nice that you came to that conclusion. I'll make it easy on myself and believe you since I don't know what to think."

Seamus did not know what to think. He only knew that he did not choose *this*.

"Seamus, please," was the last thing he heard as he turned and left the room. For someone so emphatic that he needed to leave it was strange she wanted to prolong it any further.

Seamus rolled the words around. He was thinking again.

She did say, "please." Maybe she wanted him to open her window? He could not have been the only one to feel such a draft.

Maybe she was going to ask him to "please remember to recycle." She did not like it when he threw away plastic bottles in trash cans. It did not matter if there were no recyclables bins around. He could carry it until there would be, or better yet, not buy products in plastic bottles at all.

Or maybe she discovered an ounce of sympathy not used entirely on Imogene. It was a little late for that.

Or maybe she wanted to ask him to please be quiet as he left. He stalled in the small carpeted space outside her closed door and the other two before him. Tight walls, a flickering darkness. No lights on anywhere, but the outlines of things prominent. Door jambs, door knobs. The edge of a hallway counter space, the top of the banister. He looked longest at the staircase. There was nowhere to go but down.

He looked back before turning down the steps. He thought he might have heard something, but even he knew that was imagined. Not a crack of light anywhere, nor a murmur exhaling through the thin walls.

Below, Seamus unlocked the deadbolt but was sure to keep the other lock in place. He checked the door when he was outside. It was shut, alright. He walked a few steps and stopped to consider which way to get back to the dorms. It did not really matter, just depended on how long he wanted to walk.

He heard a sudden and defined noise behind him. It sounded like a deadbolt locking.

Fuck it. He would just take the short way.

As he got moving, and did so quickly, he repeated the weary phrase again. "Fuck it," he said to himself aloud and not aloud. Over and over until something stopped him. Fuck...it?

It...

He might be more careful with his words after all, he thought to himself. It. If there was anything that saved Seamus from getting consumed in the torrent of thoughts that follow self-righteousness, which itself is the shadow of denial, It was it. Seamus was not taken by the inevitable heartache that awaited him if he wallowed too deeply in what had happened, versus who he was. And it took the simple pleasures of his senses to remind him. He smiled once he remembered. He knew what beauty was, as people who have It do. He knew what life was too, as people who have It do.

A light rain had started not long into his walk. It grew heavier quickly. He found a covered bus stop bench and sat down, waiting indefinitely for the flash storm to lighten. With nothing to do and his stomach returning from its gelatinous sucker-punched state, he accidentally sputtered into a crying fit. He thought he had It? Oh well. He was just releasing the backed-up frustration that welled inside him the last few hours at Rachel's, he reasoned.

Looking up from his hands and into the bleariness of the

yellow lit street snaking ahead of him, sparkling with rain-water, he was able to isolate one streetlamp and stare beatifi-cally into its amber glow.

The rain was coming down hard. The drops were long and thin, like needles. But they shot down at a forty-five degree angles. It was as if an army of thin hornets were spearing towards the earth at kamikaze speeds, assaulting the road. It remained unblemished from their restless assault. If anything, their war against it only added to its power. Their effect on its hard, long body was transmuted upon impact. The army of rain hornets turned the grayness of the asphalt into a glit-tering effluxion of micro explosions, each birthing golden riv-ulets whose lives spanned only seconds. They in turn bore their own shining offspring. And so entire raindrop families cycled in and out of existence, the only constant was the alive-ness of the whole mess in its sparkling entirety.

So Seamus knew. If nothing else, he had this. It was enough to still his mind, and Seamus held a deep reverence for any-thing that could accomplish that. And unlike heartbreak, the ecstatic moment was familiar to him. And it could never wear out its welcome.

This was beautiful and this was life, and so this was It. Seamus had It, if nothing else. If he could not be the boy-friend he needed to be to Rachel, and the friend's boyfriend he needed to be to her roommates, then perhaps he simply did not understand death. And if this were the case, he did not care. He was going to give everything he had to under-stand life.

PART II

BARRY'S CREW

1

The morning was cool and bright, the kind that makes people happy to be alive, recall fond memories, and smile privately. Jamie and Seamus and Cameron were together, getting stoned, and reflecting on their mortality. Stationed in the empty parking lot of their alma mater, they passed around a joint and looked out the windows of Jamie's Saturn, eyes wandering, inner narratives doing the same, and remembering times recent and not so recent. It was as though the culmination of their lives to this hour could be found within the crystalline dome at the end of the kaleidoscope, the instrument angled perfectly to reflect all that had come before into a pattern of perfectly placed colors, a hallucinatory testament to their experience that was apprehended by each on a purely individual basis, the cohesion of their accumulated knowledge vague but felt, as impossible to describe as It and just as real. Indeed, Its connections were popping up everywhere.

A sense of solidity in their lives thus far notwithstanding, the more grounded implications of what was yet to be remained murky, both in the immediate and long term. This particular morning was the kind with little to do save for one big thing, and once that thing had been done, whatever was next was yet a phantom. So they idled and waited for its apparition. It would come, they knew. It always did.

In a role typically carried through by Jamie, it was Cameron who broke the silence.

"You should have seen the faces this chick was making, oh my goodness!" Cameron yelled suddenly from the backseat. Conversations this morning flowed this way, abrupt, violent in volume or meek in tone. Wistful. Hopeful. The sum of experiences.

He leaned forward over the console, his hands on each of the front seats as though he was pulling back a curtain, his eyes pink but glowing.

"And I kept going. She doesn't smoke pot and didn't like that I did. But when I was still going 45 minutes into it she didn't give a shit anymore, that's for sure."

"Right on Camo. I'm happy for you," Jamie said.

"I'm happy for me too! I didn't even want to fuck her, either. I wanted Jennifer. That's why I went over to her apartment in the first place! But dudes, Jennifer's a tough nut to crack, Jesus Christ."

"She'll come around," Jamie said.

"Yeah? You think so?"

"You're a good man, Camo. Good men are hard to find."

Cameron smiled at Jamie's encouragement. Then, "Hey… think Melissa will tell Jennifer how good I was?" Cameron asked.

"Girls always talk about that stuff," Jamie said.

"Hell yeah! I'm calling Jennifer tonight then. She at least likes to blaze. But girls don't fuck you when they're high unless they're already going to. I should bring a bottle of wine."

"Bring champagne. This one's on me," Jamie said.

"Yes!" Cameron shouted and shook Jamie's shoulders. "Sometimes shit just works out."

Cameron was beaming. But a stray dark cloud ran through his mental circuitry, and he said, "But then sometimes shit doesn't."

He sighed a heavy breath.

"Fucking George," he said.

It was quiet again for a while except for coughs and a subtle crackle from a breathing cherry. The streets had little traffic. It rained the night before but the storm passed quickly and the morning cover burned off early. The sky was nearly cloudless and the football field was glistening wet. The boys were parked just to the left of the bleachers. Sunlight enlivened its edges. In a few minutes the sun would rise higher and pour unhindered into the car. The boys would go then. Jamie had laid that rule down already as a means to get them going, to prompt behavior on an early Sunday whose mission was over but eerily so.

"What a morning. It's like the most beautiful morning ever except that we just came from a funeral," Cameron said.

"George was a solid cat," Jamie said.

"As good as they get," Cameron agreed. "But you have to keep living."

Seamus looked back at him. "Yes you do."

George was in their graduating high school class. Jamie and Cameron knew him better than Seamus did, but still neither were close to him. But all of them liked him very much. Everyone had.

A creeping glare rose along the edge of the bleachers, flashing against the top row's corner edge.

"You gotta live. The sun rises again," Jamie said and started the car. The boys all put their sunglasses on and Jamie drove slowly out the parking lot. He waited for a semi to pass, and then pulled out after it.

"Days like these, gents, and you remember not to be in a hurry," he said.

"Amen," Cameron agreed.

"Right. Hurry to what? Our own dirt naps?" Seamus asked.

"That's right. I think I'll just let everyone just take their turn," Jamie said. "Cause you never know," his voice distant.

Cameron heard him though, and, "No sir! You never know!" Then, whistling, "I'm sure glad I got laid last night."

Jamie drove to a street fondly familiar to Seamus and him, home to what they named Victory Hill. They parked along the sidewalk where the houses ended and walked up the dirt trail until it gave way to a wild hillside, unmarred by human habitation. They climbed up its steepening terrain until they had to use their hands for aid, settling eventually at the base of a tilting tree. Most of its roots were exposed as though it were ready to rip from the earth and bowl them over. They trusted it though as a large boulder was stationed nobly near the tree's other end, keeping it locked in place. They leaned against the tree and looked over the horizon and continued to say little as they got higher.

On a funeral-centric morning, the boys felt called to spend time in nature. Before the service started they met early to drive to a hiking trail in the mountains and split a six pack. The beers were mismatched and clinked against each other in a cardboard box, sounding loudly in the early morning and competing only with squawks and chirps from the birds. None of the boys could legally buy beer, though they could get away with it at the Mountain Lodge. But it did not open on Sundays and they had to be resourceful. Seamus brought the three beers left remaining from his dorm room, Jamie snuck two from the back row of his parents' refrigerator, and Cameron helped himself to one from Jennifer's apartment.

Seven a.m. was a rare time for a two beer buzz, but the boys were adamant that nothing was more appropriate. They had among the three of them one completely shared memory with George and it was a vivid one. It was their senior year and Seamus was talking with Jamie and Cameron in the quad about something forgettable and light-hearted when George, in his typical friendliness, approached them silently and pantsed Cameron.

"Son of a bitch!" Cameron yelled and then, "Oh, Georgie! What's up man?" as he pulled his shorts back up to his waist.

"Chillin, chillin. Moran's final was whack! He didn't say shit about it being cumulative."

"Dude I know! It killed me, man. I got way more to think about than whatever the hell I learned in September."

"Right? It's like March already. If I wanted to remember what I learned in September I'd read about Chaucer on Wikipedia. Remember this gents – knowledge is fluid, not static. We're in the internet age."

Seamus shook his head and smiled. "It's one big brain. That's the internet. It's the one mind Buddhists talk about, and it's here."

"Yes!" Jamie yelled. "One and done, dudes! Fucking George. What are you up to now, brother?"

He shrugged, said, "nothing but I don't want to feel too sorry for myself over that final. You shouldn't either, Cameron."

And so it happened. The four of them took a spontaneous drive up the mountains together. The initial plan was just to get high, though no one could tell George that. He insisted that they hike first.

"Getting loaded is always better after you earn it," he had said.

The boys were two miles in when they excitedly discovered a waterfall. George was right. The boys hailed his insistence on the hike and patted him on the back, bumped fists, hollered into the open air. George smiled. He knew he was right all along.

There was a steep but accessible pathway up the right side of the waterfall to gain access to the top of it. Jamie and Cameron excitedly charged ahead, not looking behind them. Seamus followed, and after a short spurt up the incline he turned and saw that George was still at ground level.

"Coming George?" he shouted.

George appeared to be staring at the waterfall, but looked up at Seamus and gave him a thumb's up. Thinking nothing more of it, Seamus continued up the pathway to catch up with Jamie and Cameron. He would remember that decision.

Though when the boys got to the top, George was only halfway there. He had taken the left approach.

When the boys reached the top, they all looked down at George, who was no longer at ground level but had a considerable distance to travel until he caught up to them. The trek to the top had another approach, a much steeper one at that. About eighty feet of vertical face climbing, and George was in the middle of it.

The face was full of jutting rocks, many large and blocky. The boys were so silent when they first watched him it seemed the slightest indication of instability would have rung loudly across the mountain. All they heard instead was a steady rhythm of breath. George was in full control.

George made fluid maneuvers in a fairly straight line, his movements measured and deliberate. As he progressed, he studied the rock with sober focus. When it appeared he could afford to look ahead, he would calmly steady himself in place, straighten his arms and lean back to look up into the immediate, vital future. There are shoes made for climbing but George was in Converse sneakers. As he stood there studying what lie ahead, his legs were grounded on the nubs of rock beneath them as though they would never budge. Once he saw what he needed to, he continued.

"You got this buddy."

"You're the man George!"

George was maybe twenty feet away from the top when he stopped again and stared. The boys watched him scan ahead, his face remaining calm, but determined. As they looked down, they saw what he was seeing: the jutting rocks did not jut out so far up here, and their large sizes were not so large, either. The wall was far from blank, but passing safely would require a kinesthetic understanding of how to utilize treacherous looking features without falling.

His first move was a high reach to thin rail of rock above his head. He pinched it with his right hand. He brought his left hand up next, but not as high. Instead, he pulled against an exposed triangle of rock, and slowly turned his hips to lean back slightly. He raised his left foot above his left hand on something small but apparently worthy, and pressed up slowly, and brought his left hand up with him as he did so until he was able to reach for a prominent, but not exactly large, horn of stone. He dropped his right foot off the wall entirely and let it dangle, then brought his right hand over to meet his left hand on the same handhold. He did a semi pull-up and reached for a hold higher yet with his right hand, planted his right foot, and reached better climbing.

He topped out over the lip to hardy back pats, applause and cheers, whistles, laughter, fist bumps, and onlooking faces returning flush with blood. He looked back over his conquest and enjoyed the commanding view over the treetops, winding trails, and the white, gushing spray at the bottom of the fall. He was not speaking yet as the boys continued to sputter away in relief and disbelief both.

"Boy you had me going, jeez man, what a fucking guy!" Cameron yelled.

"What were you thinking, dude?" Seamus asked.

George smiled his broad, easy smile to their acclamations, but now he regained some of his earlier focus as he offered, "You want to know what I was thinking?"

"That's the first of a few things I want to know about," Jamie said.

"Well okay. The only thing I was thinking the whole way up was..."

Nothing yet, the boys waited in his pause. Then...

The hero let out a squealing fart. And no one laughed harder than him, he was so delighted in his own irreverence.

Standing beside the rushing waterfall, the boys finally got high. George took two hits only and refused any more. Each time the blunt came around to him in rotation, he only pounded his chest twice with his fist and flashed the peace sign, saying, "Just two hits."

The boys would implore him to keep smoking with them. After cheating death, as they called it, how could he be so conservative?

"Just two hits a day, fellas. Everything in moderation."

And when the boys made their way down, each going the easy way this time, they all spoke beatifically about the day and laughed giddily over small missteps along the trail, rec-ollections of their senior year's highlights so far, and slips of tongue that gave way to sexual innuendo and other variety of dick and pussy jokes.

When they reentered the mountain's small village they ate lunch at the lodge and drank illegal beer. The boys ordered three pitchers while George nursed a single pint the entire afternoon and covered his glass with his hand every time his companions tried to fill it.

"Everything in moderation, fellas."

"If you did coke you'd only have one line too? I'd like to see you try!" Cameron bellowed, drunk.

George shook his head. "From everything I hear about coke that's damn near impossible. One reason I'll never do it, too. Plus that shit's so bad for you. I need my heart to beat steady. Couldn't have climbed that way if the ticker was getting ahead of me. You have to be ahead of your heartbeat, see. Your mind has to be able to outrun it. Otherwise forget it."

The boys did not know about It back then, but it was obvious now that George was attuned early in life. Cameron, who had come to understand the philosophy as explained, or not explained, by Jamie and Seamus, suggested that George's death was not in vain. He had It. Once a person has It, death can come any time. It has already been figured out.

"Cameron...that's brilliant!" Jamie shouted.

"I'm just saying. It is everything. When you have everything, what's left to lose?"

"Jesus! Where have you been all my life?" Seamus asked. "I know a few people you should knock some sense in to. They sure as hell won't listen to me."

"Shoot. I'm no prophet or anything. You guys turned me on to It in the first place."

"We were just recognizing what you already had, my man."

"Damn! You know how to make a guy feel good!" Cameron laughed.

Seamus stood up and walked a few steps down the hill. By the time he had his camera on and focused, the wren he was trying to capture flew off its tree branch. Seamus lowered his camera away from his face and looked at the vacant birch in front of him. At least he had captured the moment live. These days, he reminded himself, that mattered most.

Besides, he was still buzzing from a shot he captured earlier that morning in the mountains, when the fog was still thick and milky, and the sun was barely a white specter. A thick cluster of snails huddled together, there could have been as many as eighty, in and around the fork of a tree. The divided trunk grew into separate directions, a straight left and a meandering right. The snails' habitation of its center, none of them committing to go higher in either direction, inspired him. The soft, white daylight provided all the lighting that was necessary to turn the fog into a serene backdrop. The tree was a neutral gray color, but dark enough to contrast against the gloom surrounding it. The snails were the darkest element and brought life to the shot. He instantly regarded it as one of his better pictures, if not his best.

It took several attempts before he felt he was able to encapsulate the immovable happiness of the mollusk orgy. He shuffled inches forward, backward, to the left and to the right, and back at the starting point again. He stood straight and crouched down, held his camera up over his head, level with his navel, stretched out straight from his heart. He took the camera off of automatic and adjusted the aperture. This would lead to more trial and error but he had the time to experiment. Such was the luxury of having snails as a subject.

When he landed what he thought was a shot that brought

the snails their joyful justice, he was standing a few feet removed from the tree, hunching slightly forward, his camera cradled in his hands and held close near his Adam's apple, his eyes fixated on the screen rather than the viewfinder. The shot flashed onscreen immediately after he snapped the shutter and he felt a vibration in his chest. He immediately flipped over to display mode and studied what he just captured.

A gap of white expanse on the left, and a layered amoeba of mountains and mist on the right. A bright orb shining through the tree's split. The snails were most identifiable farther from the center where the light offered better definition for the twirls and speckles on the surface of their shells. Those in the center were considerably harder to make out save for their shape, but this was a contrast he appreciated deeply. They looked like the tree's heart, an external, multicellular heart, quiet and still, but very much alive.

Shelled Serenity?

He would sleep on the title. It would come when it needed to, when he sat down and got to the tedious but joyful work of researching literary journals online, looking for a place where his latest work just might find a home.

Seamus had been taking many pictures since Rachel decided she did not want to see him romantically anymore. She did tell him, however, that she still wanted him in her life. Once the dust was settled, and she no longer was mad at him, she had come to the conclusion that they were not right for each other but that she thought he was a great person and she did not want to lose him. So she invited him to lunch, and even more committing activities like attending a concert and an art opening.

He did not want to do any of these things, and since Seamus did not do what he did not want to do, consistently dismissed her invitation to occupy the anesthetized, sexless position as the friendly ex in the periphery of her life.

Running into Rachel around campus provided an acute and immediate sting that nothing else in his life could give him. He found it strange that the farther out of sight and mind she was, the easier the wound healed. As he walked solitarily along the campus or sat by himself in his dorm room or shot a picture of a cactus, alone as he was, he could come to great conclusions why he was better off without her. And yet, it took one glance at her in real time, one moment of catching her smile, assured and light, for the stitching to burst open and his heart to sink. Her smile was so agreeable in fact that it communicated to him that she, too, believed they were better off without each other. She had surely come to the same conclusion with much less trouble than he had, and with much more immediacy. She was so preoccupied with the death of Imogene's sister that she probably thought about him little whereas she occupied a considerable part of his mind even on his good days. And so, far removed from even the fantasy of possessing some kind of upper hand, he would bristle once they had passed each other and dive inwardly to reconvene the process of scraping himself off the sole of her Converse sneaker.

However, there was a proverbial silver lining, as all dark things are purported to have. If Seamus' inclinations to take and edit pictures were equivalent to the stoking of a healthy flame, he now had a bonfire on his hands. Even if he took shoddy pictures, doing so at all was a purging of the lower talents so that the bar would raise, and one day the best of what he took now would be considered the worst later, and on and on, spiraling upwards towards some level of, dare he fantasize, mastery. He would settle for striving towards competency in the meantime, and had the good sense to not get too wrapped up on visualizing his name in the contents of National Geographic, though such daydreams did enter his mind with some regularity. They might visit him as he bused plates at work, or as he sipped coffee in the morning or smoked a cigarette in the moonlight, looking, nodding, hidden vistas to him alone open and spreading.

There were other improvements, too. He was working out now, going to the gym three times a week and running on two of his off days. In order to maximize the effects of exercise, and to make the whole process easier on his body, he was taking significantly fewer drugs. He was smoking a few more cigarettes lately, but they were still occasional at most and typically at work. He smoked much less pot, which had also primarily become a diversion to keep his spirit buoyant while on the Singing Pines clock. His alcohol consumption followed a similar pattern. Indeed, if not for his job at the country club, he might be damn near sober.

He did allow himself to enjoy some diversions as they fluttered randomly about the semester. He had been laid only once since the break up, and almost twice but he got too drunk to begin. This angered his new bedmate, his sole lay since Rachel, and she did not have much of an appetite for him again. He did not care much though, since bedding her before was awkward for him and transformed, at its worst, a happy activity into an unpleasantly foreign affair. He had to think about porn to stay afloat, and even then it took a Zen-like focus and a dose of struggle not to get so turned off by her stupid noises and idiotic posters and scentless sheets and not round-enough ass to ensure that he came.

Maybe she knew he was disinterested when he came over the second time. Or maybe it was the gin stink of three home-made martinis in red Dixie cups that oozed through his pores like disinfectant on a urinal. Either way, he was relieved, even with a splitting headache, to be pushed out of her room in the morning, hearing her tell him with disdainful sarcasm how amazing he was, followed by a haughty proclamation that he need not "worry" about "having to come again." He wondered if she was being punny or just literal, but gradually as the day beat on so did his memories resurface, notably of the previous night's failure to launch. The better part of him was happier than it was sad. It was too much work to have to call her and text her and smile in passing. Now she ignored him if she ever saw him and he did the same. She had few friends and was not someone who he worried too much about when it came to gossip, though there were moments when having caught wind of her petty accusations behind his back bothered him some. Still, the lay was not worth hearing her voice and looking at her face, not to mention spending time in that room that was so unlike the one he fell in love in not many weeks removed.

The girl was so unlike Rachel, so not Rachel, that he developed a severe aversion to Kermit the Frog. All he knew was that he did not want to fuck anyone under a *Muppets Take Manhattan* poster ever again in his life. He got the irony, really he did. He just wanted to rip it off the wall and drape it over her face, backside up, so that he could finish in peace and be just a little less reminded that the one person he wanted to sleep with above all others would never want to do so with him again for as long as he lived.

And so, as odd as it seemed when he thought about it conceptually, walking from the campus gym to get a biodegradable cup full of coffee from the dining hall, looking like a regular addict on the mend, he decided that he was actually enjoying the clear-headedness of sobriety as though it were in itself a new high to explore. He did not miss the drugs nor did he even think about them much. They had become predictable, and perhaps he should be ashamed that they had reached the point of becoming almost boring. What that said about the state of his nervous system he did not know, but he did understand that he was young and if there was any damage done, his body would repair itself in due time. He was already breathing better without powders of all forms funneling up his nostrils. When he blew his nose his snot was a neutral color, not blue or green from smashed uppers and opiates made in Pfizer laboratory that mimicked filthy, low-class street drugs that only hoodlums buy, sell, and take.

He felt he knew himself at this point well enough without needing to take a sledgehammer to his ego whim after random whim. Acid and mushrooms were exciting at first, but it became clear after a while that the only thing they really did was make him think a lot. Since this was Seamus' normal state, it made little sense to take them at all. The color of the thoughts induced was slightly different, yes, but during his last few trips the most striking sentiment was a deep sense of guilt, especially when he skipped class to ingest them.

Experimentation had its place but not all results were pleasant, much less memorable. Ketamine had been inter-esting the first few times he indulged, up until he arrived at the place that either scares people off the drug completely or intrigues them to return more frequently: the K hole. This heavy, tunnel-buzzing mutation of his aural perceptions and the trancing wonderland sent him flushing down an endless drain where he was not sure if he was hallucinating or was simply unable to move, where his dorm room looked just as it always had although he could not be totally sure he was actually there, feeling like he was stuck in a prolonged ver-sion of the fuzziness one encounters the instant before falling asleep, or was it the instant before waking? Regardless, he came down finally after what felt almost like a night's sleep a mere half hour later. He then realized that he *was* in a dorm room, just not his own. It took a longer time yet to ascertain that he was in a different dorm building than his own, but around the time he got outside was around the time he was finally coming back to his fuller senses. Sobering from the stupefying effects of a too fat K rail, it was a slow walk home, but he found his way eventually and promptly did some coke to better wake up so he could search the internet for articles on photography versus doing the homework he said he would since the previous night.

The company he kept had changed somewhat now, too. He never delved deeply into the world of injectables, yet his right arm was not a virgin to the needle. A friend of his persuaded him that blowing Oxycontin would never deliver the same effect as shooting it, and that if he really wanted to get the most out of the drug he would need to take the next step. On his walks later he scoffed at her promise. "Get the most out of the drug." The higher he got was simply the higher he got. There were no added signing bonuses or rises in his IQ score. Ultimately he did get higher shooting it, but he decided with rare wisdom not to get the most out of Oxycontin any more, and as a result saw that much less of the young woman who probably thought Seamus was a pussy. Regardless, that young woman had ended up just sort of disappearing, dropping out in the middle of the semester, never to be heard from again. Seamus was a poor student, but he was not the school's worst. If he wanted to keep his academic standing, it would be prudent that he did not convene with those who were.

Then there was opium. That was a treat. It smoked smoothly and burned slowly. Its smell was nostalgic, but he could not place why. The high was light and pleasant. In fact, there were few drugs as good for taking walks and thinking about things as opium was. Maybe some time he would make an allowance for that as well.

But nothing gave Seamus the charge that snapping a good picture could give him. He brought his camera with him everywhere. He had even taken it to Singing Pines where he snuck a shot of Barry brewing coffee. It was a candid moment as Steve had abruptly stormed into the frame, his veins like ropes and his teeth clenched, eyes bugging and face red as a stop sign, and twice as arresting. His wrath was unmasked, unavoidable, unstoppable.

But a part of him awakened upon witnessing this work-place tempest, transforming the regular into the irregular. He realized immediately that it was a perfect shot. Silly, full of raw fury from Steve and worker's mundanity from Barry, who looked like a downtrodden underling poised for an earful from his tyrannical boss. If someone had not known the men were equals, it could elicit genuine sympathy.

But Seamus knew they were equals and laughed at it. He printed it out and stuck it on his bulletin board. It cheered him up when one of his landscape shots had been rejected yet again by a literary magazine. He was submitting often but he had yet to land his first acceptance. But it was the journey, not the destination, or something like that.

Still, reading, "We wish you luck in placing your work elsewhere," for a countless time always gave him reason for doubt. The "elsewhere" that journals encouraged him to find was ever elusive. There was no clear destination to which he might adjust his hopes. Looking into the expanse of his aim-less landscapes, their wide mountain panoramas and winding trails that gave no indication as to where they were going, Seamus felt at home. That no one yet had found reason to print them made him wonder if he was even any good. Maybe he was not. Maybe he was still purging the lower talents, the bar yet to be raised to an appropriate level.

But sometimes he had a happier thought. Perhaps he was just reaching the wrong people. Perhaps no one with It was receiving his work, but only those aligned with the pervasive and stinking forces of Them. In fact, what else could it be?

Them. Afflicted with a virus of the spirit.

Seamus looked at his submitted photo after each rejection. He wanted to find out who felt at home when they did not know where they were going. Each rejection made him want to find them that much more.

He remembered what Rachel said during one of their last nights together when their lovemaking was tepid, her feelings and focus in another room, and the distractions of her room-mates' world blowing like a kettle whistle, calling her away from him as she disappeared for a spell, returning much later than she said she would.

When she returned, and finally looked over some recent landscapes he shot, she said, "These are really nice, but they're just not going anywhere."

Since when did "going anywhere" become a virtue? Seamus was beginning to wonder if there was anywhere to even go. Where did George go? Where was he now?

Arrest at the Fork.

That was the title. Cheeky. Lighthearted. Its play on words worked well with the Hi-Brow Review's mission statement. Moreover, Seamus was proud to put his name on it, as he was all his work. But this, *Arrest at the Fork*, that was something! That was him.

What if taking neither path was the best decision? The more as well as the less traveled were both born from the same split decision. What if movement was nipped in the bud? Was that not It, content already, seams tied shut, wounds healed, stasis realized?

The fog was clearing. Seamus knew it.

2

The sun was brightening at Singing Pines, too. Angela was changing, and it was for the better. Everyone knew it.

She had become a recluse in her little office, its bizarre location in the water room where cubicle walls gave her the illusion of separation. Though the water cooler collected sporadic traffic throughout the day, she had learned to feel no impingement on her privacy. She simply sat at her desk and completed her work. As such, no one could see much beyond the fuzzy, gray fortitude of her cubicle from the vantage point of the cooler. About all that was visible was her frizzy hair tied back in a ponytail, a sliver of her body, and her elbow moving back and forth, left and right, accompanied by the swooshing sound of turning pages and the chatter of round fingers pecking at a keyboard.

Her work, which used to encompass holding regular pre-reception meetings with the banquet staff, giving them wooden pep talks, and being "available" throughout the night had been reduced to an endless stream of paperwork and product orders. This was by her own hand. She found peace in reviewing liquor supply numbers and going over the memos forwarded by Wanda. She drew floor plans slowly and carefully, the circles representing tables traced precisely and spaced evenly so that the drawings were as true to form on paper as the rooms were in person. She determined how many chicken, fish, beef, or vegetarian dinners the chefs would need to make and always triple-checked her numbers. She wrote up schedules and assigned workers and captains every Monday, which at this point had become so rote she never bothered to make any changes but simply copied whatever had happened the previous weekend ad infinitum. If there was any need for the upstairs crew to help the downstairs, she noted it, otherwise everyone essentially stayed put. Beyond that she left her office rarely, and only when it was absolutely necessary, like when she picked up her lunch or used the bathroom.

She spoke to others in the office as she had to, when the realities of their jobs forced interaction, or they happened to cross paths during one of her uncommon departures from her desk. She spoke to them as a quiet cat lady does to the checkers in the grocery store while her cans of soup and kitty litter are being rung up, her demeanor amicable but impenetrable.

Most noticeable of all, however, was that the strange look which inhabited her eyes had diminished so considerably it was barely detectable. The jumble of anger, sadness, spite, and self-consciousness were all gone. There remained only a dark tinge of confusion, as though she wondered why she was here, what had happened, and how much longer this would go on. Yet nothing in her verbal nor body language ever hinted that she had any intention of doing anything but work at Singing Pines for the rest of her life.

The banquet servers shook their heads and pitied her as best they could, namely through collective ridicule.

"The bitch has gone crazy," Alfredo said.

"She's spooky, man," Felipe said.

"She's finally gotten off my nuts about my hair," Seamus said.

"She's really turned it around," Jamie said, followed by, "Our job is just to put plates on tables and pick them up afterwards. I think she's finally realized that."

"Amen. Don't worry Angela, we've got this," Seamus agreed.

While they never shared in the gossipy banter, no one in the banquet department was happier about Angela's distance than Steve and Barry. Angela, not wanting to spend any more time at Singing Pines than was totally necessary, especially on the weekends, surrendered the liquor room key to Barry without him even having to ask her. In fact, he had given up trying to pry the keys from her and thought he was being pranked when she simply said, "Here you go, you can take them. Just put them in my office at the end of the receptions." Her attitude was so lifeless that he looked around, wondering who was watching, knowing that after months of complaining and arguing, this outcome was too absurd to be true. But it was no joke, and now Steve's bar functioned so smoothly even he had to just shake his head at Angela and think, "Poor girl. She's finally lost her will and the place couldn't be better."

However, while every dark cloud may have its silver lining, silver can tarnish. Christine had been appointed captain since Mack left, and to where no one knew. He gave only a day's notice and apologized for the rush but said he had "a good opportunity somewhere." Then he was gone, as people sometimes are.

Christine worked the upstairs banquets and some shifts during the week, but she proved to be a tenacious busy body. While Jamie and Seamus only worked downstairs, her shift in tone and attitude the past few months were rankling to their better selves. She came downstairs much more often now since there was only one key and she was now dependent on Barry to open the liquor room for her. Apparently noticing the fresh air of Angela's absence, she did her best to sully the more peaceful environment by carrying the torch of unnecessary, invasive authority in reprimanding the servers.

"I know Angela is gone already but that doesn't mean you boys just get to wander off outside."

"Thanks ma'am."

"Ma'am? Don't be a smart ass, Jamie."

"Sorry sir."

But the battles were petty and her spine was weak. She made threats about ratting the boys' "poor attitude" out to Angela. If she ever said a word, no one knew. While this meant a great deal to boys like Jamie and Seamus, Barry had learned to be just a little careful what he wished for. The captain's reports meant nothing now and despite a long string of P's, Chris, a new hire and the weakest employee in the department, was still regularly scheduled to work with him.

Always the last to finish serving his tables, perennially unable to completely bus unnecessary glassware, plates, and utensils, and always dragging his feet when it came time to clean up afterwards, Chris was the final thorn in Barry's side. Fortunately, there had been some shake-ups after a few other employees left. There were two new and promising hires, Fernando and Alonzo. They were Alfredo's cousins and better workers than he was. Alfredo was no slouch, but like Felipe, would lapse into stagnation when the dance floor was particularly full with good looking women. Some young men are able to manage, others lose focus. They belonged to the latter, and no matter how many times Barry caught them – shook them by the collar, shouted in their ears – they were never able to break their penchant for long stares that would have been palpably creepy if any of the guests actually noticed them.

Alonzo had his own demons with the women. In fact, as

an 18 year old, it was only through sheer will that he was able to conscientiously clear his tables with consistent speed and diligence. He would run around the room, working doggedly, and in a weak moment would pause to look up, wipe his sweaty forehead with his sleeve and smile, big and toothy, at the youngest women on the floor, always hoping someone would look back.

But of course, no one ever did. So once he got his small eye-full, he was sated enough to return to his duties, and when he was done with his own tables, he would help Chris. Though his brother was usually already doing so.

Fernando, in fact, would help anyone when he had the time, a luxury he almost always had since his pace was so quick and his determination so absolute. It was like he owned the country club, ran the banquet department, and captained all at once. He was 23 and had graduated college the year before with a degree in agricultural science. He had yet to find a job that related even peripherally to his major. The only "professional" position he had found at all was to be one of the Spanish speaking telemarketers for a credit restoration firm. The sales were hard, the commissions far lower than promised, and the work depressing.

Singing Pines was a welcome change. He at least had his brother and his cousin, and he quickly got along with everyone else, making friends easily. Though it was difficult to find much time to talk to him. He was seemingly always on the floor.

"Whoever knew we'd have ourselves an ace," Seamus said during a self-designated break, passing a joint to Jamie.

"You're telling me. He makes us all look like aces. I've never seen the tables looking so good. If I miss something he's Johnny on the spot."

"His brother isn't bad either."

"Nope. A couple of nose-to-the-grindstone kind of guys. I tell you my man, we've needed that for a while now," he said and killed the roach, wheezing, eyes watering, while he leaned over a railing and spat into the darkness. "God that's harsh at the end."

"I told you, man. This bag wasn't my favorite."

"Well see to it that the next one isn't an insult to us both. If there's anything I've got little patience for, it's cut corners."

Though it was not a subject they ever broached, Barry would agree with Jamie that cut corners are nothing but offensive to all involved. Fernando and Alonzo helped make up for Chris' slothfulness, if not virtually eradicate its worst effects, but that still did not sit right with the captain. The job got done, but he hated that it did at the expense of having to carry faulty parts. After watching young people come and go over the past few years at Singing Pines, he had seen all kinds of behavioral patterns that were largely similar even if the agents in question considered themselves unique. The only kind of person who ever bothered him, however, was the one who could not, or would not, pull his weight.

Barry was not the only one who noticed, either. Even Steve had gotten wind of the schism the crew was suffering, some of its members like Jamie and Seamus defensive of Chris while others like Felipe and Alfredo picked on the boy whenever he moped around the service area, sucking on ice cubes, checking his phone, staring at the cutting table's pen graffiti to no end, and all other manners of antisocial and slothful behavior.

One night on the porch Jamie and Seamus were smoking cigarettes and telling Chris he needed to step up. They liked him enough as a person, but people were talking and it was not positive.

"The things they say man, not that you should care too much, but you should care a little," Jamie said.

"It's a matter of pride," Seamus said.

Both boys were stoned now and Chris, unaware of this as he was most things, just brushed them off.

"So what if people talk? This job is just beer money for me anyway."

"Well man, if you're cool with guys calling you a donkey and going hee-haw every time you walk by, I'll just shut up about it," Jamie said.

Chris only laughed. "I think that's funny! Alfredo looks so goofy when he does that. He has big teeth."

Chris laughed harder, his stout body swaying and his eyes shutting sweetly like he was off of work already, chewing tobacco and spitting under the eave of his mother's porch, listening to his friends talk about fighting and fucking, as they put it, like every story was the first of its kind.

"I even told him he had big teeth, and he just grabbed his balls and said that wasn't the only thing! I like Alfredo."

The boys looked at each other to determine who was going to cover this one when a voice boomed out, "But he doesn't like you!"

They turned and saw it was Steve, who was looking particularly stern.

"Who doesn't like me?" Chris asked.

Steve's brow relaxed and his neck muscles did, too. He chuckled as he lit a cigarette and said, "Barry's looking for you dude. Better get inside."

"Ah man, Barry's always looking for me. Who doesn't like

me though?"

"Yo mama."

Chris laughed like an idiot. "I heard that in the third grade!"

"Yep. Hey for real Chris, Barry's looking for you. Get inside."

"What about Jamie and Seamus? And you don't tell me what to do. You're not the captain."

"Well even if I was you'd ignore me too so why don't you just pick your donkey ass up and get in there before I lose my fucking shit!" Steve said with rising intensity, his neck bulging back into tightened form, his jaw clenched, eyes angry.

"Okay, okay. Don't have to get all mad."

Steve ignored him as Chris finally walked back into the building. Then, "Boy, that kid's dumber than shit."

Jamie sighed. "The guy doesn't have what it takes, I'm afraid to say."

"Ha! I'll say. Meanwhile he's got Fernando in there doing all his work for him. Hell, if I were Fernando I would just let Chris go to the wolves. Get that kid outta here. But what do I know. Angie's gone as AWOL as someone can for never leaving her office. Whatever brains or heart she had took a long walk off a short pier."

"Tell me about it! I'm not one to want to see any of us get in trouble, but something needs to inspire Chris," Jamie said.

"I don't know if something will inspire him but something will catch up to him. I tell you boys, I worked in restaurants a long while back before this place. Worked at the Bartleby Inn, you know, just down the freeway, get off on Carnation. And one thing I learned was you never wanted to be the worst and you never wanted to be the best."

"And why is that?" Jamie asked.

"You're the worst and all kinds of crap gets piled on you. You're the best and people are gunning for you. They talk, slander your ass. Try and set you up to fail anyway they can."

"People are so nefarious," Seamus said.

"I don't know what that means but if I had to pinpoint the truth of the matter is people look for mistakes whether you're the best or the worst, and both get amplified equally as bad. Stick to the middle and you're golden."

"My man!" Jamie said and high-fived Steve. "Take notes, brother."

"Oh I am," Seamus said. "What happened?"

"At the Bartleby? Hell, I had that place by the balls, yep!" Steve bobbed his head and smoked, looked away, assumed his trance.

"There was this hot little hostess. I'd bang her straight into the mattress one night and the next she'd give me all the good tables. See some suits? Send 'em my way. See some Bronco Billies, you know, the bleached hair and the booze shirts, white fucking socks! Yep, send 'em elsewhere. Doesn't matter if I'm up in rotation they don't belong in my section. Nope!"

"Wow, you would my man!" Jamie shouted.

"Yep, and this other guy, real timid, slow, polite I guess but hell he got shit on like my backyard when my stupid ass pit bull gets into the Flaming Hot Cheetos I leave out. Dude would be kept on for as long as possible 'til they'd have to cut him if he didn't go on, and then he'd get all the beater tables. He'd almost always have to close, and they'd stick him on the no-tip bullshit events like the Chamber of Commerce and

Rotary banquets. Just grunt work and hourly, that's all that was. Yep, one of life's losers boys. Never knew what hit him 'cause for all he knew...hell I don't know if he knew anything. Just went with it. Just a regular dope."

"Huh. So if you were the best what bad shit happened to you?" Seamus asked.

"The best? I never said I was the best."

"You just said you had that place by the balls."

"Oh, well yeah. That was because of the hostess though. I tell you this, I was sure as hell the best at banging her!" With that Steve opened his eyes wide and his mouth into an 'o,' nearly imploring the boys to say, "No you didn't!": which they did.

"You better believe it, boys," Steve said, and proceeded to box the air overhead with his fists, his cigarette pinched by his squeezed lips.

"Life's losers, boy. Well my man, you're one of life's winners," Jamie told him.

"She-it. Don't have to tell me twice."

The boys smiled down to the dark corridor towards the parking lot to get higher while Steve finished his cigarette lost in his revelations. "Old Freaky Firecrotch. Yep!"

The boys were impressed with Steve's line about life's losers, the notion about going through the motions, oblivious.

"Well man, I hate to say it but Steve might be onto something," Jamie started.

"Hey, you said it yourself. Chris may not have what it takes."

The boys philosophized as they smoked about the virtue of

being able to pick the right battles. Understanding each other and It deeply, they agreed that Chris was not their problem any more and they had done what they could. Some people had to learn the hard way.

Coincidently, Chris would solve the problem that was him later that night during clean-up, sparking the line that began as a flicker only to explode the following evening, sending all traces of his involvement with Barry's crew into the hazy residue of unimportant afterthoughts, cleared quickly by time as though they were never there.

It started when Chris wanted to go home early. He apparently had glaucoma in his eye, a dubious claim that Barry would have ridiculed if he were not so fed up with all the heel dragging, yawning, and pointless small talk that emanated from Singing Pines' weakest link at all times.

"Why don't you just put the broom down right now, take out the cell phone you've been texting on all night, and call your mommy to come pick you up?"

"Barry! I can drive home."

"So you can see well enough to drive home but not well enough to finish setting the room."

"It's not that I can't see. It hurts like crazy, I told you. Have you ever gotten shot in the eye with a paintball?"

"Paintball, sure! You know you just missed the towel," Alfredo said.

"Shut up." Barry deadpanned. "Chris, I don't give a shit how much pain you're in anymore. I just don't feel like looking at you. Go home and take tomorrow off too."

"Really? Won't you be short handed?"

"No. We have Fernando now. He can probably take six

tables if he feels like it."

Fernando stopped setting table cloths for a moment, his eyebrows raised.

"Don't worry man, I won't really saddle you with six tables. I'll just spread Chris' around a bit because he's being a bitch. I'd put B on the captain's report if anyone actually read it anymore."

The following night Chris heeded Barry's demand and stayed home. It came as a surprise to everyone that he would be foolish enough to do so since Barry had no such authority. Even Angela noticed and upon hearing just why Chris was taking the night off, could only chastise Barry weakly while at the same time tip her hand that this might be the end of Chris' line.

"Well Barry, you're short-handed now because of your own mouth but if Chris is going to actually listen to you than maybe he shouldn't work here anymore."

"You're exactly right, because that's probably the first time anyone has listened to me ever. Nothing good comes out of that."

"Oh Barry," Angela said and smiled meekly. "I'll talk to Chris tomorrow."

She would too, but not until Barry saw him first. As it turned out, Chris had spent the night getting drunk with his friends. He lived close to Singing Pines, so close in fact that he could jump his backyard wall and land on the tenth. With a thirty pack of Budweiser under their belts and a few stray shots of Jaeger, his little group did just that and wandered to the clubhouse late at night. Two of them stayed behind to smoke Marlboros on the deck while another walked in with Chris to the dining room.

"Hey everyone. What's up?" Chris slurred.

"What's up?" his friend parroted, hands in his pockets, his eyes flitting around quickly for a drunk, observing everyone. He wore a tank top, shorts and sandals. His head was shaved almost bald and his arms were large but not defined. He had tattoos of two mudflap girls leaning against each other, and a roulette wheel burning on fire with pistols firing beside it.

When Barry entered the room he dropped the tablecloths he was carrying onto a chair, assumed the position with his hands on his hips, and stared. The banquet crew snickered and elbowed each other.

Chris' friend was visibly uncomfortable with silence, or had a finely primed reaction time to apparent authority. He stuck his hand out and said, "Sup dude. I'm T.J."

"Get your hand out of my face, I don't have any fucks to give you." Barry's eyes shot to Chris. "What the hell are you doing here? You smell like a bum."

T.J. meanwhile backed away and lit up on the deck. It was dark and the only thing Barry could see was his cigarette cherry...all three of them.

"Oh shit..." Barry ignored Chris' babbling about wanting to say hi, and that he was sorry for last night. Outside, three young men smoked and spat over the railing. One of them was in the middle of saying, "I just went 'Boop,' stuck my finger right up her butt," when Barry shouted, "I'll stick my foot up your butt if you don't get the hell out of here!"

They laughed. One of them said, "Sup dude. I'm Bryce."

"Get out!"

"Barry C'mon," Chris said, waddling out.

"Get your friends and get the fuck out or never come back

again. God, it takes a moron to get fired when he's not even on the clock!"

"You can't fire me!"

"I'll see what I can do."

The fourth friend approached Barry and said, "Got a problem, bro?"

"Four."

"Yeah? Well we only have one between us."

One by one the crew piled out onto the deck, each oblivious to the mounting tension and the fact that one of Chris' friends was trying to initiate a fight against their captain.

"Shit," the one named Bryce said.

"Everyone get back to work!" Barry yelled.

No one listened. Chris' friends, sensing an impending battle they lacked the appetite for, retreated. The fourth guy had to be tugged away by T.J. and Bryce, and calmed down by Chris.

"Fuck that little bald dude! I'd kick his ass!" the crew could hear, as Chris and his friends disappeared back onto the course.

In the morning, the grounds crew found an empty Budweiser box on the tenth. It had the words "C NUTS GET TWIZZY" written on it with a black marker. A couple of smashed cans lied beside it. They thought nothing of the garbage, it was not their course, they only worked there, and threw the evidence away in the dumpster. Chris, meanwhile, thought very much about it when called in to speak with Angela. He did not know what she knew, and knew even less about what she did not, and gave himself away needlessly though conveniently as he gave Angela an easy answer to a pair of issues that were disturbing her. And these days, having to confront someone over a disturbance was harder for her than it was for the perp in question.

Still, Chris was sweating. Hungover and scheduled to work a banquet with what he imagined was going to be an irate Barry, he apologized immediately to Angela like a child does after knocking something over off a table and fearing the atomic sting of a belt whip.

"I'm so sorry Angela, I'm so sorry. I just wasn't thinking," he began.

Angela sighed, her arms crossed and elbows on the desk, hair frizzy and pulled back into a sloppy ponytail, eyes tired. "Okay Chris, calm down. I just need to know why you didn't show up yesterday."

Had Chris been a smart boy he would have quieted his mind and listened to his boss' question. It was a simple question and his first clue that she might not be privy to the whole of the drama. He just might have found out had he taken his time to choose his words, sit tight and find out just what cards he was holding.

But Angela beat him without even bluffing. He charged ahead.

"Barry said not to come in so I didn't."

"I know he did. But you were still scheduled to show up."

"Yeah but he's my captain and my eye hurt real bad so I listened and nothing was going on so that was when my buddies came over since I had the night off."

Angela titled her head. "Alright."

"And then they wanted to see where I work so we hopped the fence. I didn't even know my buddy had the beers with him still but we just had a few left so we pounded them and I tried to find a trash can but couldn't. So I'm real, real sorry about littering. I didn't mean to."

Angela looked at him coldly. What she was hearing was a full-blown confession of fireable offenses. She had every reason to tell Chris to go home yet again, only to stay there this time and search Craigslist for a more suitable gig.

But if she did that she would have to go out of her way to hire someone else, something she already had to do since the busser in the restaurant quit via keying Jeff's car.

She decided to stay calm and play it simple, see just where the conversation went. She continued, "You didn't mean to but you did."

"Angela I know! But it could have been so much worse! I stopped my buddy from clocking Barry, just clocking him!"

"You stopped your friend from - " She stopped herself.

"That's not what I heard," she said.

"Well jeez!" he said and hit the desk. "Oh! I'm sorry! I didn't mean to hit the desk."

"But you did," she said.

"I know, I know. I always do that stuff. Anyway, you gotta believe me. Maybe Barry thought I was just...I don't know what he told you. But I was holding my buddy back, telling him to stop. He was going to get all crazy and I just told him to stop. I'm sorry I even brought him to the deck, but I didn't think Barry was going to get all crazy on us like he does."

Chris looked at Angela soberly, his eyes red but less pathetic looking, and said, "Barry gets crazy, too. He said he'd put his foot up my friend's butt."

And then Angela laughed. How long had it been? Wanda's

assistant startled in front of the copy machine and twisted her body around to look. Was that who she thought it was? She turned to see Wanda standing up from her desk. They eyed each other, shrugged, and smiled coyly.

"Barry has a way with words," Angela said. Something like relief, very subtle, hardly noticeable, washed over her. She leaned back, slouched, knew what to do.

"He made my friend so mad," Chris continued, shaking his head, looking down, looking distant.

"Well you made Barry so mad," she said, and then said nothing else for a while. She twitched her nose and sniffed. She stared at Chris. He lifted his eyes and stared back. Then, "You won't be working with Barry anymore."

Chris blubbered pitifully and said through his tears, "Please don't fire me."

"I'm not, Chris."

He sniffled heavily, sat upright in slow, rigid motion. "No? You mean it?"

"I mean it. But you are going to be getting…not a demotion. We're just going to try something new with you. We have an opening to bus in the restaurant."

"Oh no! You mean work with Jeff?"

"Chris, if you want to work here, I don't see another alternative. Do you want to work here?"

After a pause, Chris nodded. "Yes, I still want to work here."

Angela smiled, then stopped. "Good. You'll have different hours. The restaurant's actually open tonight and you're overdressed but we should have a few loaner shirts on hand. Jeff was going to go solo tonight but it'll be good to have some help. This'll be a training day. Next shift you'll actually get tips. You'll like it."

"I bet I will," Chris said under his breath, snorting.

"Good." She rose and extended her hand like he was a new hire. "Thanks for coming in early to have this talk, Chris. I think this'll be good for everyone."

"Okay," he said, defeated, and walked slowly out the office and to the restaurant. It was a short but a doomed walk. It was a walk into a bleakness that offered no return. Chris did not know what Angela did, that the reason Jeff pulled up in a beat-up red '95 Mustang with the torn canvas roof was not because he was trying to go Hollywood. That was only half of it. Rather, Jeff's Geo Hatchback was keyed beyond repair by the last busser. Jeff spent his insurance check and whatever was in his paltry savings account on the new car and drove down the streets where the old busser lived but never found him. He demanded to his friends that "The little creep should get time!" But of course the little creep got released the same day he was arrested. He had fines and community service hours and needed a new job, but he was happy. He would never see Jeff again, though his former coworker would look for him every now and again, less and less over the months, but would never quite let it go.

The trouble for Jeff was that life let it go for him, and a new charge was under his control now.

"Well okay, Chris." Jeff said. "I know you don't want to be here but let's make the most of it. It has to be better than working with Barry, right?"

Chris, reeling, looked angrily to the club's only waiter and said, "Yeah, I hate that little bald dude."

Jeff smirked. "We might get along after all."

But like Jeff's unfruitful pursuit of his former busser, so too would this grudge bare any satisfaction for them. Barry could not give two shits about "Pizza Face and Little Chubby," as he referred to them. His Singing Pines world was finally in order now that *he* had what he wanted: his own, set crew without a single screwup in the bunch. Only at Singing Pines could boys like Jamie and Seamus shine so brightly. They did their jobs: putting plates on tables and picking them up afterwards. Even if Angela never considered this simple reality, Barry at least understood it. And he understood that all the horseplay and laughter, the stupid jokes and eyes towards the dance floor were simply the permutations of late pubescence and were to be expected. The hollering, the lustful eyes, the rapping, the moonwalking, the mischievous smiles, the clapping, the knocking into each other, the back talk, the dancing - all of it was his duty to stifle, and yet none of it was anything more than the underpinnings of a young person's sanity when faced with an endlessly menial workplace. As far as he was concerned, they had plenty of time left to lose their sanity. Life would beat it out of them in due time. He saw the difference in Fernando versus the others, and it was not only age and work ethic that separated him. It was something lost.

And though everyone simply shrugged Angela's dreariness off, he saw her behavior differently. She had lost herself quickly and horribly. The thread of decency and a gratitude for the breath that filled her lungs was slipping. Her spirit was potentially terminal.

Nonetheless, she asked Barry if he would be understaffed but he only told her to send help from upstairs for larger party dinner rushes. That would be enough.

"I've got Fernando, Isabelita, Alfredo, Felipe, Alonzo, and that newb Cody. And then my favorites and yours, Jamie, and Seamus."

"Oh boy," she rolled her eyes.

"Somebody's got to handle the gazebo site."

"Yeah," she sighed, nearly cathartically. "You're sure that's enough, Jamie and Seamus withstanding?"

"I'm sure, Angela. That's my crew."

And so they were, at least for a while.

3

When spring break finally arrived Seamus simply stayed on campus. This was a popular choice among poor kids and malcontents alike but for the chronically lazy, it was a no-brainer. Seamus' college enrolled nearly 4,000 students and all but roughly 200 of them opted to take some kind of vacation, whether it be an outdoors camping trip, a flight back home, or even a quick jaunt out the country. Meanwhile, the campus became a virtual ghost town for a single, eerie week. And for a young layabout like Seamus, he could not have felt more at home.

Putting effort into anything required an energy output that Seamus was not always comfortable committing. Being a well-adjusted member of the school community certainly required effort. Not only were there trends to be aware of, such as the goofy illustrations and jokey captions that adorned student clubs' printed posters that advertised things like dance parties, guest speakers, or charitable causes to back and prove themselves not only caring but in the know, but there were cliques who had trends all unto themselves. The former could only be apprehended as a reflection of the culture at large within the microcosm that was his student body, while the latter was an impossible language that presented itself in real terms a fragment at a time, thus serving as a wellspring of fractured relationships that existed among people who attempted friendships beyond their most immediate kept company. For to abandon having a clique in order to be close with people of truly diverse backgrounds, one would have to compromise his or her own social identity to the point of dissolution, therefore rendering him or her irrelevant within the context once occupied.

And if not irrelevant, mysterious. For the rare handful, moving strictly to the beat of one's own proverbial drum was the best thing he could possibly do to reel in some pussy. Or in the case of that loopy girl who always wore the sundresses and John Lennon glasses or the stoic thing with rubber ducky safety pin tattoos on her back with the bookshelf full of politically dissident books, being mysterious meant having guys talk with them wherever they went, including small talk over lunch at the dining hall, *Breaking Bad*, the weather, and whatever the hell score she got on her test in that class that she and this overly chatty dude have together.

Not all who bucked the trends were desirable sexually, or really in any other sense, and a handful of them also stuck around the campus rather than get away for a week. There was the girl who always filled a paper cup with peas before she left the dining hall, smuggling it back secretively, holding it close against her stomach under crossed arms, which were also a touch hairy. And there was the spastic boy who had either done too much acid or was legitimately schizophrenic. He was an art major and wore tie-dye t-shirts and mumbled to himself, never combed his hair, and sometimes lay stomach down on the grass to look through its itchy blades as though he were a cat prowling after a grasshopper. Then there was the daughter of the billionaire heavy truck and trailer distribution company CEO - a skinny girl who wore all black and chewed gum loudly in class and would occasionally fall into bouts of crying as she became overwhelmed with the implications of her own responses, those which nearly always had to do with gender and oppression.

Fortunately Seamus had a few friends and acquaintances roaming about who provided him with company when he felt like having it. Among them were the boys he shared a bathroom with, the one he spoke about Beat literature with, and the other he played occasional video games with when nothing else presented itself as a viable way to fritter away his time in the most pleasurable way possible. Seamus was not much of a gamer, but he had grown up in a generation full of many who were, and at times he allowed himself to toggle away on a complicated controller and get his ass handed to him on *Call of Duty*. This at least took his mind off of school, his parents, and Rachel on more than one afternoon so far this semester.

More importantly to him was the fact that a well-represented group of druggies decided that they would rather be nowhere else than school so they could yell openly as they liked, break things, blare music, start fires, and engage in all sorts of miscellany often aided, or at least transformed, by whatever it was they felt like ingesting to fuck themselves up.

Seamus stuck true to his recent ways and had a few hits of weed and even opium a couple nights, but kept his body largely pure otherwise. He was still staying away from psychedelics and narcotics and was continuing to work out in the gym, which was not only open over break but never closed since the student in charge of the room had left town without locking up its doors.

For Seamus, the break was practically perfect save for a few thoughts of self-doubt and troubled memories, but that was par for the course and in fact his mind was far less troubled than usual. For all he knew, he was as happy to be alive as were the dancing Hare Krishnas he witnessed many months ago. Life was good for Seamus, or at least it was while everything was put on pause. No classes, no homework, no Rachel nor her stupid friends, and no responsibility of any kind. Someday, he vowed, he would learn how to pattern his entire life off this golden week.

He did not know how though, and as he strolled through the downtown area within walking distance of his campus one morning on the Friday of his spring break week, sipping a latte and looking around, thinking seriously, he could not help but wonder if he really knew where even to begin. Something very strange had been happening since he had been getting high less frequently, and it was not pleasant. Something was nagging him that hitchhiking was perhaps unrealistic. Whatever this thing was that told him so seemed like a formidable opponent. Indeed, it raised points of contrast against his wide-eyed wonder by bringing up arguments like money, modern technology, rules, and of course his fucking parents. Really, he may have been a legal adult but were they about to allow him to start wandering around like a derelict and foot the bill for *his* student loans? Not likely.

This thing, what was it? It was doubt surely but it felt like something else. It felt like something more real than doubt, which by its nature is always a matter of perspective and not necessarily something to be taken seriously, at least according to the yogis and teachers of conscious evolution with whom Seamus was familiar. But what those sages did talk about was the "way things are," and lately Seamus could not shake the fact that he might be glimpsing it in all its oppressive ugliness, and dreams of thumbing his way through life might be just that, dreams, and no more real in possibility than his winning the lottery despite having never bought a ticket.

People hitchhiked and Seamus knew it. But he had enrolled in school, and once ensnared in this pathetic Ponzi scheme, the exit came with a price whether he graduated or not.

Seamus was going to be in debt and there was nothing he could do about it. Though he was only halfway through school, or would be at the end of the semester, he was getting that much closer to an adult world of obligations and regularly scheduled payments he still could not believe were real.

But they were, and he needed only look at Fernando to prove it to himself. There were other examples too, like the educated barista who made the very latte he was drinking this self-reflective moment! The miserable prick was talking about the job board openly with a coworker, telling her that his degree in anthropology wasn't impressing anyone yet, while she spouted off some faux metaphysics about continuing to hold his desires close to his heart and mind and they would happen some time. He only rolled his eyes and said, "never mind," before he handed Seamus his latte wordlessly and sighed over the series of cups, endless as they piled before him, and got to work.

Seamus was concerned, and he might have fallen face first into a bummer spiral had he not crossed paths with his school's great loner, known as Malcolm the Malcontent, painting on a bare white column.

He and Seamus were friends, in a peripheral sense. A moody young man, Malcolm was not friends with anyone in the conventional application of spending consistent time with another human being. This may have been due to the fact that he had slept with over fifty female students in not quite four semesters. Lately they had begun to turn on him. His reputation was finally solidifying among the small student body, and it was not positive.

"Look who it is, wearing his camera around his neck like some cheesy fucking tourist."

Malcolm was painting a rubber duck. He stood barefooted on a step ladder, his blonde hair tussled and overlong. Seamus observed him but looked down the corridor, and something clicked. He turned his camera on.

"Don't you take a picture of me."

"Just look at the duck. Keep painting."

A few hundred yards down, just coming into view, were a trio of administrators in suits. Seamus rarely shot people but this was something. He did not know what yet, other than the fact that he had to take this shot. He would not have another chance.

"I don't want this to be turned in to any of your stupid literary journals, Seamus."

"I never get accepted anyway. Besides, I'm a landscape photographer. This shot's for me."

Malcolm continued to paint but shook his head. "So you're going to jerk off to it or something?"

"Keep your eyes on the duck for Christ's sake! And yes."

Malcolm took his eyes off the duck.

"Jesus man, for such a free-spirited dude you're so sensitive," Seamus shouted.

A tiny smile crept on Malcolm's lips. It was serene, but rebellious. His eyes were focused on the duck but his mouth was either opening into a slow laugh or getting ready to release a gob of *fuck you* spit right over his shoulder in the direction of the suits. It was not totally discernible what emotions were spinning through Malcolm's heart, but it was at the very least cockily defiant. And it was perfect.

"You're one to talk, Seamus. I don't have to get shit faced just to bone someone who's not my ex. You still seeing her, anyway?"

"You can take your eyes off the duck now."

"I was already painting it, you fucking narcissist."

"Yeah yeah. And no, I'm not."

Malcolm dipped his brush into a smattering of orange paint. Strands of his sandy hair fell over his blue eyes. He shook his head and applied the tip of his brush delicately to the wall and outlined the beak.

"Can't believe what a pussy you are."

"I didn't like her."

"I heard she didn't like you either."

"Yeah whatever," Seamus said and looked away.

"Hey, cheer up. This chick I fucked last weekend asked about you. I think she's liked you for a while, too."

Seamus looked back to Malcolm. "Who's that?"

"Oh! The man can get a boner."

"C'mon. Who is it?"

"Karen Cordi."

"What? Not her! The only chicks who want my cock are the druggies."

"Well the apple doesn't fall far from the tree and neither does it land in a pile of oranges."

"I bet she did coke with you, huh?"

"No. But she had to leave right after I nutted. It cracked me up."

"Dude. I don't need that. I need someone a little more... shit. Health conscious."

Malcolm laughed. "Yes, because you're such a stud. Not even any numbers from the gym bunnies yet? I mean, do any of them want to go out not with a college athlete, but a stoner who likes to do bench presses?"

"We're a fucking Division III school! Why should any of them get their cunts all wet for those douchebags?"

"The apple doesn't fall far from the tree..."

"Maybe so. Maybe so... I tried to flirt with a volleyball player the other day and she laughed at me." Seamus cleared his throat and imitated her in a nasally voice, "'Ah, I have a *boyfriend.*' Man, she sounded so dismissive."

Malcolm laughed. "I've fucked lots of girls with boy-friends."

The suits walked by. "Nice duck," one of them said. The others laughed.

"It's a self portrait," Malcolm told them.

The suits spoke to each other flippantly and laughed as they kept walking back to their offices. Whatever rules he was breaking by painting on campus property they could give a damn. Seamus watched them disdainfully and figured they were probably preoccupied in counting how many Fullbright Scholars were coming out of the school this year.

"Well maybe you need to start doing drugs again. Though, you haven't really stopped. You're just a poser."

"What do you care? You're just a poser yourself. I've never seen one painting from you I thought was worth two shits."

"You think anyone thought that about Jackson Pollack at first? Maybe just his wife. But he didn't care about her anyway. She was lucky. She survived because of it."

"So did his mistress."

Malcolm finished the beak and said, "You talk about shit, there's shit. She's a so-called artist. Real life affirming, pale boxes overlapping each other. I'll take Alex Grey any day. There's actual spiritual art."

"You like him? God, now I see it. All your squiggly little lines you draw over people. Way to be original, you ass."

"One to talk, Seamus," Malcolm shook his head and pulled a thinner brush out of his pocket. "Have you ever been in a waiting room, by chance?"

"Very funny. Man, I just wish some of the artsy chicks would dig me."

"Oh God, you just want Rachel to dig you."

"No! Maybe I just found my type. You get all kinds of chicks. You're a painter. Being a photographer has to count for something."

"Never mind about getting ass, Seamus. That has less to do with painting or cameras or whatever it is you think makes pussies wet. Your photography is a problem all on its own."

"You're such a miserable prick. And you get laid like the world is going to end tomorrow."

"It gets harder and harder. It's why I'm transferring next semester."

"No shit!"

"Yes shit. I can't stand it here any longer. This town is nothing but strip malls and smog."

"You're telling me. I've lived here my whole life. Maybe I should look into getting away."

"Please."

"What?"

"The kinds of people who grow up in a place like this

never leave. Everything's too convenient, and tame. It's too engrained in you. This isn't even personal, Seamus. I've just seen your type, living here. I can't take another day of it! Without sex I'd have gone insane. You have to dull your spirit to stand it."

"Bullshit. You have no eye for beauty considering that you're a so-called artist. I think you're just in it for the pussy. What the hell are you painting a rubber duck for, anyway?"

"Why not a duck? And who said it's rubber?"

"Very deep. And it's yellow."

"It's a certain breed of duck. And now it's finished."

Malcolm stepped down to ground level and looked up at his miniature painting. His brow was wrinkled and his thin face fixed. He had very defined cheekbones. Seamus imagined he would grow up to be a gaunt old man.

"It's a rubber duck," Seamus said.

"It's the most fun I've had painting in a long time," he said.

"You're kidding me."

"I need to get out of here. I need to get the fuck out, I'm sick of this shit."

Malcolm put his supplies quickly into his backpack and headed off, saying to Seamus, "Don't put that goddamn picture in one of those journals."

"I already told you I won't. Besides - "

"Whatever. No one cares about trees and rocks, you dummy. That's probably the best picture you ever took right there."

"Give me a break."

"It is. Better even than that sad man versus angry man picture you've got. Do what you want with it but don't put it in a journal. It would probably make it in and I'm private, even if no one but the contributors looks at those journals anyway. I don't need my face anywhere except my stupid Facebook profile. God, I need to take that down before I transfer."

Malcolm headed up the corridor talking aloud though he was alone. He often ended conversations with others by beginning them with himself. Seamus knew that he would not see much more of him. He might try to, but it would be useless. Malcolm was impossible to find if he wanted to be.

Seamus would miss him.

Later, when he printed out the picture, he saw that Malcolm was right. That smug prick!

There was something illuminating about it. The contrast between Malcolm and the men down the hall was so clear. It came close to being overly obvious, and maybe it was. But the focus was all on Malcolm, his striving, his inching up slightly at the toes with his arm raised, reaching for the duck, which was just barely recognizable as a duck, the thin neck and ball-shaped head. As for Malcolm, Seamus had to shake his head and curse him for cutting such a striking image. That defiant smile, what a bastard! No wonder the women threw themselves at him. They would never have him, until they did, and suddenly the mystery was gone. But until then, he was as he was in the picture – a messy-haired boy painting cartoonish images on the walls of conformity, not grown-up, and not interested in doing so. The fucking guy could transfer if he wanted to, Seamus knew. His parents were paying his full tuition. He had a while to go before growing-up was going to matter very much.

Seamus looked at the picture and smiled. When he thought

about his own impending adulthood, at least he could take solace in the fact that it was not here yet, and he still had time to figure out a plan.

The suits were a little out of focus. They could not have been captured in a better light. Adulthood imposing upon youth, but not without a fight. No, the young man was clinging to his rubber ducky the way that weird girl clings to her peas. For those that did entirely as they pleased, college was a different experience. Why would any other time in their life, the future and all its naked horror, be any different?

Seamus was going to find out. He knew it.

4

Seamus did not know Lawrence Farley, and it was just as well he did not. Lawrence Farley was dead. He never made it back from his spring break camping trip.

Alcohol poisoning along the Colorado River. Passed out under the stars. Of course he could have drowned to death, too. No one was sure what came first. The canoeing and kayaking club members found him face down in the water in the morning, the bottom of his shirt plagued with vomit. The best of them dazed in the topsy-turvy wonderland of a stupefying, sun-blasted hangover. The sky was overwhelmingly wide and blue and the ground felt uneven under their shaking legs.

CPR was useless. No - still no pulse. And no, for the last time, no one remembered anything unusual.

It was a small trip, eight people and as many kayaks. They had finished kayaking for the week. It was party night in Laughlin, where they started their vacation. Full circle, minus a spoke.

The students were questioned by deans, counselors, police officers, parents, other students. Seamus connected with them, but they never knew it. He did not know any of them and none of them knew him.

Seamus knew they dropped the ball. Now the spotlight was on them and it had to burn hot. He was walking by a group of four girls, his camera in hand, when he noticed that one of them was a member of the kayaking trip. Her thousand-yard stare isolated her from the other girls in the circle. They were all holding notebooks. One of them had a purse, another a knapsack. They must have just gotten out of class. They were probably talking about something school related, or something else just as mundane. Seamus wanted to shatter their privacy and snap their picture, capture the two worlds the girls occupied, three on one side, one hovering, disconnected from gravity's normal pull on the other. Shooting people required intruding into their personal space, whether invited or not. What Seamus wanted was to capture authenticity. He wanted genuine joy, genuine rebellion, genuine anger, genuine vapidness, genuine sorrow. It did not matter the emotion, it just had to be real. It is always real. When the faces of It were coupled with the faces of Them, he had a shot.

He had found his voice.

Still, he never took the picture of the girl in the circle. He could not do so without someone spotting him, unless he were to hide like a sniper, which even then might bring more attention to him rather than less. So he walked on, feeling disturbed that he was passing by such a rare and perfect moment, but he calmed himself with the happy thought that he was finally published. Barry would never know he was pictured in a literary journal, and that made Seamus' smile even larger.

He had forgotten to title the picture he sent to Black Watch Review. He had never even considered titling the piece until they asked him about it in their acceptance email. So he typed back in embarrassingly quick response time, he had never been so punctual in all his life, the title that came immediately to him: "Losing It."

Seamus knew it was an obvious choice. Steve was clearly losing his cool. But it was not just the cool he was losing in giving in so ferociously to his temper. Would anyone else see the title's deeper layer?

Seamus did not care if they did or not. He realized the communicative power of the shot for the first time and now had a subject. Photography was not just about the wide angles and readymade panoramas that the natural world provided him. Those required an eye, even Seamus knew that. And he knew that some of the best photographers in the world spent their lives hunting down the best the planet had to offer as it expresses itself in foggy mornings and lighting flashes and crashing waves and distant fires and insects lifting legs gingerly on arcing fawns and dew collecting on twisting tree branches.

But was It found in a tree? Ultimately, of course. But It as it applied to human beings was a social phenomenon. A tree has no choice to have It or not. A tree can only do its best, can only mature according to the blueprints of its species and the conditions that surround its growth. But a person can grow any which way, can evolve or devolve, can spiral into the uncertainty of life's essential chaos or anchor steadfastly to illusory dogmas in order that he might sleep at night with a clear conscience and an almost clear sense of security. A person is constantly faced with the simple choice: does he reach towards It, or sink to the ground and crawl with Them?

More than a voice, chasing It in its social permutations was Seamus' mission. As another stupid tragedy struck, another young person dying from having a good time, a cause Seamus knew all too well, the sorrow that surrounded the event was intoxicating.

Seamus was able to witness the involved students with detachment. None of his close friends were tight with them, either. There was no woman in his life crusading to lift the spirits of the grief-stricken. There was only the pure pain of loss, and the heaviness of guilt felt to varying degrees by a group of people who believed they could have influenced the accident to turn out differently. Whatever their experience, there were moments, such as the one Seamus experienced walking by the girls, where he saw a new side of It, and the rabbit hole deepened. It can also mourn.

And so Seamus' extrasolar death toll rose. Young people were dying around him, but not near him. Of course the effects were a different story. He was more affected than anyone knew.

5

Seamus was haunted by the picture he did not take and one lucky afternoon he made up for it. He spotted another one of the members from the kayaking trip in the dining hall and took a candid shot. For all he cared, this one was It in tears. This one was the pain of life. This one, he knew, offered a clear view of the shame and guilt experienced by those that could have saved a life had they not been so consumed with their own.

Seamus had recognized the girl with the thousand-yard stare instantly. But he was troubled later to think that she was the only person from the trip he could identify. And so he felt the sinking pain that comes from having missed an opportunity and fearing that another one like it may never return.

He worked out later that evening and felt the positive emotions that come from endorphin release. Suddenly something struck him: he would simply have to keep his eyes open. He would be aware and he would watch for that look. He would have his camera with him wherever he went, and he would take a picture – his self-consciousness be damned – that would capture what he had eyes to see and wanted others to see, too.

Seamus did not know Lawrence Farley but his death obsessed him. He did not care if it was the booze that did the boy in. He drowned, as far as Seamus was concerned, and in spite of other people around, it happened all the same. Seamus could almost see the bloated face being turned over in the morning, the paleness of his life-lost skin, his eyes vacant but bearing the distant impression of a formerly sentient being, the embers of a campfire finally smoldered to a blackness no longer providing any warmth or color.

Indeed, Lawrence Farley was the most removed from Seamus of the three recent deaths that circled his life, but it had by far the greatest impact on him. Seamus had no stake in the mess that was the boy's demise, only a toxic but irresistible attraction to swim in its wake and understand all he could about it.

And so, when much of the dust was settled in terms of the questioning of the students involved from all shades of authority figures, those same guilty parties held a belated memorial service of their own for their dead friend on the campus quad. Those that knew Lawrence told stories, read poems, littered a papier-mâché headstone with pictures of him taken in lively, boisterous times. He was apparently an impossible extrovert, and had Seamus known him before, he may have dismissed him as another asshole belonging to the self-absorbed class of Them.

But standing in the back of the memorial service he harbored no such judgmental feelings. He only watched with devoted attention as he picked out from the speakers and attendees who the troubled seven were. He wore a jacket though the weather did not call for it, and kept his hand concealed over his camera. And for the entire hour, he questioned his nerve. In the end, his nerve won out. But now he had faces to look for, and he knew if he was patient the better time would come.

And so, while eating a quick lunch by himself in a corner of the dining room so not to be disturbed, Seamus watched a morose, lanky, red-haired young man walk along with his head down and shoulders swinging. The portrait of isolation, the young man took his own seat alone in this corner of the dining room, at a table opposite from Seamus, and began to pick slowly at his food as though it was made of rubber and sand.

Seamus knew who he was from the memorial service. He was in the front row, carried an oar in the opening procession, but never said a word.

Seamus had his camera on the table, and turned the power on with a shaking finger. He watched the boy pick away as his sorrowful image appeared on the LCD screen, but after a while he just turned the camera off and sat back in his chair. He needed contrast, otherwise the shot had no power. It just looked hokey, the glum boy and his sandwich, the sunlight coming through the big square windows, the round table plain and boring.

But then it happened. Three chipper girls came walking towards them. They were ebullient. They were pretty. They chattered over each other in a language from a world that possessed no trouble. They were perfect.

Seamus turned his camera back on and waited for the moment. This would be taken on automatic setting, no time to play. He watched the LCD screen and felt his heart beat as the girls walked behind the red-haired boy. He clicked the shutter and squinted at the image that flashed onscreen. The heads were small but the focus was clear. He just wondered where the eyes were. It was too small on the screen to tell just yet. He would have to upload the image on a computer to get a better look. He would be skipping class again, that was for sure.

He looked up, smiling, excited, eager. The red-haired boy was staring back, holding a French fry between his fingers and angled towards his temple. Gone was the sullenness. All Seamus could see was anger.

Seamus had understood up to this point that being a voyeur was necessary for some photographers. It was a fine theory and one that encouraged him to carry his camera with him everywhere. He had not put the theory into true practice until now, and his head was too foggy and his skin burning too hot for him to consider whether he was glad he did. He only stood from his seat, rigidly, and so not to be an utter coward acknowledged the boy with a head nod, and started quickly towards the door. The boy never nodded back, nor did he look away. He only sat in his chair and watched.

That close call behind him, Seamus clapped his hands aloud in the computer lab as he laid eyes for the first time on his shot. It was just what he wanted! The girls walked by gaily in sundresses and holed jeans and flowing shirts with breezy strides and smiling faces and bright eyes and sunlight washing over their hair! The red-haired boy was staring straight at his plate, French fry angled at his temple like it was a gun to his head, his body defeated, speaking volumes of enacted language that gave meaning to the wordless. Suddenly the empty dining hall was no longer an arbitrary backdrop framing an unimpressive and gloomy sap but a place that transcended emotional dimension. And Seamus had captured it, just as he captured the contrasts before with Barry and Steve, and Malcolm and the blurry suits.

Seamus shook his head and felt the warm patter of gratitude spread from his chest throughout his body, his head tingling, his mind anxious, his heart excited. He felt this way in the corridor during spring break and the feeling was even better now.

He leaned back in his chair, arms up and head cradled in his palms, smiling at the wall, seeing vistas no one around him was seeing. The private joy of realization, yes, he knew he had found his voice. And he liked how it sounded.

6

No one had accepted *Open Face Sandwich Day* yet. Seamus sent the picture to four different journals and got rapid responses from all but one, and the lingering purgatory of anticipation had left him room for uncomfortable yet viable hope. But waking one morning as the semester continued to eek towards its close, he looked in his email inbox and saw that Lucy 51, a Journal of Images and Letters, "didn't quite see" what he "was going for."

So Seamus cut class and took a walk. He had not read any of *Wintering Out* yet, and while he attended the screening of *Sunday Bloody Sunday*, he was not prepared to draw from any of the assigned poetry to confirm or embolden his reaction to the film in any discernible way. Further, the dining hall was once again stocked with biodegradable coffee cups after a quick and brilliant reprieve into reintroducing the pedestrian paper cups that it offered his entire Freshman year. Indeed, the recycled corn material was rough on the lips and made the entire experience of sipping unpleasant. It was indeed a morning of disappointments, and that meant walking by himself and thinking was not only deserved, but necessary.

He was in the middle of considering the difference between Taoism and Zen Buddhism as they related to the principles of allowing stimuli to come and go, arise and pass, when he noticed a gorgeous light beaming off the school's clock tower. Zen or Taoism aside, he knew how to take a look when it mattered.

Then he heard someone shout, "Hey," turned around, and wished he never stopped to look at some stupid sunlight reflecting off an ass ugly clocktower.

"Hey," Seamus returned, petrified at first. Having been tuned in to the effects of body language more readily lately as he ran around campus trying to expose it, Seamus caught himself quickly and readjusted his posture. He straightened with his shoulders back, assumed a position of near possessiveness over this spot in the corridor, and readied himself for a conversation he could imagine going any number of awful ways.

The red-haired boy said, "Hey," again, unnecessarily, in the same halting bark he had before, and looked at Seamus with flitting, sketchy eyes.

"Chillin' man."

"Word. So I know we don't know each other but I saw you fucking around with your camera the other day in the cafeteria."

Seamus swallowed and nodded his head. "Yup."

"What kind of camera is that anyway?"

Seamus fiddled his hands around, suddenly aware that he did not have his camera on him, a rare separation, and said, "Just a rad SLR. Sony." He nodded his head and shrugged. "Works."

"Cool cool. Anyway man," the boy looked around with his eyes but never moved his head and continued, "like I said we don't know each other but I was wondering if you could help me out."

Seamus leaned against the pillar again and considered, eyes serious. "You're uh, what, looking to take a picture or something?" He nearly bit his tongue after but did not know what to say.

"Chh, no. I'll just be blunt but you know Imogene, yeah?"

"Unfortunately." The answer was without any premeditation.

"Right? That girl has been all on my ass, thinks she's Mother Theresa or something and that I need a hug or whatever." The red haired boy suddenly reddened and looked away, his body posture now timid. "Shit, I mean you know what happened right?"

Seamus exhaled, nodded. "Saw you at the memorial service."

"You knew Lawrence?"

"As much as anyone, I guess. He got around."

"Goddamn yeah he did! Would have to be the one everyone liked who fucking drowned."

Seamus relaxed and said with revived animation, "I know it man, doesn't it kick you in the nuts? Had a guy from my high school who was just hit by a car a little while back. Same kind of thing. Everyone loved him."

"Right. I bet Imogene's sister just hated her."

And so rang the high note of Seamus' day. Whoever this guy was, he knew the truth. Imogene sucked ass.

That's good man, that's good. Don't say that too loud though," Seamus said.

"Believe me, I know it." The red haired boy looked behind him. "Anyway man, the girl's our degree of separation and I gotta be honest, even though it doesn't sound good. You know some place I can get some blow?"

And so dropped the high note. Seamus remembered quickly tight embraces as vividly as he did time alone. Looking at the kid in front of him, he knew they were connected on a level far deeper than Imogene, their scale of separation thinner than believed by this stranger, this voice for things never heard but felt. As far as Seamus knew, Imogene probably told everybody he was something he would not recognize.

"What's your name?" Seamus asked.

"Oh shit man, fucking rude, I'm sorry dude. Peter," he held out his hand, and then over shaking continued, "Dude I know how random this is. Dude, for real, just say fuck off and I'll get out of your hair. I'm not trying to be a dick or anything. Things have just been bad and the truth is, shit, I can't go off and get it from the dude I always do 'cause that fucker's got a loose mouth and no real concern for me and who knows if someone would hear or not but if they did, god man, what a shitstorm that'd be. I just need to go off the beaten path here, you know?"

"I do," Seamus said. "You've been through a lot."

The mood changed again and Peter said, "What's that supposed to mean? Like you know?"

"Hey! Don't come at me like that, guy. I'm alright with giving you a hand but don't get all down on yourself and then show your teeth. If you haven't been through a lot then get away from me. I don't owe you anything."

Relenting the chip off his own shoulder, Peter said, "Alright, sorry man. I'm just, you know, it's the kind of charity shit Imogene says. 'You've been through a lot,' shit. Sorry man, you may think you know, but you don't."

Seamus thought back, looked at the world via his life, his experiences, and what he knew that others knew and did not, reminding himself that, as Thomas Nagel said, he did not know what it was like to be a bat. "Fair enough," he offered.

"Okay, well just forget it then I guess."

"No. If you want blow I'll get you blow. I've got a buddy who lives off campus and is so in his own world no one here will ever know."

Peter smiled gratefully and let his shoulders hang down as he shook his head. "Just what I need. Bless you."

"Cool. Do you drive? I mean, you have a car here?"

"Yeah man. Just tell me where to go."

"Alright dude. Let's go."

On the drive to Seamus' dealer's house he talked with Peter about photography while Peter talked with him about growing up in Washington, and specifically about boyhood and teenage trips to Mount Rainier National Park, "right where Adams took his dentist office pictures."

"Nice shots man, but who gives a shit? It's a mountain, dude. Just go there."

Seamus considered. "I know what you mean."

When they arrived, Seamus led Peter up the brick steps to a rundown rental house on a quiet cul-de-sac. Across the street an old woman with saggy arms and brown splotches marking her face stared at them while she watered her lawn and looked unhappy, tired, and angry.

"Okay, I see Byron's car which is a good sign."

"He still didn't text you back?"

"He doesn't always."

"Sounds like bad business."

"We're friends, I think that changes things sometimes."

Seamus knocked on the door and considered. He was

friends with Byron in the way he was friends with Malcolm. And he was friends with him in a way he imagined he would be with Peter, though that thought was hopelessly short-sighted. There are always those on the periphery, he realized. And one person's periphery is another person's inner circle, or last lay, or sketchy drug dealer to call when the the first guy is unavailable. Seamus thought there was more to it than this, but settled into a quiet reflection on It and its contrasts, Peter and the happy girls, for instance. Whole worlds apart, but brushing against each other with no impact dealt to either party. Instead, a third agent was struck deeply, and captured it all on film. Degrees of separation, chance encounters. Buying blow before noon. It was all memorable to Seamus, it was all life. It was rain passing through the haloed light of a street lamp, it was the sun visiting the corners of bleachers and clock towers. It was a subtle, constant blooming, and one that bore no fruit anyone but the beholder could digest. It was good for nothing, but here he was, following its lead. As resolutely as ever, Seamus still believed that It was leading somewhere, and hoped for the best.

Byron lived with his girlfriend in a three-bedroom rental house. Two football players occupied the other bedrooms. Seamus wondered if the football players did as many drugs as Byron did. He knew they smoked pot throughout the day. That was how living with Byron was.

One of Byron's football player roommates opened the door. Seamus looked into the house out of habit. It was always a gloomy place for Seamus. It recalled memories from the summer after his freshman year, just before he started working at Singing Pines, when he stayed with Byron for four days straight to keep the boy company. Byron moved into the house during finals as he was in the process of swearing off the dorms forever, unable to get along adequately with his hall mates, resident assistant, or even the cafeteria workers.

"Seamus, don't see too much of you lately."

"I know it. How've you been?"

"Same old."

"Yeah.

"Yeah. Does Byron know your friend?"

"Honestly, they haven't met."

"Hold on."

The roommate shut the door but not all the way, and Seamus continued looking in and thinking back, remembering, seeing again a scene just like he saw it then, only now with the addition of a lazy girl stretched out on the couch.

The last summer, Byron was also having a problem with his girlfriend. They had gotten back together since, and apparently very little had changed in her personality. She did not rise to say anything to Seamus or Peter. She only lay nearly still, dipping a naked foot against the tiles, staring at the TV. She sipped a soda through a straw, made delicate, soft sounds, and then coughed hoarsely before lighting a cigarette.

The door opened wider. "Because it's you, Seamus. You know Byron doesn't like visitors though."

"I can wait in the car," Peter offered.

"Oh, and make the place look like a 7-11?" the roommate asked.

"Forget it," Seamus said to Peter. Then to the roommate, "Thanks man. You, like Byron, are a good dude."

"Tell him that. He's in his room."

Byron was huddled over his drum machine when Seamus and Peter entered. Though he had plenty of warning, he still acted surprised to see he had company. His back to the door and headphones snuggly attached to his large head, Seamus picked up a dirty sock and threw it at his shoulder. He jerked his head around at once and tore his headphones off, then stood and said, "What up, playa?" They hugged with a jerk and back slap, and then Byron said to Peter, "Yo."

"Peter."

"Peter Peter Pumpkin Eater. You and Seamus are homies?"

"Yeah."

"You're not a cop."

"No!" he said, laughing.

"I don't think it's funny if you're a cop or not a cop, just a question."

"He's fine, Byron."

Byron nodded. "Alright Pete. Seamus says you're cool so you're cool. Want some coconut juice?"

"No thanks."

"Shoot. When a man brings you into his home..."

"I'll have some," Seamus said.

"Well I know that, shoot. You always be drinking my Zico. Especially now that you're getting all swoll and shit. You're looking good playa, I'm proud of you even if you don't think we need to kick it anymore."

"It's not like that man, miss you dude."

"Well stop the presses! One homie misses his other homie! Nice of you to drop by then! Cheers, brother."

Seamus and Byron drank juice while Peter took a seat on the edges of Byron's bed.

"Make yourself at home, shit."

Peter stood up.

Byron then went on to talk with Seamus about nothing that had to do with anything drug-related while Peter stood back in the corner, growing restless but staying quiet. Seamus saw his visitor eye Byron's rebel flag on the wall, something that always drew negative attention when it hung in the dorms the previous year. Byron rationalized it as a part of his southern heritage, but no one ever saw it his way. Rebel flags were not popular at Seamus' school, but PRIDE flags were. Tibetan prayer flags were too, and even the occasional pirate flag because those weren't considered violent, just playful.

Finally, Seamus dropped the hint that he was there to buy something, and Byron came around and Peter reentered the circle, standing behind Seamus.

"Anyway man, I've got to get going pretty soon because Peter's got class. But we were going to pick up some blow and get ready to have a fun weekend before finals come up here."

"Oh, so you're not just coming by to see my sword collection? Shit, say something next time, even though you hurt my feelings."

"Sorry man, you know - "

"I'm playin' playa," Byron slapped Seamus' shoulder. "But one little wrinkle in your program here is that I don't sell blow anymore."

Seamus dropped his head and could hear Peter fidget behind him. Byron's eyes moved, watching the visitor, and Seamus said, "Oh, well man, good I guess. I know your girl didn't like having it around."

"Hell no. Girl tried to act like she was going to dump me and she pulled that moving out shit again. I just said fuck it, whatever...but I got some Oxycontin."

Seamus brightened. "Yeah? Shit, that's actually better. You never had that last year even when I asked for it."

"Nah but my girl likes it so fuck, happy wife, happy life." Byron looked suddenly thoughtful. "Though if I marry her I'm probably a dumb-ass. She even say hi to you when you come in?"

"No. But she never does."

"Shit! I tell her to keep her goddamn chin up! She's going to make people uncomfortable when they come here when she just lays out like she's cooking in the oven."

"Well, it's not exactly a Wal-Mart here, dude. I'm not hurt, for one thing."

Byron looked up at Peter, breathed through his mouth like he always did when something or someone bothered him, and Seamus looked back agitatedly and mouthed to his companion to shut-up. But it was too late.

"Well shoot. Guess you're the only one that matters, too. Standing back there like a goddamn junkie. Shit, you really kick it with this douchebag, Seamus?"

"Dude, he was just trying to be funny."

"A laugh riot."

"Hey man, I wasn't exactly making a joke here. I really don't care if your girl says one word or offers me pineapple juice or whatever. I just came here with Seamus to pick something up and I gotta get to class or I'm going to be late."

"Oh. Sorry to keep you waiting."

Seamus looked back again and shook his head at Peter.

"Whatever. Just, Seamus, I'm cool with Oxy."

Byron clapped his hands. "Oh well praise the lord! Stranger in a Strange Land approves! Why don't you tell me what you think of my flag up there on the wall, huh? I saw you eyeball that a few times, you got some fucking opinions rolling around there in that apple head, fire crotch?"

Peter rolled his eyes. "So now you're grilling me on your bullshit racist flag? Fuck man," he said and pulled out a hundred dollar bill. "Just can you sell me some shit and I can go? I don't care about your flag."

"Well you sure as shit said some things that make me think you do."

"No. Well, yeah. That's a bullshit thing to hang in your room. What, you support slavery? Think blacks should ride at the end of the bus?"

"You people. You people always think that a rebel flag means I don't like black people. You don't know what it means to be from the South. Where you from, anyway?"

"Jeez man. Olympia."

"Oh! Olympia, well never mind. That means you're better than everyone in the world but they just don't know it yet. Please, just take my drugs, I don't even need your money. I want to tell my grandkids that I had a visitor from Olympia come to my home and tell me what he thought about my flag."

The boys looked at each other tensely and Peter changed directions by saying, "Seamus man, can we just get some stuff here and go?"

Seamus looked at Byron. Byron nodded at him and said, "This isn't your homie."

Seamus shook his head.

"And you bring him into my home. You don't come around, and then you bring this piece of shit, good-for-nothing, ungrateful, holier-than-thou asshole into my home."

"Hey," Seamus said. "I don't know him, but guy's been through something okay?"

"Oh, well why didn't we offer him tissue when he came in the door? Or a hug? Hell maybe my girl well get off her ass for once and blow him."

"Fuck you Seamus, I told you about that shit!"

"Fuck you Peter, you're embarrassing me."

"Fuck it all. Fuck the whole damn thing," Byron said, now smiling madly. "We got the prodigal son here with his new best buddy who thinks he knows best."

"I don't think I know anything. I just wanted to buy something. What, you don't like money?" Peter said.

"I don't like money from cops."

"Jesus Christ, Seamus. Will you just get this going?"

"Why do you keep asking Seamus to talk to me like he's some kind of translator? I think you and I are having our own conversation right now, stranger. And personally, I don't care what Seamus has to say, either."

"Well that makes two of us," Peter said.

Seamus turned around, demanded, "Then just fucking leave. Try to do a guy a favor. Byron's right, you are ungrateful."

"And Imogene's right, too. You really are a loser." Peter turned to Byron, flipped him off, and thanked him for "high quality nothing," and left.

Seamus was stranded. But that was a reality that did not yet offer him any trouble. He heard what Peter said loudly and clearly, and he sat still for a while absorbing it, his stomach warm and his temples pulsing, his mouth dry and thoughts slushy. If Imogene thought that...

Byron stood and yelled, "Woo!" He lit sage and waved it around the room, yelled "Woo!" again and shook his head, and then his arms, and then his legs and his feet. "Gotta shake the bad juju off. Man, it's like a negative spiral vortex just left the premises. I love you my brother, but you ever drag a piece of shit like that around here again, we don't kick it anymore. That's the truth."

"Don't worry. I won't be. You can count on that."

"Alright then. Shit, you still got that soft heart, don't you kimosab?"

"What are you talking about?"

"You said the boy had been through something. Hell I remember when you kept me company while my girl left me. You were there my brother, don't think I forget. It's why I'm not getting out my sword collection right now and going all Benihana on you."

"Fuck Byron, I benefited too. Wasn't the worst few days of my life."

Seamus looked back. In truth, it was not an easy four days, either. So many movies watched, too many of them about kung fu. Byron talked about nearly everything but his problems with his girlfriend, made many strange noises and referenced movies other than those they were watching. He sniffled, he coughed. He yawned and farted, sometimes at the same time. He temporarily dozed off, only to come to a few minutes later, muttering some glib one liner like, "Snoozin'," or "It's wakey time." Then there was the pot. Byron smoked him out from morning to night for a gray stretch of indulgence that was excessive even by Seamus' standards. The sloshy come down never ended, and the highs reached gradually lower peaks, until the end of his prolonged visit when he felt like he was dealing with little more than a mildly disturbing head cold.

Byron packed a bong and Seamus was about to get ripped out of his skull. He did not protest as it would be worthless to do so anyway. When Byron insisted, it was best to go with it. Seamus always had before and was not going to change the course of their history now. As of the coming afternoon, his Ethics class already dodged, he had nowhere else to be.

Byron put on a movie called *What the Bleep Do We Know*, and then asked Seamus, "'Cause, what really do we know? We think we know it all. You know what we really know? If so tell me. 'Cause I don't know, and I'm not going to say I do." Byron stopped talking, looked at the wall, and then continued, "Shit. World is wacky."

Seamus then said, "It. You know It or you don't know It. There's nothing else."

"It? Damn, dog. You're getting all mysterioso on my ass now. Chill and watch this shit. You might learn something. Like, you're not really who you think you are, and I'm not really who you think I am. In fact, I might not even be real!"

Byron pretended his fingers were a gun and shot himself in the head. He then dropped to the floor and played dead for around ten seconds before rising and saying, laughing, "Nah, I'm real as fuck. But still, you don't know what real is."

"Byron, if there's one thing I like about you, it's that I never know what to expect."

"Fuck, cool man. Greens it, bitch."

Seamus did, and as the movie began he paid little attention

to it or Byron's bizarre noises interjected throughout as he considered in no uncertain vagueness that for all he knew, he did not know who he was after all, or Byron for that matter.

Despite all this, he watched an ugly woman onscreen tell him nearly two hours later that he could be his own God, and nothing had changed. He hated what Peter said, and despite all his rationalizations, all his conviction about It and Them, the red-haired boy's words still stung. He knew, deeper down, that whatever he wanted Rachel to think of him now was out of reach. She thought what she thought. And Seamus was helpless to change it. And feeling as low as he had at any point lately, he told Byron he had to go home.

Byron was back on his drum machine, Seamus had to throw another sock at him to alert him to the present moment. The boy looked at Seamus, then at the screen, smiled dumbly, and said, "You see what I mean? You do whatever you want to, my brother. Just a big playground out there."

"Yeah I guess," Seamus said, though on another day he would have run with the conversation ad infinitum, excited, merry, sincere. "I gotta go man. You're a true soldier."

"Uh-huh. That I am. And to make you know who loves you I got you a present."

Byron scurried to his closet and pulled out a Tupperware box of brownies. "Left over from 4/20. Three left. Two for you and one for a special homie. Maybe whatever new chick you're boning, eh, eh?" Byron elbowed him.

"Yeah, thanks man, but I don't have anywhere to put these."

"Shit, that's not true!" Byron returned to his closet and pulled out a trench coat. He dropped the Tupperware into a front pocket and opened his mouth wide like he had performed a magic trick. "Look no further, your brownies are safe, discreet, and ready to be enjoyed at a later date. But not too late. Shit gets stale. Just because they're magical doesn't mean Betty Crocker enchanted them with a longer shelf life."

"Very thoughtful. I'm good man, really. I'm just tired and I need to get home."

"Fuck! Well wake up then!"

Byron, now moving to his treasure box, pulled out a bottle of tequila and two shot glasses. He poured them both to the top said, "Cheers to the fucking man!"

"I don't feel like the man right now," Seamus grumbled, and took his shot reluctantly but quickly and for a moment had a state-dependent memory of a party he attended his previous year which resulted later in him getting head from a flighty but cute girl he had met only once before in the cafeteria. It was an outstanding evening, and for just a moment, he nearly felt better.

But reality returned as it always did and Seamus' mind kept moving. He remembered that he was butt-hurt, that it was late, and that he wanted to go home to brood. He said goodbye once again to Byron but was once again stopped. His host was not cutting the cord yet. There was more tequila to drink.

"Nope. You're not even picking up my jacket. You're not leaving here without it. You're taking another shot as a punishment for your bad manners."

"Dude."

"Dude. Cheers."

They clinked glasses and again Seamus drank. "Okay, I need to sit down for a second."

"Well of course you do! What are you, some kind of

machine? Sit, chill. Listen to this!"

Byron went to his drum machine and began tapping furiously away when Seamus rose quickly, grabbed the jacket, and said, "Cool, I'm better. Thank you man, really has been a pleasure."

"Well good on you man, you're my boy." Byron pulled Seamus in for a hug and without further hesitation poured two more shots.

"Man! No! I mean thanks, but seriously."

"Seriously nothing. You don't leave without a goodbye shot."

Seamus was feeling the tequila already and despite his conscience took a third drink and then needed something to eat. Byron gave him beef jerky and a granola bar. Which led to a fourth drink, the true goodbye shot. He then helped Seamus into the jacket opened a couple of Corona's and shoved them into the jacket's inner pockets.

"What are you doing man?"

"Watch." Byron had many straws in his closet and spared two to put into each bottle. He looked Seamus over, whistled, and said, "Perfie! You look like a million bucks."

"I feel like I could get pulled over."

"No way, homeboy. Just remember that cops are like animals. They respond to sudden movements. I've sipped on beers out of this thing so many goddamn times. Check it, especially down at the beach around these drum circles. Fools be getting drunk in public tickets left and right and I'm just sippin'. You're straight. Remember, it's a playground out there."

Seamus was going to protest further but the last shot

caught up to him, a sudden sense of saying fuck it did too, and he sipped beer through a straw out of a trench coat jacket and felt content enough to just go with it. If the world was his playground, he would be best suited to not resist its urges.

Finally departed, Seamus swayed outside and realized he felt better. Whatever Peter thought was irrelevant, and Seamus thought about things that made him happy. That girl who gave him head and other such encounters. He thought about Jamie and how happy he would be to see him at Singing Pines. He thought about the brownies Byron gave him and what a perfect treat that would make after serving dinners some night. He thought about the semester ending soon and the whole summer he had to look forward to to break from school and focus on his stupid but beautiful job putting plates on tables and picking them up afterwards. He thought about photography, the shining light in his life. If he made any-thing, it was a few decent pictures. Maybe sometime soon he would make some more. Get another acceptance or two. Most importantly, capture the subject matter he wanted to capture. Raise his voice, dial it in, get better, always get better.

He walked like a derelict, taking subversive sips from a straw sticking out near the jacket's collar, looking periodi-cally over his shoulder. The cars that drove by were just pairs of white lights coming, or red lights going. He saw a cop pass, too, but was ignored. He shuddered at first, spotting the black and white Ford, realizing it too late as it ran parallel to him. The cop looked at him, his face emotionless, if not men-acing. But he only drove along with the rest of Them, leaving Seamus alone in his intoxicated solo trip along the suburban sidewalks, noticing the details of front yards he never did before because he had never come this way on foot. His heart and mind were host to all kinds of drunken pleasantries, ideas for photo ops brimming to life. He wanted to see the kids in the kiddie pool splashing and screaming in delight, while their mom watched them pensively as she sat on the front steps, talking on her cell phone or smoking a cigarette, rolling the bad news of the day around in her head. He wanted to see the mailman delivering a package on the doorstep of the house with eclectic garden decorations, the glass blown orbs and oversized, plastic boulders, the hanging plants and rusted wagon wheel, the red painted fence and the round, paper lanterns hanging from the short tree. What would be in that box? The cat in the window would be watching, wondering.

The streetlights were blurry, his step swaying. His tolerance had come down a little, for pot and liquor, since he was not getting quite so hammered anymore. He was still hungry, but each sip of beer sustained him, made him think about food, like everything else, that much less. Drunk but eyes open, he watched the still life world, with only the cars moving in the quiet town night, and imagined all the daytime life he wanted to capture through his lens. He wanted contrasts, but he also just wanted visual oddities. He wanted the mundane world around him to sparkle with the gilded edges of It's illuminating energy. He wanted to show, through his pictures, what It was, and moreover, what It was not. He wanted his photography to break away the layers of daily failure he was becoming so accustomed to, each class more questionable than the last, each future day more distant, more uncertain, more unrealized.

He was in school, doing all the right things, and how could he ever know if that was really true or not? Seamus knew that he knew a thing or two, as those with It do. He laughed thinking about how stupid his thoughts sounded now, again into the night, a mad bum in a trench coat stumbling home, to the dorms, to the college campus, to the seat of rightness, where he belonged as a young American man, paving the way for his future, one report card at a time, with mounting loan debt rising each semester.

When he did get home, he was relieved to see that his roommate was gone. He picked up his camera, felt his eyes water, and in his cups had an uncommon thought of pure love regarding his parents.

He called them and thanked them for the camera. His dad sounded happy to hear him, and did not ask him much about anything. He never did. His mom, when it was her turn on the phone, asked him all kinds of things, none of which he wanted to answer. Her voice shook with concern at the conversation's end. She had pauses between speech, as did he. "Are you there?" she asked him.

"I am."

They said goodbye finally, and he wished he never called. He felt like she was invading his privacy now, asking him about school and his classes and all the things he did not like to think about at all. She wanted to make sure that the right things that he was doing were still right, were working properly, and that he still had his place on the conveyor belt.

He was too tired to eat. Still holding his camera, he laid on his bed and shut his eyes to think.

He did not remember his dreams when he woke up. Jimmy was back, snoring in bed, and the lights were out. This was disorienting to Seamus, who was still in his trench coat. He went to the bathroom and looked in the mirror. He had what was the start of a penis drawn on his cheek. Jimmy...

Seamus washed it off, carefully, slowly, his head hurting. He undressed and went back to bed, but had trouble getting back to sleep. He tried to remember his dreams, but felt like he had been anesthetized. He looked at his cell phone, what time was it anyway?

Three in the morning. A long time until the daylight.

7

Finally, the semester ended. Seamus regarded the 2.5 G.P.A he received as a surprising success. He earned an A in "Who Moved by Banana?" which he expected, and of course the W for withdrawing from Logic. He was pleased, even touched however, to see that he earned a B- in Ethics. He initially considered the mark to be considerably higher than he deserved, though upon reflection he did realize that the papers he turned in were serviceable. Since there were only two all semester long, it was the kind of work load that fit squarely into his wheelhouse. While some students might feel intimidated by such a shallow pool in which to sink or swim, Seamus laid skywards and backstroked towards adequate competence. And so he suddenly loved his Ethics professor, even though the man was the most colossal drip he had ever met, and only weeks ago, served as a source of inner mockery and derision as the poster professor for stuffy academics too full of themselves to see that the vast majority of their students were lost, bored, or desperately searching their backpacks for a marker to sniff. The class lectures were endless exercises for the man to practice speaking without pause, his little eyebrows moving up and down, his lips curling, puckering, flattening, the faces he was making a potpourri of expressions equal in smugness and delight, his impressions upon himself endless and epic, and his learnedness so complete he could play devil's advocate with himself all day long with little need for any of his students to suggest their two cents much less form any serviceable dialogue. And the class indeed saved all their intellectual pennies for themselves save for a pair of obnoxious ne'er-do-wells who could not seal their traps should a gunman demand their silence. One of whom made many of the same self-righteous looks as did the professor as he ended most of his points with a question, volleying back to the pompous man behind the desk with hands that never seemed to unclasp. There, Seamus knew, was a future professor. Meanwhile, never the first to raise his hand in any class discussions outside of his photography courses, Seamus was entirely quiet even by his own low standards. He uttered two scant words the entire sixteen week semester. The first was his name and the second was "whoops" after he missed a free throw attempt with his breakfast sandwich wrapper into a wastebasket.

Ultimately, nothing was more wholly satisfying than notching a D in Irish Nationalism. This outcome was inherently dicier because he never wrote his final paper. He scored well enough on the in-class final, apparently, to save his hide. An F in that class and he would be two in the hole considering he withdrew Logic. With only two credits recorded that would mean part-time student status despite having endured a full-time pain in his ass.

And so, once his report card was received, his parents' usual disappointment absorbed and released, Seamus was at last free to get on with his real work taking pictures, wandering, and thinking. There was so much to wonder about now that he did not have to waste his time explaining himself, as college professors often demand.

He also had the time to pick up extra shifts at Singing Pines, which was just as welcome as he thought it would be. Singing Pines never failed to transport him away from his school life, and now that it was his only source of responsibility again, he was able to move past the demons of the previous semester quickly and healthfully, if not repressively. But then out of sight and out of mind, and so troubles with

Rachel were as distant as the moon. Had he felt half this content during Finals week he would have completed his final essay for Irish Nationalism without the slightest trouble. But life had not been so kind to him leading up to the final assignment, and due to his decision to attend a last-minute art show Rachel threw together late in the year, his final days on campus were marred by all shades of bummer.

His only saving grace was that he did not see Rachel again after the show, and that she probably never knew just how much of a head spin her show put him in. He did, after all, show up to offer his "support." A loser never would do such a thing but would instead hide away in his dorm room and suck on the ice cubes of a get-better cocktail as he continued to try and nurse his broken heart back towards basic health. Indeed, if appearances had any impact on consensus opinion, than he had at least done his best. And certainly, the fewer people there were who regarded him as a loser meant the farther he was from actually being one.

The evening began without pain or malice, but had its share of nerves. Rachel's show was called "Interpersonal Space." Student body-approved 8.5x11's had advertised the show around campus, which was held in a small room inside the multipurpose building. The moment Seamus laid eyes on one he knew he would be there, and when the night came, he was so nervous he started at a hall mate's get-together to get a little liquored up before he showed his face. He would have to go to her show alone, since none of his friends gave a shit about his ex's art. He did not blame them. She was not necessarily that good. At least, that was what he had determined in recent months.

He reached the multipurpose room and gave himself a final break in the bathroom, which was thankfully empty. He took a piss and stared into the toilet, feeling his brow sweat and his temples pulse, the excited gallop of Brazilian dance music thumped through the walls. The Capoeira kids were fluttering and leaping around, clapping, yipping, congratulating, encouraging, rolling their tongues and whistling. They sounded like they could barrel through the walls, trampling Seamus and dislodging the toilet, sending a geyser of water sprouting in their wake.

He flushed and washed his hands slowly, looked himself over in the mirror. His sweater fit snugly. His hair hung over his shoulders, clean and not too frizzy. His eyes were white, not pink, and his skin was clear. His partial sobriety was becoming even more so lately, but a semester of taking it easy had been good to him.

He was ready.

And so the anticlimax of Rachel's no-show sounded in his ears. There was a decent turnout of students, nearing twenty, wandering around the square room sipping wine from plastic cups and looking cute as they did on weekend party nights. They looked at the paintings, they spoke to each other, they laughed, they took pictures, and then posted them on Facebook from their phones. "Interpersonal Space," meanwhile, was nothing but tits, ass, and the occasional cock. There were balls, too, but they were always an afterthought, an ellipse peeking over a leg, designating anatomical completion. The colors were muted in the bodies, which were drawn on sandpaper and painted over with black, gray, and navy blue lines. The sandpaper sketches in turn were pasted over canvases painted in multiple, bright colors.

Seamus considered. Their signification of lust and sex was so overly obvious, and the friction of bodies implied by the sandpaper such a short-reach into creative expression, that he nodded his head and thought to himself that yes, Rachel was but artistically pedestrian from an intellectual level.

But then another thought struck him, and his chest filled gaily with the warm feeling pride brings, and his penis enjoyed a touch of blood flow, encouraging him and his understanding. This was, after all, a show devoted to sex. And Rachel, being his ex...well, it was obvious. He had left a mark!

Indeed, Rachel had told him when they were together that he was the best she had had. Knowing that was just a few short months ago, he felt renewed, as though he had tapped that and was free now to explore other castles. What doors could he open, should he have been opening? It was finally time he really gave himself a healthy chance.

Then Rachel finally showed up, walking in carrying some clear plastic cups, and Imogene beside her carrying a box of wine, as apparently the first cube of white Zinfandel was tapped. Rachel walked with the gaiety of a master at her craft, her round cheeks puffy like her lips, her hair almost straight except for a few flirty curls, and her jacket short to reveal her mandolin hips hugged by her tight slacks. She looked good. "Seamus, you made it!" she said and gave him a hug that was neither tepid nor warm. It had the strength of a hug she meant, but the quickness in delivery of an obvious obligation. Yet at the end she held his arms for just a moment, looked in his eyes, glanced quickly over his body, and let go as she stepped back, paving the way for an all-business one-armer from Imogene, who asked in a sleepy, bored voice, "Hey Seamus, how are you?"

"Great. I like the sandpaper, Rachel. That's clever."

"You do?" she asked. She was smiling.

"Yes," he said. "Everything looks good together...it's a good series of images."

"Thank you, Seamus. How's your photography?"

Seamus nodded his head. There was so much he could tell her, but he knew this was not the time nor the place. Tonight was her night. He had to be gracious. "It's going really well, thanks."

"Good," she said.

He stalled, seeing her look away, and said, "I just got a piece accepted in a literary journal."

"You did?" Her teeth were so white, better than his. He could see her tongue. He wanted to feel it again.

"Yeah, I've got a few more pieces out, pending responses. I'm moving on from landscapes, getting more in action shots, people shots. I think I'm finding my angle, or voice, whatever you want to call it."

She nodded thoughtfully. "That's good, Seamus."

Imogene looked at Rachel and walked away, though she did so with a nimble slink. It was classically dorky, and thus was cool, as she snuck up behind a boy with dark hair, arms in the process of being tattooed totally, and a striped polo shirt. She threw her arm around him and shouted something in his ear. He laughed and pulled her in for a quick dance. Seamus knew it was forced and hated Imogene even more than he usually did, and also the tatted boy though he had never met him.

Rachel brought his attention back to her, saying simply, "Thanks for coming, Seamus. I have to go make my rounds. You look great, by the way," she gave his arm a squeeze. He watched her catch up with Imogene and the dark haired boy, who leaned back jovially and waved his hands delicately over the room, no doubt feeding her a line similar to what Seamus had moments ago.

Seamus, realizing quickly that he was standing there

watching her walk away, grabbed a cup of wine quickly and walked back over to a wall, looked at a few paintings he had already looked at, sipped his drink, and left. He caught Rachel looking over when he left, and he waved with a smile, as did she, before she returned her attention quickly back to a scarfed and mustached boy taller than Seamus and far skinnier, irking him all the more soundly.

As he left it began to dawn on him that he was walking away from an art show that was devoted completely to sex. He did not think about much more than that, letting the thought wash over him. His mind was priming itself for a sprint, stretching its legs, getting accustomed to the position it needed to hold over the blocks. He knew this feeling. He could feel something holding him back, like a bouncer at a bar. But that something was only temporary, was only the passage of time that it took for him to digest a fear, a worry, a malevolence towards the life he was living and the faces of the people who populated it.

And then the shot sounded. Seamus went back in time.

Rachel was so sexless their past couple of weeks together that the final impressions she had of him could hardly be so colorful in her mind as the canvases that littered that small gallery room. In fact, the thought of sex seemed to offend her. At least with him.

He rounded the track's curve, the first 100 yard dash behind him.

It had been a few months since they had been broken up. He had been, even in spite of his own disinterest, with another girl. Rachel had to have at least had one casual encounter with a boy.

The next straightaway emerged beneath his frantic feet.

That dark haired boy was sure comfortable with her. He stood close to her, practically touched his stupid, squat nose to hers when he spoke. And that tall asshole, for all Seamus knew Rachel was trying to get to know him better, or some other such nonsense.

Seamus almost stumbled but caught himself and now his stride was sloppy, his arms beginning to flail.

She grabbed his arm too!

Round the bend, closing in on the tape.

In fact, he had caught her winking when she first walked in, but not at him. It was off to the side somewhere. It could have been anyone, but maybe it was him. Him! He did not even know who that was but the wink could not have been aimed at anyone with a vagina.

The last few yards were ahead of him.

None of the dudes in the paintings looked like him, that was for sure. Pulling ahead, bulbs flashing.

Rachel was always a sexual person. Did he really expect her to stay chaste for any great duration of time? After all, who broke up with whom?

He was exhausted. His feet stuttered to a slow, small-stepped march towards stillness. He doubled over, caught his breath, felt the sweat drip down his eyes. He could think clearly now, the adrenaline calming as his body strove carefully towards homeostasis. He looked around him on the track. He was alone. The photographers had disappeared, the people in the stands a mirage that evaporated into the night. He won a race no one else was running, and taking his place on the podium, handed himself a medal.

He had made his appearance. And there was only one person with whom it left a mark.

So he had been her best? Was he still? He stood and raised his head towards the sky, looked around, saw other people moving about on the warm Friday night, and he kept walking some more.

Her best...for all he knew, he had long since been dethroned as the King of Fuck in her life. Once her finest, he was now chucking pebbles at the castle walls, looking at her eyes for clues, her body language, damn the body language! There was no picture worth taking tonight. Unless of course he wanted to position himself as he had Peter against a backdrop of happy people. Then it would have fit right in with his latest efforts.

Returning to his room, Jimmy was gone again and he was relieved. He drank the few beers he had in the fridge as he listened to music and searched the internet for journals seeking submissions. After getting fairly sloshed on his own, he knew this misery could not go on forever without company. He called Malcolm, who in what might have been a twist of divine fate, actually answered his phone.

When Seamus got to Malcolm's room, he immediately saw a bag of coke with two lines sitting beside each other on his desk. Malcolm had one of the rare singles in his dorm, even rarer given his class. But when three separate people request new rooms after having endured the same initial roommate, the guilty end up winning the greatest prize.

"I see your greedy eyes...take one."

Seamus looked at him with disbelief. "I don't know."

"The hell you don't! I'm sharing with you, ya cocksucker! I got a whole ball. Think of it as my going away present."

Seamus was getting hit left and right. "Where are you going?"

"I'm transferring moron! I told you last time I saw you."

Malcolm took one line cleanly up his nose, pinched his nostrils shut, and breathed in hard, the nasal, choking sound sending Seamus tittering along the past's boundary lines again, but he was too inebriated to start another race now.

Malcolm motioned him over and handed him his cut straw. Seamus held it in his fingers, looked it over like it was an artifact from times in man's earlier history.

"It's just that, I haven't had any since Rachel and I -"

Malcolm laughed delightedly. "'Rachel and I?' What - broke up? How about since 'Rachel dumped me.' You can fool yourself all you want but I know you better than that. Obviously you haven't got any other play, either."

Seamus felt his temples throb, and a rush of confused, sulking anger rose up through his belly. He leaned over and took the gift Malcolm offered him. He could tell immediately that it was garden variety, cut with something benign but done so liberally. Still, once he tasted the acrid drip in the back of his throat, he knew he could not care less how much baby powder he was ingesting. It was going to be a better night.

Seamus hit the ground running after another line and told Malcolm, who was only interested at all because of the coke, about the art show. While the open ears were comforting in the most basic sense, the lack of sympathy was to be expected and only poured more fuel onto his jealous fires.

"Of course she's fucking someone, or some people. That's what people do when they break up, Seamus. Or especially when they cut someone off."

"There was some tatted guy there that really got to me. He was feeding her so much shit his eyes were turning brown."

Malcolm cocked his head. "Tall, short? Stocky? What color was his hair?"

"He was like, average height I guess. Decent build. Dark hair."

"He had a bunch of tattoos, some Hindu monkey god and asshole alphabets on his arm?"

"Yeah! You know him?"

"I'll be happy not to after next week. Tim Redfield. That guy's one of the biggest tools in the whole art department. He's everything that's ruining men today."

"A real metrosexual, huh?"

"No, a real puss. It's Generation Puss among men today, Seamus. That guy does it all. He's such a low life he'd bend down to kiss the ring on a girl's pinky toe and lift his head back up to tell her how good her feet smell."

"I hate guys like that!"

"You're a puss too so don't get excited. You're still creeping around your ex's show seeing if she still loves you."

"Fuck off dude. I was curious."

"Curious. No, you weren't curious. But you were trying to do the right thing, which I guess is why I like you. A fucker like Tim doesn't know the meaning, or even that there's a difference. He just follows his mousy nose to the nearest opportunity, pokes his head around, sniffs, and doesn't leave a fart. Just comes and goes. You, you're too stuck in your own stupid head to at least not show your face. It's a sad goddamn face a lot of days, but you show the thing." Malcolm nodded his head contemplatively. "You and your stupid pictures. You might fail at trying to be something good, but you're not going to succeed at being something bad."

Seamus took another line. He was chemically insulated against taking offense.

"I like you because you're the most miserable, depraved asshole here in a school full of faux-optimists. You have the balls to stink like a rat. No showers, and no cologne. Just angry, antagonistic foulness. And for every hundred people that show up to class all made up like they're going to the prom, or every other hundred who try to look down and out even though their parents are paying the tuition in full, you just walk around in that same fucking t-shirt and jeans combo you've worn since day one. How the fuck you've gotten laid for owning like ten plain white t-shirts is beyond me, but at least you've never tried to match it with a smile. I don't know if your paintings are going to get any play anywhere, but I saw tonight that it's better to be influenced and at least try to make a point than to just throw some bullshit on a canvas that tells the same story everyone in the world has been telling since the beginning of time. Sex, so what. You don't paint it but you do it and that's probably the way it should be."

Malcolm took another line.

"Maybe we're not so different," Seamus said.

Malcolm paused as he cut a line and looked at Seamus.

"Oh we're fucking different. One of us is going to get laid tonight."

"Who's left in this shit hole that would sleep with you?"

"She's not from this shit hole. She makes coffee at Starbucks."

"You kidding me? What, are you sleeping with high school students now?"

"Yes but she's a senior."

Seamus laughed. But Malcolm did not.

"Like I said, one of us is at least getting laid."

"You're serious?"

"Dude, pussy is pussy. What do I care? Next semester nobody will even know my name. This is just for the road. Hell, I'll fuck her through finals. I don't care. I'm tired of this place."

There was a knock at the door. Malcolm, perched on his wooden bedpost, answered, "Yes?"

"It's me."

"Okay."

Malcolm's newest flame came in, a green apron still around her waist.

"Shut the door," he told her.

She did. "I didn't know you had company."

Seamus was pushing one nostril shut and breathing in deeply through the other, and could not help but think that this poor girl in this absurd situation was sweet and well-meaning. That he was "company" made him feel warm, like a guest at a well-set table. He assumed from the outset that he would be viewed as an intruder by the girl, but it was clear to him by her slinking shoulders and soft steps forward into Malcolm's careless arms that she viewed herself that way instead.

"Take off that apron already, work was a long time ago."

"I've been off for like fifteen minutes," she laughed nervously.

"Take off your apron and help yourself, then. Seamus! Get away from the desk, you greedy fucking pig."

Seamus laughed.

The girl held the straw nervously to her nose as Seamus sidestepped her and watched. Her hand shook, but just a little, and after she took her line she sat on Malcolm's lap and looked up at him. He stroked her hair, thin and unwashed, and she began to talk quickly about her parents going out of town the next weekend. She asked Malcolm, more than once and in the middle of multiple sentences, if he would come. She invited Seamus, too.

"Can't, sorry though."

As Seamus looked at the young girl taking her share off Malcolm's square mirror, he sensed that he might be over-staying his welcome. Seamus knew what he wanted, and wanted it very suddenly and strongly.

"Malcolm, you think Karen is up?"

He gave Seamus a sinister look.

"Who in the fuck would know?"

"Because you're friends."

"Who's Karen?" the young girl asked Malcolm.

"The chick Seamus wants to bone."

"Oh," she said.

"Yeah," Seamus said.

"Well, seeing as how this has been fun but it's time for us to say our goodbyes, I can text her if it gets you out of here."

"Hey, that's mean," the young girl laughed and slapped at Malcolm. Her voice was nice but not overly animated, coke and all. Seamus kept looking at her, listening to her, trying to take away something interesting but never could. She was, he knew and felt cruel for the fact that he did, the last strand of daylight in Malcolm's stand down south. He was from Northern California and he would be back there soon. He would return to his element, but at a new school be a stranger all the same. There, Malcolm would be less a malcontent and simply another face. Or maybe not. But whatever he would be, he would be a student without history. And if he were to begin another winding trail of misery, he would only have two years until he graduated. If two years was his shelf life in a small school where everyone knew each other, or at least believed they did, than certainly it would be enough to sustain him in a state university.

Seamus waited for Malcolm's phone to vibrate a response. He looked at the girl, a stranger out of place in this room. She might be a senior in high school, but it took less than Malcolm's esoteric standards of time to determine that she was a long way off from fitting in here. And so she was a human symbol of Malcolm's welcome worn thin. His once mysterious personality now a frayed effigy to sleaze, devalued among the female student body. Yes, it was time to go, Seamus knew.

Then the phone vibrated, and a little while later, Karen let herself in.

Bubbly, loud, walking with swinging hips and bright eyes, she said, before anything else, "Nice of you to think of me, Malcolm. I've wondered where you've been."

Funny, Seamus thought. One of the last few people remaining, and a woman no less, who had not given up on the malcontent. Then Karen squeezed his shoulder and said, "Hey stranger," to which he said, "Been a while."

"It has," she said and took a line without ceremony. Seamus took another too, and they started talking as people around cocaine do. Malcolm smiled on, and said soon afterwards, "Okay, good seeing you Seamus."

Seamus was going to answer but a surprised Karen did for him and said, "What? You call me over just to kick me out? Some host Malcolm."

"I didn't say you had to leave."

"Ha ha. Seriously, are you going to lose your boner if it gets later?"

"My penis is going to turn into a pumpkin at midnight. No Karen, I wanted to say seeya, I'm getting out of here."

"What do you mean?"

Seamus answered for Malcolm, and everyone chattered over each other until the end which was quickly upon them all.

"Malcolm decided he's too big a fish for this pond. He's going to swim upstream at Cal."

"Malcolm! You can't leave!"

"Really? You mean you're moving?" the girl on his lap asked.

"Thanks Seamus, a guy can't break his own news. Some pal, after all I've done for you."

"Why are you going back there?" the girl asked.

"Because everyone knows his name," Karen said. She smiled. It was devious. Seamus was horny.

"Because I'm sick of clowns like these," Malcolm said.

"That's mean!" The girl said again and took another line.

"And we're all sick of him. It's quite mutual," Seamus said.

"Less than you think. Who's going to be your friend when you're getting all moody like you do, Seamus? This time next year, no one's gonna want to hear how butt hurt you are that your girlfriend left you, when you're still holding your tail between your legs."

Seamus reddened as Karen looked at him. Before taking another line, he stammered, "I say one thing to the guy that's halfway human and he acts like he never shed a tear in all his life. So macho for a painter."

Karen smiled, teeth, bright eyes, said, "Malcolm's just so tough, gets all the girls, has all the friends in the world."

As she took a line too Malcolm stiffened, bucked the high schooler off his lap and stood to wave his visitors out the room. "Aright, alright this isn't a coke buffet! I call you two over for a goodbye kiss and you take all my blow."

The girl, unfazed by Malcolm's shoving her away, took another line herself. Malcolm then snatched the straw from her fingers while she was gaining competence plugging one nostril and inhaling in the other. He took a line, threw down the straw and Karen said, "Goodbye kiss, huh?"

So he kissed her. Lips, tongue, and wide open eyes from both. They laughed, Karen more than he, and then, without warning while the girl in the back was looking uncomfortable, Malcolm grabbed Seamus gruffly by the head and pulled him in for a kiss. Lips, tongue, and his eyes closed while Seamus' were open.

"Malcolm! That looked more romantic than mine," Karen said.

"I just didn't want to see the twinkle in his eye."

Seamus said, "I always knew you loved me."

"Yeah yeah. Hey, you could be a good kisser," Malcolm said.

Karen turned to Seamus and cocked her head with play in

her movements and asked, "Are you a good kisser, Seamus?"

Seamus looked to Malcolm, who winked.

Seamus smiled, "Better than him."

Malcolm swatted the air, "Give the guy an inch..."

"You can give me an inch," the high schooler said.

Malcolm looked mortified and Karen bubbled, "Good 'cause that's all he's got!"

"Wow!" Malcolm yelled. "Give the people cake and they ask what year the wine you're giving them will be. Fuck off, you two."

"We will," Karen said, and Seamus, opening the door for her, looked back to Malcolm and mouthed, "Thank you."

Malcolm nodded his head, held the high schooler to his chest, and gave something like a smile, the kind he did when he painted the duck on the pillar, and nodded his head.

Malcolm was gone from Seamus' life as soon as he shut the door but he was high as fuck and not sentimental yet. Plus he had an apparently eager woman with him. He would miss his friend soon, but before he had much time to grasp that this was the end, as life is abundant with, he was in Karen's room and she was turning on a single light with a pink light bulb and bringing out her own coke supply from a drawer.

"I've got some Veuve in the fridge," she said.

Seamus pulled it out. "This is a nice bottle. A really nice bottle. I see the bride and groom drink it sometimes at the weddings I work."

"It's nice but not that nice. It's still on fucking Vons Club." She took a line, continued, "No man I marry will be drinking Veuve with me on my wedding day.

Seamus shrugged and opened it, as he knew how to do, without a pop. Karen twisted her head and looked at him. "Nice!" Then she took the bottle and handed him a straw.

He took a line and before he could put the straw down she was handing him back the bottle, and before he could put the bottle down she was wrapped a leg around his and kissed him.

They made out for only a few moments when she stopped and said, "Malcolm was right, you are a good kisser."

"You are too," Seamus said.

"Malcolm also said you're a good photographer. I tend to agree. I saw your picture with the snails on the tree. It was gorgeous."

"Malcolm said that?" Seamus asked, incredulous.

Karen pulled her face back. "Gosh, you want me to call him over so he can kiss you some more?"

Seamus smiled. "You would just never know. I'm glad you like it though." He kissed her a few times on the lips, cheek, neck. He pulled his head back and said, "I read some of your poetry in *Open*. Most of the assholes at this school can't write their way out of..."

"A paper bag?"

"As long as it's recycled."

"Very clever. Listen to you, making a joke. You're not all in here," she tapped his head.

"What are you talking about?"

"I always see you walking around. You look so serious, so deep in thought."

Seamus reddened, reached for the champagne, drank. She continued.

"Such a thoughtful boy. I wonder about what though, always wonder if I can get in there and see myself."

"You'd think we knew each other," Seamus said and regretted it. He was about to get laid and he did not want to point out the obvious, as though she had forgotten somehow, and that this would all evaporate if she was reminded that she was about to let a stranger into her bed.

But Karen showed she had other feelings that preceded such a reality. Crushes are like that.

"No, I don't, and that's the point."

She took the bottle and only put it down on her desk and kissed him some more, and he walked backwards, spun, and collapsed with her onto the bed where they whiled away kissing, groping, but not undressing until a sudden moment where she had him back on his back and she rose over him, put her hands on his chest, and looked down seriously. She then knelt over and turned on a Sonic Youth album, *Daydream Nation,* and grabbed the mirror and offered him some before she took some too. She put the mirror down and smiled at him with all the knowing in the world as "Teenage Riot" began to build in its melody, its warm-up sounding instrumentals, its dreaminess. She smiled as though all his secrets were spilling out in front of her in material form and she could pick through them as photos in an album and determine exactly what he wanted, and she straddled over him while the guitars, warm and ready, ripped awake. She in turn ripped off her pullover sweater and then his pants, smiled one more time while her tits jiggled, and sucked him off decidedly.

His body was thoroughly coked but aroused and somehow, after a while but eventually, he came. He might be a good kisser but she was something else entirely to him. Lying there with the nearly ugly, almost angry, but constant and hammering "'Cross the Breeze" beating through the pink lit room, more coke and more champagne and a naked chest all offered to him though he did nothing to earn any of it, he wondered just what his aversions to this girl ever meant.

In the morning, or rather the afternoon when he woke up, having nearly watched the sun rise the night before as he and Karen stayed up for hours talking and kissing, at one point he ate her out, he woke up before she did. His head hurt and his chest felt weak, and he slowly rose out of bed. The pink light was on, some album by Tom Waits was on, and and looked at Karen, who rolled over to her side in her sleep. For as quickly as time goes by in bed, it goes on that much longer in the bookend moments before and especially after. He would see Karen again, he knew, and then wondered if even that was true. He was hungover, tired, sad, and weak. He needed to eat and he left her alone to sleep, feeling nearly confused and whatever elation he experienced the night before gone and drained, distant, not coming back for a good while.

He did see her again, the night before his final in Irish Nationalism was due. More cocaine, more booze, and this time sex. More elation. And somehow more thoughts about Rachel. The next day he tried in vain to start his paper for the fourth time. It never seemed right, and try as he might he could not turn in something embarrassing, which his lifeless response to *Examining Irish Nationalism in the Context of Literature, Culture, and Religion,* felt to him. The book was by some Mick named Eugene O'Brien, and Seamus felt no more Irish than he did before taking the class. The book's subtitle was "A Study of the Epistemological Structure of Nationalism." It was a perfectly appropriate summation of whatever the class was supposed to teach, and meanwhile all he could think about was how to expedite the bettering of his hangover and how of all people he actually enjoyed sexually might just be the worst thing that ever happened to him. His liver had been doing so well lately.

Finally, out of juice and out of hope, Seamus watched the time turn to five in the corner of his laptop screen, two and a half pages into his five page final. Had he really felt the burning need, he probably could have slammed out the remainder of the final in an hour. An hour was only an hour and that should only irritate his professor, but not bar him from turning in his assignment. Most deadlines, Seamus had found out, were in name only, with professors taking as many as two days after the fact to finally go to their mail box and pick up the loose ends.

But Seamus, realizing the futility of the class and regarding it as a painful reflection of the arbitrary nature of his education as a whole, said "fuck it," quite literally and aloud to himself, and lit up a half-eighth joint he had been saving for the end of finals and smoked with his roommate and hall mates. He allowed his fate this semester to seal, and just wanted it to be done with itself already.

And so, weeks later when his report card relieved all his great academic fears, and he marveled looking back on his previous assignments that he had apparently done better than he had thought he had all along to get a D even without a final, he rejoiced in the same way he nearly pissed the semester away: getting quite stoned. He would be doing that a lot this summer, his cutting-back-from-partying period over and done. All he had to do for the next few months was put plates on tables and pick them up afterwards. Over the summer he would even hear from Karen a couple times, getting laid both times, and one of those without cocaine involved. He would still take pictures, some of her, and he even texted Malcolm who texted him back. There was little to say and so he did not contact him again, but he did not regret that he had in the first place at all. Malcolm was hard to get a hold of, but his reply back meant that he meant it when he told Seamus he was trying to be something good.

For a while, Seamus felt damn near invincible. But given the narrow confines of his summer world, school a memory and Singing Pines a joke, his parents supporting him for his annual warm-weather stay, life was easy again, made sense once more, and his brooding selfishness a charming quirk. Life was good when he had what he wanted, and for just a little while longer, he wanted for nothing.

8

Meanwhile Angela got what she thought she wanted: some attention from a man. But halfway through their first time alone together the reality of the situation smacked her in the face. She was on a first date. And oh dear, it had been a while.

She looked at him. His name was Bryce and he was 23 going on 13. Angela watched him struggle with his chopsticks, sticking his tongue out of his mouth, furrowing his brow, and staring with the fixed concentration of a surgeon at work.

"Bryce...Bryce, hey!"

"Yo?" he asked and looked up at her.

"Try it like this," Angela demonstrated, her form perfect and the rice remaining solidly intact as she raised it up and out of the soy sauce.

Bryce mimicked her as best as he could and managed better than he had thus far. He laughed a tumbling, blocky chuckle as he chewed, and said through muffled words, "Damn girl! You really know how to eat!" He then put his hands together and bowed to her.

She poured herself more sake and ignored Bryce's cup. She thought about Michael, who she had dated for four years. She thought about him constantly, and sometimes with more severe regret than usual. It had only been two months since they had broken up, or rather, since he dumped her. But the end came sooner than that. The end came many months before, and despite her leaving Singing Pines earlier, allowing her to have more time with him on weekend nights, he only pulled farther away, not closer. And there she was, still leaving early, only to go out listlessly with friends or return to her apartment alone, drinking wine and seeing what was on TV. It seemed like nothing was on, ever. Just a parade of emotional faces, babbling chatter, synthetic music, listless laughter, product close-ups, forced fights, crocodile tears, yelling, confusion, and the endlessness of a fixed world that offered a sterile but magnetic company. It was an endless stream of stimulation that did not stimulate, it only lulled her, along with the wine, into the depths of survival mode. And while all her biological and financial needs were easily met, it felt as though any sense her life had was swept away in an ice storm while she huddled inside her home, warm, buzzed, and breathing. She was getting by.

While she never awoke in the middle of the night, watching her date order another bottle of Sapporo, his third, made her feel as though she was awakening from some dull, depressing dream. And yet, given reality, the dream was better.

"You're having another beer?"

"You're taking all the sake, girl. Hey, how's this?" His chopstick abilities were improving but his sushi often fell apart, too saturated by soy sauce, and the sticks too loose, too close together, too shaky.

Still, he managed the entire bite in his mouth. "Konichiwa, bitches," he said while chewing.

Angela finished the sake and asked for a second beer glass. Bryce watched her as she poured half his bottle into it and took a long sip. When she finally shook off the creeps of his staring eyes and met them, his dumb smile arrested her. He was having a *great* time. How could anyone be enjoying this?

"Ah yeah, crunk time," he said and raised his arms up at

ninety degree angles, twisting at his hips. "Drink that shit, girl. More the merrier."

She breathed in and out quickly. Suddenly, she felt a surge of power well up inside her. It warmed her cheeks and kindled a fire of resolve deep within her. This heat was not simply alcoholic courage, but the rise of a power already within her, primal, and until now resting dormant. It felt similar to anger, but was stronger, and cleaner. Her thoughts were less hazy, and her intention more focused. She was able to look at Bryce and clearly determine that he was too stupid a human being, too obviously an oops baby to warrant anger. Further, he reminded her of other boys, for despite their age they were far from men. And he was a nuisance, utterly. An oops baby... he was an oops in her evening. He was a detour in the road. No matter how boring that road might be, it was hers.

She wanted to get home. Even if to just watch TV and drink a little bit more before calling it in, she wanted to get home. And Bryce was in her way.

"You need to drink your own shit, too. I have to go."

"Oooh, you said a naughty word."

"You've been swearing since I picked you up."

"Yeah but you're a lady. Where are your manners, girl?"

She could feel her breath power through her nostrils. Like everything else, it too felt hot, determined.

"Stop calling me, girl. I've told you already."

"Yeah but then you stopped asking me not to so I thought you got over it."

"I'm not over it. Drink up, I have to get going."

Bryce reached for his beer gingerly but kept his eyes on Angela as he drank. She watched him icily, and he finished the beer quickly. His brown eyes were indeed a window to his soul, his stupid, backwards soul. And Angela had no doubt by the concerned look within them that her message was being received loud and clear. Konichiwa, bitch. Not into you.

"Yo Sensei! Check please," he asked the sushi chef. Angela could feel the fire lessen, by just a crackle. She pitied him. But it was too late for those feelings.

After signing - thank God he did not ask to go Dutch, she could feel it coming all dinner long - Bryce did a curious thing.

"Wait," he motioned to Angela to sit down. He ripped off a square from the customer receipt and began folding it. Angela did not sit, but watched quietly. The fire hissed and she stroked her keychain.

Bryce, tongue out as it had been while he labored with his chopsticks, was creating some kind of origami from the small paper. And when he was finished his face relaxed, as did his whole posture, and throwing his shoulders back against his chair he clapped his hands and pointed to the tiny paper crane resting in front of him.

For all the fire, Angela could giving nothing more than a shrug of her shoulders and a listless "That's nice," in response. It lasted only a single, wild second, but the feeling was profound that something had gone crazy, and she was not sure if it was the world or her.

Bryce stood and waved the crane around her face and over her head. "Damn girl, this bird likes you!"

Angela avoided eye contact with everyone and left promptly. The wait staff said something in Japanese to her followed by "thank you," to which Bryce turned and bowed. He then followed quickly after his date who was already in the car.

He tumbled into the passenger seat and asked, "You in a hurry, sunshine?"

Angela reversed hard and broke quickly. The crane, which was resting on the dash, flew out the open window, and Bryce yelled "Shit!" and jumped out as she began to drive forward. She braked and watched him flop through the parking lot in her rear view mirror, chasing a crane that scooted through vacant spaces carried by the wind.

He retrieved it and powered to her car, breathing heavily.

"You're a personal trainer. How are you out of breath from that?"

Bryce stuck up his index finger. "Passion, plus resolve, are an adrenaline cocktail."

She put the car in drive and realized that she would be in her car alone with this man for roughly ten minutes. Ten more minutes of her life would be shared with this strange person whom she met at a bar and gave her number too flippantly during a rare night out with friends she had not seen in a long time.

And thinking back on that night, the best of her friends among them visiting from back east and hence the celebration, she remembered little but the laughter, of which was great and plentiful and rang best of her recent memories.

And why had she given this strange man her number? She could not remember what he said to her. She just remembered that he made her laugh, and that she laughed with her friends after he left their table. Thinking on it now, they were not just laughing with him.

So, if it was survival mode she was in these days, then survive she would, including this car ride.

"That creation of yours is certainly something to be passionate about, too. I'd have to travel to the Far East to see something remotely like it," she told him.

"Oh shit, girl, I'm pretty much the whole world in one dude! I train at least one person from each race. I even train some Navajo cat! I'm like versed in all kinds of different shit. All mixes together, too. We're like, basically the same person."

"Wow. Well, did you know that all the land on earth used to be connected? Every continent was just part of one great, land mass. It was called Pangea."

"That's me! That's fucking me!"

"Which foreign countries have you been to?"

"Shit, none of them. I hate airplanes. Motherfuckers fall from the sky." Bryce looked at her. "Hey girl, what you smiling at?"

"Nothing."

"Only crazy people smile at nothing. And clowns. Those fools never stop smiling. Shit, except the sad ones. You ever seen a sad clown, girl?"

She could not hold it any longer. "Stop it!" she said.

"Now you're straight up laughing at me, too. I've seen sad clowns. Paintings of them at least. Like, I don't know where... but I have," he said and thoughtfully played with his fingers, as though counting back through the years on an excavation into his past.

"I know what you mean. I've seen paintings of sad clowns, too. And I also don't know where."

Bryce slapped his once-contemplated hands onto his knees and beamed. "Fuck yes! Why can't we figure this out? Where have we seen them goddamn sad clowns?"

Angela snickered. "I don't think we can know. It's just like a weird experience that you've had but it's not important enough to register how or why it happened."

"But goddamn you know that it did!"

"Yep. And that, Bryce, is sometimes all you have. You know it happened, whatever it was."

"Yeah! Like when I made this bomb ass stew out of whatever the hell I had in the fridge and when my roommates got home they were like, 'The fuck's our food at!' But then they ate that shit and were like, 'Damn!' And you know what? I can't remember what I made it with! But I know it was good."

"Hmm, okay. That's probably in the same ballpark. You like to cook?"

"Ohhh buddy! I'm an amazing cook. When people eat the food I make they're like, 'Wait a minute...is that my ninety year-old grandma or just some chill ass dude?' And I straight up transport people with my Chicken Carciofi."

"Chicken Carciofi. Now that's special to me, actually. When I graduated college I went backpacking through Europe for two months, just my best friend and me. She lives in Pittsburgh now."

"Pittsburgh? What an idiot! That place sucks my balls!"

"Name one thing about it."

"It's named after B.O."

"Okay, well she works for Songwhale which is based there. She's brilliant, actually, and not an idiot. Anyway -"

"Shoot. I wouldn't work for the Queen of England if it meant I had to live in that dump."

"Well, the Queen of England isn't likely to relocate there.

I heard she turned down an offer from Songwhale, anyway."

"Now you're playing with me!"

"And you're interrupting me. I'm trying to tell you about the Chicken Carciofi I had in rural Tuscany."

"I don't care where you had it. You never had it in my kitchen."

"No. But I did have it in the village of Colonnata, which is a tiny quarrying town in the Apuan Alps. The same quarries that modern people have mined for marble were once used in ancient times. They even found a relief of the Roman god Silvanus there."

There was a long hush before Bryce asked, "Girl?"

"Yes?"

"You fascinate my ass!"

"Thanks, Bryce."

"You're very welcome Angela," Bryce said, and proudly smiled at her as though calling her by her actual name was equal in measure to having traveled halfway around the world.

Angela arrived at Bryce's apartment complex, which was called "El Dorado," and was alluded to multiple times earlier in their date as he was excited to inform her it was also known as "The City of Gold."

"Ready, Freddie?" she asked.

Bryce laughed and clapped slowly.

"To get out and go home, so I can go home myself," she said.

"Ah," Bryce said, and then lunged forward to kiss her on the cheek. He immediately sprung back before she could react in any meaningful way with a push or other sign of disinterest. He left quickly but turned to look at her and gave her a thumb's up. "Home sweet golden home!" he shouted.

Angela waved and watched him retreat behind turquoise wrought iron gates, the paint chipped and flaking. As she began to drive she saw the crane left behind on the passenger seat. She picked it up and twirled it around in her fingers, as she did later that night when she called her friend to tell her about Bryce's thoughts on Pittsburgh, and the rest of the world for that matter, all apparently within him.

It was a phone call of perfect laughter, remembered rightly in the morning and throughout the day. It had been a while, alright.

9

June had been largely good to the boys, but a creeping doubt did linger. Though Jamie and Seamus and now Cody were still afforded the leniency lately they had enjoyed for some time, Seamus' growing ponytail now tied back into itself as a knotted ball on the back of his head, a testament to the boys' tenure, none of them could help but watch their concern grow that the never-ending honeymoon might indeed have a shelf life.

The truth was that Angela was making her presence felt at Singing Pines again, and the boys feared that she was starting to overstep her bounds. After a delicious quiet spell that ended far too soon, she was strutting about the club-house with greater vitality and enthusiasm in all that she did. Her posture was no longer a dreary slouch as she held her head high and her back straight. She no longer looked down at her feet as she walked, which in its very movement had changed. Lighter on her feet, she nearly strolled through the building, her hips moving with softer and more feminine turns, a quality that was lacking ever since she got in the habit of burying her head and scurrying like a rat uncomfortable outside of the darkness.

If there was anything that anyone said outright about Angela it was that she looked happier, and it began in her eyes. The dark circles still hung beneath them, a little puffy, a little tired, but the dead vacancy had been filled. By what no one was sure, though it took little sleuthing to determine that she was getting laid again. Still, sex was not something anyone felt comfortable imagining Angela having, and instead would clumsily mention to each other, "Angela's in an awfully good mood these days."

Her behavior was tolerable at first. She was beginning to leave later at night, yes, and sure, she was sticking her nose into the business of others by asking them questions like, "How are you?" and "How's school going?" She was even taking time again to tray salads and dinners and tell people lamely, "Good work." The boys allowed her these silly but harmless missteps, acknowledging that no sweat was accumulating on their backs as a result of her forced niceties and meager attempts at managerial responsibility. What troubled them was the attitude that such pitiful deeds were often coupled with, namely a preposterous sense of entitlement that after months of absence she could simply reappear in their lives and instruct them on what to do, and be a bit of a meanie about it in the process.

It was not long before she gave the boys little chores like telling Seamus and Jamie to pre-place overlay napkins on the serving trays or to wipe down the water pitchers. They attempted resistance by telling her such things made no difference, but even they had to admit to having no defense against the argument that "standing around doing nothing isn't worth much, either." Defeated, they settled grimly to their assigned chores.

Her real crime came when she began to dip deeper into her managerial hat and pull out a rabbit everyone long assumed dead: the schedule. Indeed, assigning mindless busy work was one thing. Defiling the group dynamic under which Barry's crew flourished was quite another.

The first great thorn in their collective sides came when Angela insisted that the "downstairs crew," as she called them, was short-staffed ever since Chris was moved to the restaurant. In turn, she gave Yasmine a promotion from the snack bar. She even went so far as to wink at Barry and say, "Besides, all you boys could use another woman's touch down there."

Barry, biting his tongue hard against making a profoundly snarky comment regarding a "woman's touch down there" replied lamely, "No we don't."

"Well fine, Barry. If you want to be all macho about it. You can at least use another pair of hands."

"What I can't use is a pair of butt cheeks that's going to distract my crew. Yasmine treats this place like it's a high school dance."

"Barry! Careful with how you talk. We're friends but if corporate heard you talk that way you'd be in trouble for sexual harassment."

"Gee. Thanks Angela, old pal."

"Oh Barry. Yasmine's a hard worker. She's just...vivacious."

"Is that an STD?"

"Barry! No it means-"

"I know, I know what it means. Fine. But when Alfredo is caught literally with his pants down in the linen closet don't cry to me. You know they're dating, don't you?"

"Of course I know that, Barry. And I think she'll help keep him in line. I see how he horses around with Felipe. Alonzo's impressionable, too, and he's spending a lot of time with the two of them."

"I'm telling you, Angela. You're looking for trouble and making everything harder on everyone for no reason."

"Barry, you're the best captain we have. You can handle an eighteen year old girl."

If only Angela, or anyone for that matter, knew just how

much trouble Yasmine's promotion would cause. Though no one knew it, she had eyes for more than one.

If that was not enough, Angela was beginning to think outside of her cubicle walled box and suggest bold new ideas, like special dinner nights for country club members. And before anyone knew it, the simply titled "Tequila Night" was on the Singing Pines banquet calendar. If there was one night to remember for Barry's boys, Tequila Night was impossible to forget.

The evening began pleasantly. Angela wowed the room with her date, namely because she had one. Gone were the assumptions that she had managed to bed a couple of losers at the Red Door Tavern. This was bona fide proof that she had a boyfriend already, and one that appeared happy to be with her. A veritable dummy, Bryce never stopped smiling and was immediately and obviously harmless, even sweet, to everyone who talked to him. While he made it clear repeatedly that he was a personal trainer, he was never pushy about his services as many in his field often are. He passed out no business cards, and would instead share simple accounts of the pride he felt when watching some of his clients overcome personal obstacles. By the end of the night, three people had his phone number and assured him they would "be in touch."

On all accounts, he was accepted as a lovable goofball, and probably poor as fuck. Certainly no one in the room ate dinner as quickly as he ate his.

Angela, often looking at him like he was her little brother whom she had to constantly correct and keep in line, was nonetheless as happy as she had ever been lately. She talked to coworkers and country club members alike with equal flare. She even shocked the banquet servers when she carried a tray of tequila shots to the service area.

"Salud!" she cheered.

Jamie, Seamus, and Cody took the first three shots, and later, the last three. They took other shots in between, namely from a bottle that Jamie regarded as his greatest lift of his career.

"They fucking paid for it, all these bums, just like the champagne!" he slurred.

"Fucking salud," Cody laughed, swayed, fell back against the railing, and grabbed Seamus by the collar. "We're made men."

"Untouchable," Seamus said. "And with all that drama going on, we're invisible, too." He nodded at Jamie.

Jamie pointed the bottle at him and became emotional. "You remember all that I taught you," he said, his voice cracking.

Looking like a trio of initiates fresh from Frat row, they held themselves upright after nearly knocking each other down. The made men, drunk in the darkness with tables bussed and the crème brûlée served, were easily visible to Fernando as he stood by, smoking a rare cigarette, and wondering what was going to happen next.

It had been a rocky night for him, but it was not over yet. His brother was essentially drunk, or at least as much as anyone could be from four shots. His trouble began early in the evening, when Fernando politely refused to take a shot with the rest of the crew. Yasmine also passed on hers.

"That's okay baby, I got something else you can drink," Alfredo told her. He pawed at her face with a lecherous hand, looking into her eyes.

She broke eye contact swiftly, and told him, "Later, baby."

Alfredo watched her walk merrily away, catching up behind Fernando, and when he looked behind him at the only other person in the room, Alonzo, smiling nervously and nodding his head.

"Something else you can drink, that's funny dawg," the young cousin said and offered a fist to pound.

"Nah, that girl thinks she's in charge now. I tell you something, she didn't think that the other afternoon. I had her begging me to get in her."

"Oh yeah?" Alonzo asked, his eyes glittering.

"I had her tied to her bed posts, just teasing her little pussy, tick tock, I was going back and forth like that with my peepee," he laughed. Then, picking up two shots, "Cheers cousin."

"I already had one."

"Have another."

Alonzo eyed the plastic cup like it was hazardous material, rotating it in his fingers.

"It's okay cousin, drink for your brother. He's too busy wiping himself between his legs to have a toast with you."

Alonzo lifted his eyes from the shot. "No, no, my brother's a good man," he said.

"He's good, of course he is," Alfredo said. "He's good at being a fifi! Drink!"

Alonzo did but wearily, and said, "You know Yasmine is that way with everybody. My brother isn't trying to take her."

"He couldn't take her if she drank that whole bottle of tequila. She only wants me. But I don't think he thinks that."

"C'mon man, he's your own cousin! Show him some

respect!"

"Shhh. Have another drink, cousin. I'm kidding with you. Don't be so uptight."

And Alonzo drank again. His stomach felt warm. He felt happy, but guilty. He always looked up to Alfredo, loved him. Of course he loved his brother too, but his cousin possessed characteristics Fernando did not and never would. The trouble with Alfredo, as Alonzo knew however, was that no one could really know him. There was a wiliness there, a slipperiness that even those closest to him wrestled with, forgot about, and wrestled with again, his moods fluctuating, his motives appearing mixed, hidden, beguiling.

Alonzo only needed to hear the sudden brusqueness Alfredo's tone adopted to be reminded of this slithering nature. But still, he always gave his older cousin a chance.

"Just keep your head up now, I haven't seen you drink since Miguel's birthday. And then I didn't see you for a long time!"

"I'm fine, cousin." Alonzo tottered across the room to grab a hand tray. "I'm just fine."

"You're fine like my culo after I eat Sancho's habenero sauce. You're shit faced and you've only had three shots!"

"Bull."

"Bull?" Alfredo laughed meanly. "Bull! Tough man, oh shit. Who says 'bull' around you? It's not your mommy or daddy. Maybe your brother thinks he sounds like a cowboy when he says 'bull' to you when you ask him about Yasmine."

Alonzo frowned. "I don't ask him anything about Yasmine. There's nothing to ask."

"Bull!" Alfredo mocked him.

"Bull," Alonzo mocked back.

Yasmine fluttered into the room, smiling, bright-eyed, happy.

"Wanda and Angela are really drunk!" she said. "This is a funny night!"

"Girl, you think Alonzo is handsome? Like, you think you would be his hyna?"

"Alonzo is so handsome," she said. "I would be his girl-friend."

Alonzo looked shy but smiled.

"What about his brother? You think he's handsome?"

Yasmine still smiled, but quietly. Alfredo smiled, but sinisterly. The three of them shared a tense triangle of broken glances and awkward postures.

"I think I work with the most handsome boys in the world," she said. "I'd be lucky to be anyone's girlfriend here."

Alfredo rose darkly away from the wall he was leaning on and looked deeply into Yasmine's eyes. "Well aren't you lucky then? Have a shot with me, girl."

"Baby I don't drink." Her voice was hushed. She resisted his arms around her and headed out the room.

Alfredo scoffed. "Two days ago cousin, and she's my valentine in the summer time. You'd think she wanted to wake up next to me everyday."

Alonzo shrugged. Here he was, in the nether regions again. What was his cousin after? He did not have long to cook up a response, though. They were interrupted.

"Jesus! Is it butt-picking hour at the Singing Pines Cantina already?" Barry said when he walked in on the two cousins doing nothing together.

Alfredo started, "Barry, I'm just giving my cousin a talking-to about tonight. He gets a little tequila in him and then he starts getting stupid, looking at chi-chis everywhere and dropping plates and -"

"No way dawg!"

"I see you out there, your eyes are as big as your hands when you touch yourself at night."

"Stupid!"

"You're both fucking stupid. No more tequila for either of you or you'll have to escort Wanda home tonight. She needs two men tonight, maybe three. Her husband can't handle all that woman on his own."

Though Barry was joking, Wanda's husband, known behind his back as Mr. Wanda, was not when he told her assistant's uncomfortable boyfriend that he hoped his wife had something left for him when they got home. He said this calmly while Wanda hooked her toned, 53-year old leg around a speaker and pulled in close to feel the bass vibration from *Flesh for Fantasy*. Mr. Wanda nodded his head along, smiling his lazy but large smile, his teeth so white they nearly appeared to glow.

The boyfriend excused himself from Mr. Wanda and joined his girlfriend at the bar.

"That's two caddys," he said, catching the bartender in time.

"Sweetie, I was just getting one for you," she said.

"Have one with me. I finally got away from that creep Wanda married."

She looked delighted. "I remember when you said the Christmas party was enough Singing Pines for one year."

"Don't get excited over it or anything."

"I'm just happy to have you step into my world." She kissed him on the cheek and leaned her head onto his shoulder and secured her arm against the crook of his elbow.

Then Alonzo smacked into her sending her margarita all over her.

"Hot damn!" Mr. Wanda said, rushing over with a napkin. "Hey Bucko, that busboy made your girlfriend wet before you did."

"Yeah," he said, glaring at Alonzo, who stood still, speechless, and shaking.

"It's alright, it's alright," she said, wincing as she dried herself with the napkins Mr. Wanda had brought over.

Alonzo began to back up, and stammered, "I didn't see... my head was down...I'm so sorry."

"It's alright Alonzo, you have a tough job."

Her boyfriend was ignoring Alonzo now and covering his girlfriend with his jacket. "Well you didn't want a margarita anyway."

"No but I sure got one."

"Yeah you did."

Alonzo looked around him and saw Angela and Wanda looking at him. Their eyes were bleary but demeaning. He felt like he did when his mother caught him puking in the backyard after his cousin's birthday, his throat burning and his knees shaking, hearing her voice rain on him with threats of punishment and rising exclamations regarding his disobedience.

He went back to the service area not knowing where else to

turn. When he got there, Cody and Jamie were laughing over the bus tubs, and then, Cody started, "Just the motherfucker I was looking for!"

"Guys, I made Wanda's assistant spill her drink on herself."

"But did you feel her tits?" Cody asked him.

"No...maybe," he considered. Did he? Actually, yeah, he probably did. It was a quick but full contact collision and carrying a hand tray his hands had certainly been up. The irony! The only silver lining of such a folly and now it was a mere ghost of a memory relived in the minds of others.

"Ah, you guys don't even know her," Jamie said. "I've gotten the gazebo runner from her plenty of times. Her name's Crystal and all I know is she's chill as fuck and won't even trip."

"Yeah. And you touched her tits! Fuck, I wish I didn't look where I was going when I walked around," Cody laughed.

"Hey man, tough dance out there with the Wedding Planner's Assistant," Seamus said as he entered the room.

"It was a dance alright," Alonzo said.

"Looked like you got a feel, though," he said.

"Yeah, I think I did."

"He's the fucking man!" Cody yelled.

There were four shots left on the tray. Jamie handed one of them to Alonzo.

"To making all the other guys jealous," Jamie toasted.

"No, no, no. That's how all this started."

"Your hands are shaking, man. You need to chill out. Have a shot," Seamus said.

"Guys, no."

"What if we take them with you?" Cody offered, as though that should be significant.

"Guys..."

"I got my shot ready," Seamus said. He handed the last one to Cody. "So does Cody."

Alonzo looked at the boys. They wore the friendliest faces he had seen all night. Shrugging, he said, "How much worse could it get, I guess?"

"Now you're making sense," Cody said.

"Cheers, fellas," Alonzo said.

"Cheers killer," Jamie said. They all drank.

"What a night," Alonzo said.

"What a night is right, cousin," Alfredo said, looking concerned.

"What's wrong?" Seamus asked.

"I have to talk to my cousin," Alfredo told him.

The boys looked at each other and nodded their heads. This was a family matter. They excused themselves to the dining room and got back to work walking around with dirty plates on their trays they took from the bus tubs.

"Barry's looking for you. He's pissed."

"Man! But Crystal said it's alright."

Alfredo shook with nervous laughter. "She said that to *you*, cousin."

"Oh no, oh no! Shit man, fuck me, oh no..."

"Shhh! You sound like a fifi! Now Listen to me. Go outside

and sit on the stairs. I'll cover for you. Hell, even your damn brother is taking care of your tables. Just make yourself hard to find. Barry will cool down and his peepee will go down again. Right now he's looking to fuck you."

"I don't want to get fucked! I need this job!"

"Shhh! I told you! Get outside. Your cousin and your brother have this."

Alonzo did as he was told. In the dining room, Fernando asked his cousin, "Where's my brother? I didn't see him in the back or upstairs. I checked outside too."

"How would I know? Fool is probably puking in the bathroom. He took shots like he begs for pussy. You can't stop him."

"Shut up. This is serious."

"Oh? Why so serious?" Alfredo tried to sound like Heath Ledger. It was butchered, but Fernando got the point.

"You are a real joker, funny guy all the time."

"Hey, watch out for your own brother. He's not my responsibility."

Fernando went to check the bathroom. He saw Isabelita in the lobby.

"Fernando, there you are! I'm looking for your brother."

"That makes two of us...at least."

"He's been talking to Alfredo all night but now Alfredo said he doesn't know where he is. Listen, you know I have younger brothers. I know how it is."

Fernando shook his head. "Thanks for telling me about Alfredo. Hey, I'm checking the men's bathroom upstairs. Can you check the women's bathrooms? You never know."

Isabelita rubbed his shoulder. "You're a good brother. Yes, I'll look for him."

Meanwhile, Alonzo shivered outside. He was not cold but he was dizzy, and he struggled to determine when it was right to go back inside to work. He shook with the thought of it all, the purgatory he was in now, wondering when it would end, how it would end, and would his face ever be a welcomed sight inside again? The stair steps were a hard seat and he squirmed on them, looked at the dark course, a swallow of unseeable land that gave the deck a floating quality. He was alone, all right, washed up on the shore of a bad day at work. He never had one when he worked in a local store as a child in Mexico, and he did that for four years. It took hardly more than four months at Singing Pines before he erred, and in such a high profile fashion.

Finally Barry came outside to smoke a cigarette. He looked queerly at the shape on the stairs, and then approaching slowly, relaxed his shoulders when he got close and said, "I thought it was a drunk from the party." He dragged on his cigarette. "I was right."

"Barry, I'm so sorry."

"Well I understand that but I don't really think that hiding in the dark is a good way to show it."

Alonzo swallowed. "Barry, please don't fire me. I made a mistake. But I'll be better!"

Barry smoked and said nothing for a while. Other people were used to this, but Alonzo had not felt this nervous in a long time.

At last, Barry asked him, "Alonzo, are there moles in Mexico?"

Puzzled, Alonzo said, "Yes."

"Do they dig holes that make problems?"

"Yes."

"And can those molehills seem like bigger problems than they are?"

Alonzo considered. "I don't understand."

"Can a molehill sometimes seem like a mountain?"

Alonzo laughed, and felt some relief. "Yes. Sometimes in my mind they are."

"Yeah. Well sometimes in America we say things like 'Don't make a mountain out of a molehill.'"

Alonzo smiled. "C'mon Barry, I didn't move here yesterday."

Barry nodded. "Sometimes you're a fish out of water, that's all I'm saying. Have you heard that before?"

Alonzo nodded and smiled. "Yes, Barry."

"Okay. Then get back inside. No one's complimented the rose Yasmine is wearing in her hair in the last three minutes and she's getting worried."

Alonzo laughed again. "I told her she looked beautiful twice already!"

"Yep. Thank Angela."

"What did Angela do?"

"Lots of things, Alonzo. Get inside. I just used up all the nice guy I had in me for the year."

Alonzo said little more to anyone for the rest of the night. Except when he talked to his brother, and said, "You were right about our cousin."

And so later in the night, standing outside and smoking a cigarette that an excited Cody gave him, Fernando watched his drunken coworkers revel. What world did they come from that they could act this way? Fernando was not old but he was older than them, and yet they were older than his brother. Somewhere in this whole mess of a night, probably a big success for the clubhouse but a disaster for the crew, the iceberg had lifted finally from the ocean. And watching one part of the crew sway outside carelessly, he thought about his brother swaying inside dangerously, and the evil look on their cousin's face, no doubt the chief instigator in this terrible ordeal. Perhaps Barry would tell him too that this was but a molehill, but Fernando never sat down, this simple break now so rare that had Barry opted to smoke just a bit later he and the captain might have their first honest talk. No, Fernando was a man of action even if the action was menial. And when it was not, when the action required had implications larger than workplace routines and simple customer service, his mind went turning along a dial that could not be stopped.

Above all else, because it was in the back of his mind and formed the spine of all his thoughts, he thought about Yasmine.

She had asked him for another ride home.

When Fernando walked back inside, the mood was as he feared it would be. Alfredo, taunting his brother, was saying, "Oh? You're growing hair on your nuts all of a sudden? Let me see, I can't believe it."

Alonzo was pushing his antagonizer away. "I'm not playing with you. You got me in trouble out there, dawg. I didn't think you would ever do that to me."

Alfredo laughed. Fernando hated the sound!

"You got yourself in trouble - I've seen five year old girls hold tequila better than you."

"That's enough!" Fernando barked, his shoulders raised and his back arched.

Alfredo did not flinch. He turned on his heels, smiled deviously, and said, "Oh? You've got hair on your nuts now, too?"

"Wise guy. Funny man, huh?"

"It's a little late, cousin. I'd give you a shot to celebrate but your fifi brother beat you to them."

"Listen. You say whatever you want about me."

Alfredo clapped his hands hard. "What do you think I'm doing now?"

Fernando continued, his voice throbbing. "But you leave my brother out of this. You hear me?"

Alfredo took a step forward and developed his own air of firm authority. "Then next time you go near my girl, why don't you tell her how big and strong you were for little Panchito over there. I'm sure she'll be just so impressed. 'Oh Fernando,'" he said, in a mocking voice. "'Oh Fernando, how brave! How strong! Oh Fernando!'" His eyelids fluttered like butterfly wings.

Alonzo wanted to speak up, to say something that would not divide what was already a broken relationship. And he wanted to stick up for himself and not allow Alfredo the pervasive thought that only Fernando could save him. He knew he had picked sides already, more than once, and had a foot on each side of the line in the sand so what good was he? He needed a diversion, just something to end it.

"We need to mop up in here," he said, feeling stupid, weak, and guilty.

"Then let's go then," Fernando said, still staring into Alfredo's eyes.

Alfredo put his hands out and took a sideways step. Fernando walked with Alonzo soberly upstairs, their thumping footsteps disappearing into the Mexican rock music blaring from the kitchen. Alfredo got to work wiping down the counters around the sink and coffee machines, the ice machine, and the cake cutting table. He rapped to himself. He nodded his head like a rooster. He was alone and felt like he burned with the peace of God. He was at peace, deeply so, with his own actions. That was enough for him.

When the evening was over he said to Yasmine, "C'mon girl. I'm taking you home."

"I thought you were going to the races?"

"Not tonight. The races are boring. I don't need them."

"Please! You live for the races."

"What if tonight I live for you?"

"Tonight...what about next Saturday night?"

"Then too," he kissed her and she weakly accepted. He laughed and put his arms around her. She rested in them, looking uneasy. "You getting shy? Like when I first met you."

"No. I think you should go to the races. You love going, I know you do."

"Nah, girl. I told you! C'mon. I'll take you dancing."

Alfredo started c-walking in place, rapping to himself, and Yasmine had to giggle. When she saw the side she loved, she loved him all over again.

Fernando walked in to the service area but backed out quickly. He was going to tell Yasmine it was time to clock out, to go home, but he knew better.

He knew his head would ache in the morning, but he asked Cody for another cigarette and smoked on the way home, all the windows down and the air rushing into the car loud and warm. He and his brother would have to shout to hear each other, but it was just as well. Neither said a word.

10

Other than the incident between Alonzo and Crystal, none of the behind-the-scenes drama of Tequila Night was made evident to anyone involved with the event, which was widely regarded as a success. Attending members who filled out questionnaires were all highly positive in their comments, and nearly every one of them said they would attend another like event, such as a night devoted to a different spirit. Even unapologetic Wanda, immune to shame even after mounting a speaker, paid Angela a compliment. The Food and Beverage Manager, in all her giddiness, called Bryce first, even above her own father, who knew much better than her boyfriend just how difficult it was to cause Wanda the Ice Queen to thaw.

For their own part, the boys used Tequila Night as a way to galvanize their standing in the club and to remind themselves just who was in charge. They needed to let loose the way they did to cement the fact to themselves that no one was going to take away the driver's keys once they had their hands on a BMW. This was their club, and their hubris was so great that just days later, when Angela and Wanda both had days off, Jamie and Seamus went to the driving range for a spell. There was something buzzing about Jamie and not even the mad man himself knew just what his own buzz meant. There was simply a desire and it burned, and whatever it was Jamie wanted, he was going to get. They both knew that.

And so, taking a piss after finishing a bucket of driving balls each, Jamie's dad's clubs already back in the Saturn,

Jamie paced listlessly, thinking. And then, looking into the mirror and asking himself, in all seriousness, "What's in your wallet?" he stood back and blinked at his reflection, as though an epiphany was hatching from its egg within his skull.

"Seamus," he said and removed his wallet, from which he produced a grocery store club card. Seamus, still considering what relevance a Capital One ad campaign had to do with anything, nodded his head, questioning.

"Just an ordinary card. Right? And this," he said, knocking on the door to the liquor room, "is just a ordinary door, right? And this," he said, jiggling the locked knob, "is just an ordinary knob that won't open because of an ordinary lock."

"That's a whole lot of ordinary," Seamus said.

"Exactly. And ordinary works with ordinary. Earthlings breathe Earth air, round pegs go in round holes."

Jamie slid the card into the slat of the door and made little work out of the lock. Opening the door and smiling at Seamus like a realtor inviting a married couple to have a look at a hot property overlooking the canyon in which Singing Pines itself was located, said, "Ordinary is right. This place didn't exactly spring for Brinks when it came to the liquor department."

"Hell no. They put it in the fucking bathroom after all."

"Yep. Now what'll it be? Goose or Kettle?"

The following night Jamie and Seamus stood outside the cart garage during a break and passed a fifth of vodka to each other, swaying and drinking like a couple of bums on a warm, summer night. Cody was somewhere on the driving range, pissing and laughing, and swaying too. When he returned, his voice was alive with innocent joy. It made Jamie and Seamus feel alive themselves.

"It's fucking beautiful out there!" Cody wailed.

"It's beautiful everywhere!" Jamie agreed.

"I was pissing right in the middle of the goddamn thing. Like 200 yards deep." He laughed hard. His laugh was a reckless, party boy wallop. It had the carelessness of a child's - the only difference was puberty.

"Stars everywhere," Seamus said.

"Yeah! I was spinning around looking at them, thought I was going to puke," Cody said.

Jamie shook his head. "Drink up. It'll settle your stomach."

Cody nodded along and took a long pull, stuck out his tongue and shook his head. "I'd hate to drink fucking Popov." Then, looking back up at the stars, "Hey. Do you guys think the Greeks were drunk when they made up the constellations? I was looking at Cassiopeia and I was just thinking how in the fuck is that a woman?"

Cody was sincere but Jamie and Seamus were leaning against each other, laughing. It was contagious, and Cody laughed with them, his voice lifting above theirs. It was loud. It was wild. And most of all it was free. It was a laugh like Jamie's, identical in spirit. Seamus loved him for it.

It had been a couple months since Cody began tagging along with Jamie and Seamus on their smoke breaks, the hidden varieties that no one else knew about, or at least bothered to stop. Ever since he ate an extra brownie that Seamus brought to work one night, Cody had been an inseparable member of the Jamie and Seamus clique. It was about time. He had often been an odd man out at Singing Pines, an agreeable boy who got along with all and had his share of friends outside of work but never managed to make a close one at the clubhouse.

Still, Cody had remained for a long while, knowing that

however tedious his role as Singing Pines was, it easily beat out having to work for Mr. Wanda. That was his first job, and one that thankfully did not last long.

Wanda and his mother had been friends since their high school days. Her husband repaired copy machines. Cody assisted him as they drove all throughout Los Angeles and its suburbs, finding work like a pig finds truffles in the muddy earth. Mr. Wanda was successful even in unsuccessful times. This was only fitting, as from his outdated hairstyle to his flippant dismissal of ever tightening law enforcement, Mr. Wanda had the gift of endurance.

Always around five or six o'clock, driving back from wherever their calls were on horribly congested freeways, 101, 110, 134, 5, 60, 210, the 10 - he went everywhere - Mr. Wanda would tilt his seat back a few inches, ease his rubbery-looking face, adjust his Ken-doll hair and open up a tall can of Steel Reserve beer.

"Yep, I think it's a time for a beeh," he would say in his Boston accent. He would look so relaxed that Cody expected to see him light up a cigar while he was at it and put on Jimmy Buffet. But Mr. Wanda never listened to music. He only talked. On and on about subjects ranging from a selective version of libertarianism to sports and all too often about copy machines themselves. And traffic. There was always talk about the traffic. When it was especially slow-going getting home he would amuse himself with diatribes that likened the traffic to a sports event for which he was the commentator.

"Ooh, got a Corvette here, hot stuff coming through but no luck...Bronco says nope and shuts the door. Sorry Mr. VIP, you'll have to wait your turn with the rest of humanity back here, sheesh. What's that? Oh ho! Sees an opening in the diamond and takes it even though he's a party of one! We'll be seeing a timeout called if the Chips catch on to him. But that's a big 'if,' ladies and gents. They're never there when you need them," Mr. Wanda would say, and take another sip of his beer.

"Why don't we take the carpool lane?"

"Cody, the diamond is a joke. You see those taillights up there?"

"Way up there? Yeah."

"It's no faster than any other lane," then he would laugh and say, "Backseat driver, yes sir."

Cody did not understand why someone would be in denial about the advantage of carpooling. He wondered if the lane, always being watched by the Highway Patrol for strays like the Corvette, put Mr. Wanda in a more vulnerable position given his penchant for drinking through rush hour. Mostly, he just wondered if Mr. Wanda took some bizarre kind of pleasure in traffic. Maybe it meant he got to spend that much less time with his wife. Maybe he relished the extra time to bend Cody's ear.

Every once in a while Mr. Wanda asked Cody about his life. He asked him how school was going, how his girlfriend was doing, or what he thought of the Dodgers. Unfortunately, it was usually the last question which most interested Mr. Wanda. Cody was not familiar with the Dodgers, and was only a fringe fan at best when it came to any professional sports team. But Mr. Wanda was never able to notice.

"It's not pitching that's the problem, Cody. That was never the issue heading into this season, though Lilly stunk up the place any time he took to the mound. That was a disappointment."

"He had a bad season, huh?"

"You can't just divide things that way, a bad season, a good season - c'mon Cody. There's more than one side to any story and it's not that he was bad. He wasn't getting much support, either. But he wasn't stealing any, that's for sure. He only won seven games."

"So maybe it wasn't that bad a season for him, then."

"Oh so now you're making excuses for him? He didn't have the support but I just said Cody that he wasn't stealing any for them, either."

"Oh. Well, I guess they just needed more from him."

"Look, you can call it whatever you want but Lilly was the least of the Dodgers' problems. They needed more, as you toot you horn about, from a lot of guys. One thing you gotta get straight here is that pitching was never the issue, I said that already. You can't win games if you don't score. Can you?"

"No."

"In any sport, right?"

"Golf."

"Ah," he would swat the air with his beer can and take another swig. "Those jokers are just being gimmicky with all this lowest score crap. I love my Wanda but the hoity-toits she's working for over there can keep their game."

"Oh yeah, she works at a country club, right?"

"Yeah yeah, listen if you want to talk about Tiger Woods or whatever I'm not your man, Cody. Okay? Excuse me if I don't know much about golf."

"I don't either I was just-"

"Well your ears perk up when I just mention the place. But you're not getting out of this easy, no sir. You're sitting here waffling around on Lilly and I'm trying to tell you that the pitching was fine for the Boys in Blue, just fine. You watched the playoffs last year, didn't you?"

"No."

"Okay so here we are in the great era of Mannywood. Dodgers make everyone in Chavez Ravine feel something they haven't felt in a long, long time as they sweep the Cards."

"Nice."

"Nice? You're telling me! It was just a few years ago St. Louie shot the Dodgers down in a heartbreak series where the Dodgers lost games scoring only 2, 3 runs. Now what did I say?"

"You can't win if you can't score."

"Yes Cody you are right. Now all of a sudden they're hitting and they sweep an old foe but then goddamn Phillies, same team that took them out in '08, does it again. And the Dodgers just got lit up! Just lit up! Eight runs, ten runs, eleven runs. No good. No good at all."

Cody considered. "So they do need help on pitching?"

"Goddamn it Cody, that was last year! Okay big shot, you think it's all on the mound, what move do you make?"

Cody would look at Mr. Wanda. "I don't know. I really don't know anything about baseball, or the Dodgers-"

"That's fine, Cody. I'm not talking about how much of a baseball fan you are. You're telling me though that offense is a problem and I'm merely wondering what you think they should do about it? I'm just curious. Believe me, I'm over here scratching my head, too and meanwhile you're a regular Ned Colletti here so why don't you tell me what the next move should be?"

Cody would consider the question. But his mind was

somewhere else. He did not like golf but he had come to realize that there was nothing he liked less than fixing copy machines.

"They should probably look at the free agent market."

"You always look at the free agent market Cody, that never changes. Oh-what's that? You want to cut me off Honda? Go for it, I'm a patient guy. Mr. Motorcycle is on both our tails though so he's going to have his opinions...What? Hot damn! Boy!" he would whistle on top of his commotion and take a drink of beer. "You see that Cody? That Honda almost took out that motorcycle! But Moto Mike's mad now, picks up the speed and makes Honda eat his dust, off to the races sir, yes we are!"

When Cody got home that evening, he asked his mom to call Wanda. He was curious if the country club was hiring. He had an interview the next day and was hired immediately. And while it had been a long road to get here now, he was finally rubbing elbows with the clubhouse's best and brightest, and the thought of a different job never crossed his mind anymore.

"What if we started making up constellations today?" he asked.

"Dude, there'd just be a bunch of cars and shit. It'd be a goddamn traffic jam," Jamie said.

"Yes, and computers and cell phones and copy machines." Seamus looked disgusted. "One big work trip, man."

"Fuck that," Cody said.

"We're doomed," Jamie said quietly, and looked into the distance as he stole another drag at the bottle.

"Doomed," Cody repeated, wide-eyed. "Think we should head in now? We've been out here a while."

"Yeah, Barry's probably about to notice we're not around," Seamus said.

"Fuck it. He doesn't give a shit anymore. He's got Hotpants to worry about."

"Jesus Christ. It's a regular Mexican soap opera in there," Seamus said.

"I know!" Cody yelled. "Yasmine's hot, she's cold, then hot again."

"I've never, ever, seen my man Alfredo get clowned this way by a girl," Jamie said. "And now that I'm seeing it, I don't think this place will ever be the same."

"There's a rift with the Latin Lovers." Seamus shook the bottle at his friends. "And for the first time in a long time there's drama back in the clubhouse."

"This place has never had girl problems with Isabelita," Cody said.

"It never had boy problems before Fernando, either," Jamie said. "He's the last person I'd expect mixed up in workplace controversy but maybe there's more behind the curtains than we know?"

"Shit," Cody hiccuped. "Whatever it is it keeps us on the other side of the curtain."

Jamie pointed at him. "Sounds like he's one of us, huh Seamus?"

"Invisible here is everything, isn't it?" Seamus asked Jamie.

"Amen," Jamie said and shot up the side of the clubhouse to stand tall on a railing. He hid the remaining vodka on a brick window ledge underneath the second story.

The boys caught up to him and Cody whistled at the bottle's hiding spot. "This job!" Seamus beamed.

"This life!" Jamie yelled.

They were nearly arm-in-arm making their way back to work and would have worried about being too obvious if it was not for the ugly scene that awaited them. In the service area, as the three sloppily walked in single file and to pick up hand trays, Barry was scolding Alfredo.

"Just because you have your girlfriend running around here shaking her ass at you doesn't mean you can let your tables go to shit for your cousin to take care of. You'd think he had enough on his plate getting coffee for the helpless gray-hairs at Dumb, Dumber, and Dumbest's tables."

"But Barry! I don't make her kiss me on the cheek or grab for my nuts. She wants me all the time." He shrugged. "Bitch is horny."

"So you have nothing to do with it when you're making out in the elevator?"

"Barry! I can't hurt her feelings. You're a married man, you understand these things."

"The last time my wife wanted to make out with me was five years ago at a Rod Stewart concert. Don't tell me how to treat a woman."

The boys left the two of them alone and patted each other on the backs as they casually scoured the room for dirty bar glasses. Invincible, vital, and young, they felt as though they had built the clubhouse themselves and worked weekends because they felt like it. Neither Barry nor Angela nor Wanda nor Howard nor the owners themselves held any fear over their hearts. They were students and they had jobs. They were doing what they were told they should be doing, but as long as that was the case, they would do it on their own terms.

"When I come to work I do what I want," Jamie had said before to Seamus. It resonated with him then and now the sentiment had rippled towards Cody. As long as they were together, it did not matter what transpired at the clubhouse so long as they were left to their own devices.

Splitting off and joining again, crisscrossing the banquet room and meeting in the lobby, in the service area, upstairs in the kitchen, the boys joked with and heckled at each other, planned their next exit outside, determined how many bottles of champagne to take tonight.

For Seamus, he was essentially reliving the golden summer he had enjoyed a year before, though now Singing Pines was like a familiar getaway he toured in the warmest weather months, escaping the confining madness of a clockwork world he had little respect for and even less a clue about. School was leading somewhere, but he was less sure that it was leading anywhere near where it promised. It took one look at Fernando to remind him bitterly of that unsightly pill, and his throat was too dry from partying to swallow it whole just yet.

Instead he held tight to these fleeting high times, even more clockwork than his school life, but transcendent in their Sisyphean absurdity. Every night was putting plates on tables and picking them up afterwards...

But at least the rolling boulder of Singing Pines was straightforward and laid bare in its drudgery. Seamus feared a much more deceptive game, one that he was only halfway through. Sometimes, when crossing paths with Barry or Fernando, spotting Angela trudge up the stairs to leave for the night, Seamus was reminded that unlike Sisyphus' sad plight the real rock he was pushing, at least on paper, was bound to settle at the top of the hill eventually, and he would have to move forward again. At least Sisyphus never had to go to college.

Seamus could not help himself but question life after the next two miserable years. Would It still be relevant? He shuddered when considering. It would remain the only thing that was relevant. The bigger fear for him was that he would lose sight of this holy mindset in pursuit of something strikingly absurd and watch himself wander fruitlessly with no stones left to turn, instead forever looking back at his rock left idle behind him like all the rest. One by one, boulders sitting at the tops of hills, abandoned by their pushers, who had come to the apex only to savor the ecstasy of a job completed, ready to crash back down to earth harder than they ever did before when chasing the rolling stone, when they had hope for the future left turning in their stomachs. The great disillusionment of a waterless campaign through a desert of ideas and theories would bear no tillable soil, and he was seeing this, or fearing it, at hours he never wanted to be awake.

Perhaps others were waking up in the middle of the night, too. Though his roommate never did. And instead Seamus would settle back down to a restless toss and turn until sleep came finally again, like a weak dog submitting to a barely stronger master. Sometimes he wondered if getting better grades would ease his doubts, but to this lunacy he could only scoff. He might as well stay sober while working at Singing Pines. He never asked for the system, but he did agree to play by the rules, or at least most of them.

Later in the night, finishing the vodka, the boys smiled and laughed again and the fears of tomorrow were gone from Seamus' mind. Summer was good for that. Though a largely repetitious season, more so even than the school year, it blotted away the doubts and concerns that otherwise plagued him.

Of course, as often happened at Singing Pines, there were other distractions apart from a head full of booze that helped mute the chatter of a troubled spirit. Shortly after killing the vodka the boys heard a frightening sound cast a ripple in the silence that had surrounded them. They were heading inside when they heard what sounded like a snared animal, its moan husky but pierced with a high timbre that signaled the hellishness of inescapable distress. Instead of entering through the back of the banquet room, they turned the corner and headed towards the deck where they spotted Chris leaning over the railing of the exterior stairway to the restaurant, his face in his hands and his shoulders shivering. He was crying in jolting, pained spurts. Behind him Jeff stood shaking his head, saying, "C'mon Chris...Chris...Buddy, c'mon."

"Leave me alone," Chris lifted his head to groan.

"Chris, just come back inside. I'm sure this was all just a big misunderstanding."

"Fuck you."

"Hey buddy, I'm on your side."

The boys had gotten close now as Jeff could make their shapes out in the darkness. He said, "Hey look, it's the asshole patrol. Get inside boys."

They laughed. "I don't think we need to head inside unless Barry says so."

"I say so," Barry said.

"Holy shit, Barry! You're trying to scare a guy or what?" Jamie asked him.

"Where'd you come from?" Seamus asked.

"From around the back, where you idiots were doing drugs."

"Actually we were drinking," Jamie said.

"Just get inside."

The boys obeyed. Barry looked at Chris and Jeff and began, "Now what the hell is going on here?"

"It's restaurant business, Barry. You should take care of your own crew."

"You have one guy to look over and he's crying like a three-year old."

"It's not my fault! He just flipped out and started wailing."

"I didn't just flip out Jeff! You're always picking at me and picking at me and picking at me!" Chris said as he beat himself wildly with his fist.

Though neither of them wanted to share the burden, Jeff and Barry nodded their heads at each other. They were in this together.

"Chris buddy. You want to cool off?" Jeff asked.

"I am cooling off!" Chris moaned and slid his back down against the railing. Jeff half-expected him to stick his thumb in his mouth. He was cooling off in that he stopped hitting himself, but it was obvious that he was a loaded gun. The waiter and the captain remained careful with their words.

"That's good bud, just breathe in, breathe out. I'm going to -"

"Stay fucking there!" Chris cut Jeff off as he started to walk down the stairs.

Jeff froze so Barry came closer.

"You stay there too, Barry!"

Barry proceeded but slowly.

"I'm warning you."

Barry stopped this time, at the foot of the stairs, and said, "Chris, the best you can do right now is make the most out of a bad situation."

"You can fuck off."

"I can. And I will."

Chris let out a giggle. It sounded innocent but eerie.

"Fuck off, Barry," Chris said, giggling yet.

"I'll fuck off first thing tomorrow morning, Chris."

Chris's giggles grew to a shaking laughter.

"That's too late."

"Then I'll fuck off tonight. But first you need to drink a beer."

It was difficult to tell who looked more surprised, Jeff or Chris. Barry pulled out a cigarette and before lighting it paused to hold his pack out to Chris. He took one and said, "Thanks, Barry."

"Sure. Jeff, please don't tell me you have tables left."

"No. We've been closed for a little while, thank God."

"Go up and get Chris a beer then."

"Very funny. I get it now."

"Glad you get it. Coors Light is fine. Bring two. Shit, bring three if you feel like letting your shoulders down for once."

Jeff cocked his head and chuckled arrogantly. "What the fuck?"

Barry looked at him.

"You're serious."

He realized Barry was.

"You're telling me to steal three beers and have a little party down here?"

Barry considered. "You're right. That is absurd."

"Uh, yeah. And you're rewarding Chris for losing his fucking mind?"

"Fuck you Jeff!" Chris started again.

"Bring two beers. You get to go be a captain while I'm here with Chris. I know that's what you've always wanted."

Jeff studied Barry's face. There was no bluff. Barry only smoked and broke eye contact, looked away into the distance, squinting even in the nighttime as he dragged his smoke.

"You'd let me look over your own crew, huh?"

"I think different talents are needed with respect to what you and I both have on our hands. Bring us our beer, please."

Jeff did. He gave Barry an evil smile and said, "Okay boys, hope you know what's good for you," and walked inside to the banquet room. Fortunately for the banquet staff, the guests were leaving and it was time to clean up with no reset afterwards. Jeff's authority would be limited and short-lived. But he might not have known that himself. The smile he shot Barry outside sat on his acned face all night. In between insults to the crew he filled them in with accounts of how Chris was obviously under the influence of drugs and Barry's solution was more drugs.

"Of course, he's got Huey, Dewey, and Louie running around here all the time stoned out of their skulls so it really shouldn't surprise me," he told Yasmine.

Yasmine scowled at him and said, "They're good guys, Jeff. You should take notes some time," and walked promptly away.

Jeff smirked and said, "Hell of a crew, Captain Barry," and

started pulling tablecloths in the corner of the room by himself.

Outside, Chris was calming, if not coming, down.

"Thanks for everything, Barry," he said. "I'm really, really sorry. I'm not getting fired, am I?"

"I'm not your boss."

"Will you tell on me?"

Barry lit another cigarette, after giving one to Chris, and exhaled deeply.

"No."

"Do you know what I did?"

"Something stupid."

"I guess. I ate mushrooms during my shift. I'm still tripping now. Just not as bad. It got mellower after I cried. Fuck, don't tell my friends if you see them, that I cried."

"I won't."

"Are you mad at me?"

"I don't care enough to be mad at you. I think you should probably start looking for a new job though."

"So you are firing me."

"No damn it, I can't do that. But you came to work on fucking mushrooms. How do you expect not to get fired?"

"Jamie and Seamus didn't when they came to work. They said it was a spiritual experience."

Barry rubbed his eyes. "I wish I didn't know that. But those two are pretty much the last people you should ever take your cues from."

"Why are they still here, then?"

"Because for the most part they do their jobs. It could be worse. They obviously hold their shit a lot better than you."

"So Jeff's going to tell on me?"

"What do you think?"

"I think I'm fucked."

"Yeah. Just don't start laughing when Angela tells you to fuck off. Being sober tomorrow when she calls you into her office will probably help."

"Yeah...Barry, one more thing."

"Ok."

"Why'd you stick up for me like that? I mean this beer is making everything so much better! How'd you know that would do it?"

"I'm not a fucking boy scout, Chris. I've seen better people, smarter than you, do worse things. And I already told you. You put yourself in a bad situation. Your best option wasn't good anyway so you might as well do what you can."

Chris considered. "Barry?"

"What now?"

"One more thing."

"This better be quick. I have to go switch places again with Pizza Boy. Can you handle him?"

"He'll probably just tell me to clock out."

"Probably. You're leaving your car here, aren't you? God knows you can walk home."

"Oh yeah. I'm hopping straight over the wall."

"Okay. What then?"

"I fucked up tonight, so I probably won't see you again. But no hard feelings from before when you kicked my friends out, or sent me home early."

Barry gave him a rare look in the eyes.

"Just do better next time, bud."

"I will," Chris said.

Barry headed inside like nothing ever happened, his thin body impatient and his feet clapping on and off the ground. Chris smoked the last drags of his bummed cigarette and stood to look over the fountain.

Just what was he thinking eating mushrooms?

He probably was not thinking at all, like his teachers used to tell him in school. Oh well. It had been fun, at least sometimes. Part of him would miss Barry. A bigger part of him wondered what he should do now.

When Jeff stepped out, gingerly and stone-faced, Chris giggled again.

"Why so uptight, man? Wasn't that fun being captain?"

"Yeah. Chris, I think I got it upstairs. Why don't you just clock out, call it a night, and I'll see you tomorrow?"

Chris nodded his head and smiled. It was the most clear-headed he had felt all night. "It's a night alright. Sorry for what I did. But...I'm not sorry for what I said."

Jeff nodded. "Well it's all good, buddy. See you tomorrow."

"I'll hold you to that."

Jeff looked away but answered, "Of course."

Chris realized he had made a reckless, nonsensical decision.

But somehow he felt it was still worth the price of admission. He clocked out without saying another word, and looked forward to when he would see Jamie and Seamus again.

11

Chris was Angela's first fire. Barry told Jeff to give Chris a second chance, but Jeff countered, "Working with me was his second chance. You've really gotten soft, man, if you forget you wanted him gone in the first place."

"Your restaurant is dead all the time. He can handle that. Just lighten up on him and try not to act like you're banging Jennifer Lopez or something."

"Wow! Are you losing it or what? No wonder Jamie and Seamus and now Cody are the laughing stock of the place."

"At least they know what age they are. Someday they might even act like it."

"Yeah like when they're thirty."

"If all goes well."

"That's exactly my point," Jeff smirked. "Whatever, Barry. You're just like the creepy, lonely uncle who never got married and is trying to make friends with his nephews."

"Except I am married, Jeff. And I'm plenty creepy to my nephews without trying to be their friend. They just think I'm an old loser. You'd love them."

These were the kinds of conversations Barry was having with Jeff lately, who had finally gotten his wish. He was going to be a Singing Pines Captain.

The news was broken at a staff meeting, the first Thursday in August. It was the first of its kind since many months ago.

Then Angela was meek and an open target for her unruly staff's assault on her authority. In her current incarnation, she was robust and lively. She stood beside her familiar easel and oversized paper pad with marker in hand. She was back, and worse than ever.

"Hello! So good to see everyone bright and early today."

Cody leaned back in his chair and yawned. Others laughed.

Not to be outdone, Angela said, "Oh you know what Cody? I forgot to brew coffee this morning. Please get some going for us, would you?"

Cody was confused. What in the hell was she trying to pull?

"You want me to brew some coffee?"

She smiled, clearly drunk on some depth of power she was just beginning to realize. "I'm sure you're not the only sleepy-head in here. Now, the first thing I want to do today is apologize that it's been so long since we've met. That's my fault and I should have...Cody? Are you going to brew the coffee today or tomorrow?"

He had no choice. He got up and did as he was told. And when he returned to his table minutes later, carrying a carafe, Angela was explaining why "attitude is everything."

He hated her. Looking at Jamie and Seamus, he was not alone.

"Since most of you only work banquets, you take for granted that your guests aren't exactly as demanding as they are in the restaurant."

Seamus felt his throat tickle with a mounting protest, but he kept his lips sealed. Apples and oranges. Besides, the banquet guests could be quite demanding sometimes. The boys in particular just ignored them.

"They don't come into a reception with the same expectations. This is actually a good thing. This is how we win their attention and get them to recommend us to other people they know, or even come back for their own wedding."

Steve laughed. "Yeah, because every woman wants her wedding to be identical to the one her cousin just had."

A voice of defiant reason, Jamie, Seamus, and Cody applauded Steve. They nodded their heads furiously at Angela to further demonstrate their support of the number one bartender.

But Angela only smiled back, and in a way that did not totally look different from the smirk Jeff made when he was riding high on some convoluted sense of self-importance.

"That's one way of looking at it. But that's not the way I look at it, and it's not the way I want any of you to look at it. We want to surprise people with how awesome we are. We want them to feel welcomed and we want their expectations to be blown away. This isn't just a banquet, this is a reception at Singing Pines Country Club. Who knows? They might join the club. Guys, this isn't just about weddings."

The boys looked to Barry but he was staying quiet. The warrior that defended them in the last meeting was keeping stoic with his arms crossed, taking sips of the coffee that Cody was traduced into making.

"So if we have the attitude that we're working in the restaurant, than the banquets themselves will be better, get us repeat business, and everyone will be better off," Jeff said.

"Thank you, Jeff. That's what I've been saying."

"I understand that. The service we give in the restaurant is really the benchmark for the whole club. Anyone in banquets is welcome to observe me sometime with my tables for fifteen minutes or so before their shift," Jeff said.

"Sign me up for when you make the next guy cry," Jamie said.

Jeff looked over and was about to speak, but Angela intervened, saying, "Jamie, that's completely inappropriate. But, since you brought it up, we don't need an elephant in the room."

Everyone looked at her, waiting to see how she was going to make this one politically correct. She fired a kid because he lost his shit high out of his mind and cussed out Jeff. What was she going to do? Tell them "it just wasn't a good fit?"

Alfredo looked at Yasmine. It was an off day. She sat opposite him at the table instead of beside him. His hands were in fists, and he had little interest in how lame the meeting was. He could think of bigger liars than Angela.

"As you all know, Chris had a bit of an episode here. If it was just stress we could forgive that, but he did a very foolish thing and came in under the influence."

Steve scoffed. "Well don't hold back, Angie. Dude was trippin' balls, that's what I heard." Laughter, head shakes, blushed faces. If Barry was going to remain mute, at least some one was standing up for truth, the boys knew. "What? That's what you're getting to, right Angie?"

Angela smiled. She was as in control of her emotions as she had ever been.

"It's no secret that Chris acted inappropriately. I wouldn't say anything but you're all close, from Barry's crew to Christine's crew to the restaurant crew. It's not like we have any secrets."

She paused to give square looks to Jamie, Seamus, and

Cody. They stared back. They were not scared, and they feared no evil. This was as much a microcosm of the man impinging on their freedoms as anything they had experienced. This was clearly their moment. If Barry was not going to speak, then they must.

"So who's next? Somebody's gotta have something else to say. Chris' ears have gotta be just about on fire," Jamie said.

Seamus shook him vigorously by the shoulders, he was so proud.

Angela remained unfazed. "I appreciate that Jamie. But let's remember that there are good examples and there are bad examples. We need to know the difference."

Cody began to laugh at the absurdity but reined in his enthusiasm. Angela tilted her head up and smiled at him, but that was all.

"Now, speaking of examples, we're starting a new policy here at Singing Pines. Fernando!" she said his name spiritedly. He blinked, which was strange to see.

"Shit," Jamie whispered to Seamus. "She's got Cool Hand Luke looking spooked. We're all done for."

"C'mon," she motioned to Fernando. "Come up here, please."

When Fernando stood before his coworkers Alfredo looked at Yasmine, who was sitting opposite at the table, her back facing him. It had been a week since they saw each other much less had sex, though they talked over the phone since. Some of their conversations bore the semblance of intimacy, her "too" particularly pronounced after the "I miss you." He had believed her.

Fernando took his place at the front of the room and Angela pulled out a star-shaped pin from her pocket and held it in the air. Steve laughed now and covered his mouth, his eyes bugging over Angela's theatrics. Angela ignored him and said, "This is the service superstar pin. Whoever gets it passes it on when he or she thinks someone is ready for it. Our very first service superstar is Fernando, and no one deserves it more."

The room applauded. Alfredo clapped slowly, Steve clapped while rolling his eyes, and Barry clapped with near-silent apathy. Yasmine whistled. Jamie, Seamus, and Cody, said things like, "There you go, there you go," "My man," and "Nobody better." Jeff smirked. All the while, Fernando reddened, looked down and away, while Angela pinned the star to his polo shirt.

"Now, Fernando exemplifies what a service superstar is. He's always early, but never clocks in until his shift starts. His tables are always the first served and the first bused. He helps out everyone else when he has time, and he always has time because of how hard he works. Fernando is the ultimate good example and has the best attitude."

"Oh my," Alfredo said under his breath. "The best attitude. Well, well, well."

Angela frowned at him but quickly said with a smile, "Thanks Fernando. You earned it."

"Yay Fernando!" Yasmine said and hugged him with exaggerated zest for the minor magnitude of the accomplishment.

He hugged her back and could not help but look at his cousin, who was sneering at him. Fernando, showing a strength he lacked in his embarrassment of recognition upfront, kept his eyes fixed on his cousin. They both knew. Had Alfredo not gone to the races Saturday, they both would have been better off.

This was not the time for a rehearsal of boiling blood, at least not for the cousins. In a moment, all of the Singing Pines banquet staff would be reeling at the news that was coming next, that Jeff was going to be anointed as the next captain. Worse, he would be taking Barry's place.

For Jamie and Seamus and Cody, the news nearly stopped time. The shocked gasps surrounding them slowed to a muffled groan. Angela's pose - her all-teeth smile, her jittery step backwards and the bend in her waist, her clasped hands and swaying keychain hanging from her pocket - was frozen on their eyes, only to be burned away by the self-congratulatory zeal with which Jeff stood up and smiled his own damn smile, the smirk gone, the evil only now revealing how powerfully it could darken a room, while Barry just sat there, unimpressed, unmoved, and looking impatient as always to move on to the next chore of mundaneness ahead of him, whatever it might be, so long as it was not here.

"Thanks guys, thanks everybody," Jeff said as though the gasps were cheers and applause. "I know that everyone's going to miss Barry, myself included, but he'll be around for another month while he trains me. I can just promise that I'll do my best, listen well to Barry, and I won't let you down."

Steve cracked and let out a rumbling explosion of laugher. He covered his eyes but not his mouth, which he seemed unable to close. He laughed even as Angela asked him to stop. She had no choice but to ignore him, and continued to talk again anyway, seeing that the barman was a lost cause, and hopefully, down the line when she could find a replacement for him too.

As she talked, her closing remarks rehearsed, rote, she was somewhere else, soaring along the stretches of a hidden horizon. Her heart pounded. She knew not long from now there would be more Tequila Nights, more special holiday buffets, more golf tournaments, more teacher-of-the-year receptions, more graduation receptions from all sorts of institutions, and more of anything else she had not yet imagined. Why had she fought this for so long?

She thought of Bryce while she watched Jeff sit there and smile, smug as a stormy day pouring rain on the best made plans. Bryce was nothing like him, and she was grateful. If Jeff even wanted to, which he never would but that did not matter somehow, she would never let him near her. That was power enough for her. Bryce, with his physique and genuine confidence despite his intellectual shortcomings was a man. Jeff was a weasel, a fact made more obvious when she compared him to her boyfriend. But Singing Pines needed a weasel. It was full of them already. It was weasels that made the club spin forward on its hidden axis. This was not just an affluent country club in a quiet Californian suburb, but an extraordinarily minor investment for an ownership group overseas. And if not a weasel, everyone was at least a liar, as the company line told to all inquiring guests was to wax beatifically about the club's beginnings in the town when there were more orange groves than houses. The explicit reality of its current allegiance was never denied, but simply forever ignored. It began with Crystal who was the trophy of the organization, charming, attractive, and genuinely kind. Exploited for her positive assets, she was a perfect liaison for anyone first inquiring about holding a banquet at Singing Pines. Wanda was a choice closer, and Howard a phenomenal example of reserved, beady-eyed timidity, a spineless man who doled quiet, short-sentenced approval but never criticism. He was too scared to confront even his own employees. He blinked his eyes, stuttered in place, and hummed some type of sound to remove himself from the situation, turning awkwardly to his office to make a note, cast a shadow, or cut a cord. But he never did so publicly. So long as the bottom lines were met, and ultimately exceeded, he was a mouse in the wall, a few faint scratches sounding from his office but remained otherwise nonexistent. The accountants, the secretary, the HR people, all weasels. Faceless, soulless, living cadavers pretending that they were doing exactly what they wanted to when they grew up, paralyzed in place by an economy that no longer offered upward mobility the way it used to, much less options for work.

Angela knew she was stuck, too. She knew she was enjoying an ironic stroke of luck. All along she was making good money doing something she hated, but these days the animosity was dissolving.

Suddenly the job she did was not so bad anymore. It was not a chore, it was not a sentence, and it was not a trap. It was a bizarre kind of freedom. It gave her wings. And now people took notice. They no longer treated her like the dorky girl in the cafeteria who might melt to a puddle of red-faced horror if given prolonged attention. She was a productive member of the office staff, and a vital gear in the Singing Pines machine. The job did not matter any more, but the position did. Though she never thought that this is what she would want, she was lucky enough to see what she had while she had it. How close had she come to to the latter? She shuddered to think.

All she knew was that she had more tools than she realized. A fall guy in a perfectly worthy life boat in a corporate tempest. And washing ashore on dry land was transformative, indeed. She had heard that people never appreciate what they have until it is gone, but she swore that she could appreciate her job just as much without having to lose it. Indeed, though she would admit it to no one but Bryce, that was the secret to her new success.

12

It would be a short while before the boys found out that Barry was fired. All they knew was that Barry was going to work somewhere else, in what they imagined was a better position. It was uncomfortable for them to hold a grudge against him, but they did.

Jeff's training period was a long, dry month. The boys had to take solo trips to the dumpsters or the deck to get stoned. Jeff was more adept at showing up unexpectedly than even Barry, and he certainly knew how to pick his spots. He passed out champagne bottles before the toast, and wasted no time in returning all uncorked bottles to the refrigerator afterwards.

"What if they want more champagne later?" Jamie protested.

"They only paid for these for the toast."

"Yeah exactly, they paid for them already!" Jamie pressed.

Jeff shrugged, as he did often. "Maybe they ordered too many."

"Damn it Jeff, they only order as many as Wanda tells them to."

"Jamie, I'm not the wedding planner. I'm just your captain. Take it upstairs if you're that upset about it."

There were other problems. Seamus and Cody no longer cut the cake. Jeff did. Jamie and Seamus no longer had gazebo duties. Felipe took care of those. Further, the escalating drama between Fernando and Alfredo was dragging everyone else in the crew down to their embittered level. While Barry used to get caught up in the issues, bearing the burden for everyone, Jeff laughed it off, dismissed the feelings of everyone else involved, and told Alfredo "your puppy love isn't my problem." The spirit of the place was depressed, and even Steve, often isolated in his bar, noticed the thickness of tension whenever he took a smoke break.

"Jesus, you people are turning this place into the Heartbreak Hotel! I've seen happier looking people in a morgue."

Jamie scoffed. "This place used to be *thee* place, I'm talking about the place to be, my man. Ever since Jeff came on board everything's changed, everything."

"He's just a kid, no older than you. You boys need to have some balls, tell him to fuck off."

"We've tried, but he just reports everything to Angela. I was gone for ten minutes, ten of them, and he couldn't find us so the next night I'm sitting in Angela's office getting versed on my Miranda Rights practically."

"Your Miranda Rights, huh?" Steve dragged on his cigarette and nodded his head. "Yep, I've been told those before."

Steve had a story to tell but was interrupted by the man of the hour.

"Jamie! It's time to serve the cake. I can't look for you while I'm cutting it so do everyone a favor and get inside now. Chop chop."

Later that evening, as the boys smoked a joint in Jamie's backyard, Seamus said, "Chop chop? He said chop chop?"

"He said it, my man. He fucking said it."

"What a douche! Like, he's the wettest, sloppiest bag of douche in the world," Cody said.

"He's the worst person I know. And Barry just holds his tongue," Seamus said. "It's awful guys. Our club has been ruined."

"I was just telling Steve that!" Jamie shouted.

"Yeah man. I need this place. It kept me sane last semester. School's starting up again soon, too. I don't know what I'm going to do."

Cody said, "We need to find new jobs. Or..." He trailed off. Was he that stoned? He looked like he was receiving an epiphany. The boys leaned over the table, sensing his energy.

"What if we started our own business?"

Jamie whistled. "Well man, that's the dream of many but I can't claim I'd know where or how to start."

"You don't have to. Just come up with an idea and go for it. People start their own businesses all the time. It works for them."

"People go under all the time, too," Seamus said.

"Fuck that! That's not your attitude! Singing Pines is getting to you man. I see it in your eyes! You too, Jamie. You two are all about bucking the system. We gotta figure something out!"

Jamie and Seamus considered. They had It, but some nights they did not even bring the topic up anymore. They were distracted. Jamie was getting bored, Seamus was having bad dreams.

The next night the boys were dealt another blow as Angela switched Cody with some boring stiff named Bill who got along with Jeff more than anyone else based on their shared strength of reference to popular cartoon TV shows. The move came without warning, and Cody was simply told that he would be "working upstairs from now on, thanks."

Jamie and Seamus passed Cody in the kitchen. He dropped all traces of entrepreneurial aspiration and said, "I'm looking for a new job Monday. Maybe a restaurant, maybe a bank. Hell, I think I'd like working at a bank. If I'm going to be at work I might as well be at work, wear a suit and tie and handle important shit like thousands of dollars everyday."

"That's the spirit my man, can't let this place call the shots all the time," Jamie said.

"That's right. You make the next move. Make it count," Seamus said.

They would see little of Cody the next couple weeks, and knew it. Downstairs, they said nothing to Barry and he said nothing to them. It seemed that he talked to Jeff only, and blandly, about whatever it was that captains did. Jeff seemed to listen, but it always looked like he was more interested in watching the actions of his new crew. When Fernando made a wrong turn with a dolly and sent a stack of six champagne glass racks toppling onto the dance floor during cleanup, he was the first person to chime in with, "Oh that's just great."

Barry was not around. He was in the office or something, doing paperwork probably. Jamie and Seamus did not care where he was. They were more concerned with watching Fernando stand silently in place, absorbing what he had just done. The rest of the crew stood by with them, looking on with the sorrowful eyes of passersby over a car wreck. Alfredo laughed wildly and clapped but no one else said a word.

Fernando knelt to the ground and stared at the piles of glass sprinkled over the floor like they were a thousand yards away. When he looked up he asked, "So is anybody going to help or are you all just going to stand there and stare?"

Steve was walking back to his bar and said, "Well, at least he's taking it *so* well!"

The words awakened Jamie as he quickly retrieved a broom and dustpan from the service area. Seamus picked up racks and shook out glass fragments over a trash can. Yasmine gave Fernando a hug, but he barely touched her in return. Alfredo started pulling tablecloths on the other side of the room, rapping to himself. His voice was the only human sound against the clanks and jangles from a galaxy of broken glasses getting swept up and thrown away.

Jamie went with Fernando to the dumpsters. When he returned, he told Seamus, "We're taking a detour tonight, my man. Hope you're hungry. We might be sitting in Denny's for a while."

"I have a joint for the drive home. You think Fernando - I'm guessing the man's involved - would want to share it?"

"I don't think so man. I think he just needs to talk. And by the sound of things, and the look of things, it's been a while since he's done that."

"No shit. The ace has gone John Wayne on us lately. He's a regular Quiet Man."

"Well, the Duke is ready to speak."

The boys met Fernando at a 24 hour Denny's far down the street from Singing Pines. It looked like an imaginary version of the fifties as seen from a kitschy, corporate design team's point of view, though contemporary Top 40 songs played from the overhead speakers. Jamie and Seamus were only a little stoned. They ashed out half the joint to save for later. They figured they would need it then. They were right. Fernando took a while to get going, but once he did it poured.

For Fernando, it seemed like anything that mattered always

took a while.

The first few minutes he was in another place. He wrapped his hands compulsively around his coffee cup, which was all he ordered, and looked down more than across the table where his coworkers sat, making small talk, drinking water, smiling, nodding, breathing audibly. Together, they shared all the mannerisms of a shitty first date.

Fernando knew that accidents did not happen on their own. He knew that he did not make a wrong turn with his dolly because he was careless. He had only to reference the many recent nights where sleep took so long to come he woke up in the mornings groggy and spent as though it never did. He tried to remind himself of his father's favorite pseudo Zen line when days did not go as planned. "Life is life," he would say.

Fernando always smiled when he thought of that, remembering how they would laugh together. "Tomorrow is tomorrow," Fernando started to say as he got older.

These days it was bearing little fruit. It was not the season for a folk simplification of human pain, the everyday doldrums and insecurities of his age, nor of the promises he was still waiting to cash in on, or the alien behaviors of women. He remembered thinking that English was difficult to learn but not as much so as everyone said it was. It was easier to learn how to speak a second language than it was to do so in any words to women. Actually, it was just as hard, he was finding, to speak with family.

When he finally got out with it that a girl was at the heart of his current troubles then Jamie and Seamus knew they were finally free to talk straight to him. It was not like Yasmine's love triangle with two proud cousins was a secret. But to a young man like Fernando, it damn well felt like one so long as he kept his own mouth shut. His feelings, his real take on the whole ugly affair, was after all as secret as everything else about him. The strong one with the upright posture and the firm but positive demeanor, sullied only by recent familial tangles and a little lust. No one knew exactly what happened, they only knew that something did.

Jamie and Seamus realized as they spoke to him that the only source that would give them the straight talk on it, as much as could be realized by an inherently biased source, was going to come from the trio's most characteristically straight member. When Fernando acted, others followed. And now that he spoke, the chattiest and staunchest dreamers of all of Singing Pines were rapt with every word.

"If he had only gone home instead of the races, like he was doing, then none of this would have happened," Fernando started.

"The past is the past," Seamus cautioned.

Fernando leaned back, smiled unexpectedly. "You're right." He looked out the window, held his coffee cup, took a drink. "And tomorrow's tomorrow but today's still today. And I don't know what to do."

Fernando sat for a while, rubbing his coffee cup, thinking. The boys let him. They watched him talk in fits and starts, braking to contemplate, to examine, and choose his words carefully. Whenever he began speaking again, his dark eyes would implore them, his head cocked sideways, asking as much as saying. He was in it deep, clearly, and it seemed almost that he was talking to himself as he talked to them.

"I mean, what can I do? I kissed my cousin's girlfriend... ex-girlfriend. I made out with her, thinking okay, she wants this, I want this, I mean, she's gorgeous! What could I do?"

Jamie nodded his head vigorously. "You can only be a human being my man. You had a layup. You took it."

"No. It wasn't that. I thought she really wanted to see me, to be with me. You see how Alfredo treats her? He's such a jerk!"

"I know, I know he is. But that's not your concern."

Fernando breathed hard. "No it isn't. I wish I thought about that before. To me, when Yasmine reached over, grabbed my leg, pulled in and hugged me, God, I hadn't felt that in a long time."

"Yep, yep," Jamie nodded. "She's got that ass, too! I'm saying Fernando, I'm saying!"

"I know!" Fernando loosened, smiled again unexpectedly. "But if I thought that was all it was, I would have pulled away, said goodnight, been a gentleman, see you tomorrow. I thought with the way she always talked to me she wanted more than that, did not want to be Alfredo's fuck buddy. That's all he ever saw her as, even though he was, as he says, only with her. I don't know if that's true or not, but the only time he ever treated her like he even liked her, I mean for more than to lay, was when she started hitting on me."

"And that was when you gave her rides home," Jamie said.

"Yes. I remember Alfredo, even then, saying to her that she could ride with me all she wanted, that I wasn't going to do anything, that I was more scared of women than Felipe. It made me mad, so mad, when she told me he said that."

He finished his coffee and looked around for a server. No one was available yet and Fernando sat quiet, contemplating. Jamie and Seamus left him alone, sat with their own thoughts until the waitress brought their meals and filled Fernando's cup. He continued.

"If I knew that it was that, not even sex, I mean, not that *that* matters, a kiss, a lay...it's all the same thing in his eyes so long as it's not him she's doing it with."

"Right, that's his ego. But don't let his perception become your reality! Make it happen with Yasmine! Make her happy!"

"But my friend! She won't give me so much as the time of day! I call her, I text, whatever. Email. Email chat. And it's all pleasant but the minute I bring up anything, anything at all about, I don't know, us, it's done. She has to go all of a sudden."

"Ah...so you only kissed her that night?" Seamus asked.

"That night. Then it's like it never happened."

The boys considered. Fernando was fucked.

"Can't say I envy you this drama, man," Jamie said.

"That's what I'm saying. I told you I needed to talk it through Jamie, and you're here. Thank you. And thanks Seamus for coming, too."

"I've been yanked around a little too," Seamus said. Then he wondered if that was true. It probably wasn't, at least like this. But heartache was heartache, and that he knew. Soon he would be back in school and he worried about how his first time seeing Rachel would unfold. He did not know what he would say or do or feel. And it worried him whenever he considered it.

"Yeah?" Fernando asked him, shaking him out of his own trancing thoughts.

Seamus considered quickly. "Yeah," he started and chewed his spinach omelette. "You let a woman see your cards and you're done. Don't call her like this anymore. You see her at work, and man that's gotta be hard. Just leave it at that. Do your best. I don't know what else there is to do."

Fernando nodded, confirmed to Seamus he was right. Seamus, sensing often that he knew a thing or two about a thing or two, was always gladdened immensely to be told that he was right. Except this time he was not. It pained him to think that the best thing for Fernando to do was ignore someone he cared about, even wanted to be his girl. But that was the truth of it, and Seamus picked away at his omelette, thinking bitter thoughts about the truth of the romantic world as he knew it, as he had learned, that people move on whether they are loved or not and the only appropriate response is to look straight ahead as possible and not make eye contact unless absolutely necessary. Seamus knew that some people apparently got along fine, even became friends with, their exes. But Seamus did not know how. Seamus knew he knew some things, but every now and then like tonight, he was a little less sure what he knew after all. Whenever he admitted that to himself, the world seemed that much smaller and the air that much tighter and harder to breathe. When he awoke in the middle of the night from a dream and saw it was four in the morning, the mental claustrophobia was worst of all.

Fernando raised his cup and said, "My friends." He had no food to eat and swore he was not hungry. Seamus gave him his fruit anyway, which he accepted, and dug into over the course of the rest of their conversation. Little more was revealed other than the fact that Alfredo hated him, his brother seemed to resent him and his cousin both, and Yasmine wanted nothing more than to talk pleasantly about things he cared little for and the occasional ride.

"She even left this in my car the other night," he said and pulled a gaudy dangling earring from his pocket. "It's a little big not to notice you dropped it, no?"

"Well, when I wore earrings I rocked iron crosses. And you better believe I felt lighter when they were off my dome," Jamie said.

"Yeah but these things are light, man. Feathers and beads. I've lost like eight pairs," Seamus said.

"You two are assholes," Fernando smiled. "I'm happy I know you. And thank you, I know I said it already but I meant it."

"We know you do, my man," Jamie said.

"The feeling's mutual," Seamus said.

"This is nice. Good coffee, good friends," Fernando said. "Good conversation too, even if the topic isn't nice."

"Life isn't nice, man," Seamus said.

"No. Life is life," Fernando said.

Jamie and Seamus never knew Fernando had It, but they had their suspicions. His simple statement rocked them, and became a mantra later as they finished their joint. And when Jeff gave them hell at the club, they reminded themselves about the golden phrase again and again.

"It, life, fuck man," Jamie said a week later while driving home from another difficult shift.

"You said it," Seamus agreed.

Cody had found another job after all. Fernando, for all his catharsis at Denny's, had clearly made no progress with his cousin. Yasmine remained distant, and even his own brother lukewarm. Life was life, and in the final days of summer at Singing Pines it was hard on everyone.

13

As quiet as Fernando was at work lately, he was feeling better. He was thinking, and doing so often. He was watching his thoughts, waiting for them to clear up, make sense. He was waiting for Alfredo to cool, for Yasmine to ask for a ride again, or at least her earring, a subject he never initiated himself. And he was waiting for other opportunities, a better job, actual responses from the countless employers he contacted on job boards. The only interest he received were from unfamiliar companies with generic looking websites and hopelessly broad mission statements. They always seemed to be looking not only for one person, but a team. And they were only hiring "now." He was encouraged not to wait to get back to them before it was too late. Fernando was waiting for a lot of things, but these jobs were not among them. He had been down that road and knew it well.

Fernando had a strong memory but recalling any separation between his days at Imperial Credit was difficult. He gave six months of his post-college life to this company which promised to make homeowners out of the bankrupt and foreclosed-on, while its employees made upwards of $50,000 a year. All he had to do was convince callers, each ingoing only because Imperial Credit received their numbers through an online survey company, to pay a one-time fee of $59.95 for a complete credit check and *free* consultation with one of their National Association of Credit Management *certified* credit analysts. For each caller that bought the credit report, he received a small commission. Every once in a while he would get lucky and achieve a first tier level bonus. All higher tiers were based on impossible numbers he would never hear about anyone actually reaching.

It did not take Fernando long to resent his new job, but he stuck on for a while because of the initial positives he gathered when he first started. He was told by the man who hired him, Wesley, whose position was vague but apparently important, that his degree in Agricultural Science was a big part of why he was hired. This seemed strange to Fernando but he appreciated hearing it. No one else had said that to him. Secondly, he spoke Spanish. He had all his life of course, and knew that this would be a positive most places. He actually found it curious that it had not helped him more until he got to Imperial Credit, an interview that he practiced and rehearsed as though it was the chance he had been waiting for since he graduated.

When he was hired, he sat hopefully in his pressed pinstripe shirt and tie, looking around at a dozen men in the conference room where they waited for Wesley to show up and lead their orientation session. Wesley was an unblinking man who stood 6'5" and spoke in pronounced, ringing words that could be heard just as easily from one end of the room to the other. He leaned in closely when having one-on-one conversations with others. He showed his teeth often which were large and perfect and white and square.

Fernando smiled mildly, his posture perfect and his hair combed neatly, his gray slacks pleated. He was apparently a day early with the dress code. They would not be on the phones just yet. This was an easy day, a relaxed day, a get-to-know-everyone day. Wesley teased him about it, his voice booming and his laugh hollow, and the men in the room laughed too, as did Fernando to be a good sport. He knew his laugh was forced, but by the sounds of it, he was not alone.

Some of the men looked nervous, some looked bored, and

some simply looked tired and spent. Some were younger, some were older. One had bad skin and yellow teeth, one wore heavy cologne and spiked his short hair. A couple wore t-shirts that were far too tight. Whatever anyone looked like, there buzzed an inner chaos within them each, manifesting itself in rambling voices, nail biting, and constant cell phone checking. One man in particular was obviously confused the entire time Wesley spoke. A former animator and father of two, he looked and sounded desperately out of his element. His questions about the housing market crash were met with whispers from other men in the room, making Fernando feel out of place too. Apparently these guys knew all about just what had happened and why banks gave loans to people who could not afford the houses they were buying. Because that was all Fernando knew about the situation himself, he hoped the orientation would help solve some of his questions, that his new job would teach him about modern finance and how to recover the economy. When he walked away from the orientation feeling just as uneducated as before, he hoped that he would learn as he went. He would wait it out for a while, listen well, speak well, read the employee handbook.

It was a long wait.

One of the new hires, the oldest among them was named Charlie, and he apparently knew so much that he was unsure if he even wanted to work for Imperial Credit. He had a long career in sales and had his options. He said as much when he consistently challenged Wesley throughout the orientation. Each time Wesley answered rapidly with a voice that mocked him, though politely. Charlie would nod his head and say, "Okay, I like that. That's why I chose you guys." During their midday break, Charlie loudly told a story to the brash, late twenties man next to him about a time when he nearly put himself in jail if it was not for his coworker being such a pussy.

"After I smacked him in his little pea head I held him by the collar and told him he dare tell anyone or call the cops I'd kick his ass so bad the next time he'd be collecting unemployment checks. The chicken shit didn't say a word. Yeah, I knew he wouldn't!"

The following week Fernando spotted Charlie on his knees and grunting by himself near his cubicle. It was late in the day and most people were gone already. Instinctively he approached him and asked if he was okay.

Charlie looked back with equal parts confusion and defeat, but gathered a smile on his face as he stood up, stifling a wince and showing Fernando a can of soda.

"Just dropped my Pepsi, guy. Hey, don't ever get old. Your knees go to shit," he said and patted Fernando hard on the back. "But I can still kick your ass, son!" He laughed wildly and walked away with a hastened jerk in his step. He turned back to see if Fernando was watching. Fernando was watching, but he was also smiling. He hoped that Charlie was not embarrassed. He did not know why he liked him, but he did. He had never felt that way until just then, either.

He would not have a chance to get to know Charlie since the old man was the first of the new hires to be fired. He could not close four calls in the first two weeks, a number everyone had to hit or they would be relieved. Fernando doubled it. This was good for a new hire, but as Wesley told him, "Eight ain't nothing. Give it a month. If you get eight in one week you'll be sweating bullets. But it takes time."

Fernando nodded. Wesley made him sweat even without thinking about numbers. He took an hour to sit with all of the new hires during their first two weeks. Fernando had dreaded when his turn would come, but once he got through it he felt relieved. It was one of the only moments that stuck out, this faint feeling of arrival. He got a job that his degree helped him to get, he wore nice clothes to work, and his cubicle was located near a window where he looked out over Westwood Boulevard and thousands of cars in constant motion below, the sunlight caressing everything in the living city that had much more to offer than humble suburbs where he lived in an old neighborhood near railroad tracks.

More than anything, he was no longer in the hospitality industry which he had worked in throughout his college years. He was doing something semiprofessional, and knew that it could only be the first step towards something else, something greater. Who knew? He could become a Credit Analyst one day himself as Wesley promised everyone would have the chance to become if they earned high numbers and proved themselves.

But after a while the feeling of future hopes with Imperial Credit and of arrival both faded. The repeated habits of Wesley became difficult to bear. And the sit-downs with the new hires turned out to be more of a periodic regularity than a single, introductory event.

A couple months in, Fernando encountered his second sit-down with the boss. He shivered as he worked his way through a call and felt his tone instantly lilt, his confidence sag and his back go rigid. Wesley just sat back in a chair next to his underling, smiling, watching him work, and staying totally silent for ten minutes.

When Wesley did speak, after listening to Fernando struggle through five calls without a close, he stuck his finger prominently in the air as though to make a point but instead pushed a button on the phone, releasing the receiver from its cradle and rendering Fernando temporarily unavailable.

"Fernando, have you always been this polite?"

Fernando squirmed as he sat back, readying himself for a conversation that he was fearing. His numbers the previous two weeks had dipped from what was a steady but unspectacular pace.

"Yes, I suppose so."

Wesley smiled and shook his head. "I suppose you're a regular gentleman, aren't you? A man from another time. Is that because you're from Mexico? I don't know, I'm just a big white boy and I'm curious. Keep in mind, the only time I've been down there is in Cabo for Spring Break back when I was listening to Nickelback and drinking Tecate Lite, okay?"

Fernando nodded. "When you learn a language as a second language, I suppose you speak formally. You learn how to speak that way."

"Yeah. Well you don't sound like it's your second language. You sound totally biracial."

"You mean bilingual?"

"Ha!" Wesley belted mirthlessly. "Sharp as rhino's horn. Just testing your ESL, compadre."

"Okay, well..."

"Okay, well nothing!" Wesley yelled and leaned forward. Fernando jumped and felt embarrassed but he could not help himself. Wesley startled him.

Wesley, still leaning forward, smiled. And then he sat back and said, "Now I'm just testing your reflexes. You're a better English speaker than you are keeping your cool."

"Sorry, I didn't expect it."

"Don't worry about it. I like you. You're a nice guy."

Fernando felt his back relax for what felt like the first time in years. "Thank you."

"You're welcome. But I've got to tell you that nice is, well, nice. But not everyone we're talking to needs to hear something nice. Hell, they've lost their home. They've maybe lost their job, perhaps their spouse. We're talking shit sandwiches all the way around here, you know what I mean?"

Fernando did. If there was anything he knew about his job, it was the kind of people he was talking to on a daily basis. They made him uncomfortable from the minute he spoke with them. He was waiting for that feeling to subside. It had, but it had yet to go away completely.

"Right, you're right."

"I know I'm right. Otherwise I wouldn't have sat over here to say it. Now when you first came in I thought, okay, here's a good employee. I still think that, don't get me wrong. I mean, your numbers are good, they're not great, but they're good. You're never late. You've never missed a day. You've got a lot going for you."

"Thank you," Fernando said, waiting for it.

"But then I see some returns last week office-wide that aren't so good and I see your numbers are down too, and it's like, jeez! Here's a guy who should be picking up the slack, not dropping it with everybody else!"

Fernando considered. He felt strangely guilty and proud. He did not know Wesley saw him that way, but now that he did, he could not help but take the numbers personally.

"So I come over here to listen to you anyway, give you the benefit of the doubt, figuring you're on track and maybe I can share with other people what you say, see how you do it, and suddenly it's like listening to my little brother ask a girl out for the eighth grade dance! And yeah, I've got a brother that young. My family's huge - there's six of us. I'm in the middle if you can believe it, so maybe being assertive and in your face just comes naturally to me, I don't know. But hey, don't think it's because anything came easy."

Fernando nodded. Sometimes Wesley made so much sense even as he said little in serviceable content that Fernando really wanted to do better, really felt the need for greater numbers, to stand out among the others. He did not feel competitive so much as he felt a sense of duty. He understood that life did not always come easily. He wanted Wesley to know that.

"Wow. That's a big family alright. You've worked hard."

Wesley beamed and then roared. "You patronizing my ass, boy?"

"No! No, not at all."

Wesley put his head on his hand and stared at Fernando. He then sat up, looked gravely at him, and asked, "Fernando, do you have everything you've ever wanted?"

Fernando looked away, had to, but could feel Wesley's eyes groping him. He said, "No. Well... I'm here now, so sure."

It was the first joke he had made in his entire employment at Imperial Credit, but Wesley did not laugh.

"Do you want to own your own house one day?"

"Yes," Fernando said immediately, moving the conversation along.

"But since you don't now, you don't have everything you've ever wanted. And what makes you think these people are any different?"

Fernando shook his head. "Nothing. They're not different."

"No they're not. They all want to get into a house they can

call their own again, they just don't know how. They wouldn't be taking these surveys online if they did. And we wouldn't be forking out big bucks to get their numbers if we couldn't legitimately help them. I know not everyone's going to do the right thing for their future and get that credit report, but I swear every call you let go is costing us money. You're playing with the house money here, Fernando. Don't bet lightly. Don't be nice when you put your chips on the pass line. Fucking roll those dice like you got a pair!"

"You're right."

"Don't just tell me I'm right!" Wesley slammed the receiver back in its cradle. It rang shortly after. "Pick up that phone!"

Fernando did and and tried his best. He spoke more assertively, felt his stomach turn as though he was fighting against himself but urged the caller that he could not make the decision for her, but said that if she realistically wanted to be a homeowner someday she would not wait until it became a seller's market again. When she again refused him, he asked her, "Are you happy where you live now?"

She must have heard the cowardice in his voice because she gave him a curt response but spared him much anger. She was the one being assertive now though as she asked him to put her on the "do not call list," and knowing damn well she would be called again he hoped with all his might that her number would not show up on his call list the next morning.

He hung up and looked at the staring Wesley who only shrugged his shoulders and said, "I can't make the calls for you. Or maybe it's the decision. What was that you said?"

For Fernando, the meeting with Wesley ended then but his feelings about Imperial Credit and his place within it were lower than ever. He refused to ever try to strong arm another caller and in the following weeks his numbers were leveling back to normal, but he knew that he would need to leave as soon as he could. He went home each day searching for new jobs online. He had some hopeful leads and even got an interview with a paper packaging company to work as an administrative assistant. The interview was promising as he was told the company had received over 400 applications! But despite his follow up phone calls he never heard from Jim who interviewed him.

Finally one night when he got home, dejected and too weary to think optimistically as he had been training himself to do the last few weeks, his brother told him happily that he just got a new job. He would be working on a banquet staff where Alfredo worked, and apparently they were still looking for someone else.

As was his reflexive response Fernando opened his mouth to dismiss working with food again but no words came out. He was struck dumb by a kaleidoscopic recollection of all the familiar sights and sounds of the Imperial Credit office. Other workers saying with practiced and forced enthusiastic sympathy, "Oh, then I'm *so* glad you called us today!" Wesley clapping his hands and parading around the office around noon saying, "We're almost there to 30! C'mon boys, let's get halfway to our quota by the time you bring out your lunch boxes and sippy cups! We can do this!" And worst of all was the memory of those dreary days when they did not reach their daily 60 closed deal quota and Wesley would say, "We're behind boys. We've got to crack that whip tomorrow to gain some ground and mama won't be here to rub Vaseline on your bum bums."

"You're working at a country club? What's the pay?"

"Ten an hour. Alfredo said we get overtime though most weekends."

Fernando considered. He would make more at Imperial Credit but not a significant amount more, and then there was that awful commute. An alive city or not, it had lost its luster over the last few months. He only saw it through windows, after all.

"Can you put in a word for me?"

"Of course! Man, that'd be so cool with all of us working there together!"

Fernando smiled and agreed. He could not think of anything better. He emailed Wesley his resignation that night and never showed up again. Like Jim at that paper packaging plant, he never even heard a response. He realized that maybe he was foolhardy in quitting before he secured a job at Singing Pines, but he did not care. It was time to go. Things could not go on that way.

And now, months later working a job that he thought would at least be completely free of stress, he knew that things could not go on this way, either. But as he admitted to Jamie and Seamus before, he did not know what to do.

So he waited. And before long, a curious thing happened when Angela hired someone to replace Cody. Life just took care of itself. Life was like that, Fernando knew. It just pained him to think that waiting, rather than doing, sometimes ended up being the best option.

And so, working at Singing Pines, continuing to look for more meaningful employment, he prepared himself to wait for as long as it took.

14

Angela sweat profusely at the gym in a fashion more akin to someone in her mid-forties grunting through creeping existential doubts than a young person waltzing gaily through each blissful day in the honeymoon stages of early romance. She was dating Bryce now, that much was official. While his worldview betrayed a radical shift from her own, it had become consistently entertaining. Watching him work in the gym, however, stoked her amusement into fondness.

He instructed his clients to lunge forward with their feet facing specific angles, or to lay down towels on the benches for "hygienic purposes," words he spoke loudly, slowly, and clearly but never explored further. If questioned, he might just say, "I ain't no doctor. Just no one wants that stuff slick like...anyway, just like bring a towel. Pretend you're going to the beach or some shit." He pushed his clients to "dig deep," like they were "searching in the back of their sock drawer to find change to take the bus home after work." Bryce's energy never wilted. In between clients, if Angela was in the gym working out, he'd stride over and espouse yet another mantra pushing personal advancement. Her personal routines well-established by now she did not need his guidance, but she would always giggle at his enthusiasm.

"Oh? You see that? She's laughing at you!" he scolded a five pound weight. "Here. Let's see how funny she thinks ten pounds feel."

She grunted while she raised her arms, keeping them straight the whole way through, until they reached ninety degree angles from her sides.

"Yes," Bryce clapped. "Just like that. Be like that naked dude in the circle."

"Are you talking about that drawing by da Vinci?"

"Shit, I ain't no art major! But you clearly know the dude I'm talking about so be like him, only be a chick. But same posture. C'mon, do this! One! Two!"

Angela continued to be like the dude in the circle until Bryce left. She was finishing her next set when a young girl walked up to her and asked, "You know Bryce?"

Angela pushed through number ten and felt the tiny jolt of ecstasy that every concluded set brought.

"I do," she said, catching her breath. "I sure do."

"Do you train with him or just know him?"

Angela looked at the girl. Tank top, sports bra, high runner's shorts, tennis socks, running shoes. And not an ounce of sweat anywhere.

"You want his number or something?"

The girl shook her head, "No! I mean, he's really sweet. But no, no thanks."

Angela wondered if she was being rude, but then did not care. Why should she? Still, in the interest of politeness, she said, "He is a sweetheart."

"He is, and has his own brand. I give him that. Sorry, I'm Britney by the way."

"Angela." They shook hands, and Angela thought she might apologize for the slipperiness of her palm, but then did not. Why should she be sorry?

"I'm a trainer here, too, so that's why I was curious how you knew him. He gets more clients all the time."

Angela looked over at Bryce, who was across the room drinking a bottle of water and talking quickly to a coworker, which probably meant he was rapping. He did that sometimes.

"Doesn't surprise me," Angela said. "He has a way of worming his way into your life. He's like...a lovable parasite."

"A lovable parasite? That's perfect! Oh my god!"

Angela's last boyfriend was not lovable but neither was he parasitic. He just went to work and came home, and on the weekends took it easy until they were over. Though he never paid a bill late or let his hair grow too long before it was due for a trim, he would never have an excuse had he not done these things on time. He was simply always ready whenever these types of details reached the necessary point of action.

"He's a free spirit," Angela continued. "And thankfully for him he found a good place to work as one."

Yeah. Could you imagine him at a bank?"

"Outside and rapping, yes. Inside, no."

Britney's eyes went wide and she covered her mouth. She said, "You're funny! I like you."

Angela smiled. "You're sweet. I hope you have good luck finding more clients. It sounds tough."

"It's crazy! I swear all the men in here find clients easier than I do."

"That's not fair, and that's strange. I would think you would find a lot of women clients."

"I would too but overall people just hire men to be trainers.

Definitely men don't hire women. It's rare that they do. It sucks. I was hoping maybe you weren't training with Bryce but you don't seem like you need a personal trainer anyway. You're obviously working hard."

"You're saying I messed up my hair?"

"Yes! That's exactly it. Seriously, if you're not sweating, you're not working."

"Well, you might want to consider that," Angela smiled.

"Hey! I'm working out later."

"I'm giving you a hard time."

"I know you are. It's okay. Anyway, I'll let you get back to working out. It's been nice meeting you...Angela, right?"

"Yes Britney. Here, take my number. Give me a call if I can help in some way."

A week later Britney was wearing a tux and working upstairs in a newly fashioned crew. She was Cody's replacement on paper but was a better worker. She worked weekdays at the gym which opened up her weekends and nights for Singing Pines. She was reluctant to contact Angela, but given her meager list of clients and no substantial employment alternatives, a second job would not hurt at least in the interim. And should she get more clients and need to work fewer shifts, Angela assured her she would not only accommodate but would congratulate her, too.

Shortly before Britney's first shift Yasmine had been shuttled upstairs and Fernando with her. Yasmine and Alfredo were over, and since she and Fernando were not dating either, they were as chatty as monks in chapel. However, Britney's place upstairs would serve not only as a catalyst for positive change as she and Yasmine quickly became friends, but immediately took Fernando's mind off the pain of working with

Yasmine. Britney, after all, seemed to take a quick liking to him, too.

Britney had graduated with a Bachelor's degree in sociology and a minor in history, so she was largely fucked. And she had a natural understanding for Fernando and his underemployed position as he did for hers.

And as quickly as they met was as quickly practically as they kissed. Right in the walk-in refrigerator, rows of cheese behind them and boxes of champagne at their feet, it was almost romantic. And as they pulled their mouths away to look into each other's eyes, the frosty exhale from their mouths dancing and disappearing as they caught their excited breath, they knew without asking what both were thinking about asking and decided that yes, they should be doing this, and kissed some more.

And this was how Fernando learned that yesterday was yesterday.

After Yasmine broke up with Alfredo, Fernando swore he was in. He drove to her house and returned her earring, but her reception was less than lukewarm and never would he forget the stillness of her mouth as she spoke, and her hand patting his back in a hug that not even teachers give their bad students. He was dismissed.

He needed to talk to someone, but never brought it up to Seamus and Jamie, not this time. He spoke to Isabelita out of the notion that perhaps she knew something he did not, could decipher woman, could tell him where he went wrong.

"Listen Fernando, this isn't a man-woman thing. It's an insecurity thing. Kissing someone and then asking them about their feelings after isn't sexy."

She told him not at Denny's over a long reflective talk, but

over the bus tubs, her proclamation to the point and immediately received. Short-lived in time, it stayed with him for
days.

So when he volunteered to take the champagne bottles to
the walk-in with Britney, help she did not need but her smile
an assurance he was reading everything right, he leaned in
first this time to give the first kiss.

They kept their romance quiet initially but quickly
everyone knew. And once the word was out, there was a
ripple effect that spread throughout the clubhouse. Yasmine,
relieved of all her pressures from Alfredo and now Fernando
too was able to enjoy being single without feeling the need to
live up to others' expectations. Felipe, in all his hopelessness
with women, asked Fernando how he got a girlfriend.

"I mean, no offense, but you're kind of like me," Felipe
told him.

Fernando, taking no offense at all, said kindly, "Don't ask
too many questions, my friend. Even of yourself."

Felipe, inspired by this cryptic message, repeated it to
Alonzo, imploring him to decipher what his brother meant.
Alonzo, not knowing about the seconds-long revelatory conversation Fernando had with Isabelita, could only shake his
head and say, "My brother surprises you sometimes. Really
surprises you, just when you think you know him." Indeed, it
was not Alfredo whom Alonzo looked up to most of all, but
his brother.

And for his own part, Alfredo, too, was able to get past the
troubles he had with his cousin. With simple admission, he
told him, "Okay dog. I give up. That girl is *fine*."

However, in the midst of happy endings that gave way to
new beginnings, or new beginnings that made happy endings

possible, not everyone's story was reaching a cheery climax. Seamus and Jamie were split up without warning as one day Angela moved Seamus upstairs. While the initial silver lining appeared to be that Jamie would finally be able to coordinate their smoke breaks together, the sad reality was that Jeff and Christine monitored smoke breaks intensely and made all such meetings impossible.

And so, realizing with great agony that the writing had been on the wall for a long time now and seeing clearly how hard he worked to look past it, Seamus saw that his once-beloved place of employment, the training ground for the fundamentals of It and a window to the real world that existed on the other side of his ivory college walls, was now nothing more than another fine example of the routine madness of the modern American world in which he lived. There were no longer portals to invisibility and ultimately invincibility. There was a clockwork order of business run by a captain well sutured now to the mindset of Them, and likely forever lost to the great race of gray people who consider the mundane duties of their insignificant lives greatly important not as means to themselves but as means to giving their irreversibly shallows lives the appearance of bearing depth. Among Them, Seamus knew, the stone never sat at the hill nor rolled down, but continued moving always, pushed by the will of the masses for whom nothing but the momentum of their own blindness was needed to keep this routine world rolling, no matter how suffocating, limited, and hopeless that routine continued to become.

It was with considerable necessity then that Seamus, along with Jamie, was able to reconnect with a pair of old friends, one of whom would share the truth finally. Fernando and Alonzo threw a party at their house when his parents were out of town. Every server and captain from the current Banquet staff was invited, along with Cody and Barry who both showed up, to the surprise of everyone. After initially catching up with all sundry, Barry snuck off with Jamie, Seamus, and Cody to have a reunion in the Trooper. Sitting parked in the driveway, with Jamie and Seamus in the back of the car and Cody sitting upfront, Barry reported on his new job and shared that, despite the odds, he was still gainfully employed.

"So now I'm working at a hospital supervising the lunch ladies in the cafeteria. I thought I'd get fired from there, too, only for getting a boner. But I'm still there."

"My man! Breaking hearts everyday! Speaking of, you broke ours when you just let Jeff take over the goddamn place."

"I was let go by then. What was I supposed to do? I fought my fight plenty of times before that."

"You were let go?" Cody asked. "And they kept you on for a month?"

"Yeah, that's their version of a golden parachute. They paid me so I could train the heir apparent. At first I agreed to it because I needed money while I looked for a new job but I got hired at the hospital really fast."

"So why didn't you just leave immediately?"

."Because I'm a fucking loser and kept my word to stay on for the month. Besides, watching Jeff act like he knew what he was doing after one night on the job made me worry about all you little dweebs. I should have known you'd all get new jobs anyway though."

"We're still working there, just not on the same floor. Place sucks," Seamus said.

"I just assumed you left like Cody did."

"We're trying to, my man. There's not a ton of jobs out there right now," Jamie said.

"Sure there are. Where are you working now, Cody, a bank?"

"That's right. Pays the same as Singing Pines. And I think it's making me into an adult."

Barry laughed one of his rare, genuine laughs. "I'll believe that when I see it."

"It is, dude! I couldn't just fuck around at Singing Pines all my life! That place makes you not give a shit."

"I think that's a prerequisite for working there. None of you were what I would call a Johnny Do-Gooder."

"Johnny Do-Gooder! Fuck! I need to put that on my resume!" Jamie yelled.

Seamus agreed, "It's way better than saying 'dynamic' and 'reliable.'"

"Fuck yeah it is. I got lucky getting hired at Wells because I said both those things on my resume," Cody laughed.

"No. Don't ever lie about being a Johnny Do-Gooder when you're not one," Barry warned them. "That's what got me in trouble."

Jamie tugged him on the shoulder. "My man, please, you gotta tell us seriously what did get you in trouble. You were an institution at that place."

Barry stared off into space and said, "Pretty much word got out that Chris came to work tripping out on drugs and someone needed to take the fall for it. Why it wasn't Jeff I'll never know...actually, fuck that. I'll always know. He's young and tall. I'm old and bald."

"Barry! You're like 32! And you've got a lot of hair left!" Seamus said.

"33 now. And my bald spot is getting bigger each year."

"Seriously, how did they really pin this on you?" Cody asked.

"I think it had something to do with me talking to him while he was tripping. They were already talking to Jeff about being a captain so I told Pizzaface to just get in there and captain. Chris seriously needed to calm down or he was going to hurt himself or someone else. He was crying and hitting himself. It was weird guys. I've taken acid maybe 15 times and I can't even stand being in the same room as myself but I never tried to beat my own face in."

"Man! You're holding out! When was the last time you took acid?" Jamie asked him.

"Probably around the last time I smoked pot. I used to be young once. And I almost thought I was cool before I stopped lying to myself."

"Shut up! You've always been cool," Seamus said. "And you were cool to be Chris' sitter. What were you supposed to do? Turn him in to the authorities?"

"Basically. They said instead of reporting him I just let him sit there and stay high."

"Sit there and stay high!" Jamie yelled. "Yeah, 'cause bringing in the fuzz would have mellowed him right out!"

Barry nodded. "I guess I could have called the cops and ruined his life but I knew he'd be fired anyway so I let him go when he proved to me he was stable again. That was kind of dumb but whatever. Nobody there liked me anyway so I'm better off now nodding along while old ladies talk about their dogs and grandchildren."

"Actually, Barry, nobody understood you," Jamie said. He looked to Seamus and Cody, who both nodded. Jamie then pulled out a joint. "Well, almost nobody. C'mon, Captain, light one up with the guys who always believed in you."

Barry raised his eyebrows. "Woah buddy. That's like... drugs."

"Yes man, yes!" Jamie yelled.

"He's in! Look at that fucker's eyes!" Cody smacked his hands down on the floor.

"This fucker hasn't done drugs since his wife -"

"Yeah, yeah, yeah - since his wife wanted to fuck him. We get it. Just get high," Seamus said.

"My fucking man!" Jamie shook Seamus by his collar.

Barry said nothing but thumbed through his CD case and emphatically pulled out his selection. He turned his car on, loaded the CD, took the joint and the light with little ceremony, and waited. The moment Quiet Riot's *Cum on Feel the Noize* blasted through his speakers he lit up.

If there was any way for the boys to remember Barry, they could think of no better goodbye. Seamus ran into him months later and the former captain admitted to waking up in a parking lot using a hamburger as a pillow. It was only natural later when Seamus used Barry as a job reference. Who else could he trust?

15

Angela heard about Fernando and Britney's fledgling relationship from Crystal, whose own painting of the picture
was adorned with the words "adorable" and its synonyms
many times over. Indeed, Angela agreed, the concept of two
employees finding romance at Singing Pines – a country club
yes, but also the scene of around 40 weddings and 250 wedding receptions a year – to be a feel-good story that could be
nothing but good for department morale.

While walking around and through the building, a new
practice that was part meditation, part exercise, and the rest
a practical application in keeping tabs on her employees, she
noticed Alfredo talking lightly with Felipe and Alonzo during
a set-up shift. He was back to his old self again. Even in his
angry incarnation he rapped to himself and spoke in voices,
but those acts were pierced by a malevolence towards those
apparently so close to him that she considered firing him at
one point. It was his seniority that saved him, not to mention
her own blossoming busyness at the time with new ventures.
Even currently she was already cooking up ideas for another
theme night. Lately the often-popular idea of a gambling
night was being bandied around between her and Wanda and
Howard.

Walking away and outside, the sun shining and her dreams
brightening with it as they revealed scenes of festive nights
ahead and a staff to go along with it, Angela realized Britney
was not just a hire to replace a friendly but troublesome Cody,
but a symbol of a maturing staff. It was as though Alfredo

had been unburdened not because his cousin was happy, but because his cousin simply was not after "his girl," whether that title was current or expired.

And so, thinking about Cody's departure, it was no wonder that Jamie and Seamus, too, were better behaved. Two miscreants she could break up, but three would always be impossible. That said, she noticed moments of absence from them both that she was having more and more trouble tolerating. But then again, those absences were never shared by the boys at the same time. Jeff and Christine were excellent about ensuring that no one from the crews mixed. It was a department policy they took seriously and it showed. Truly, they were examples for the others whether the others knew it or not.

At the tail end of her walk, it struck her that she should take Jeff and Christine out for drinks. There was no event planned this Wednesday, and it would be a fine time for her to show her appreciation for them in the name of morale. They were banquet captains after all, and she wanted them to know that meant something. The clubhouse was different without Barry as a captain, a man she would never have a drink with to save her life.

She even told them as much when they did agree to meet with her, and unknown to them beforehand, Bryce as well.

"Well yeah. Besides, Barry only drinks with losers who do drugs. He and Chris are probably down at the Red Door Tavern right now with all the other jerks," Jeff said.

"Shit, I like the Red Door," Bryce said.

Ignoring him, Angela said, "Now Jeff, I wouldn't want to have a drink with the man because he makes me want to die a little. I didn't say anything about Chris."

"I don't know," Christine said. "I'm the only person at this table who can say I did have a drink with Barry. And, to your point, Jeff, Seamus and Jamie were there too."

"Losers who do drugs!" Jeff grumbled.

"You two!" Angela intervened. "They still work for me, and for both of you, too."

"Ah," Jeff swatted the air. "If I could fire and hire...anyway, thanks for taking us out, Angela. I won't dwell on the...I don't know, I'll call it the weeds. Weeds get weeded out eventually."

"That's not much better sounding than losers who do drugs," Christine said.

"It's the word that came to mind," Jeff smirked.

Bryce finished the remainder of his Jack and Coke, courtesy of Angela, which was itself a step-up from his more well-known acquaintance, Jim. He looked for a cocktail waitress but there was none. There were servers and there were bartenders. There was a host and there was a bouncer. But if he wanted another drink he would have to get up and stand in line. So he did, and surveyed his surroundings as he waited.

It was a busy night, especially considering it was a Wednesday. Bryce had never met Seamus, but this particular bar was not far from Seamus' campus. As such, it was good for a crowd most nights. And as such, Bryce saw bougie-looking young people he never saw at the Red Door. There was not just makeup, but makeup done perfectly. Men wore gel in their hair. Tattoos were colorful, intricate, and placed not an inch too far from shirt sleeves rolled up to reveal them. Jeans, if worn, were designer. Plaid, if worn, was the same. Facial hair was only wild if accompanied by clothes free from wrinkles. Not one boot worn had a visible scuff, and no piercing that sparkled in the low lights was likely bejeweled with fake stone.

Bryce, a foreigner here, recalled the atmospheric differences between the places. Both were similarly dark, but in this bar strings of white lights shone through the dim lighting. At the Red Door, appropriately red lighting splayed forth from conical fixtures, and more than one of them were broken. Here, a tiled floor. There, a mildewed carpet. In his ears clanked a dancey contemporary number with disco drum beats and tinny keys. The last time he was at the Red Door, or, two nights previous, the patrons selected Buckcherry's *Crazy Bitch* three times on the jukebox, its collection of burned CDs rarely adjusted.

As he received his drink and took a final panoramic look around the room, he thought to himself, "This place sucks." And surely, if Angela had not invited him to join her this dull evening, he never would have known it existed.

A funny thing happened on his walk back to the table, however. Seeing Angela sitting at a round table talking to others triggered a state-dependent memory from his past... near past? How long had they been fucking again? Anyway, that was beside a point that was revelatory and crested his mind with sudden authority. He *had* been here before!

Ignoring the ongoing conversation rattling around the table, which at this point featured Jeff saying, "I don't care, when you're down in the trenches, you have to give a smile," Bryce raised his glass to make an announcement.

"Hey everybody, look at me," he commanded.

That stalled even Jeff in his waxing. Bryce said, "I know where the hell we are. Girl, we fucking met here!"

Jeff looked at Christine first, who was already turning her head to look at him. Their intentions of looking their boss in the eye apparently non-existent, it was Angela who spoke first to say, "Yes, we did meet here. And boy, what an impression it made on us both."

Bryce said, "Hell yeah! This is the shittiest bar I've ever been to! This stupid chick has a tattoo that said, 'This too shall pass' with two fucking o's! A bunch of wannabes but they're dumbasses."

Jeff and Christine laughed. "Hey Angela," Jeff began.

"What?" she pressed.

Jeff paused. "Never mind."

"What, Jeff? You're going to suggest Bryce go drink with Barry?"

Jeff shrugged and opened his mouth which emitted nothing intelligible at first until he finally settled into saying, "You said it, not me."

Christine kicked him under the table and Angela glared. Bryce said, "Who's Barry and what does he drink?"

"Did you miss that part of the conversation earlier?" Jeff asked.

"Jesus, Jeff!" Christine shouted.

"You son of a bitch," Angela said.

"Chill, girl!" Bryce yelled.

"I'm not talking to you!" she snapped.

"Oh," Bryce said. "Oh! Holy shit. Woah! Like, damn!" Bryce continued to put his hand on his chin and rub it as a monkey does when grooming. He drank from his glass and continued, "First time for every fucking thing."

"Listen Jeff, you need to remember that you work for me,

not the other way around."

"Of course Angela -"

"No, not of course. If of course then you'd never say what you said. Bryce is an accomplished physical trainer who only gets busier. I love how seriously you take your job, but you need to understand that you're not the only one who's good at what he does. I took you out tonight to thank you for that, and I brought along my boyfriend because believe it or not, you have something in common, and it's one of the most important qualities anyone can have."

Bryce, who was enjoying watching Angela get fired up more than he did hearing her defend him, became quickly aware of one keyword he did not expect to hear. And while no more drinks were ordered but apologies from both Jeff and Christine flowed like wine, Bryce spent the remainder of his drink and his time at the bar wondering just what he had gotten himself into this time.

When they all parted ways, amicability well-returned among the coworkers, he said his goodbyes dopily and seemed much drunker than he was. That one word and all its strings dangling before him, Bryce staggered through the contemplative place he rarely ventured unless things had gotten really strange, which now they had. It was not that Bryce was thinking so much as trying to understand.

"You're quiet," Angela told him as she drove them away from the bar and back towards her apartment. When did he even say he was coming over?

"You made a left," he said.

"Yes. That's the way home. How drunk are you?"

"Listen. I was going to go out with my boys later."

"Well why didn't you tell me that?"

"Because I forgot. But those fools just texted my ass and were like, yo!"

"So you want me to take you home?"

"I don't know. They're not picking me up for a while."

Angela, used to this type of wishy-washiness from him, decided that she would do what she always ended up doing and that was take over the conversation and thus the direction of the night. She put a hand on his left thigh and told him, "Then why don't you come over for a little bit?"

He shrugged. "I just didn't know that's what we were doing."

"Well, is that what you want to do?" She rubbed his thigh higher up and massaged her fingers deeply into his jeans. "I know what I want to do."

Bryce did not know what he wanted to do. And while his friends were picking him up later to go to a party at a girl's house, he could still go for a lay right now. So that settled it and eased his mind. He would deal with the word Angela used at another time. He did not know when. But thinking he had to know now became entirely stupid to him as he came to an understanding that life was good and he just had to enjoy it. That was the main point in the book he read which he could not remember the name of but had a colorful cover and was one of the only books he had read in his life. Realizing that he was about to get laid by two different people in the same night assured him that he was thinking the right way after all. After all, the last time this happened, which was two weeks previous, it was fucking killer.

"Well cool. But my boys have to pick me up later. Can they come to your spot?"

"Yes, you know they can pick you up there as long as they

stay in the car."

"Damn, girl! You know they know that already."

"They've been good lately but still. If your neighbors called you about some stranger pissing on...actually you wouldn't give a shit. But trust takes a long time to earn."

"Hell. If I saw some fool pissing in front of El Dorado I'd be like asking him what the fuck? Fool probably came from some party on the other block."

"My point exactly. Anyway, do you have condoms? We're out."

"No. What do I look like? A 7-Eleven?"

"You look like a hot mess but what you are is my boyfriend. You should probably think to bring condoms some time."

Bryce shook his head around. That word again! Damn, girl. Was she trying to kill his mood?

"Detour," Angela said and made a quick right and then a couple of lefts and pulled into a convenience store parking lot.

"You must really want to get laid," he said and got out of the car.

"Are you actually buying them this time? What a gentleman."

"All good," he said and stormed into the whiteness of the brightly lit store. Angela watched him point at a big box behind the counter. He was actually thinking ahead, for once! She was proud of him, even if this was a silly, trivial decision.

At home, they began with little foreplay and not far into it he rolled her over for doggy-style sex that he was so fond of with her. He came before she expected him to and hurriedly removed himself from her and rolled the condom off before she could turn around lie back against the headboard, disappointed and not even sweating.

He whistled. "Always a pleasure. Thanks girl."

"The fuck was that?" she asked.

Bryce stalled in pulling up his underwear and looked. He slowly nodded his head and asked with a toothy grin, "That good, huh?"

She shook her head. Her initial reaction was to ask him if he was kidding but she knew he was not. "You've got the entire night to get wasted all over again with your buddies. I ask nothing from you and I give you everything."

"Wait. So you weren't down?"

"Why is it that you're really this stupid? I swear, I hear you in the gym and the things you say to people are at least somewhat creative. Then you get here and you're a goddamn knuckle dragger."

Bryce was pulling his jeans on now and his cell phone vibrated in his pocket. "Ooh! Almost rang right up on my dome," he said. "I'm cooling down, fellas. Hold on," he said and pulled out his phone.

"You make a good point. I will consider everything you just said. Thanks for clearing this up so eloquently." Angela rolled her eyes and put her hand on her head. This was her boyfriend...

"Damn! They're down the street. Thanks again girl," he said and kissed her on the forehead.

Angela, though in no mood to forgive, would have some serious thinking to do. But Bryce saved her the effort. Clothed and leaving her bedroom, he picked up the box of condoms from her dresser and threw a final, "Bye, girl," before she stopped him.

"Hey! Why don't you just leave those here?" she asked.

He turned. "Uh, well shit, girl. I bought them."

"Amen. But you never have any so why don't you just leave them here? You'll just forget them next time."

"No I won't."

"Yes you will and you know it."

"Girl, I've never forgotten the condoms before. You've just always bought them."

"Just leave the fucking condoms here. Save us both the hassle."

Bryce was in it now and that stupid word was beating within him. It was heavy, but he dug deep in the back of the drawer and looked for bus fare. And then inspiration struck.

"Listen, girl. My boys and me are going to a house party and there are going to be a bunch of chicks there. And those fools never bring condoms but I'm going to totally hook them up. They're going to get laid. And it's because of me. And even you. Like, you can totally be with me on this."

Angela said, "Okay. But the first thing you said was that you bought them, meaning you should have them. If you needed to bring some for your buddies, who even though they're going to get laid like it's a 90-day guarantee are too absent-minded to bring condoms, you could have said that upfront. But you didn't. And there are eleven left."

His phone vibrated again. He checked it. "Yo, they've been outside for like an hour. I gotta go."

She got up from the bed and pushed the door closed. "Yes, you do gotta go. But we're talking first."

"Girl! You're like, pissed off."

"Unless you're the twelfth person in your group of assholes, what's going on?"

Bryce shook the box of condoms at her. "Girl, that's the crazy part. I actually am the twelfth guy."

"Bryce, cut the shit. No you're not."

"How do you know? You just imagined that I might be."

"No. I intimated, that's the word by the way. Jokingly."

"So you were making a joke? Damn girl, okay. I thought you were pissed."

"Bryce, just leave the condoms here. They are for us, right?"

His cell phone vibrated again. He reached for it but she snapped at him to ignore it. Bouncing up and down on the balls of his feet he turned and paced through her room, his shoulders swinging with every step, his head down and face turning bright even in the dark.

He pointed to the trash. "Of course they're for us. Who the hell just wore that thing?"

"What about the rest of them?"

He sat down on the edge of her bed and moved his head around as boxers do trying to regain a clearer consciousness after leaving themselves all too exposed. If he had gotten himself into this, he should be able to get himself out of it. Thinking positively and remembering that the power was his, inspiration struck yet again. Maybe he should fess up a bit, but only about one person. Suddenly he wondered if Karina, the bisexual tattoo artist, would want to get involved in a threesome. His mind raced. He had seen pictures of her with chicks before. And if Angela was asking like she was now, he might be onto something. He could not blow this. So he took another deep breath, realized he was a genius, and asked an innocent question.

"Girl, have you ever been with another woman?"

Angela's voice cracked as she asked, "What the hell are you talking about?"

Bryce remained calm. "Life is full of adventure. What I need to know is how cool are you with another woman?"

Angela let out a low moan like the kind an injured cat would. Bryce had to turn away. He brought her tissues from her bathroom.

"Don't come near me," her voice shook.

"What? I didn't do anything, girl."

"Who the hell are you fucking?" she demanded.

Bryce realized that he was caught. Angela was not interested in other women, and above all else, was deeply hurt. He felt responsible somehow, and a little sad.

"This wacko chick Karina who does tats out of her garage. She likes chicks, too. I thought maybe you'd be up for an adventure."

Bryce's phone rang now and as he answered it and told his friends to "chill" among other expressions, Angela put a hand to her eyes and wiped away the tears. She felt her eyes burn, but there was something other than self-pity making them feel this way. As she listened to Bryce stumble through his words and reassure his friends he would be out "faster than a v-dog goes in his condom," she considered that she had another option, other than sorrow. And this amused her.

Bryce hung up. He said, "Girl, why don't you sleep on it."

"No Bryce, I'm not going to. I don't have an interest in other women or even another man if it meant having a three-some. I'm just not that adventurous, as you put it."

Bryce shook his head. "Hey girl, different strokes. I'm sorry to hear that but, well, I gotta go," he said and started towards her and the door.

"Is Karina going to be at the party tonight?" she asked and stopped him.

"No. Why? Are you -"

"I'm just curious. Are there any other women who are going to be there? Women you might have, you know, interest in?"

Bryce was careful as he could be as he asked, "There are like...there's women and...why?"

"Because I'm afraid I'm just a little too boring for you and I want to know what kind of women are there who get to be this adventurous with you. You don't have to be with me, but you don't have to be with a crazy woman who inks people out of her garage, either."

"Wait, what?"

Angela smiled inside. "You said she's wacko. Karina is her name?"

"Yeah, or K-girl. I call her that when I...that's my name for her."

Angela stifled a wince. "I don't think you need to be with anyone you'd call wacko. You're worth more than that, Bryce."

Bryce nodded. "Girl, you may not be the best lay I've ever had but you have the biggest heart." He nodded more, thoughtfully.

She put a hand to her heart. "Thank you," she said.

They hugged. He said, "You really do care about me, don't you?"

"Yes, and I want to make sure that if it's not me you're with, it's someone who deserves you."

Bryce did not want to hurt Angela but judging by the way she was talking he guessed that even if it stung, she could probably take it. Truly, he thought, he could tell her anything.

"There's this chick there tonight who I fucked the other night, and like, we had a connection," he said.

Angela bit her lip as long as she needed to. She could only nod at first. "Mmm-hmm," she said through burning lips.

"Her name's Marissa, and like, I think I'm going to fuck her again tonight. She's like, so down."

"Do you care about her?" Angela was able to ask.

"Yeah. Yeah I do."

"Does she care about you?"

"Shoot. I don't know. She doesn't say it. But she looks at me like...like she wants to know my mind or something."

"Well Bryce, if you care about her than she probably cares about you. And if she wants to know your mind, God, that could take her a lifetime."

"Shit. You know me, girl."

"Yes. But you don't know women. Not like you think you do."

"Hey! I thought I gave it to you good."

"I'm not talking about that, Bryce. But trust me, when you give it to Marissa later you can win her heart if you talk to her during sex."

Bryce clapped his hands and hooted. "Fuck yeah! Chicks love dirty talk!" He gave Angela a high-five. "Man, you're good."

"I'm just telling you the truth. But the trick is not to stop after you start talking dirty."

"Like keep going. I got that."

"No. Change the subject. Start talking about yourself. Start by talking about a memory from your childhood."

The general confusion that accompanied Bryce whenever something unexpected was said or happened returned with force. "Hold up," he said. "Talk about my childhood? During sex?"

"Yes. Sex is about intimacy. And there's nothing more intimate than being honest about yourself. It's something you never did with me and I know now that's because I wasn't right for you."

"No, I never said stuff like that because it's crazy."

"Actually Bryce, what's crazy is not doing what I tell you to do. If you really care about Marissa, you have to talk about your past. She will melt."

"You're being for real?"

"Have I ever been anything else?"

Bryce thought. "You're pretty much the most straight-up person I know. Almost too much. Like, you need to chill most of the time."

"Okay, well there you go. Listen, after you talk about your childhood, you need to ask her to meet your parents."

Bryce lost it. His phone rang yet again and he picked it

up to scream, "One goddamn minute!" He looked at Angela, dumbfounded, and asked, "Is this just some sick shit you're about?"

"Bryce, this is what every woman wants. We just don't go around telling guys, they need to know for themselves. But I have special feelings for you and am willing to tell you because I want you to get what's coming to you."

"So, even if all this is true, what if I don't want her to be all in love with my ass?"

"You said you have a connection. And I didn't say she'd be in love. But if you care about her and you don't know if she does about you, you'll definitely know now. What are you going to tell her about your childhood?"

"I don't know. This is crazy."

"Women are," she said.

Bryce looked at her with full trust. "Yeah they are," he said and rubbed his chin thoughtfully. "I'm going to tell her about my pet turtle. Fool ran away."

Angela turned her head and covered her face. She was fortunate to laugh so hard as to cry, and that with proper muffling, it sounded like she was bawling.

"Girl, hey!"

She turned around and said, tears streaming, "That's so beautiful it breaks my heart. Bryce, you've got this."

"Yeah? For real?"

"For real! You go. Go with your boys. But more importantly, go for Marissa. Who knows, she might even want to meet Karina."

"Fuck!" Bryce wailed and hugged Angela again. "Thanks

girl! And girl, I hope you find someone special, too. You deserve it!"

Bryce was leaving but Angela had to stop him one more time to say, "Bryce," and point to the bed. He left the box of condoms sitting there.

"Oh shit. You're right girl, I can't remember a damn thing." He picked them up and said, "But I won't forget to bring up Sammy."

"I'll assume that's your turtle."

"Chh. You're smart. Always remember that."

"Bye Bryce. You're special. Always remember that."

Bryce sprinted out of her room and out of her apartment. She listened to him slam the door and enveloped herself in the sound of her own gushing, glorious laughter afterwards. When she finally caught her breath many minutes later, she went to the fridge and pulled out a beer. She opened it, took a long sip, and sat out on her balcony.

Draped in a bathrobe and feeling cool night air on her toes, she tilted her head back and searched for stars. There were not many of them in the streetlight sky. She thought back on starry skies over Italy. When it was clear on the coast, she would always sit outside at night and look for shooting stars. Thinking that there would be no better place in the world to see one, she finally did one night but never made a wish. Looking back, she saw she did not have one.

Here on this balcony, she had a wish or two. But they did not gnaw at her like unfulfilled dreams. Instead she smiled just thinking about them, felt her heart gallop in anticipation of making them come true. That was real adventure, she knew.

16

Angela was in an iron-fisted mood when she fired Seamus and raised a heavier hand yet when she fired Jamie. At least Seamus, though his deciding offense was highly trivial, behaved explicitly against the rules. As far as Jamie was concerned, there was no rule against being on the roof. No matter. When Angela spotted him in an inconvenient position during a freak episode where she was showing some tight-lipped jerkface from the Health Department around the property, she fired him on the spot.

"Just like that man," Jamie told Seamus when he visited him in his dorm room and smoked a bong load. "She was white as the picket fucking fences that must ring around her house." His eyes lit up with fond recollection. "Jamie. Get down!" he strained his voice. "It was nuts, dude. She was like a wild animal."

"Dude. She had to be spooked to see someone up there like that."

"She was. She mumbled some pleasantries into this square's big ass ear and looked me right in the eyes like I was holding a bow and arrow and aiming for them both. It was actually pretty cool."

"Shit man. Did she catch you with pot up there?"

"I wasn't even stoned. And that's what really gets me. When a man can't climb up to a roof and think, then we've all lost."

"It's a police state man, and that's a cultural thing. Not all authorities are cops."

"But everyone wants to be the sheriff. Oh well Angela, you got your man."

"The warrant was out and the perps were nabbed."

"That's the truth my man. Beats me how it all works but hey, it's not our problem any more."

"Amen. I make shitty money at my work study job, and it's boring as fuck, but at least my principles aren't being assaulted anymore."

"We rode that horse 'til it had nothing left to give us, my man. And I'm proud of you. I told you long ago what you needed to do to succeed at that place and you soared. While the getting was good, you got it alright."

"You showed me the way, man. And you know what? You were damn good. At least when you got fired you got the last laugh. You got one final rise out of her."

Jamie packed another bowl. "Hey. You stood your ground to the end. That's all anyone can ask."

"I guess. You'd like to think you leave a mark, not the other way around," Seamus said.

Seamus' firing was fairly quick, but still more drawn out than Jamie's, whose routine action led to a direct and final reckoning. Seamus' wrongdoing landed him in Angela's office, and for all the pettiness of his crime came an equally petty interaction. Seamus had been in the snack bar eating an English muffin when Angela was walking down the hall looking for him. He thought he heard something but looked out the window and saw nothing. A moment later he heard tapping and looked again to see Angela's listless face Seamus was reminded of a koan about a monk hanging onto a vine, and the vine was beginning to break so that it was only a matter of time before he fell to the jaws of man eating tigers below, and there was a strawberry on the vine. And the monk picked the strawberry and savored it, dangling there over a cliff. Standing there chewing the muffin, Seamus did his best to enjoy his forbidden snack. When he opened the snack bar door and Angela told him, "Seamus, let's talk in my office," he knew his vine was about to break.

He was wearing the service star that Jamie had given him, who had received it from Alfredo. A controversial choice since he and Jamie no longer worked together, Seamus beat her to the punch by saying, "I suppose Jamie's support of my efforts are called into question here, as well."

"You really think that's what this is about?" she asked.

"I don't know what this is about."

"You probably know it's against the rules to eat food from the snack bar."

"Yes, but if you fire a man because he needed to eat, then that's on your conscience."

"Okay," she shrugged. "I'll try and get a good night's sleep. I don't know how, but I'll do my best."

What in the wild hell was this? Angela was getting smart with him?

"Angela, look -"

"Where?" she interrupted.

"I'm serious, listen -"

"To what?" she asked.

"Are you kidding me?" Seamus asked.

"No Seamus. And I'm not in the mood for your philoso-phizing, either. You know perfectly well it's against the rules to take food from the snack bar. On top of that, you skipped out on the prep meeting to do it. What do you really expect me to do?"

"I'd expect you to think I'm in the wrong. But what does the prep meeting even prepare us for that we don't already know? And really, what are rules?"

"There you go again. Sorry, Seamus, but that horse has left the barn. I'm not in the mood for sparring with you over your make-believe ideals. There have been times, believe it or not, when I've defended you. You've worn out your welcome kid, and I can't save you from your own bad decisions."

Seamus knew this was his moment but did not know what to do with it. He only said, "I was hungry."

Angela sighed. "I'm sorry, Seamus. I'm going to have to let you go."

Seamus got up and nodded and looked her in the eye before he left. There was nothing more to say. The finality was one thing, what she said was another.

Sitting outside the clubhouse he called Karen and waited for a ride home. What Angela didn't know was that Seamus was searching for different jobs anyway, and that she merely beat him to the punch. What she knew even less about was that she trampled over freedom in the name of progress, stomped down personalities for the cause of conformity. Every time a place like Singing Pines changed, or at least got the better of those who represented its true potential as a workplace, those aligned with Them won. And that was a reality Seamus could not bare just yet.

He knew what he had to do. He had to find a place where things stood still, where what was, was enough, and where the illusion of progress was seen through as the flimsy facsimile of purpose that it was. He was going to a place where nothing happened.

PART III

THE LOSER GENERATION

1

Jamie walked on stage and turned on the microphone. It was silent save for his footsteps sending coarse echoes into the room. He exhaled into the mic - it was on all right. He took a sip of his Seven and Seven and breathed the dense air. Slowly, looking up from the ice cubes in his tumbler, he swirled his glass casually and began his routine.

"So I picked up this job at a department store selling purses, and let me tell you: it's not exactly what I dreamed of growing up to be putting bags in bags for a living. Hell, I was selling bags to bags!"

There was no response and Jamie took another sip, walking across the stage a little to his left and engaging another part of the room.

"Tough crowd…let me know if I'm bothering anyone here and I'll see what I can do. This is a comedy club, but if that's not what you're looking for I swear there's a great movie theater down the way."

Not a whisper. Jamie walked to right side of the stage.

"But back to this purse business. I'm sitting with my girlfriend the other night, and her phone rings. It must have taken her five minutes to find the damn thing, and I'm thinking, what is it with these goddamn purses? Maybe I should get one. It's like I lost my keys and it may take a while to find them, but at least I know where I lost them."

Silence.

Jamie continued, laughing, "I can tell my buddies, 'Yeah man, you've got to get a purse. They're great for losing things and a lot lighter to carry around than a couch.'"

He wiped sweat from his neck and took a look up at the white light heating up the stage.

"I feel like I'm auditioning for the Witness Protection Program under this thing, Jesus Christ. 'No Officer, the last time I heard them laugh was when the comic before me was onstage.'" He laughed himself.

He paused from his routine to look over the room. It fascinated him just as much today as it had the first time he saw it. Pink and blue lights washed lightly over empty cocktail tables, which were situated on a tapered floor. It was a mini-amphitheater that raised his pulse to a jackrabbit's sprint even when no one was watching him.

He loved it there.

And of course he loved his lunch breaks, when everyone, including his manager, left the building for an hour and left him perfectly alone to his own devices. The rest of his hours he spent largely on the phone, working as a ticket rep and daydreaming through half of his conversations, his mind thinking about the room, about his new girlfriend, about his years at community college he might never finish, and about all the private jokes he encountered with such bountiful regularity, the observations about the world no one else around him knew he saw, unless they stumbled into the right conversation with him to find out.

He shut off the lights and recovered the well bottles with the blanket that kept the fruit flies out of the pour spouts. He killed his cocktail and washed the glass out in the bathroom. It still made him smile that there were two doors to get to the comic's bathroom, just like Singing Pines, and even more so that the countertops were black granite. He did not have to elaborate when he told his friends.

"You just know what goes on in there," Seamus had suggested. Jamie only nodded, smiled, and leaned back as though he had taken a peek behind the wizard's curtain, the proverbial tricks of this uncharted trade open before his eyes.

Whenever he reentered reality and the office, checking the messages from people who called while he was performing, he felt lonely again, but that always passed. It was no Singing Pines, but it was no Nordstrom either where he lasted just three months selling purses before he got fired for coming in one day smelling just too strongly of pot.

While the Improv had no replacements for Barry, his twenty-somethings coworkers had no problem self-deprecating themselves with varying degrees of snark. They lamented, with both dark and light humor, the small paychecks they earned and the paltry dinners they ate. Their grocery carts home to nothing more than eggs, lunchmeat, bread, noodles, and booze of any stripe. They took to the same stage as Jamie, only on Amateur Hour on Wednesday nights, collecting themselves in the box office after their routines to punch tickets for people coming to see the real comics.

Sometimes, if Jamie had a Wednesday night off, he would watch his coworkers try their best. Their receptions always lukewarm, he gave as much pitch to his laughter as he could. Because he knew them, he truly did find them funny. He knew what they were trying to say.

Jamie harbored no illusions about taking his lunch-hour routine to Amateur Hour. The stage and his own footsteps pacing back across it was enough for him. As he watched his coworkers live and in full color, he caught each droop of the eyebrow, every sideways step that was almost a stumble. But they always lifted their heads and caught their balance, and in spite of tepid responses, they give it their all. And Jamie could respect that. What else, in that circumstance, did they have?

Nothing, he knew. They were taking their chances no matter how bad the odds. And when Seamus told him he was moving to Big Sur for the summer after his junior year in college, and that between the two of them maybe he might just stay there, Jamie could only acknowledge that Seamus was taking his chances, too.

"But my man, you'll need a job down here for when you get back."

"I know it. I'll have to look again during the fall. There's always a job on campus."

"But those things are weak! You know that."

"Yeah, but I've got to give Big Sur a chance. It's a special place dude."

"Fair enough my man. I know how you like your hippies. I hear there's one or two of those up there."

"There's a handful," Seamus had smiled.

And being the friend that he was, Jamie had smiled too and agreed immediately to give Seamus a ride. Cameron Cooper joined them and they made a weekend out of it, getting high, making sudden stops at fruit orchards and casinos alike, hanging out, catching up, and laughing, always laughing.

When Jamie picked up the phone at the Improv one day and heard Seamus on the other end, he expected more laughter. But Seamus said little other than the fact that he could use a ride again. Jamie agreed just as readily as he had before, and they said goodbye without further discussion.

Jamie hung up, stopped writing down the jokes he would soon be telling to an empty room, and leaned back in his chair. Something had happened.

2

Seamus thought about thinking often, but he spent most of his summer in Big Sur remembering. And for long stretches five days a week he spent his time making small talk with tourists, families and couples, Californians and New Yorkers, Koreans and Germans. He worked in a store and lived in a cabin tent. He ate employee meals for lunch and cooked simple dinners on a two-burner propane-fueled camping stove which he borrowed from a college friend who wanted to avoid paying for a storage unit over the summer. Throughout the summer, cooking dinner was his happiest ritual. He ate a similar kind of diet that Jamie's coworkers did, but prepared his meals under the shade of redwood trees and on a wooden bench. It beat the confines of a studio apartment, until he went back to the musky heat of his tent cabin and lay on his cot, shut his eyes, and watch the memories roll in, whether he wanted them to or not.

Some memories were inconsequential and near – conversations in the dining hall; the light squeaking onto the quad on an overcast day, a sight he could appreciate only because he was skipping class to see it; Jamie and the look on his face when he rolled through yet another stop sign, or rather the total lack of acknowledgment that he even did so at all. Other memories ran deeper - his first introduction to the sour reek of chemicals in his high school dark room; the similarly bizarre smell of pot the first time it burned and the infinitely difficult concept of properly using the carb in a glass pipe; not driving when his classmates started earning their permits; still not driving when they had their licenses. Then childhood. Of course childhood - moving, and moving again; learning, and often failing at, how to pay attention; learning to swim and then not swimming for a long time.

Seamus would rise from his cot and walk around again. He would try to walk before it got too dark out, because then it was really dark and there were no streetlights on the road to make him visible on the One. When he did walk at night he brought a flashlight, its light a fuzzy circle at his feet. When he walked in the dark it was because the night was really long and there was nothing else to do but walk with it.

The day time, mercifully, was different. And on his days off he walked often. When he could, he made his way to a trail that gave him access to a view of the coastline. There, Big Sur was its truest self. Severe cliffs dropped violently into a hostile ocean, its surface deceptively flat but always in subtle motion. The waves assaulted the cliffs in white spray. The wind caught them, carried them through the shrubs and weeds and poison oak living along the cliffs, indigenous and proud. The air smelled so clean it could almost be tasted. It smelled like morning all day. Indeed, it smelled like the morning of the coastline's creation, smog and industry a presence in their own absence like silence that rings when someone is gone and does not return.

At many of these high vistas there were beaches below that sat lifeless and perfect and impossible. Physically reaching them was its own daunting dilemma. Further, it was illegal to do so. Seamus looked out at their sand untouched by people that only the birds and the wind knew. Down the road, people and cameras, taking pictures of these fantasy shores as he did. After a while, the pictures were no less real than spying on them from above with the fragrant, pure air blowing across his face. They were just as touchable either way.

A person could only enter Big Sur and leave Big Sur along

the One, and Seamus was becoming just as single-minded. He walked with it, or at least along it. He could never walk with it. It was always out of reach even at his feet. It had its own inner-life and history, its own grandeur and romance. It carried lines and lines of cars and RVs, saw plenty of cyclists, and every so often a highway patrolman making his rounds. Even the authorities kept their distance in this place, he thought to himself.

The more Seamus walked, the more he remembered. Soon, the One was not just an escape, whether it was day or night, from the past. It was just another stretch of time that passed. Walking or lying down was the same thing. All around him, no matter what curve he was rounding or stream he was crossing, the scenery was the same. The One, singular indeed, was the path to and from the same place.

3

The first time Seamus visited Big Sur was during a spring break trip he took with Karen. It was in the middle of their 3rd year and, just as he thought he might, he had gotten involved with her, though never with commitment. Still, neither of them slept with anyone else. They simply regarded each other with a distant kind of romance, or at least Seamus did with her. He went to sleep with her when he wanted and practiced leaving early in the morning so that no one else on the hall would be up yet, would see him, would expose him. He never held her hand in public, and though they spent time together visibly, in the dining hall or walking each other occasionally to class, he gave quick goodbye kisses and always walked hurriedly away.

Finally in Big Sur he could be more expressive of how he really felt about her, and stumbled into saying, "I love you."

As was the case with Rachel though, he did not say it first.

Still, he shuddered riding home with her now that they were a couple, and he would have to do the couple things he did not want to do. Seamus feared the gossip that would circulate at school where who was sleeping with whom was by far the chief topic in talks about others. He hated all the talk that he was going around with that "druggie," not taking the time to think that his own reputation bore a similar description. Yes, Karen did drugs, but not as many as people said she did. She also made him use condoms even as she used birth control, so she was hardly out of control. He remembered bitterly having to answer people over and over again when asked if he and Rachel were still together. And more loathsome was when someone said something back, their inability to pick up on the social cues of his shrug and tight lips as an invitation to exit the conversation, not press further with whatever worthless sentiment they harbored regarding business that would never be their own. Apparently, other people's feelings were public property.

In spite of all his stabs at privacy in what was a failed attempt to conceal their relationship, Karen never asked him to behave any differently. Instead, she greeted him opened armed each night, sometimes wearing lingerie and other times with fresh fruit for them to share. Every night an occasion.

And she always asked him how he was doing, as he did her. And then they would talk, sometimes before sex, sometimes after, but they would talk and he would always lose sleep. She knew more about books and movies and art than anyone he knew, and her references always colored their conversations about whatever it was they were talking about. She quoted Henry Miller, telling Seamus, "Art is only a means to life, to the life more abundant. It is not itself the life more abundant. It merely points the way."

Love got him nowhere before but disguised itself as something more. If he was going to go nowhere he would prefer to do it on his own.

But in Big Sur – even in the intimate moments where they took naked together to a stream, his eyes never leaving her, whether in real life or through the viewfinder – something else gradually took hold of his attention. He loved her, yes, there might be a different kind of love here. There might be a love of the land, a love of the culture, a love of the way of life. Here might be a muse.

Along the One occasional travelers. From the trees giggling. In the shops and bars, settlers in this small town, pil-grims in self-exile from the conformities of their past lives, was a lightness of being and persuasion. The interconnected-ness of everything that existed came up casually when ringing up a necklace. Snickering at the Highway Patrol man as he drove past the gas pump. An aversion to materialism at the Henry Miller Memorial Library. The people of Big Sur.

Seamus loved Karen, but then what? Fall in line with Them? Graduate and get his meager degree and wake up to reality the hard way? Eek out an existence like Fernando and Britney were doing? Karen was a Psychology major. The times ahead were not lined with flowers yet to bloom but more likely weeds ready to multiply.

And holding her, his arms crossing over her stomach and his chin on her shoulder, under her lifting jaw he kissed her neck. They looked into each other's eyes and then the ocean. They got into the car and said goodbye to the coastline. It was a long while before Seamus had the nerve, but when he told Karen he was going back there, for longer this time, she only encouraged him. She loved him too, and she denied him nothing. When he told her that he might not return, and pulling deep into his own growing narrative, said he probably wouldn't, college loans be damned, that he might just find his muse, find his community, find his home, he found some-thing else along with it: he would not have to worry about holding her hand in public after all.

4

What Seamus wouldn't give for some pussy now. Never mind that he and Karen actually said they loved each other forever ago. That was a different conversation, a separate lament. Right now, he could use a warm body.

Then again, even someone being just a little kind would be cool, too. People smiled, no doubt. People talked about the "connective fibers of all that is," too. But since he was not a tourist but a new co-habitant, people were different with him than they were when he was on spring break. He was, after all, inserting himself into the intersection of their interconnected world. And that was fine, but they were holding the place down before he got here, thanks.

He talked more to people who were passing through than people who had laid down their wizened, wrinkled roots which sunk deep below the Earth's crust and to its center, intertwined with the heart of the universe. Many of his personal interactions came from those who picked him up for rides.

There was at least one glaring positive in his experiment into this hidden wilderness world: he finally got to try his hand at hitchhiking. Indeed, if there were any truly exciting moments during those tenterhook days in Big Sur, they came when he stopped inching up and down a mile or two along the One and stuck his thumb out instead. What else did he have but the sights of it all? It would take some wheels to make sure he saw all he could.

Provided that he had pot to pass off to those that picked

him up, he always had currency to get a ride. Some refused his offer, apparently giving him a ride out of the goodness of their hearts. Others maybe did it because he was part of their Big Sur experience. Hitching around Big Sur was not rare. Seamus had seen people thumb their way along the One plenty of times himself. There was one local drunk who made a regular habit of it on his way out the bars. Living simply wherever it was in the woods where he lived, he did not even need a bicycle. His reputation served him well enough.

Seamus, as he came to understand, was more or less a lone traveler only with a job. Big Sur attracted many of his kind, and many more who were passing by for less time yet, without income, let alone other essentials for a modern life, like goals and prospects. Seamus met them regularly along trails, in bars, or stretching out on the lawn at the Henry Miller Memorial Library, a place so magically lax in rules that locals and wanderers alike would come to get high, do yoga, play guitar, read a book, or settle on the grass to do nothing at all. It was a place to come as one was, and leave when one wanted. It housed a book store but those who worked there never sweat if anyone spent money or not. It was a place with permanent art fixtures sitting unceremoniously outside with old, faded placards summarizing its namesake's life. It reminded Seamus of the "chill houses" he knew in high school, havens for drug use and living room speakeasies where girls from the sister schools came over to visit their "friends." Except at the Memorial Library the curfew was much later than four in the afternoon and there were no stern parents who would come home to bust the good time. On the other hand women were grown and not looking to continue exploring their bodies with unexperienced stoners. They came as the men did: to be. That was the ethos of Big Sur and some people had it boiled down to a science. Big Sur had a playful and unofficial title as "the place where nothing happens."

Mining for a moment where something just might happen, Seamus would keep wandering. South of the Library to Partington Ridge, Limekiln, Julia Pfeiffer Burns, or north to Andrew Molera, Point Lobos outside Carmel, and the many scattered trails that sprang from the One all along the seven mile stretch that comprised the heart of Big Sur and its residents.

Seamus walked often along the Big Sur River. It cut through several campgrounds and roadside inns. It was less a river than a mellow stream that sometimes widened, sometimes deepened, and in some parts was so shallow that Seamus would see children getting up from their inner tubes to drag their inflatable transport a few feet forward until they could float again, unhindered by jutting rocks.

And in watching the children float in the water, shoot water guns, and swim where and when they could, his attention was at its most arrested. He would pick up burritos from a store just off the river, sometimes getting two or three at a time so he could save them in his ice chest and ration them out over a few days, and while he was waiting for his order he would sit on the grass and watch the water and the young, thrashing bodies peopling it. Sometimes he would get a tall bottle of beer and drink it casually on the grass, looking quietly and without a word to anyone, much less the children playing.

If he ever said anything, it was to parents, to say that their children looked so happy. In this particular spot, one of the town's inns, the parents were always from out of town, and they would nod happily and agree, and move along. Some of the adults sat away from the children in wooden chairs that were positioned in an ankle-deep portion of the river. No matter how many children played, there were always a few adults drinking a cocktail, watching as Seamus did, though at much closer reach and greater serenity. He was always happy to see them.

Seamus enjoyed Pfeiffer Beach more than most places in Big Sur. He never got in the water there, and thankfully would only see children running up and down along the sand, getting splashed by incoming waves but otherwise staying dry. Locals cautioned against swimming there. The currents run strong at Pfeiffer, and the undertows are many and violent. Tall rock formations forbid entry in much of the beach's half-moon shore anyway, so it seemed obvious to most to enjoy the horizon but to stay otherwise on the sand.

He occasionally saw adventurous visitors scale one of the rock formations, its left face littered with knobby foot and hand holds. They appeared to have easy times with it, and thinking of George, he wanted to join them and get a look at the ocean from up high, imagining the view.

He was too scared to climb it to have a look for himself. He allowed himself to get halfway up at best, but climbed down. It was unnerving. It felt clearly within his abilities, but the "rock" in the middle of the face was really just hard, compacted sand. He worried it might give way, might break and send him to his death, since he was high enough that losing his life over a slip was certainly within reason. He was fluid in that reality as he found himself clutching positive holds and looking at the short but necessary traverse to the left where hard rocks would greet him below should he fail. Death was not inevitable, he gathered, but that was after he came back down to shore. In either circumstance, he felt that being maimed and crippled was not a best-case scenario worth chancing.

He remembered the night he came back to his home after getting halfway up, when he did a push-up session and drank a bottle of cheap, screw top wine afterwards. He had a pack of cigarettes and removed himself from his cabin tent to look at the stars. They were everywhere. There were no street lights to blot them out. There were no nearby cities whose lights would pollute his view. He knew he was looking at only a handful of the universe, and that most of it was dead already, light just catching up to his eyes on Earth. So much had happened, but like days and nights in Big Sur, nothing had at the same time. It was just time unfolding as time always did, beautifully, peacefully, and without friend nor enemy. Time was burning slowly through the summer that he was trying to enjoy, and he was running out of ways to pass it. As silly as it sounded to even himself, he was doing his best to make it work. It had been a while since he had given anything his best, and now that he was largely doing nothing, his job ringing things in a register and stocking shelves to simple to fail or excel at, he wondered just how good a job he was doing. He wondered what his best even meant or how it worked.

Seamus badly missed having a gym to frequent. He never wanted to pass his time in one so badly as he did now. But his alternative was decent. He did push-ups outside of his cabin tent and in tree shade. He breathed in the soil every time he lowered himself to the earth, and exhaled sharply as he thrust himself back up into starting position. The endorphins from working out mixed with the potency of the fresh smells from clean land. The air was clear here, and he took lungfuls of it like water from a well. He had never spent such a prolonged time away from the Los Angeles sprawl and the smog that came invariably with it.

Seamus knew why people liked Big Sur, in fact why they loved it. It was the "Church of Big Sur," as he told his friends later. The residents bought in to the program. They revered the land in a way that others might kneel in Jerusalem or bow in Mecca. Their actual spiritualities varied, though most were some kind of eastern-themed plurality. But what each possessed was a burning sense of protection over their home in the woods, along the cliffs, in the mountains. They called themselves "stewards of the land," and they took their work seriously. A couple years prior to Seamus' arrival a wildfire had burned brutally through the Ventana Wilderness, destroying hundreds of thousands of acres. The entire town of Big Sur was evacuated for ten days, while monks at the Tassajara monastery high up in the mountains and detached from the Big Sur town proper held their ground and agreed with each other and their truth that they would burn with the building should that be the way universe manifest its unknowable will.

The monks survived, and so did Big Sur. Some residents lost their homes but most people went on with their lives as usual. What was more important was that the area experienced a wildly mild winter afterwards. In season's past, rains fell heavy enough to roll mud onto the One, causing road blockages for weeks on end. With a mountainside denuded of trees and the underbrush whose roots acted as a net under the surface, keeping erosion at bay, similar storms could have leveled the town.

But as locals who told Seamus a much abbreviated version would say, they were "blessed."

Seamus agreed: they were. His own beliefs did not negate that.

In Big Sur, it took some poking around to learn about what really happened, in the past and present alike. Seamus walked along the periphery of a town and community, a church service that never adjourned, wondering what was going to happen to him. The more he walked along the road, the more he held his thumb in the air, the more he ate burritos alone at night in a camp chair outside his cabin tent, drank beer and smoked cigarettes, toked out of a cheap, glass piece as he sat wearily on the edge of his cot, retiring to read a book or look through a National Geographic he checked out from the library though he lacked membership, the more he saw that things were always happening. Something had to. It always did.

5

Seamus was getting tired of having little to do with anyone. People answered questions he asked them at bars but never asked him any other than where he was from and where he worked.

Seamus talked briefly with a man along a trail leading away from the Big Sur Ranger station. The man was ahead of Seamus by a few hundred yards and had looked back behind him several times along the trail. Seamus caught up to him when he saw him standing on a ridge staring into the distance. He appeared sheepish as Seamus approached, and they began talking as Seamus asked him about the trail they were on, for which he was apparently well-versed in traveling. It was another nine miles to the hot springs, and Seamus laughed at the notion of continuing on that far, his only equipment being a camera and a metal water bottle dangling from his belt loop on a carabiner.

The man was from Philadelphia, nervous but friendly, and burning through his savings as he drove through the country - parking for days at a time to go backpacking or bike riding. He always traveled alone, but never liked to be the only person in camp. It scared him to be that isolated.

Seamus watched the man's fingers grope the straps on his backpack while he quickly spoke. The fingers would take breaks to wipe away forehead sweat, and would then pull unnecessarily on the straps to pull the pack tighter. He excused himself after a few minutes of conversation by telling Seamus he would "let" him get along with his hike, and that he was going to keep going himself. Seamus decided that was as good a time as any to turn back around.

The man from Philadelphia was not a local but reminded Seamus of everyone else who was, though they were all much less on edge and of course had their roots. When he hitched rides the people picking him up never had much to say to him, either. They continued to talk amongst themselves and were gracious in taking his pot.

The man he bought pot from was a chipper and musically inclined coworker at the campground. He sometimes played guitar at night and sang. Seamus went to watch him play in early August at the campground bar where they worked. It was "Storyteller's night," which meant the lineup consisted solely of singer-songwriters. A dreadlocked girl wearing tights and a high-cut shirt went on after Seamus' coworker. She played guitar and blew in a didgeridoo simultaneously when she performed. Seamus thought they were sleeping together but he could not tell. The pot seller was as normal as anyone he had ever met except for the fact that he said no more to Seamus about anything other than the a-list topics of the weather, how his day was going, and what he thought of the weed. The girl on the other hand said nothing at all. She had even walked away from Seamus at the bar after she had played a set and he complimented her abilities to "really blow into that thing *and* play guitar. Wow!"

Sure, he could have known the instrument, but he reflected that she could have told him what it was. Instead the guy who sold him pot laughed and told him what it was for her while she sat in a chair and closed her eyes.

"She's got another set coming up with this other dude next. She's zoning in right now."

"Yeah," Seamus said. "I stepped into that zone and almost

lost a leg."

"Nah, she's harmless. Just into the music," he widened his eyes and smiled. "What'ch ya' drinking?"

"Racer 5. It is absolutely delicious. And dude, I could use the extra percentage tonight. I'm not getting along well with that massage chick over there or that chick by the jukebox."

"Nah," he dismissed him.

"She invited me to Dance Church though, but she also left the bar after that. I think it was a polite 'fuck off.' I know those, I've given them before!" Seamus laughed and drank his beer, thinking back and remembering again. Big Sur was good for that.

"Hey, here's to you," the pot seller said, rubbed Seamus' neck warmly, but then also walked away, leaving Seamus standing along the wall drinking his beer and being alone.

"Smoke 'em if you got 'em," he mumbled to himself. He went outside to the porch and pulled out a pinner joint from his cigarette pack. He stood off the deck and found a darkened spot by a tree away from the other smokers. He was taking his second hit when a large-bodied man with dark hair hanging just past the bottoms of his ears came up and said cheerily, "Yo man, you care if I hit that? I just got in from a drive all the way from Chicago. It was nonstop, dude. I'm like a zombie right now."

Seamus wondered if the man was tweaked as he seemed remarkably alert and animated.

"You know dude, this is all I have left and if this thing was bigger than a toothpick I'd love to share but, you know, I'm out basically."

"That's fine, man. You don't have to share your weed. Not everybody does. I get you."

Seamus thought back to every ride he had hitched over the summer.

"No, I really would like to share. And I usually do -"

"Whoa bud! You can rest your case man, you are what you are. It's all good. Adam," he said and put out his hand.

Seamus introduced himself and shook Adam's hand firmly as he always did anyone's.

"Dude! Okay, you've gotta just chill it back."

"What?"

"Here," Adam took Seamus' hand and pushed it back and forth in the air. It was less of a shake and more of a loose but steady roll. "Can't just go around grabbing people's hands like that man, you're going to scare them. It's too intense."

Seamus considered. "Like this?" He tried to emulate Adam's handshake.

"No man! You're still doing it! Like this," he said and repeated his lazy manual greeting.

"It's still firm."

"Of course it's still firm. But I'm not shaking the shit out of your hand like I'm a politician."

Seamus hit his joint and tried again.

"No dude! Like this!" Adam took over and shook Seamus' hand again. "I think you need more than that needle dick you're smoking dude 'cause you need to chill out!"

"Dude," Seamus grunted. "I shook your hand, looked you in the eye, was cool."

Adam shook his head. "See what I mean? Now you're all defensive and shit."

"Yeah, yeah," Seamus said and turned around to walk away into the tree shadows.

Adam had other ideas. He started after Seamus and said, "Yeah right, dude. Just walk away, walk away!"

Seamus turned and looked Adam in the eye again. He said, "Either I'm walking away or you're walking away. I'm good to ignore an asshole like you but if you want to keep giving me your goddamn handshake clinic you're obviously the idiot who needs to chill out. What the fuck do you seriously want from me?"

The corners of Adam's lips reached up to his eyebrows. "I wanted to hit that little piece of shit you're smoking but you're too good to share it or even shake my hand like a real man. You want me to walk away? Fine dude, but that's only so I don't knock your fucking face around. I gave you a bunch of slack, loser."

Seamus had every intention of standing back and watching Adam reenter the light of the porch alone. But that was not what happened. Seamus was out of slack himself.

A couple drinking cocktails looked over. Seamus inhaled deeply and stood up into the light. His body was shaking and his face felt hot like he had just broken out with a sudden fever. He blew smoke into Adam's face and kept his shoulders back and ready, though for what he had no idea.

"You shit," Adam said, though incredulously. The smile was gone, as was the animation. He was just alert, but with a new and menacing focus.

"What? You wanted a fucking hit, didn't you asshole!" Seamus said.

The couple walked over now and took Adam aside as he was lifting his chest and his head and probably his arms as

Seamus had already raised his as though strings from the sky had dropped down and reeled him up like a puppet getting ready to put on a show for everyone sundry.

The couple, mysteriously, said nothing to Seamus much less looked at him. They only pulled Adam away, took him inside, and disappeared. He resisted but not with all he had. He was big enough to break free if he wanted. The couple were probably part of the Chicago, nonstop car ride together. How they had Adam's respect Seamus would later marvel. Somehow the brute had respected them in turn enough to submit to their insistences.

Others on the deck had looked over too and still watched Seamus. He looked to a table where he left his beer and took a drink. He hoped his hand was not shaking nearly as bad as it looked or felt, but he did his best to ignore everyone's eyes as he fished out a cigarette and smoked. He realized that he had dropped his joint. It was not at the roach yet but wherever it was the cherry was out and he had lost it in the darkness. He was not about to go searching for it now, sifting through the dirt for the last hit that very well could have been Adam's. Though that awful bastard would never have taken just one hit, and if he did it would have dusted half the entire thing. Seamus knew it. He would not consider otherwise. He knew little these days, but that was as an important a thing to know as anything he had ever known his whole life.

After he was done with his cigarette he went inside, ordered another beer, and went out front to smoke yet again. He wanted to flag his coworker down to buy more pot but he could not find him. He found Adam but their final inter-action was fleeting and restrained by a safe distance. Among his other good fortunes was the fact that no one who saw the near-fight said a word about it to him. For once, he was grateful to be alone.

And as life often likes to play, circumstance threw him a companion when he was feeling his least social. What started as a question about directions transmuted to a viable conversation. At first though, cursing that of all miserable moments it had to be this one when a sweet old lady asked him where she was, Seamus only pointed flippantly around and told her, "Big Sur." She could have damn well walked right past him at that point, or driven off, and left him as alone as he apparently wanted to be. But luckily for Seamus that was not her style.

And luck, as Dr. Marsha Harbinger said, was a lot like timing: it meant everything.

6

Dr. Marsha Harbinger was born in St. Paul, Minnesota and enjoyed her childhood until she was seven, which was in 1956 when her parents divorced. She rarely saw her mother, only twice until her adolescent years and once after that: her high school graduation. Her mother had become a kind of ascetic in a time when abandoning one's family in the pursuit of spiritual knowledge was not yet in vogue.

Marsha's mother nearly died on a doctor's operating table but blinked her eyes back to life as Jijnasa, though that name would come years later once her guru found her appropriately enlightened.

But Marsha never knew her mother as enlightened, especially not as a child. She just remembered the earthiness that seeped through her pores and the softness of her linen dress against her cheek. She remembered her mother bringing her flowers for her hair and candy that she could eat immediately without having to wait for dinner. Her mother was different after the experience, mainly she was happier and quieter. She was serene. Her visits were each short lived as she was just "passing through the neighborhood," and her father forbade her to stay and visit. Each time Marsha had to sneak off to take a walk with her mother, laughing and crying and talking endlessly as they "sauntered without direction or purpose," as her mother put it.

"It's important to know that nothing is truly important," her mother told her, smiling cryptically but affectionately. Her mother always doled out hugs and kisses when Marsha was younger, but now Marsha was the one going to her, burying her face in her dress and grabbing at her side until her mother calmly peeled her away.

"You're such a beautiful spirit," her mother told her, smiling the same way. Everything had become a mystery, yet she had no answers to her daughter's questions about why she could not go with her.

On occasions when Marsha returned home from her walk she was hit with a belt. Eric Harbinger never remarried and spent most of his time alone. He raised his daughter, his only child, to be serious, rational, and cautious. He implemented a strict set of chores that included scrubbing toilets and washing dishes when she was younger and chopping wood and performing basic maintenance on the truck when she was older, though never on the Galaxy. Her father worked at the Ford plant in St. Paul and though her home life was full of stern directions from her father and quiet evenings where she retreated to her room to read, she never wanted for anything. She went to private school where she learned to play the flute and speak French. She read *The Stranger* in its native language her senior year and despite her father's sternness, she had the same curiosity that so consumed her mother it became her namesake. In the fall of 1968 she attended San Francisco State College based on scholarships, grants, and a bit of her own nest egg. Her father refused to pay for her to go to school in the same city where her mother was living communally with other Hindu-named, reborn luminaries, so she took a year off from school, lived with a boyfriend, and applied for financial aid while registering her taxes as a non-dependent adult. The budding existentialist that she was, she knew all along that she was essentially using the boyfriend since their relation-ship was doomed to fall apart once she had a ticket booked for California, but all the guilt faded in an instant when she refused his marriage proposal and found herself paying her dues by living out of her car for two months, though those were in the summer and provided little hardship but rather provided her with a sense of freedom she had never experienced before in all her life. Had she not been on the college track she might have gone the way of her mother and driven to San Francisco not for the education but for the enlightenment. Instead she spent the next ten years graduating three times and becoming a licensed psychotherapist during the Carter Administration, a president she campaigned for and continued to laud years later for the fact that he never went to war with anyone. She saw her mother only twice more in San Francisco, the first time was a homecoming of sorts and the second time was a goodbye. Her mother died from ovarian cancer shortly after Carter was elected. She died peacefully with her daughter by her bedside and friends from the commune surrounding her, chanting, reading excerpts from the Tibetan Book of The Dead, and adorning her face with oil. Dr. Marsha meanwhile lamented the years between that they lived so close to each other but remained estranged.

The homecoming had not been what either had imagined, and the truth hurt. Jijnasa said it was the Universe's way that she leave the family and find her truth. Dr. Marsha said she abandoned her.

"I haven't now," her mother said, eyes glassy and blue.

"Are you going to leave The NewWhere House?" she asked.

"Marsha, this is my home."

"Then you've still abandoned me," she said.

Before she was a doctor of the mind, Marsha was a student, and she spoke as simply as she could. Meursault had taught her that it was none of anyone's damned business why she did anything at all, and when her mother pressed her for reasons why she could not accept her role in the commune, she found no reason to explain herself other than reiterate *her* truth.

"You abandoned me. And living here you still are," she said.

Marsha knew being closer to her mother was only one fraction of her reasons to move to San Francisco. She prided herself on her independence and had forgiven herself for using her boyfriend the past year, but knew that in the end it had been his choice to invite her there and his choice to ask her for her hand in marriage.

And yet, when her mother looked at her with such steadfast determination, and even something that resembled mercy (though it could have been sorrow, it was tough to tell) Marsha realized that she was not as good of an existentialist as she expected others to be and that perhaps the fraction of a reason for moving to San Francisco was a bigger and faultier part than she had recognized.

Her truth was that her mother abandoned her. And instead of devoting herself to a major in the classics with a minor in French literature, Marsha explored her pain by delving into the field of psychology. Realizing rather quickly that she had more wounds than she ever imagined, and that none of them could be patched over by adherence to philosophy alone, her worldview shifted.

Once she graduated late the next decade, she would make a living by helping others shift theirs.

7

Seamus was not a stranger to shifting world perspectives, though he had gone through a dry spell over the summer in terms of entertaining new thoughts. When push came to a listless shove and most days felt routine and lonely, emotion trumped revelation. When Dr. Marsha pulled up in her green Jaguar, Seamus' attention was fixed solely on the emotions flying freely out the window of a gray Ford Explorer. Adam was hanging halfway out the car from the backseat, cursing, "Fuck you ya' greedy fuck! You uptight asshole!" He spit on the ground. "Fuck!"

Whoever was driving the car reversed onto the highway and quickly pulled into drive, speeding south and out of Seamus' life.

Dr. Marsha wheeled her Jaguar convertible with its top down into the open space. It was the only one available in front of the bar. "Where is this?" she called out.

Her friendliness bubbled with an immediacy that denied the theatrics that just blew over. Still, Seamus was not in the mood and he pointed a noncommittal hand around over his head. "Big Sur."

"Thought so," she said in a singsong voice.

She shut off the motor and got out, smiling. "Sounded like you made that man pretty mad."

Seamus smoked. "Yep."

"Well, whatever it was over, I'm glad you got into it with

him. I got a perfect parking space out of it."

"You know what? That is true," Seamus admitted. "And you have no idea how busy this place gets on the weekends, either. The locals love this place."

"The locals! How wonderful! If you know that, then you must be a local yourself."

Seamus considered. "I'm local enough."

"You live in Monterey then?"

"No, no. I live here, but for the summer."

"How wonderful! What a beautiful place for a summer job. You must be having a lovely time."

Seamus looked over the bubbly woman talking to him. Her hair was straight and thin and white. It went to her shoulders and because her skin was so pale she almost looked like an albino save for the rosiness in her full cheeks and the brightness of her blue eyes. She was slender and Seamus imagined that her body must have been tight when she was younger. She wore a blouse with multi-colored shapes and zig-zagging lines on it, similar in pattern to a Jerry Garcia tie. She wore a long skirt and high boots. She wore a gold necklace of strung together triangles that sunk deep over her chest. It was chunky and demanded attention. So Seamus found himself looking at the chest of a woman in her sixties. Beauty was beauty.

"I'm a solo traveler with a job," he said.

"Oh!" Dr. Marsha gushed and clapped her hands, her blue eyes radiating.

Seamus had to smile now. He said, "Glad you like that."

"It's fantastic! A solo traveler with a job. I've met many solo travelers who did not have jobs, you know. Some have ended up in my office. Pro Bono."

"You're a lawyer?"

"No I'm a psychotherapist. Emphasis on 'psycho.' I've met people like your friend in the gray car, too."

"Well, that guy was something else. We got into a disagreement because I wouldn't share my joint with him. And then he was trying to teach me how to shake his hand."

Dr. Marsha laughed excitedly into Seamus' face and brought her hands up to her mouth to stifle the sound. Her body shook, her belly contracting in and out.

"I'm so - sorry!" she said through her laughter. "But that's just fantastic!"

"Really?" He took a moment, then, "God, I guess that does sound funny when I put it like that!"

"It's absolutely gorgeous! Don't you love the absurdity of it?"

She had a point.

"I do."

"Wonderful! I'm glad I didn't offend you. I just think that's such a beautiful way to get into a fight!"

"We didn't get into a fight per se...almost did. How'd you know that?"

"Oh I didn't mean a fist fight, I was thinking of something verbal. But that's even better!"

"Yeah, yeah. It still didn't happen though. His friends pulled him away and I got lucky. I think he would have beat my ass, but then who knows? I haven't been that pissed in a long, long time."

"How amazing, then, that you're laughing now. That was a fast turnaround. You know, we all have our approach in my field but as far as I'm concerned if my clients aren't laughing by the end of therapy than they're not healthy yet. No matter what happened to them, they need to be able to have a laugh or two."

"You mean laugh at their problems?"

"Sure, if their problems are funny. But not all problems are."

"No, not all of them."

"But something else always is."

"Okay. I like that."

"Good! Then maybe I'm onto something. I've been working at this a long time. You always hope it's working, too," she winked.

"I'm sure it is," he said. "You seem like you'd be pretty easy to talk to."

"Thank you! Now, as a quasi-local, I actually need your help with some directions."

Seamus eyed the road. "You don't have many options on which way to go, so I'm confident I can help you with that," he smiled.

"Excellent. I'm looking for the Esalen Institute."

"Boy. I know where that is but it's a good ways down the road. I mean, ultimately it's pretty close but the highway is windy and it's exposed out there. It's dark and the moon isn't very big tonight so you'd be wise to take the road slowly. Plus I don't even know how they work there. It might be too late to check in."

"Hmmm. My friends I'm meeting there called me earlier and said they were going to soak in the hot springs at one in the morning and listen to a shaman play the didgeridoo."

Now Seamus did laugh, "Well you better get a move on then!"

Dr. Marsha squeezed his shoulder and said, "You may not believe this but I was stressing myself out driving into town here wondering where this place was and if I had missed it, though that seemed impossible coming from the north. There was nothing for miles. Just cliffs and trees, but I was searching like a mad woman all over the place. I wasn't taking the road too slowly either, but you're so sweet to warn me that I should."

"Oh yeah. It's a while to go still. And it's kind of hidden. Drive with your brights on. There's a sign and a little road that goes down into some, I don't know, hobbit town or whatever the hell Esalen actually is. Shamanic village apparently."

"Oh listen to you! It sure looks like I found the right local. Gosh, I don't know. I might be better off just going in the morning."

"You might."

Dr. Marsha considered. Then, exhaling loudly and putting her hands out, said, "Well time for a drink then. Will you join me?"

"I would love to," Seamus said, and meant it with everything he had.

Seamus got another beer while Dr. Marsha ordered a whiskey sour and the two went outside.

"I'm Marsha by the way," she said and extended her hand.

He shook it and replied, "Seamus."

"My. That's a firm handshake. I don't see anything wrong with that."

"Ha! Adam did. Said it was like I was a politician."

"Well judging by Adam's demeanor he'll never make it in politics. He could be jealous."

"I'll drink to that. Cheers!"

They clinked glasses and a splash of headlights washed over their faces from a car ambling past them to a cabin.

"Where's he going?" Marsha asked.

"Down to a cabin. There are a few in the back of the property. Pretty cool place."

"You know a thing or two about this town. And it's such a cool town. So small and strange."

"It's both of those alright. But I work here so I know about the cabins. They're pretty nice inside. Have everything you need. Get to walk out on the porch and be around the trees. It's beautiful here. Good place to visit."

"Ah, of course to visit. Solo travelers don't stay put for long. Where's next?"

Seamus shrugged. "Home. This solo traveler is heading right back where he started from."

"How long have you been away?"

"Hardly any time at all. This has ended up being a summer job. That's all."

"Summer job, so you must go to school. An education is a wonderful thing. What are you studying?"

"Something wonderfully impractical. Photography."

"Impractical? What are you talking about? Is the world not teeming with pictures? Have you ever opened a newspaper or a magazine? Gosh, I'm dating myself. Maybe you haven't done those things!"

"Nah, we had to do what were called 'current event reports' in grade school using the newspaper. I think my eighth grade teacher even forbade us from using online news sources. He was a real forward thinker."

"Wasn't he? Does he live here now?"

Seamus pointed his glass towards her. "You're good! They have the internet even here, you know. You can pay for WiFi in twenty minute blocks inside at the bar. There are other WiFi spots sprinkled around you can connect with on your phone for free. We're only partially off the beaten path."

"And isn't that a fine compromise? To live in such a beautiful place but not to be disconnected from the world. Monterey is only, what? Half an hour away?"

"God I hope it didn't take you that short a time to get here. More like an hour."

"You dear, I'm a good driver. I promise. Anyway, I bet you're really going to miss it here."

"Not really. This place is beautiful, you're right, but it's the loneliest damn place I've ever been. And the dumbest part about the whole thing is that I didn't necessarily plan on going back to school at all. But I sure as hell don't want to stay here. There's nothing for me here. Nothing happens."

"So you don't like school and you don't like it here. Sounds like you're not a happy camper. Sorry, I had to."

"I forgive you." He drank, looked around at the dark shapes of trees sitting against the near blackness behind them. The back porch, brightly lit with a tree protruding directly through the deck in one corner, was warm with gathering bodies. He listened closely. No vibrations from inside. A break in the music and people were spilling out as they always did to smoke and get fresh air. He made a quick, paranoid scan but there was no Adam. He was gone for good, he knew.

"But you know what? A moment like this, the place has its perks. All these people, the positivity. I almost feel like a visitor myself."

She smiled at him. "Then that's the kind of feeling you want to have! Maybe your traveling is not over yet. Maybe you can be a solo traveler with a photographic job one day. Just make shorter stops. Summer stays might wear on you."

"God, that's gorgeous, but that's just not how I see it. Sometimes, all I have is something simple to appreciate. This calm moment here with all these happy visitors is that. What you're talking about, I mean, nobody gets those jobs."

"Somebody does."

"Yeah but not me. Not me."

"And why not, Seamus?"

"Well Marsha, not long ago I wanted to hitchhike. This summer I finally did it. More than once. The way people picked me up, I thought it would be something crazy and adventurous. But it was just people, almost always around my age, who I had little or nothing in common with that gave me a ride and took my weed and we waved to each other goodbye. And that was it."

"So your first attempt at the traveling part was a bit of a disappointment. But why can't you eventually get a job in photography?"

"Because I'm not the kind of guy that stuff happens to. Even when I get what I want, to come here, to hitchhike, to take pictures, nothing comes remotely close to how I'd like it to. And you know what? It's always been that way. Moments here and there. Otherwise, not much to it."

"Always is a long time."

"Always has." Seamus considered. "All except at this one place that was pretty much the greatest, stupidest, most fun experience I had. And it was a job. A mindless, menial job. But god we had a blast. And I never in a million years saw it coming."

"Okay then! And what was this job?"

"I worked in a banquet department at a country club and worked mostly wedding receptions. That's the menial part. The better part is that I met this guy there that I became fast friends with. I loved everyone I worked with, really did, but he was the guy. He led me on these wild adventures. We snuck out onto the course in golf carts to get high. We snuck up to the roof to, well, get high! We drank champagne, priest-blessed wine. We did whatever we wanted to do. And this damn cynic who was like our boss but really just our supervisor was a miserable prick but had this hidden, huge heart. So long as we did the bare minimum, we were fine. And the manager, the one with the real power, wow. She didn't do a damn thing to stop us. Until the end of course."

"The end? Did the place shut down?"

"Oh no way. Nothing like that. She just changed."

"She changed. You know, people do. And often when we don't want them to."

Seamus nodded. "That's a funny way of putting it. But yeah, that's exactly right."

"Now other than the fact that you could be careless goof-balls, was there anything else you liked about this job?"

"No," he laughed. "That was the crux of it. I mean, sure. The people there were real. They were real, working people. Different than the kids I go to school with, a lot of whom have never worked."

"By the description of what you just told me it sounds like you haven't either!"

"Ha ha," he deadpanned. "I worked there. Just casually."

"Do you sneak off to get high at your job here?"

"God no. This place is way different. Way different."

Seamus thought back on the weeks behind him. For every cut corner and backdoor trick he pulled at Singing Pines, he had been a boy scout in Big Sur. He was always ten minutes early, found something to do even when there was nothing to do, which meant straightening things on shelves countless times a day to keep his hands moving, and left the floor and cashier area spotless whenever he was finished with his shift.

"Mainly, I'm so goddamn bored the only thing there is to do is work."

"Goodness! Isn't that funny?"

"Kinda, yeah! I don't know how I do it, either. I hate work, Marsha. I really do."

"Well Seamus, I'm not in the business of telling you how to think, that's your job, but if I may share one little secret here – it's all work. Everything you do. And that never goes away."

"Yeah, I'm sure you're right. So, like the whole bit earlier, that's also why I'm not going to become a traveling photo-journalist. It's work, but not just head down and get to work. It's super-intense networking, elbow-rubbing, full-blown hop into the Matrix and be a man of the world stuff. There's a drive in people that make it to jobs like that which I just don't have."

"It's funny you say all that. Because I think you're getting at something very important about work that you don't even realize you know."

"Really? And what's that?"

"You're not getting off that easy with me. How about this – all this networking you talk about. What is that? What happens?"

"As far as I know, all networking means is that people meet, talk, and offer to pull some shit for each other."

"That's a caustic but accurate description. Now what does that mean to you?"

"It means people shoot the shit and suddenly, I don't know, things happen."

She clapped her hands. "I don't know how either, but you're right! Things do happen!"

"But that's completely arbitrary."

"You're standing here in a place that bores you talking to me when you could be lying here in a place that bores you having been knocked out cold. Is there any reason for that? Did you make that happen?"

"So you're saying there's no such thing as work?"

"No. But a lot of what happens to you is really built on luck."

"I get that. But that means work is meaningless. People just fall into things out of sheer luck."

"It's luck and timing, but those are sort of the same thing. Now with that said, there are things you can do to better your odds. In your case, you could get an internship. Develop a portfolio. Do you go to a small school or a big school?"

"Small. And private."

"Wonderful! Then I'm sure you could work closely with a professor who might be able to be a good connection for you."

"I could. Yeah, you know, I really need to actually. Okay, but still. Odds may be an important and even alterable factor but your thesis, at least that which I'm getting, is that it's still a big crapshoot."

"You're defining luck as randomness, and I never said that. Look at it this way: you have to take some swings to get it right. And some people have to take more than others, while others barely have to take any at all. That's luck. People almost always attribute their success to hard work, but that's not really the whole picture. Nothing may be better for your odds than perfecting whatever craft you've chosen, whether that's an art form or learning how to trade stocks. Talk about luck by the way! But there are many hard working people out of jobs right now who are pretty confused about what they should be doing and have simply given up. And there are others who are applying for hundreds of jobs a month. There are some who have never lost a job in their lives. There are others yet who relocate if they have to, take their chances. All different forms of swinging the bat. Only in life it's like we always swing blindfolded, which is the real fun of it. Because life would be pretty dull if it were predictable, wouldn't it?"

"If I could have predicted how dull this place would have been I could have saved myself some trouble. It's not very interesting being bored and lonely."

"Oh no. You're bored. How could that happen to someone this day and age?"

Seamus smiled and took a drink, nodding his head.

Marsha leaned back with her whiskey.

"Now before we go off in that deep end you keep swimming out to, I want to ask you something. That person you worked for who changed. Why did she change?"

"Beats me. She had a new boyfriend. Seemed happier. Yeah, I think that was it."

"Okay, you're trying to play psychologist now! That's not at all the why I was looking for. Why did she change? Sounds like everything was working fine for you and your friend down there, getting high at every opportunity. If you did the bare minimum of duties your jobs required and your supervisor was cool with the chaos, why did she need to change her ways?"

Seamus finished his drink and thought. Who was this woman?

"If I'm going to really be honest, probably because she sucked at her job given how much shit we pulled. She probably wouldn't have lasted if we kept it up."

"So she came around and got to business. Meanwhile you had a great time for a while and memories to cherish. Did you leave that job to come here?"

"Nope. Got fired."

"Boy. She did come around, didn't she? What about the others you mentioned? Did they get the ax too?"

"Sure did."

Seamus looked back at the people on the porch. There remained a happy density behind him. Now was a good time to get another drink. He looked at Marsha's glass. Almost empty.

"Since I'm making you work on your night off, can I at least buy you a drink?" he asked.

"That would be wonderful. And this isn't work, Seamus. I haven't worked in a long time."

"So it's not all work?"

"I'm one of the really lucky ones, Seamus," she said with an angled look.

He grinned and turned, walked through a gap in the crowd. Cologne, perfume. The fetid odor of a man's dread-locks. And, somewhere in the crowd, pot. Timing, Seamus thought. Whoever was burning, they did not realize how good theirs was.

When he ordered the drinks, he made it two of the same. For all the myriad substances he put into his body the last few years, he was unfamiliar with whiskey. There would likely be no better night for his first time.

As the bartender stirred the drinks in their tumblers, he thought back to Steve and his stories, his defiances, his seeming untouchable quality that made him immune even when Angela did tighten up and get her authority act straight. He wondered if he was still there, and if so, he was one lucky son of a bitch.

Then it hit him.

Outside, he declared to Marsha, "I was damn lucky to get that job while I could. We hit the right timing, as you said, before the boss hit her stride. Before all that, we thought we were so goddamn clever. We were certain that we were evading her authority, challenging it and minimizing it. But we weren't good, we were lucky. The minute she decided to act with any degree of responsibility, we were done."

"I'll have what you're having," Marsha joked.

"Yes you will," he said and handed over her drink. "Cheers."

They did. He puckered.

"Okay. That's that," he said.

"Got some things off your chest?"

"This drink is putting something on my chest."

"Oh listen to you. It may have been the part where you admitted to turning your workplace into a frat house, but I don't think a line like that suits you."

"I've never had whiskey before."

"Oh. In that case, you should have held the sour. Then you really might have something."

"This is fine," he emphasized.

"Okay," she smiled. "If you remember this conversation, outstanding. If you remember to order a whiskey sour next time you're out, then you'll know for sure what we talked about."

"Believe me. This is the only truly memorable thing that's happened this whole time here. Everything else has been nothing but remembering."

Marsha eyed him and he drank nervously. He knew what he just said but did not see himself saying it. Sometimes, Seamus blurted things out. It was, for a long time he saw, a trouble-some habit. And whatever trouble he had with women, it was this exact flaw that beat at its heart.

"I won't press, Seamus. But when you say something like that..."

"You really love what you do, don't you? Just got in from a long drive and all you want to do is put me on your couch."

"Oh Seamus. It's actually quite easy, with just a little, tiny effort, to divorce yourself from your practice. And this isn't even a real session, believe me. But when we started talking, you didn't keep talking about how pretty the cabins were or how good a time you were having. You remember what you said?"

"Hey, you asked me where I was going next after I said... Okay, I guess I admitted some things about how stupid miserable I was up here. I'm sorry. I haven't really had a real conversation with anyone for a while and it just kind of slipped out."

"Don't be sorry. And I really won't press. But."

"I have a tendency to let things slip. I don't always pay attention," he said.

"That's something. What do you do instead?"

"Look around. Think."

"You think but you don't pay attention? Isn't that a funny combination?"

"Yeah. It's just sort of been who I am. Always has been."

"Always again. Everything is always with you, isn't it?"

"Some things do appear inherent. I didn't mean to tell you a few of the things I said. I just sort of said them."

"I understand this might happen often. And I understand it probably has happened for a long time. Inherence seems pretty real when your history is full of the same patterns."

Seamus felt dizzy but figured it was the whiskey. He smacked his lips softly, the sourness and bittersweetness lingering in his mouth.

Seamus did not feel that he was dizzy because of the memories that were readily available for him to divulge to a bona fide psychotherapist. They were coming too sharply into focus for all he had imbibed for them to be the reason the deck began to sway. For all her talk of luck and odds, here was his real shot if he wanted to venture into the true woods of Big Sur, the kind that he knew so well because there was nothing else to do. When time stops, not even thinking bears weight. The past is all.

So he stood still with it.

"Some people have the same problem. I'm not the only one," he said.

"Sure. But what does that have to do with you?"

He was sure though, that what he was going to say, was what he wanted to say. Because what else was he going to say about himself? He had shared plenty of bad news already. What was left now? That he was an awful student? An evasive son? That he never did his chores as a kid? That he spent too much time looking out the window from the time he stopped staring at a mobile? That, at an early age, he never shut the screen door when he came back inside the house?

"Because I want to talk about other people since that's what I've been remembering," he told her. "And that's how this whole segue we're on got started. So can I tell you?"

"If that's what you'd like to do, of course."

"The thing about other people and not paying attention is that bad things happen. Bad things have happened. And when you don't pay attention, then something a little bit more than luck is in play. Something like irresponsibility. Really, awful, heavy responsibility. And I've seen it. And it's not good."

"That's a start. I need a little context now, Seamus, before you give me your opinion though."

"Oh I'm getting there. I knew these kids in school and they totally were responsible for this kid dying. And that was from not paying attention."

"Seamus, you're giving me a reason for someone else doing something again, like when you said your boss became a real boss because she was happier. Frankly, I have no idea where that came from, and I don't know where you're coming from now, either." She sipped her drink hurriedly and then her eyes lit up. "Here," she said, motioning to him authoritatively. "Pretend you're a photojournalist. Just tell me as you see it."

"Fair enough," he conceded. "Okay, take this. This girl I knew had a sister who died. Her sister died hitting a tree when skiing. Pure dumb luck, just like we talked about. I get that."

"Okay. And?"

"These other kids all went on a kayaking trip together and got shit faced drunk one night. They all passed out, and when they woke up this kid was lying face down in the water. Dead."

Marsha bit her upper lip. She said, "Now. That's a picture. Tell me more about it."

"I wasn't there. No one really wanted to talk about it, but I heard from someone who heard that his face was bloated and that it was disgusting. And no one saw it coming. Had one person been sober enough to wake up when they heard him puke or roll into the water, whatever came first -"

"Seamus, your picture ended at 'bloated.' You're giving me all kinds of reasons for other people again. How can you say that had they been a little more sober they would have known? What if someone was as sober as a nun but a sound, sound sleeper? Or was so exhausted from all that kayaking a bomb wouldn't have woken them? Or that they put in ear-plugs because that was how they always slept, booze or no booze?"

"Because that's not what happened, that's why! I told

you what happened. And if someone was sober, they would have probably paid better attention. They may have noticed someone pass out by the water, or maybe they would have woken up because those other things you listed are all hypothetical."

"They're just as hypothetical as your theory that someone's sobriety would have saved the day. How can anyone really know?"

Now Seamus was seeing the world through blurry lenses, and it was not the whiskey, he was sure of that. But focus returned, and he continued, "You have to understand. I knew, just barely, one of the kids on that trip. Actually, I didn't even know him until after, and we actually got into this weird fight but anyway...he knew what he did. He felt awful. He knew that he was a part of it. He knew he didn't pay attention and was partly responsible. You could see it on him."

"You'd be surprised how many people come to me to talk about other people," she smiled.

"Marsha, I think you're really amazing but this isn't a happy thing to talk about."

"I'm not smiling about what you told me, Seamus. Well, I am, just not the content part per se. Anyway, I don't know your friend and I hardly know you but I will say that while behavior does lend itself to a degree of culpability, to take on more responsibility than is yours to take is simply disrespectful."

"What? Like he should shrug it off? I mean, I pulled that act at work all the time. Always have. Yeah, that word again. But this kind of thing, this is the kind of thing that stays with you. It shows you who you are," he said. Then, softly, "And it's not good."

"No one is shrugging anything off by accepting that they were a part of something tragic. But to lose sight of the fact that tragic things happen in which we are ourselves are tragically involved is to take on a little bit more than we should, and do you really think taking on more than you should is a good thing, either?"

"You're saying to just chalk it up to a thing that sorta was someone's fault but really was also bad luck so just get over it?"

"No one can get over something like that, and they really wouldn't want to."

"That's what I'm saying!"

"No, what you're saying is something else. Tell me what you think your friend should do."

"Oh I have no idea. My point is that he was partly responsible and that's not something that can be fixed. Whatever he does, this will always be with him. And that's horrible. Call it luck, but realize that he made his own luck in this case."

"So you're giving me a very brutal picture of a storm. And you're refusing to return to that place to give me a picture later, in the future, when things look different. Maybe still affected by the storm, yes, but different because people pick things up, or at least that's their healthy instinct. But you won't entertain that possibility. For you, this story is the storm and that's it. Does that sound accurate?"

"God. When you put it that way. But how do you pick this up?"

"I don't know. I don't know him. Even if I did I couldn't tell him how. But I'd want him to know he could."

"To pick things up?"

"To pick things up."

Seamus considered. "Because picking things up isn't the same thing as getting over it," he said. Twice, actually, because the first time was low and Marsha could not hear him.

"For my money, Seamus, yes." Marsha took a drink and Seamus did too, sucking on an ice cube. "Now you've been so kind as to tell me about yourself and this boy you know. I'll tell you myself that it's not pretty to see someone who matters to you die in a way you feel could have been avoided, and further could have been avoided with your influence. But if we're going to be honest enough to not take full credit for the good that happens to us, we better not be so foolhardy as to take full credit for the bad, either. Especially that which is really someone else's life, anyway."

"That kid who died drank, too. He didn't stay sober either."

"No he didn't, did he?"

He exhaled. Seamus said, "I guess it's disrespectful to make someone else's death your own."

"To not pick up the pieces is like dying to yourself, isn't it?"

"Yeah," he said, pausing to keep his words measured, "but it's still so fucking hard."

"Of course. But you know what's harder? That this won't be the last death this boy encounters. And whether he has anything to do with any of them ever again, if he doesn't put this one in true perspective, how can he ever understand any other death that enters his life? How can he see them clearly enough to understand them as best as he can because of what they do to other people? How can he really understand someone else's pain?"

Seamus noticed as he turned around to look at anything

but Marsha's blue eyes that there were only a couple of people left standing on the deck. It was getting late. He said as much.

"It is. Are you sleepy?"

"Yeah," he said. "Are you?"

"Not so much so that I can't make it safely to bed."

"But you don't have a place to stay. You can sleep in my cot, if you want. I'll sleep on the floor, or outside on the bench. It's the least I can do."

"Oh you're a dear!" She said and squeezed his shoulder. "But I think I'll drive down the road and find a turnout. Put the top up and lean the seat back."

"You're not going to sleep in your car, are you?"

"I'm actually quite excited at the prospect. It'll bring back memories, believe it or not."

"Good ones?"

She considered. "Ultimately, yes."

"Wow. Well yeah, like .2 miles down the road. On your right."

"Wonderful! The adventure continues!"

"You're okay to drive?" he asked, cautiously.

"After all this talk! You poor boy. I've had two, Seamus. I'll be okay and so will everyone else, I promise. I'll watch my speed, too."

"Okay, but I'm sitting in the passenger seat."

"Now what is that for?"

"To know that you're okay. It's a short walk back and I'm not too tired to do that."

"Well Seamus, you are a gentlemen as well as a solo traveler. Come travel with me for .2 miles down this beautiful road."

"I can do that!"

The drive was shorter yet and Marsha pulled slowly into the turnout. Seamus thanked her for letting him ride with her.

"This might be my last hitch," he told her.

"Thank you for the privilege," she said kindly.

Seamus nodded. "You know what Marsha? You really have It."

Her face lit up like she knew exactly what he meant and she squealed, "Thank you, Seamus!" and leaned in to hug him warmly. In the tight space his throat felt tighter still.

He got out and waved at her like he waved to everyone who gave him a ride.

"And Seamus, if you see that boy again, be kind to him."

"I will," he stammered.

Turning back up the road, slogging through the tail-end of drunkenness, he stumbled through zig-zagging thoughts of memories, seeking out the kind ones among them, before finally reaching his cabin tent and passing out cold on his cot.

8

The next morning Seamus sprung from his cot to slip his shoes on and tear down the road so quickly that he did not realize how hungover he was until he slowed to catch his breath. He stopped sprinting when he reached the turnout where Dr. Marsha had parked to sleep. There were three cars there now, but none of them a Jaguar. Panting, he jittered from side to side in an awkward ellipse before succumbing to the stirring in his stomach. He put his hands on his knees and bent over. Staring dizzily at the dirt, he waited for it to come, but it never did. So he stood up straight again and walked back up the road.

Seamus drank a cup of coffee on the back patio of the bar. He had hoped he could buy Marsha a cup of coffee as an extended thank-you, and tell her again how much it meant to him that she talked with him. Sitting alone again under the tall trees he thought about all the other things he'd wanted to tell her.

And so Seamus had a full day unhindered by any schedule and nothing to do with it. These were the days off from work in Big Sur.

The next two weeks ached by but ended finally. There was no hitchhiking and no sight-seeing. There were not many pictures taken and fewer conversations. He spoke to his dealer once when he picked up his final bag, and to whichever coworker it was who he needed to talk to at a particular time. Otherwise, his last days in Big Sur were spent within walking distance from his cot and involved little more than picking up something to eat and looking lamely about at all the beauty that bound him.

On a couple occasions, he went down to the water. Children played, adults sat and drank. He waded. The water barely rose past his ankles in most places. The floor was endless with smooth stones. Every now and then a toe caught a jagged edge or a rough-skinned twig. He felt these rough spots with added attention and time. He caressed the nearly right angle of the break in a rock with his little toe. He nudged the broken end of a stick with his big toe. He lifted a foot up to run his hand along its slimy sole. He rubbed his finger across tiny abrasions revealed on the ball of his foot. He stopped studying and walked further. During his second visit, he walked as far in the water as he could. Once on dry land he hardly walked long at all until he was back at his cabin tent. If you find yourself in nothing, Seamus joked privately to himself, then keep going right through the center.

When Jamie and Cameron finally arrived to pick him up, they wanted to have a look around town. Seamus walked them around the Henry Miller Memorial Library and had a drink with them at Nepenthe. He showed them the beach at Andrew Molera State Park but Jamie had wanted to see a different beach, the one in the pictures that Seamus emailed him. So, they went to Pfeiffer Beach.

The sun was not set but the sky was purpling. On the beach was a pool of water and boys skipped, and attempted to skip, stones across it. A yuppie couple, each in perfect white pants, wore bucket hats and silken shirts. Their topsiders were getting sandy and they walked carefully. They seemed to be having a fairly unenjoyable go of it. Photographers with tripods littered the shore. Seamus looked at all these people, so like the people he saw before on this beach, and wondered if any day here really was any different than any other. And when he looked to his side, Jamie was gone and Cameron was raising his fingers to his mouth. Seamus looked where Cameron was looking. Cameron's whistle speared Seamus' ears the exact moment he saw that Jamie was halfway up the rock formation that Seamus had retreated from weeks earlier.

"Goddamn it, man!" he yelled and ran furtively up the sand.

Jamie ignored him. His hands were over his head and he stepped his left foot onto a sandy knob. Beneath was salty air and crashing water. Above was more hard-pressed sand. At the top, the solid rock of the formation met where the less solid parts ended. But Jamie was not at the top. And when he brought his right foot near where his left was, he left the solid, lower parts of the rock behind him.

"Jamie!" Seamus wailed. "Jamie!"

Jamie kept his attention on his climbing. One hand up, one foot up. Left, right. Then a sprinkle of sand skidded out from under his foot. He looked down. A wave tumbled into the rocks below with a smack. He moved his foot. Nothing came loose. He moved his hand. A chunk broke off in his fingers.

"Jamie!" Seamus yelled.

Jamie held on to the piece that broke loose. He rolled it around in his hand, and then dropped into the water. He continued.

Seamus stopped yelling and dropped down to the sand and watched. He could keep yelling, but that was useless.

Jamie was gone. The only thing left were feet and hands, married by motion. Left and right and up. And up. And up.

"Seamus dude, he's got it no problem. You see somebody get fucked up here or something?"

Jamie stood on top of the formation and put his hands up in the air.

"No," Seamus admitted. He stood and stared at his friend, tiny at the top, and facing away from them to stare, enjoying no doubt what had to be a godlike view.

"Then let's go up there too!"

Seamus said, "We're sure as hell not leaving him up there alone."

The climb, as it turned out, was remarkably easy. The sandy part of it was profoundly solid, even if its surface area released the odd scatters of silt during their ascent. Everything they grabbed and stepped on was huge. And while the water burst below their feet, the threat of joining it was nonexistent lest they choose to end it all and jump. No one died that day in Big Sur.

Nor, Seamus remarked mentally, the entire summer.

At the top, the boys sat and talked.

"Dude," Cameron said, "if the world ended this is exactly where I'd want to be. I would just sit up here and play my guitar and get baked."

"Fuck yeah man," Jamie agreed. "This is a front-row seat!"

"I'd probably write some bitchin-ass song, too," Cameron said, squinting his eyes at the blurry line of the horizon.

"What would it be about?" Jamie asked.

"Probably about love," Cameron said.

"Shut up," Seamus told him.

"You shut up, tough guy! Down there you were pissing your pants."

"I didn't realize the sand was so solid. I went up halfway once and it seemed way less stable."

"What is and what seems are not the same thing," Cameron said.

"You should write that in your song," Seamus said.

"Damn, dude! What happened here? You were the one who told me that in the first place."

"Yeah I was there," Jamie corroborated. "That was the same night when that song kept repeating and it was like, 'Let it go,' over and over and over again?"

"We put it on loop accidentally," Seamus said. "And were too baked to realize it."

"But why was it that we put that song on loop?" Cameron asked. "Could have been any song. But it was that song."

"Well, it couldn't have been any song. There were only eleven on the album."

Cameron shoved Seamus. "I can't believe you! You're acting weird, man."

"Sorry dude. Been a rough summer."

Cameron pointed at the ocean. "How bad could it be?"

"Yeah man! This place is tits, brother. If I were you I'd move back after you graduate next year."

"I'm good, thanks."

"What else are you going to do? Get some stupid job in a bank or something?" Cameron asked. "Hell, maybe I'll move here."

"Go for it. See what happens."

"Well man, all I can say is I'm sorry you didn't get what

you were looking for," Jamie said.

Seamus shook his head. "No, I certainly did not."

"Shoot. As a photographer this would be like Nirvana," Cameron said.

"You can only shoot so many trees. If photography is the name of the game then I've got some work to do. It's not here, though."

"What do you mean? You're already good at it, man," Jamie said.

"A lot of people are. I need to come at it some different way though. I don't know, maybe invest the money I earned here into some good ass equipment. Shoot portraits or something."

"I don't know man. Not to shit on your drive but there's a lot of portrait photographers out there already," Cameron said.

"Yeah, which means it's still a viable job."

"He's got a point," Jamie said.

"Sure, but if you do that you have to shoot people doing something else other than sit there. Like, make yourself different."

"That's a good idea!" Seamus said. "Like what do you think?"

"Chhh. Beats me..." Cameron mumbled and stared. "I know!" he clapped, "You could film people having sex, like on their wedding night or honeymoon! Imagine that. Just sit back and film them and then give them a DVD copy of their own sex video that they can cherish for the rest of their lives."

"Yes! That's the business my man!" Jamie yelled.

Seamus sighed. "Don't you think people would want to have a chick doing the filming? I don't think some dude wants to hire another dude watching him bone his new wife."

"C'mon Seamus. I wouldn't give a shit if some dude was holding the camera versus a chick. If anything it might make my chick more comfortable that she's the only girl in the room," Cameron argued.

"Listen to him," Jamie said.

"Think about it, Seamus. There are lots of portrait photographers out there but not too many personal pornographers," Cameron said. "I don't know any."

"Me neither," Jamie said.

Seamus put his arms around his friends. "I can't blame you guys for thinking outside the box."

"That's right. And you better start doing that again yourself or you're just going to lose yourself, man." Cameron said.

"Give the man some space," Jamie said. "We don't know what it's like to live here. Maybe the woods are haunted. Are they haunted, Seamus?"

"Not that I know of."

"Then you have no excuse," Cameron said.

"For what?" Seamus asked.

"To be all sad about living in paradise."

"This place is not what it seems."

Cameron clapped and whooped. "That's an answer I can at least accept!" He stood up and looked down at the beach. "Fuck it, fellas. Let's go down and get high."

One by one, they made their descent to the safety and softness of the shore. They made their way back to Jamie's Saturn where they piled in and smoked a joint while making the slow drive back over the two bumpy miles, past hidden driveways and gated estates forking off the main road. They stopped at Seamus' cabin tent and he picked up his things, already packed, and stuffed them into the trunk.

PART IV

SEAMUS KNEW

Seamus took walks often, which usually meant time to think about himself. His mind was busy with other subjects, however, as he walked back to campus one Tuesday morning in mid-May. Moreover, his stride was full with bounce and vigor, his shoulders swaying with a looseness of concern and his arms cutting through the air with pronounced ease. While in the past he may have held his head to the side in thoughtful but aloof dreaminess, today it angled straight to the world, his chin raised and his eyes wide and smiling.

Seamus was going to graduate from college. He passed all five of his classes. Of his three D's, one was a shoe-in but the other two were questionable. One of them was Forensic Science, which was also the last class he learned his grade in before records for graduation were submitted.

The day before Seamus waited tensely through the morning until his professor held office hours so he could find out if this four-year exercise in learning to play ball was finally coming to a close. Today, Seamus recalled fondly entering his professor's office with grave sheepishness to ask what his final grade was. His professor groaned quietly as he pulled out a calculator and punched impatiently at the keys, looking up from his spreadsheet, and back to the calculator again. For what lasted no more than a minute but felt like ten, he finally turned to Seamus to say flatly, "60.1 percent."

Seamus was immediately possessed by a joy that shook him from his lungs out, his body quivering in relief. He put his hand out to shake his professor's as though one of them was having a child.

His professor, lips vice tight, glared at him. Did he want to kill Seamus or himself? Clearly perturbed by Seamus' well-earned pride, he nonetheless took the boy's hand and gave it a single, feeble jiggle. He then withdrew his hand with such immediacy as though giving any more of his vital energy away would cause him to have a stroke.

Seamus' final report card lowered his cumulative GPA to 2.06, or from a rounded perspective, 2.1 – a fact not lost on Jamie who saw it as an achievement worth praise and celebration.

"2.0 is average, my man. And you're above that!"

"I am man, I really am. And I didn't even try!"

Though he did not smoke or drink nearly as often anymore, and abstained from hard drugs altogether, Seamus took the largest bong rip of his career after learning of his scholastic fate. Jamie had arrived at Seamus's dorm the previous night with a joyful but reverent manner as he pulled from an obscene zippered bag a six-foot bong he borrowed from an "esteemed colleague" at the comedy club.

It was a wonder, then, that Seamus was as alert as he was this Tuesday morning in May, but he had work to do. Though one of his other D's was in a math class about fractals, which was perhaps an even greater achievement than passing Forensic Science, Seamus spent much of his last year passionately involved with basic arithmetic.

Walking back from a liquor store in the downtown area not far from his college campus, a school of numbers swam through the left side of his brain as he calculated the going rate for Durex, Trojan, and Rough Rider alike. The liquor store did not carry Rough Rider, but he carried those figures over from a recent trip to a pair of adult stores that did. Ever since he and Jamie invested in a condom vending machine, it was important that Seamus keep his accounting clear to accurately gauge the cost of overhead versus the profits earned. So far, the gap between them remained significant and only continued to surpass expectations.

The machine was located out of plain sight and in the men's bathroom in Seamus' dorm building lobby. He initially wanted to belly up and invest in two so he could put one in the women's bathroom, but was blocked from doing so by the Hall Council. And such was the luck of certain unfulfilled desires. Looking back, he realized that having two machines in both bathrooms would not have increased business any more. Judging by how many condoms the machine turned out, and having noticed the uptick in presence by students from other dorm buildings at all hours of the day, what would another machine really do but create oversaturation and cause him that much more work? And if there was anything Seamus had become downright religious about, it was only working if it was wholly and necessarily worthwhile.

Still, Seamus worked often. He had a job as an assistant server at an upscale restaurant which he walked to from campus. He also worked odd photographic jobs that he found on Craigslist. One assignment featured him taking pictures of reptile and amphibian tanks. Another saw him taking pictures of inventory at a light-up promotional item warehouse. Really, he took whatever he could get provided he could get a ride.

His favorite of them all was fairly steady and good for 2-3 gigs a month at $75 a session where he assisted a portrait photographer at weddings. Given his inability to drive, he only worked those that occurred at Singing Pines, in which case the photographer picked him up regularly as his dorm was on the way of her commute. Apart from the joy it gave him to be friendly but stern with Jeff when asking him to get out of the frame, or reminding Angela of how fondly he remembered working the gazebo site, returning to Singing Pines also allowed him to learn about a few old friends.

Fernando and Britney were out of state now, working for

AmeriCorps on a kiwi farm in Washington. Apparently they had aspirations for the Peace Corps next. Yasmine was now Angela's assistant, and though that was a new position in the organization, it was apparently necessary given the increase in special events for members and non-members alike that Angela pushed through the Banquet Department. Steve was gone, which was not surprising. What was surprising was to find out that Steve had a day job all this time and only worked nights at Singing Pines because he liked it. What surprised Seamus even more was what Steve actually did: investment banking.

Of all people to be surrounded by cars, Isabelita now worked at a car dealership during the day and picked up a couple night shifts during the week driving for Uber. Alfredo and Felipe and Alonzo all worked at the clubhouse still, but each was angling for a way out eventually. Alfredo was attending a technical school to become a mechanic. Felipe was applying for other jobs within the hospitality industry while continuing to go to community college. However, after a continued string of failures to launch romantically, his classes consisted of dance, theatre, poetry, and art history. Alonzo was going to the same college his brother did but rather than study agricultural science he opted to study biology with a minor in environmental studies.

No one knew anything about Barry, however. And when asked about Jamie, Seamus simply told them that Jamie was a lot like himself: both were doing fine.

Jamie, meanwhile, had texted Seamus. He was already on campus. The meeting was going to start before Seamus could get there, but if Seamus knew anything, it was that Jamie could talk. Besides, he wanted Jamie to feel them out for him.

Seamus took a detour through a park. Kids were throwing a frisbee. A woman was running around with her dog. A couple was sitting on a bench, just talking. They were not facing each other but looking ahead. The man talked with his hands, raised his eyebrows, seemed he was convincing himself of something. The woman began to talk but he interrupted her. She watched the man and did not look away again. The man continued to look forward.

Seamus did not have his camera. He did not carry it with him everywhere anymore. He sometimes took shots with his phone but those were never as good. In moments that he wished he had his camera with him, he chose to look as carefully as he could instead. Still the voyeur, Seamus watched. When the man looked up, it was time to go.

Seamus still sent pictures to journals. He received $50 for a shot he took in Big Sur. He captured a young child running across the beach with his hands in the air, his small silhouetted body framed by two oblong rocks rising from the water. The sun splashed between them, casting a bright wash over the shore where the child ran.

It was likely the prettiest shot Seamus had taken. A part of him wished he received more for it, but he was good about remembering the times when getting a picture published for free was priceless.

His success rate was still light, yet he was more selective now where he sent his work. By all accounts, that was success enough for him.

Besides, Karen liked his work. He was damn lucky, he knew, her tryst with the guy she was seeing at the beginning of the year was short-lived. The minute they broke up, Seamus knocked on her door, apologized, and was dismissed readily. So the next day he knocked on her door again, jokingly apologized about apologizing the day before, and asked if she would like to catch up sometime. She did not.

The third time he knocked on her door, she was not home. But timing was on his side, and as he was writing a note to leave for her, she appeared in the hallway, asking him what he was doing.

"Writing directions for you to find some place really cool," he said.

"Give me this," she said impatiently. Her eyes flitted around the paper, she flipped it over to see if there was anything else. She looked up. "This looks like a five year old drew it."

"Do you recognize the fountain? That really gives you your bearings."

"Yes," she said. "But it looks like the top of a troll's head."

"Are you at least going to follow the map?" he asked her.

She stalled as she closed the door. A sliver of her face in the crack, "Only because I have class next door so it'll be hard to miss."

She closed the door and Seamus beamed.

The studio next to Karen's sculpting class was not being used that semester, and housed a piano and a drum kit and a couple of a beaten up paintings. Seamus made sure to meet the kids who jammed there and arranged to put up pictures he took in Big Sur on the walls. None of the pictures had any people in them. On the piano rested another note, expressing how none of the pictures had Karen in them, either.

When Karen knocked on Seamus' door, she told him she accepted his apology. When he asked if they could catch up some time, she asked him, "What do you think?"

Their catching-up time was nothing but that. But it was still short-lived. And once they gave each other another shot, it did not take long before Seamus held Karen's hand in public, held the door for her, kissed her, told he loved her even if others walked by. She made fun of him, told him he had a "Come to Jesus moment alone and horny in the woods."

"Maybe I did," he said. "And you forgave me."

"Knock it off," she told him, smiling.

Seamus spent most nights in Karen's room. He spent most mornings there, too. He was not always in a hurry to leave anymore, and they drank coffee in bed, put on music, and leaned back against each other to read aloud weird news head-lines, watch viral videos, or sometimes just talk. And some times still, they talked about things they never told anyone else, and in the space of that perfect vulnerability found per-fect trust. And when Karen did not leave him when he was sure she would, he saw that he need not tell anyone ever again and that would be just fine.

When he told Karen, he retold it to himself and promised himself he would not try so hard to forget it again. He might just miss something if he did.

He had hoped to see her this morning before his meeting, but she was busy. Graduation for her meant packing bags and getting ready to fly to Europe. Taking a vacation was impor-tant to her, she said, before she began grad school in Illinois.

Seamus did not suggest that they take a vacation together. This time, as she left him for a different world, he accepted without protest and understood that some endings could not be avoided. Instead, he thanked her for as good an ending as he could hope for given that an ending must indeed occur.

Some endings for Seamus were not nearly as clean.

The last time he saw Chris, the poor boy was a tattered, bloody pile. He and Jamie picked up Chris in front of a bowling alley where his friends had deserted him. Delirious from booze and an ass-beating, it was a marvel he was able to operate his phone to call for a ride in the first place. Though he only wanted to go home, he was too immobile to resist being dragged into the hospital.

He was angry with Jamie and Seamus for taking him there, and they did not talk to him again. In the eyes of Chris, he only needed to sleep his wounds off, drink a beer in the morning, and return to work at the grocery store in the evening.

But whatever grudge Chris held was meaningless to Seamus and Jamie. That night was never about Chris for them in the first place. At least not the way it evolved.

Seamus started driving not long before the incident with Chris. Having settled into his senior year and continuing to find little reason to be inspired about his future, he hatched the notion that he should travel some more. Big Sur was a bust but certainly not every place he visited would be. He could live and work in a new place each season, pay off his loans as he did so and live humbly. Of course, if he really wanted to travel, he would need to drive. So, who else could he possibly turn to for guidance?

The night the boys found Chris, Jamie had been giving Seamus a more advanced driving lesson. They were wrapping up the night and had just bought beer and were headed back to Seamus' dorm. Seamus had been driving with Jamie's supervision for more than a month now, and though he did not have a learner's permit yet let alone a license, Jamie assured him that he was far too good a driver to get pulled over. Wanting to believe it, Seamus did. And his education continued.

By the time Seamus successfully drove them all to the hospital, nerves were shot and Jamie milked Seamus' position as the driver for all he could.

"Sorry my man but you are a true warrior of a human being for going through this. I know you've got class in the morning," Jamie started.

"To be fair, I was just going to drink beer with you at my place so I'm not exactly blowing off a study group or something."

"That's the spirit. We'll save those to celebrate for tomorrow."

"To celebrate for what?"

"Not being here. Yikes this place sucks. Who the hell actually becomes a doctor, anyway?"

"Beats me, man. People have no concept about what a gift life really is."

"For real! They spend all of theirs at work. Well man, I'm hungry as a hippo. You have any change? My wallet's got flies buzzing out of it."

"Sure. But get me some Cheetos," Seamus said and handed Jamie a couple of dollar bills.

Rather then go to the vending machine in the corner of the lobby, however, Jamie left the building. When he returned and bought snacks, he was in a reflective mood.

"You think in the future vending machines will cook food? Like, they'll have hot plates and will sling out omelettes or some shit?"

Seamus crunched his Cheetos and said to Jamie, "You're holding out on me."

"Ah," Jamie pointed at Seamus playfully. "You have to drive. Remember, you don't even have your permit yet."

"Did you drink a beer, too?"

"Two is right. Anyway, I'll smoke you out the minute we get back to your spot."

"How fast did you drink those things?"

"Seamus, get your mind straight. I'm talking about vending machines that cook food here. How cool would that be?"

"It'd be a dream. I think some primitive form of that technology already exists. They have like hot chocolate dispensers and stuff."

"That's not even at all the same thing. Anyway man, could you imagine that? Oh, dude!" Jamie said excitedly and tossed a handful of snack mix into his mouth. Chewing, he said, "Imagine if there was like a vending machine that took pictures. Right up your alley, man. What would that take?"

Seamus considered. "Jamie," he said. "Those are called photo booths."

Jamie cracked into a galaxy of laughter. He lifted a leg in the air and leaned back, twirling his foot before bringing it down and the rest of his body weight with it. "Damn, dude! It seemed like such a chill idea! No wonder someone came up with it."

"It's definitely a chill idea. People love pictures of themselves. Selfies. How I hate that word."

"Hey, people love to be loved. And they love themselves."

Seamus grinned. "Yeah. I'm surrounded by that shit at school."

"They'd probably like a photo booth then."

Seamus stopped.

"Dude? You cool man?"

"Yeah," he said.

Though Seamus had planned on putting his Big Sur savings and current paychecks towards a car eventually, he found a deal on eBay that could not be refused for an old photo booth that dispensed sticker prints of the photos taken. It cost $1300 with shipping which he split with Jamie. Though it was missing its original backdrop, Karen helped him install a shower curtain on a bent rail that protruded above the screen.

The Hall Council in Seamus' dorm allowed him to put it in so long as he gave ten percent of the proceeds back to Council itself. He obliged, and the machine was so successful that by the time he petitioned to bring in a condom vending machine that he would fill with higher-end condoms, they agreed without any resistance.

Seamus checked the ink and paper levels on the machine assiduously. When it threatened near emptiness, he quickly ordered replacements online. Because of the extra work, he took five percent more of the profit than Jamie, which they agreed upon mutually. The same system applied to the condom machine.

Seamus looked back on the wild, early days going to Hall Council meetings for the first time in his college career. No one on the Council knew anything about him. But he believed in the photo booth. And when he ordered it without their blessing, seeing as he could not allow the deal to pass him by, they crumbled.

"No apologies for driving the golf cart, my man. You remember how you handled Angela in the glory days, and it's clear to me you haven't lost a step!' Jamie had told him.

Now, something very important was in order. Seamus needed someone to look over the machines after he graduated. The job would be simple. He would still order the replacement materials and stock the machines himself. He was not leaving the area and could manage that part.

But he and Jamie also needed something else: someone with the ability to code a website replete with an application page. It did not take long to make money back on the photo booth before Seamus and Jamie decided that they needed to brand. Still having money left over from Big Sur and other jobs, and with Jamie's newfound conservation of his own funds, the boys loaned money to Cameron to buy an old but still functioning hot beverage vending machine for his dorm building. In turn, they received a percentage of the profits as did Cameron's Hall Council.

The boys knew that if they invested every so often in a good machine, they could find someone at some campus somewhere who would be willing to apply for a loan from them in exchange for giving them a cut of the profits. All vending machines purchased had to have sensors, whose readings would need to be submitted through the site and to them on a monthly basis.

And so, Seamus sent out an email to the student body looking for a student who could code a site with the necessary parameters. The student had to be entering their sophomore year, and had to be "honest, reliable," and most of all, "hard working." The pay then, likely another percentage, would be negotiable.

As Seamus neared the campus, he reflected back on his fun times with the photo booth. There was nothing so satisfying as entering his own purchase, Karen beside him, and putting money into a machine that was coming right back to him.

"Those shots are on the house," Jamie had told him.

Pulling out those strips of photos from his pocket, looking them over and knowing he might see her on campus some time before graduation, though they had agreed to keep their distance to keep the ending as pure as it could be, he knew that he not only loved and lost, but used his own burgeoning livelihood to remind himself that he had.

"Idiot," he told himself and smiled.

Seamus put the photos back in his pocket and walked. He would keep them but not for long. He wanted to remember her differently.

When Seamus reached his campus he took a look at Malcolm's duck. Another ending clean and sudden. He looked down the corridor and pictured suits cruising towards him. Was that even an ending if he never met them?

He walked past his old dorm he lost his way in, past the fountain that began his treasure map to Karen. He walked past succulents rubbery and tall, squat and sharp, prehistoric and fuzzy leafed littering the drought-friendly gravel beds throughout the campus.

He walked until he arrived, and pausing before knocking on the door of the room where the musicians jammed, its space still not being used for a class and perhaps would not be for a long time, Jamie popped out and immediately escorted him down the hall to talk.

"Man! I've been warming these kids up for ten minutes and I'm running out of material! They have no concept what it's like to work for a living. I'm wondering if this whole thing is a mistake."

"Can they code?"

"To a man. Or to a woman. There's this chick in there who rocks. But they didn't get half my jokes about the working guy. They just asked when you were getting here."

"Maybe they're all business. That's not a bad thing."

"Well hell, all I know is if we're going to find ourselves our first employee, they damn well better have an appreciation for a little labor."

Jamie, meanwhile, had the image of a local burger restaurant drawn over his cheek. In yet another venture, he had taken a cue from a story he found about college kids who used their faces to advertise local businesses. So he followed suit. No one at the comedy club cared, either. He was simply "that jackass in the window with a billboard for a face."

"Look dude. They probably just work differently, and that's exactly what we want in someone we're going to hire."

Jamie turned his head in a sigh. The other cheek had a drawing of a dancing burger on it. "I guess you're right."

"You sell both cheeks now?"

"Hey, don't tell me how to hustle. Now, you ready to meet these clowns?"

Seamus nodded. "We've got five people in there and only one has to hit. Those odds work for me."

"My man, I never tell you this but you can really lift the spirits. Now let's get to work."

Jamie stormed down the hall and back into the room. Seamus followed and shut the door behind him, ready to begin.

www.ingramcontent.com/pod-product-compliance
Lightning Source LLC
Chambersburg PA
CBHW031029030726
47497CB00004B/1065

* 9 7 8 1 9 3 8 3 4 9 3 3 1 *